CHARMED

"Well, gee! Whocked. "I've only been ab   elieves he's an Indian from   like a sack of dirty laun   f star- vation . . . but on   enough to live that long!"

"You require wooing?" he queried, still amused, though his eyes now glowed with sensual fire. "In what manner shall I court you, Neeake?"

"Flowers and candy would be nice," she said smartly.

"What need have you of flowers when your eyes are the color of the blossoms which grow in the meadow in spring and your mouth is like a wild summer rose?" As he spoke, his lips reached for hers.

Nikki's pulse raced. When his mouth retreated, she felt bereft.

"Your flesh is as soft as the petals of a rose," he continued in a mesmerizing purr, his lips now seeking her throat, "and as sweet as the sugar from the maple tree."

Nikki lurched beneath his touch, already craving more. In the small portion of her brain that was still functioning logically through the rising tide of need, she could not quite believe what was happening. This man . . . this maniac . . . had but to speak, and she was virtually seduced. A look from those crystalline silver eyes, and she was practically mesmerized. And a touch . . . a mere touch was like being branded with lightning!

"Let me taste of you, Neeake," he murmured, "that I might sip the sweet nectar buried within."

Though she said not a word, her body answered for her . . .

CHARMED

Catherine Hart

Zebra Books
Kensington Publishing Corp.
http://www.zebrabooks.com

ZEBRA BOOKS are published by

Kensington Publishing Corp.
850 Third Avenue
New York, NY 10022

First Printing: December, 1996
10 9 8 7 6 5 4 3 2 1

Printed in the United States of America

I dedicate this book to the Shawnee Nation—from which came one of the finest leaders this country has ever known: Tecumseh. Live on!

Also, I would like to thank my friend Amy—or *A-me,* as she is known in the ceramic world. Your beautiful artistry is as special as you are.

Again, I want to thank my husband for all his love and devotion and for always being there when I need him—which is forever and with all my heart. You are my heart's inspiration.

Last, but not least, to Maria Carvainis, my agent and my friend. Thanks for the vote of confidence, for your understanding, and for all those pep talks. You really know how to motivate a person!

One

1813—A cave in southern Ohio

As Silver Thorn made the final preparations for the ancient ritual he was about to attempt, he smiled in hopeful anticipation. If this spell worked as it should, it would be a spectacular coup indeed—much grander than either of his brothers had achieved. Not that he was in any sort of intense rivalry with Tecumseh or Tenskwatawa, but each of the men had always enjoyed trying to best the others' latest accomplishments in ways only these three could aspire to.

From the very beginning, the brothers had been set apart and above others by the unique circumstance of their birth, for they were the sole set of triplets born in all of Shawnee history. As if this were not phenomenal enough, each had been blessed with mystical powers the likes of which had never before been witnessed, at least not in such abundance. All three could perform diverse magical feats and were able to foresee events of the future to varying degrees. Some moons past, Tecumseh, the firstborn of the trio, had predicted the passing of a shooting star such as the one that had streaked through the sky on the very night of their birth. And last year, Tecumseh had caused a great quaking of the earth which had been felt from Canada to Florida, from the eastern shores to west of the Mississippi River. Likewise, Tenskwatawa, more recently known as the

Prophet, had claimed credit for a total eclipse of the sun, though he had simply foreseen the occurrence in a dream and used it to enhance his own importance.

By contrast to his celebrated brothers, Silver Thorn was much more modest about his curious accomplishments, though no less serious in his endeavors. Still, he thrived on the friendly competitiveness which he and his siblings had shared since boyhood, a natural contest of powers which had served to hone their unusual skills to a keen edge over the past forty-five years. Now he was about to commence the most difficult task he'd ever set for himself, that of calling upon a spirit from the far future to gain a glimpse of what would become of his people. Heretofore, neither he nor his brothers had been able to predict any event beyond their own lifespans, but Silver Thorn was sure it could be done and that he could be the one to do so.

Kneeling before the small fire he'd built, Silver Thorn carefully retrieved a clay mold from the coals. Within its earthen boundaries, molten silver rippled and gleamed, reflecting the exact color of Silver Thorn's eyes—yet another oddity of his birth. Blowing gently upon the steaming mass, Silver Thorn began to chant an ancient incantation. Softly. Reverently. Pushing aside all concerns of the world outside the cave and focusing all his thoughts and energies on becoming one with his inner powers.

When the mold had cooled sufficiently, he broke the clay away, taking care not to disturb the still-malleable disc of ore. To further solidify it, he slid the silver into a pail of water, icy cold from the stream that ran through the heart of the cavern. A short time later, he plucked the charm from the water and attached it to a leather thong. Then, with a special concoction he'd prepared, he meticulously polished the coin-shaped medallion to a brilliant sheen. One side was perfectly flat and mirror-smooth. The other was graven with concentric rings, one within another, signifying life and time to infinity. Imbedded crosswise in this design, overlaying the bands, was the image of a feather, the symbol of power.

Hours passed. Outside the cave, day gave way to night. The moon rose, full and bright over the surrounding land, and still Silver Thorn knelt and chanted, endowing the charm with all the potent magic he could draw forth. Finally, when the moon had reached its zenith, he took the amulet out into the night. Standing at the edge of a small waterfall, he held the talisman upward. Suspended from his lean fingers, it spun like a miniature moon, reflecting the light of its larger twin in the sky above.

"Created of earth and fire, formed by wind and water, blessed by the moon and the spirits, marked by time and power, I commend this charm to the world of the future— so that the person to find and claim it will enter into this time and place to impart the knowledge and learning of the days yet to come."

With these words, Silver Thorn swung the emblem in an arc and flung it into the stream below the falls. He watched as it hit the water, spun several times in its own eddy, and began to drift with the strong current. The thong caught on the lip of a protruding boulder, and the amulet sank out of sight.

Silver Thorn seated himself on the rocky ledge overlooking the stream, prepared to wait patiently for as long as he must.

1996—Seven Caves, southern Ohio

Nichole Swan exited the cave into the bright sunlight, and the heat and humidity hit her like a swat with a wet rag. For a moment she was tempted to scout out the next cave immediately. Her jeans and sweater, just right for the cool temperatures underground, were too much for this early June heat wave that even the weather forecasters hadn't anticipated this early in the season.

Her stomach rumbled, reminding her that her meager breakfast was but a pleasant memory. Since then, she'd hiked happily for hours, both inside the caves and along the woodland trails surrounding them, burning up any energy her morning coffee and bagel had had to offer. It was time for lunch, and Nikki knew the perfect spot for her solitary picnic. After removing her cardigan and tying the sleeves around her waist, she hitched the backpack she'd borrowed from her nephew into place across her shoulders and trudged in the direction of the little waterfall she'd passed earlier that morning.

With each step, she told herself that all this exercise was precisely what she needed in order to shed those twenty extra pounds she'd carried all winter like some hibernating she-bear. Of course, she was looking her thirtieth birthday in the face. And teaching Ohio history to a pack of reluctant junior high students was more an exercise in patience than aerobics. Still, she'd made herself several promises recently, and she meant to keep them. This summer, during her well-deserved and much-needed break from the classroom, she was going to turn her life around. She was going to start taking better care of herself, both physically and emotionally.

To keep herself on track, she'd even mapped out a three-month course of action aimed toward self-improvement and liberally laced with pleasurable rewards for goals met. This present excursion met all the criteria at once. It gave her the opportunity to research various historical sites, with an eye out for the best place to take her students on a class trip in the fall. At the same time, she got to indulge herself in a bit of Indian history, one of Nikki's favorite subjects—most likely because one of her ancestral grandmothers had belonged to a local Shawnee tribe. From this long-ago relative, Nikki had inherited her black hair and tawny complexion, while her violet eyes and stubborn nature had been bequeathed by a Scot ancestor on her mother's side of the family. Where her flash-fire temper and her quirky sense of humor derived from was anyone's guess.

At the moment, Nikki was content to immerse herself in her own bit of history. Last week, without even bothering with her usual bout of spring cleaning, she'd closed up her small house in northwestern Ohio and headed for the southern section of the state. So far, she'd visited several ancient mounds, including the famous Serpent Mound. Just last evening, she'd viewed the open-air performance of *Tecumseh* and had found herself thoroughly enthralled by it. By the flickering firelight, surrounded by the dark night and Nature's own stage, the drama and the actors had seemed so real—as if she'd been magically transported into the great Shawnee chief's era and set down in the middle of everything that had happened to him and his people in the same locale over a hundred and eighty years ago! It had been fantastic! Today, she was touring caves that still seemed to echo eerily with Shawnee footsteps and whisper ancient secrets, where a waft of chill air felt like ghostly fingers, raising gooseflesh in its wake.

Rounding a bend in the trail, Nikki found the spot she sought. Here, in the shade beneath the wide-spread limbs of a huge old oak, right at the edge of the small pool, was a splendid view of the waterfall, which made this a delightful place to rest and eat her lunch. However, she first needed to wash the dust and cobwebs of the cave from her face and hands.

Kneeling at the edge of the pool, Nikki cupped water in her palms and splashed it over her flushed cheeks. It was heavenly! Blessedly cool. How refreshing it would be to remove her hot Nikes, roll up her jeans, and dangle her feet in the water. Would anyone really mind if she did? And even if there were park rules to the contrary, two sweltering feet surely wouldn't contaminate the pool that much!

As she was contemplating this idea, she caught the glint of something metallic beneath the surface of the water, mere inches from her hand. "Someone's lost fishing lure?" she wondered aloud. Then she gave a rueful laugh and muttered, "More likely just a discarded pop can. Why can't people be more considerate about where they dump their trash? Isn't this planet polluted enough? Isn't ecology supposed to be the national byword these days?"

Frowning, she leaned over to retrieve the litter. As she did so, the weight of her backpack almost sent her tumbling headlong into the pool. As it was, the clarity of the water had thrown off her depth perception. Her arms were immersed nearly to her armpits before her fingers closed around the shiny object, the dangling sleeves of her sweater thoroughly soaked.

"Oh, great!" she grumbled. "I've probably ruined a thirty-dollar cardigan for a ten-cent piece of tin! Good going! Why didn't anyone warn me that clumsiness comes with turning thirty? What's next? Bifocals and orthopedic shoes?"

By now she'd regained her balance, though barely, without further damage to herself or her apparel. When she opened her hand, her irritation evaporated considerably. There, nestled in her palm, was a round, fairly flat disc of some sort strung on a soggy cord. Though she was certainly no expert, the medallion looked to her like it was made of silver. The upper side was grooved with a series of circles, one within the other. She turned it over and found herself gazing into a surface so smooth and gleaming that her own image reflected back at her. Holding it aloft, she inspected it curiously as it began to rotate slowly at the end of its tether.

Around and around it twirled, catching stray sunbeams and flashing them at her. Faster, brighter, like a hypnotist's

amulet, it spun. Fascinating. Mesmerizing. Although aware
of the effect the strange emblem was having upon her,
Nikki was helpless to stop it. There, on her knees, half-
blinded by the sparkling charm, she felt herself swaying
dizzily as she watched the engraved circles seem to coil
upward, inward, much like the designs blurring together
on a child's toy top. First the spiral pattern, then her own
reflection. Repeated again and again, with increasing
speed, until they seemed to meld into one— her face
within the rings, snared in a bright whirlpool, getting
smaller, more distant, with every turn. Smaller . . . farther . . . faster . . . trapped . . . falling. . . .

1813

Silver Thorn came instantly alert. Something was different. Had he heard some small sound? Or had it merely
been an odd vibration in the air that had intruded on his
meditation? His keen eyes scanned the area below the falls,
searching for the origin of the disturbance.

It took but a moment to identify the source, and Silver
Thorn's heart leapt with excitement. There, on the river-
bank, lay a body! Could it be the messenger he sought?
The One from the future?

With more haste than caution, he scrambled down the
rocky slope, sending a shower of pebbles ahead of him.
A few paces from the body, he halted, investigating it from
a distance. Whoever this person was, he lay on his side,
unmoving—either unconscious or dead. His hair was long
and dark, tied back with a metal fastener of some sort.
He was dressed in a coarse pair of blue trousers, a yellow
shirt, and had a blanket-like garment hanging from his
waist like a breechcloth and a bundle attached to his back.
On his feet were shoes, or short boots, of a type Silver
Thorn had never seen. They were blue and white, of some

peculiar material, with ridges on the bottoms and printing on the sides that said NIKE. Silver Thorn, who had learned to speak and read the English language years ago— though his pronunciation of the words was not always accurate— supposed this to be the stranger's name.

When the person remained still, Silver Thorn crept close and knelt beside him. Alert to a possible trap, Silver Thorn clasped one thin shoulder and quickly rolled the stranger onto his back. Silver Thorn's eyes widened in surprise as he immediately realized his mistake. Despite the manner of dress, this was no man, small or otherwise. The twin bulges beneath the shirt proclaimed the body as irrefutably that of a female. Ebony tresses framed a pale, delicately boned face with full red lips and long, lush lashes.

Had Silver Thorn harbored any further doubts about her gender, the writing on her shirt and the accompanying picture would have eliminated them. In bold letters, it said, "It's fine for a woman to put a man first, if the view from behind is worthwhile." The painting depicted a man, facing away from the viewer, bare to the waist and wearing a tight pair of trousers similar to those Nike wore.

He puzzled over this. Though he was further bemused that the spirits should send a white woman to impart the future to him, the mystical pendant lying in her limp fingers gave proof that she was the Conjured One. Retrieving the charm, he looped it about his own neck. As his fingers pressed against her throat, seeking and finding a pulse, he called to her to awaken. The woman moaned. Her eyelids fluttered open, and Silver Thorn caught a glimpse of eyes the color of the inner rim of a rainbow—the same purple hue of dawn's shadows, when the sky first welcomes the rays of the rising sun.

Nikki awoke to the sound of a deep male voice calling her name. With her eyes still closed, she was sure she'd never met this person and wondered how he could know her, for he spoke her name in accented English, pronouncing it "nay-ah-kay." Cautiously, lest she become dizzy again, she forced her eyes slowly open and found herself lying on her back, looking directly at the gleaming medallion, which now dangled from about the man's neck—a deeply tanned neck that matched a broad bare chest hovering closely above her.

"What . . . what happened? What's going on here?" she blurted out, her weak attempt at bravado emerging as more of a frightened squawk. Not sure if he intended to help or harm her, she scooted hastily away from him, far enough to lever herself into a sitting position. The abrupt movement sent her head spinning, and it was a moment more before she dared raise her wary gaze to his face.

What she saw there did nothing to quell her unease. His face was as bronze as the rest of him appeared to be, the features even and bold, framed by sleek black hair that brushed the tops of his shoulders. This she noted almost in passing, for his eyes immediately snagged her attention and held it. They were a shimmering silver, like twin flashes of lightning, and so compelling in their intensity that she had the eerie feeling that he could see into her very soul.

She shivered slightly and swayed backward. Immediately, his hand closed about her arm—whether to steady her or to keep her from fleeing, she did not know. Despite herself, she could not contain the frightened gasp that escaped her lips.

"Do not fear me, little one," he crooned in a foreign, formal way. "I intend you no harm, for it is I who have brought you here."

"Who . . . who are you? How do you know my name?" she gasped, her eyes wide with apprehension.

"It is written on your moccasins," he replied. On a curious note, he added, "Do the women of the *Shemanese* have a need to proclaim their identity to all or do your men require it of you?"

"I'm American, not Sheman-whatever," she corrected, puzzled by his strange manner of speaking. "Who are you? And what do you mean, you brought me here? I came to the park myself." A quick, careful glance revealed, much to her relief, that she was still sitting near the stream, right where she'd fallen.

"In Shawnee, I am called *Mona Kahwee*. In your tongue, you would say Silver Thorn. Can you rise now, without becoming faint again?"

Only now, as he helped her to her feet, did Nikki notice that his mode of dress was as odd as his speech. That wasn't a pair of tan shorts he was wearing—it was a buckskin breechcloth that matched the moccasins on his feet! Disoriented, she struggled to sort it all out in her mind. At last her brain caught on a logical explanation, and she released a shaky laugh.

"Oh, I see now!" she exclaimed softly. "You're a member of the *Tecumseh* cast, aren't you? Still in costume and practicing your role, I suppose. I saw the performance last night, and it really was very good. I could almost believe I was back in Tecumseh's time."

"I know nothing of this performance you speak of, but you are, in fact, in Tecumseh's time and mine," he informed her seriously. He cast a dubious eye over her small frame and shook his head. "I summoned you here, from the future, though it was my hope to recall a man, perhaps one of some prominence and intelligence—not a mere woman, and a white one at that. Better that I had been more exact in my request to the spirits."

"Yeah, well, hindsight is always better than foresight, so they say," she quipped, her trepidation restored and multiplied tenfold. This guy was really acting weird! Hitching her backpack over her shoulder, Nikki stepped back from him. She wondered if she stood a chance of outrunning him or if she could find her pepper spray in time to use it before he attacked her. Did she still have it packed away in her purse? Good Lord! She hadn't even checked it out to make sure it actually worked! Why hadn't she tried it on the neighbor's dog, at least? But as she'd told her would-be Indian, hindsight was always twenty-twenty.

"Look, I've got to be going now," she said. "You can keep the medallion. It goes great with your outfit." She inched slowly away, not yet brave enough to turn her back to him.

He stood calmly watching her, his well-muscled arms now folded across his chest in a posture of male arrogance. "Where do you think to run, little goose? At best, you would lose yourself in the forest and starve. More probably, you would become a tasty morsel for a hungry bear or wolf."

"There are no bears or wolves roaming wild in Ohio anymore," she replied, still edging away. "A stray dog or coyote, maybe, but the worst I'd be apt to encounter around here would be a skunk. Besides, it's only a short jog along the path to the park entrance and there are plenty of other visitors if I run into any problems."

"Look about you, *Neeake*," he said, again giving her name that peculiar pronunciation. "Do you see or hear any person other than the two of us? And where is this path you speak of? I see none."

His words drew her up short; her gaze darted anxiously to and fro; her ears strained. He was right! The path should have been just behind her, between the old oak and the trash can. But now, even the trash can was missing! And the only sounds she could hear over the mad pounding of her heart were birds singing in the trees and the rush of water spilling over the fall.

"I . . . I must have miscalculated," she stuttered. "It's here someplace. I'll find it." Starting to panic, she dashed around the clearing, which itself seemed smaller than before. Still failing to discover the bin or path, she opted to forge her own escape route, anything rather than stay here with this madman, and promptly bolted into the tangle of trees and bushes.

The thick brush was a hindrance, but she plowed through it determinedly, ignoring the branches and briars that tore at her skin and hair. She had to get away, to locate one of the paths that led to more traversed areas of the park. There she would find other tourists, preferably normal ones, and be safe from that fruitcake actor, or druggie, or whatever he was. From there, she could get her bearings and make her way back to her car.

With all her thrashing, it was impossible to tell if the man were following her. She paused a moment and chanced a look behind her, but could hear nothing more than her own raspy breathing and accelerated heartbeats. Nothing moved, and Nikki heaved a thankful sigh and continued on, more slowly now.

Fully half an hour later, tired, out of breath, sweaty, and thoroughly exasperated, she had yet to stumble across one of the many paths intersecting the park. Branches, rocks, thorns, vines—these she'd invariably stumbled into, but not a single trail. For the past fifteen minutes, after surmising that she wasn't being followed, she'd repeatedly called for help. Now her voice was hoarse and her throat strained.

"Damn, damn, double damn!" she exclaimed. Tears of frustration and anger welled up and spilled onto her cheeks. Sinking wearily to the ground beneath a tree, she let the tears fall freely, feeling thoroughly sorry for herself. Her friends and fellow teachers would have a heyday if they found out about this. She imagined them asking her what she did over summer vacation and herself answering, *Oh. nothing much. I toured some caves in southern Ohio, managed to keel over with sunstroke or something, met this looney-tunes Tonto decked out in a breechcloth, panicked, and got myself lost in the woods.*

"Next time, I'm bringing someone else along," she muttered. "Then if I get hip-deep into trouble, at least I won't be in it by myself."

From somewhere close behind her, a dreadfully familiar baritone voice intoned solemnly, "To quote one of your English authors, 'Misery loves company.' I am yours."

Two

With a startled gasp, Nikki spun around to find Silver Thorn leaning against the trunk of the tree, staring down at her with his eerie silver eyes. "How did you sneak up on me like that?" she croaked. "Good grief! You nearly gave me heart failure! How did you find me?"

His lips curved into a derisive smile. "Woman, you left a trail a blind man could follow, and every animal from here to the Great River must have heard you thrashing through the brush."

Squatting down beside her, he held out her sweater. "You dropped this."

She reached out hesitantly and silently retrieved the twig-riddled garment, torn between relief at not being totally alone, and fear that he now had her cornered in an even more remote area of the park. If only she could be certain that he was harmless. "Can . . . do you know the way out of this maze, by any chance?"

He offered her his hand, palm up. "Come, Neeake. It is going to storm soon. I will take you to the caves, where we can find shelter. There, I will reveal to you the purpose of this mission."

Her eyes widened in fright. The caves! God in heaven, if she followed him down inside one of those, no one would ever hear her call for help! For that matter, if he decided to kill her, it could be years before anyone found her body!

But, wait! Surely there would be other people touring the caves. And the paths from the caves to the parking area were well marked. All things considered, this might be her best chance to ditch him, once and for all. At least it would get her out of this blasted woods and back to some semblance of civilization!

"Keep your distance, buster," she warned him, declining to take his hand. Levering herself to her feet, she quoted wryly, " 'Lay on, Macduff.' Just don't try to lead me astray. I happen to have a black belt in karate." A lie, if ever she'd told one!

"Ah, an educated female. Perhaps you will be of some use to me after all, small messenger. But tell me, what is this belt of karate that I should beware of it?"

Deciding it might prove more prudent to play along with him, at least for the moment, she replied reasonably, "It's a form of martial arts, basically used for self defense, and very effective, too."

He merely nodded, as if satisfied with her answer, then turned to lead the way, evidently expecting her to follow like a pup on a leash.

With a shrug, she fell in line behind him. Only now did she notice how dark the sky was turning and how the wind had picked up. A rumble of thunder shook the earth. Ahead of her, Silver Thorn picked up the pace. Nikki did likewise, nearly loping in her effort to keep up with him. Within minutes, the muscles along the backs of her legs felt as if they were on fire and she was wheezing like an old steam engine. Then, as if she needed to be any more miserable, the storm broke, drenching her instantly beneath a blinding sheet of chilly, wind-driven rain.

Just when Nikki was sure she couldn't possibly take another step, she and her guide stepped into a small clearing. Disregarding her previous reactions to his touch, Silver Thorn took hold of her arm and towed her quickly toward a tumble of rocks.

He pointed upward at the mouth of a cave barely visible through the torrent. "Can you climb or shall I carry you?" he asked, leaning close to be heard over the noise of the storm.

She pulled back. "Neither, thank you," she informed him in her primmest teacher's voice. "This is where we part paths, sir. I can find my own way from here."

"Do not be foolish, woman. In the cave, you will be dry."

"I can be just as dry in my car," she countered.

He shook his head. "You do not understand."

Before he could continue with whatever explanation he might have added, a blinding shaft of lightning speared jaggedly to earth, mere yards from where they stood. So close was it that the fine hairs on Nikki's nape stood on end and the accompanying thunder, deafeningly loud, shook the ground beneath her feet. She let out a yelp of fright and all but launched herself into Silver Thorn's arms.

Taking quick advantage of her momentary confusion, Silver Thorn lifted her and promptly tossed her over his shoulder. He then began to climb the steep pile of rocks, toting her with him as effortlessly as if he were carrying a sack of feathers.

Hanging face down over his shoulder, with her nose bumping his back and her knapsack thumping her on the head with every step Silver Thorn took, it was several seconds before Nikki managed to regain the breath that had been knocked from her lungs.

"Put me down this instant!" she demanded as haughtily as she could manage under the circumstances. "Did you hear me?" she insisted, pounding on his back with her fist.

"I am neither deaf nor dead," he responded dryly. "Your voice is like the screech of an owl, and your talons nearly as sharp. Neither is appreciated."

"Yeah, well there's more where that came from, you latterday Neanderthal. Release me, or I'll rip your skin to shreds!" She raked her nails across his spine for good measure, just to let him know she was serious.

He grunted, stopped, and swatted her smartly on her upended backside, eliciting an irate screech that threatened to burst his eardrums. "Do not prove more trouble than you are worth," he warned darkly. "Now be still, for the rocks are slippery and I may yet drop you on your head."

For safety's sake, Nikki stopped wriggling, but continued her verbal tirade, which emerged in short, jerky segments as she bounced atop his shoulder. "I'm warning you. I have three . . . big, strong brothers. And if you hurt so much as a . . . hair on my head . . . they'll track you down like the mad dog you are . . . And by the time they're done with you . . . there won't be parts big enough to bother burying! Now set me down!"

Her captor chose to ignore her, which only served to rile her all the more. Her options at this point were few. Deciding that a tumble down the rock-strewn slope might be preferable and hopefully less painful than being raped or tortured or whatever this guy had in mind, Nikki braced herself as best she could and sank her teeth into his shoulder blade.

Again, Silver Thorn grunted. Evidently, her renewed attack, despite his warning, took him by surprise, for he lurched to a stop. His feet skidded on the rain-slick rock, and for a couple of nerve-wracking seconds they teetered precariously before he once more caught his balance. Nikki's jaws loosed their grasp on him. Almost instantly, he swung her down in front of him, his expression thunderous as he caught her by the hair, hauled her up on tiptoes, and brought them face to face.

"If you wish to keep those teeth and this mane of hair, you will cease such reckless behavior," he growled, his teeth flashing white against his bronze flesh. "Your threats and puny struggles will gain you nothing but needless distress."

Though Nikki, now nearing a state of hyperventilation, could not immediately recall whether or not the Shawnee had scalped their enemies, she was presently in no situation to argue the point, and she certainly didn't want to bet her life against it. Just the idea of dying in that manner was enough to send a violent quiver up her spine. Through chattering teeth, hot tears mingling with the raindrops falling on her cheeks, she begged, "Please. Just don't hurt me. I'll do anything. Just don't hurt me. Don't kill me."

Silver Thorn's features registered his surprise at her plea. His grasp eased enough to lower her to a flat-footed stance before him. Frowning, he asked quietly, "Little goose, why would you think such a thing? Have I not already told you that it is not my intent to harm you?"

"Then . . . then let me go!" she wailed.

"I cannot. You must come with me. We have much to discuss. Much to learn from one another. Come, Neeake." He held out his hand to her. "Come, small one. Trust me, and soon all will be explained to you."

Her eyes locked upon his, seeking reassurance, probing for indications of his sincerity and some hint of compassion, searching for any overt signs of sanity or madness. He returned her look with silent solemnity.

Hesitantly, Nikki placed her hand in his. His long fingers closed about hers, engulfing them.

Something akin to pleasure filtered into Silver Thorn's eyes as he gave a satisfied nod. "You have heart. Courage. This is good, for the path we begin may be hard. But fear not, for I will protect you."

With Silver Thorn in the lead, helping her over the most difficult spots, they soon reached the shelter of the cave. Just a few steps inside, it was dry, and not nearly as dark as Nikki had dreaded. The entrance was wide enough to admit plenty of fresh air from outside, while the roof hovered perhaps seven or eight feet above the stone floor. The walls sloped gradually toward the rear, where Nikki could barely see a partial wall and a darker area in the shadows, which she assumed to be a tunnel to another part of the cave. In a near corner, away from the mouth of the cavern, where it would be protected from wind and rain, was a small firepit. Next to it, blankets had been made into a neat pallet.

"You've . . . you've been camping here?" Nikki asked guardedly.

"Hah-hah," he answered with a bland look and a nod.

Her snide reply was automatic. "Well, I'm so thrilled to have given you a laugh, but could you let me in on the joke? I could use a good chuckle about now myself."

Silver Thorn graced her with another frown, this one openly perplexed. "Please explain, Neeake. I fail to see why you think I am amused."

"Oh, for heaven's sake!" she exclaimed in annoyance. "Surely you can't be this dense! You laughed. I distinctly heard you say *ha-ha.*"

He shook his head, a smile tilting the edges of his mouth. "You misunderstand again, little goose. *Hah-háh* is the Shawnee word for *yes.* I apologize for confusing you. I will try to remember to speak to you in your *Shemanese* English."

"There you go again," she accused irritably. "What is this *Shemanese*? I consider myself a well-educated person, but I've never heard of it, and you've mentioned it twice now."

He thought a moment and explained, "You call yourselves American colonists, I think, though you speak nearly the same tongue as the Red Coat Englishmen from across the great sea. The words are the same, but the sound of them is not."

Her unexpected laugh surprised Nikki as much as it did Silver Thorn. Her amethyst eyes sparkled with wry humor. "These days, with people relocating all over the country and the world, you're lucky if you can understand your own relatives, let alone your neighbors. A family from Delaware can move to Texas; and on top of trying to comprehend Southwestern diction, they're apt to get an Asian doctor and an Hispanic librarian."

He shook his head slightly. "Communication between us is likewise difficult, it seems."

"It wouldn't be if you'd give up this grand charade," she retorted. "While I appreciate you're trying to immerse yourself in your role, you are carrying it a bit to the extreme, don't you agree? After all, when you get right down to it, I'm probably more Shawnee than you are."

His eyes narrowed with acute interest. "Why do you say this?"

"My great-great-great-great-grandmother on my father's side was a Shawnee Indian. Too far back to have passed on the language or traditions, but her genes have survived the years. Several of us have inherited her darker coloring."

"So. This is why the Spirits have sent you. You do belong to us after all." His teeth flashed in a wide, pleased smile. "Welcome back to your ancestry, little goose."

She heaved an exasperated sigh. "You really intend to play this to the hilt, don't you? Well, don't expect me to buy into it. And another thing, I wish you would refrain from calling me goose! It may sound cute to you, but it is quite annoying to me. I didn't get my bachelor's degree in education to have someone refer to me as an addle-brained bird."

"But that is your name, is it not?" he queried in puzzlement.

"My name is Nichole. Nikki, for short."

"Neeake," he agreed, "which in Shawnee means *wild goose*."

"Really? You're not just making this up as we go along, are you? Pulling my leg?"

"I speak truly," he told her with due sincerity, "and

while I find it strange that you would need this, I shall be glad to pull on your leg if you require such aid."

"I'll take a rain check on that, thanks." Her gaze drifted to the mouth of the cave, where sheets of rain still poured down. "On second thought, let's just forget I mentioned it at all." A giggle caught her unaware as her sense of humor kicked in. "Lord, that's a real goose-drowner out there, isn't it? In light of your interpretation of my name, I suppose I should be grateful to you for rescuing me."

As though suddenly reminded of his role as host, Silver Thorn strode to his bed, caught up a blanket, and handed it to her. "You are cold," he stated, gesturing toward her arm.

Nikki glanced down. "Goose bumps!" she chortled. "How appropriate! Especially since my last name is Swan. I just hope I don't start to quack or waddle or, God forbid, molt! You know the old adage, 'If it looks like a duck and quacks like a duck, it probably is a duck."

As Nikki started to wrap the blanket over her shoulders, Silver Thorn stopped her. *"Mat-táh.* No. You must remove your clothing first, else both they and the blanket will be wet, and you will still be chilled."

Nikki graced him with a glacial smile. "I've heard better lines from some of my eighth-grade students, chief. And I'll remove my clothes when you stand on your head and stack marbles."

If her phrasing baffled him, her intent was clear. His face became stern once more, his voice like muted thunder. "You must not sicken, Neeake. There is much to be done. Now, defy me no longer. Remove your clothing and wrap yourself in the blanket, or I shall do it for you." He turned his back to her and walked away. "I must tend to the fire. Do as you are told, and soon you will be warm and dry and, hopefully, more reasonable."

Silver Thorn had spent the past several days and nights outdoors, praying and awaiting his visitor from the future.

It had been too long since he'd fed the fire to find any live coals among the ashes. From his small cache of firewood, he retrieved two pinecones. One he shredded into a tiny pile in the center of which he set the second cone. Taking up his bow, he twined a slender stick through the bowstring. Then, as Nikki watched in fascination, he began to manipulate the string, causing the stick to spin rapidly against the dry pieces of pinecone.

"Do you really expect that to work anytime soon?" she inquired.

He didn't bother to look up as he told her, "Fret not, Neeake. In a short time, we will have smoke, followed by flame."

She was already digging into her knapsack, searching for her purse. Seconds later, she approached him and said, "I have a better idea. Try this."

Silver Thorn regarded the white cylinder in her hand. "What is it?"

Nikki rolled her eyes. "Oh, come on, sport. It's a cigarette lighter, as if you didn't already know. Now, as the ad suggests, let's flick our Bic." With that, she rolled her thumb over the metal wheel and the little yellow flame sprang up immediately.

Silver Thorn lurched backward, dropping his bow. His eyes widened; indeed, his entire face registered his shock. Even as he watched, the flame disappeared into the hole in the top of the strange device.

When he finally regained use of his tongue, he murmured wonderingly, "What manner of sorcery is this? Are you a witch?"

"I've been called worse on occasion," she admitted. Eyeing him skeptically, she added, "If I didn't know better, I'd swear you're serious . . . that you've never seen a lighter before."

"I have not. Can you make the fire appear again?" he

asked, sounding much like a child enthralled with a magician.

"Of course." Once more, she flicked the lighter, making the flame dance into sight.

"It is truly wondrous!" he breathed. "Who would imagine a firestick so small and quick."

Nikki handed it over to him, watching as he lit the flame several times in succession, amazed that he seemed so thoroughly awed by it. "Hey!" she laughed. "Enough playing around! You'll use up all the butane, and we still won't have a fire going."

He grinned at her. "What is butane?"

"It's a sort of gas inside the lighter. When the metal wheel strikes a spark on the flint beneath, the gas ignites. Presto! Instant flame."

Silver Thorn turned back to the pine chips, flicked the Bic, and tossed it atop the pile. To his dismay, the flame disappeared at once. "It is broken," he claimed in disgust.

"Not at all," she assured him. "But you have to hold the lever down for it to continue working." Kneeling beside him, Nikki picked up the lighter, ignited it, and directed the flame toward the shredded cone. "This would be faster if we stuffed paper around the chips."

Silver Thorn shook his head. "Parchment is too valuable for heedless burning, woman. Will you next suggest we burn some priceless book?"

She held up her hands in a gesture of surrender. "May those words never pass this teacher's lips."

While Silver Thorn's attention was on his task, Nikki, still pondering his reaction and/or his superb acting skills, decided to take his advice. Swiftly, she peeled off her wet jeans, T-shirt, and running shoes, and wrapped up in the blanket. Though her bra and panties were also soggy, she was not about to remove them. Clammy undies were better than none, particularly since she still wasn't convinced that this guy had all his marbles. If worse came to worst, a mad dash to her car in her underwear was preferable to mooning everyone in the park.

She turned toward the fledgling fire just in time to see Silver Thorn, with his back to her, whip off his breechcloth with a nonchalance David Niven would have envied. Tossing the garment aside, he bent and plucked another blanket from his bed, in the process offering Nikki an enticing glimpse of his lean, tight buttocks. Her eyes widened in amazement. Her mouth went instantly dry. And the only thought she could form was, *Oh, my gosh! He's got the cutest twin dimples in his buns!*

Three

Nikki didn't think she'd groaned aloud, but she must have, because Silver Thorn turned to inquire sharply, "Do you have pain, Neeake?"

"No!" she managed to squeak out, trying and failing to school her gaze away from his groin.

Unconcerned with his nudity and totally ignoring her embarrassment, he took his time wrapping a blanket around his waist and knotting it loosely. "You are certain you are not hurt?"

"Only my pride," she muttered, tugging her own blanket higher over her chest.

To herself she thought miserably, *It isn't fair! This guy is older than I am by at least ten years or more, and he's absolutely gorgeous! "To die for," as the girls in my class would say . . . while I feel like an over-stuffed couch-cushion! And why the hell am I ogling him as if he were some huge chocolate brownie when he's as crazy as a bedbug and likely to kill me before the day is out?* She shook her head in an effort to clear it and mumbled, "I always thought insanity was genetic, not contagious! If I live through this, they'll probably lock me in a padded cell and make me eat spaghetti with a spoon!"

"Is it considered polite in your culture to speak in tones too low for another to hear?" he asked reprovingly. Not waiting for her reply, he gestured toward the fire. "Come,

Neeake. Sit and warm yourself while I explain why I have summoned you here."

Nikki edged toward the fire, skirting it and Silver Thorn cautiously, and seated herself on the floor opposite him, with the fire between them. "Okay, shoot. I'm all ears," she said.

"Does that curious phrasing mean that I have your full attention?" At her curt nod, he began his tale. "I am called *Mona Kahwee*, Silver Thorn. My brothers, Tecumseh and Tenskwatawa and I were all born on the night of the shooting star, one after another. Tecumseh is the firstborn, and takes his name from the shooting star. Tenskwatawa is next eldest; his name means He-Who-Makes-A-Loud-Noise. Recently, he chose to be called the Prophet.

"From the time of our birth, the Spirits have blessed the three of us with special powers, which we have tried mostly to use to the benefit of the Shawnee Nation. Tecumseh now leads us in this war between the Shemanese and the British, though many of our people have no wish to be caught up in this conflict between the whites. Both the British and the American colonists wish to claim land upon which we hunt and live. Why should we aid either side? But Tecumseh says we should fight with the British, who give us guns and bullets and will help to push the Americans back to the East and into the ocean."

"Wishful thinking," Nikki interjected. "You know that's not the way it hap—"

Silver Thorn held up his hand in a gesture for silence. "You may speak when I am finished," he informed her. "For now, just listen and be silent.

"Tenskwatawa agrees with Tecumseh, as do a number of our warriors. As a tribal sage, I am more a spiritual leader than one of war. Others come to me for advice, for guidance in their personal quests, for interpretations of their dreams and visions.

"As one accorded unique skills, and in an effort to better

guide my people, I sought a means to determine the future, that the Shawnee would know which path to take. In a vision, I was given that means. I was to create this charm," he related, touching the silver medallion on his chest. "Upon it, the Spirits would bestow mystic and mighty powers, which would bring to me a messenger from years hence. When you found the charm, Neeake, and held it in your hand, you were brought from your time to mine, that I might learn from you the fate of my people and determine the best way to guide them in this time of trial."

At the conclusion of his speech, Silver Thorn lapsed into silence. With a keen gaze, he awaited her response.

For the full space of ten seconds, Nikki remained mute. Then her words and her temper erupted like a spouting volcano. "Right!" she spat out. "And I'm the Easter bunny! What sort of fool do you take me for?" She leapt to her feet, leaning toward him over the low flames, pointing her finger at him. "You're certifiable, you know that? A grade A lunatic! A nut! A squirrel! Furthermore, your story is chock-full of holes, fella! Ha! It was just your luck to try and pull this on a history major! Teaching Ohio history is what I do for a living nine months of the year, and I'm no slouch at my job. For your information, buddy, Tecumseh may or may not have been a twin to the Prophet. There is even a theory that there might have been a triplet brother; but if there were, he was malformed and sickly and died as a child. So, Mister Smarty-Pants! What do you have to say to that?" she ended on a superior note, her hands planted cockily on her hips.

"It would appear that those who have recorded history are mistaken," he replied calmly, with just a hint of a smirk on his lips. "Plainly, I did not perish as a child."

"Then why don't the hundreds of books written on the subject relate that bit of information?" she countered smugly. "Why do they scarcely mention your not-so-credible existence and not even deign to give you a name, while they tout your brothers' exploits long and loud?"

His smirk grew, and laughter laced his voice as he said, "Perhaps because, unlike some people, I feel no need to flaunt my . . . ah . . . prominence. Speaking of such, your blanket has slipped, and your 'prominence' is bountifully displayed."

Aghast, Nikki glanced down to find one breast, covered only by its lace bra-cup, exposed to his view. Yanking the blanket back in place, she glared at Silver Thorn, as if it were somehow his fault. "Go ahead and laugh, you insufferable oaf. So I'm a little overweight. Big deal! At least I don't spend half my life lifting weights at a gym like you probably do."

"Overweight?" he echoed.

"Yeah, as in pudgy, pleasingly plump, fat. Take your pick, but I'll have you know I am a mere twenty pounds heavier than I should be. I simply don't carry it as well as some women do."

"This is untrue," he disagreed. "The person who told you this must be blind, stupid, or envious. What man wants a thin, bony woman in his bed when he can have one who is soft and warm, with bones that are padded well and do not poke sharply through her flesh? You are neither fat nor thin, but just as you should be."

Despite herself, Nikki glowed at his compliment. "If you weren't crazy, I could become very fond of you, Silver Thorn. You do know how to turn a girl's head. Of course, by your age, you ought to. How old are you, anyway?"

"I have lived forty-five of your English *years*. Do you realize that in this time, which you would call 1813, you are not yet born?"

She blinked at him, momentarily stunned, then shrugged. "Well, I suppose that could be considered an improvement over being almost thirty-years-old, divorced, and childless."

An appalled expression claimed his face. "What terrible

deed did you do to cause your husband to divorce you, woman? Tell me of your wickedness. Did you attempt to kill him? Were you so disrespectful and ill-tempered that he finally rid himself of you? Or were you unfaithful to him, perhaps?"

"Now, just hold on a minute, you chauvinistic ass!" Nikki exploded. Forgetting herself, she rounded the firepit to poke her finger into his chest, emphasizing her words with several sharp jabs. "It just so happens that he was the one who was unfaithful to me. And I'm the one who sent him packing!"

The disbelief on Silver Thorn's face magnified. "This cannot be so!" he exclaimed. "A Shawnee wife does not set her husband aside, as you say you did."

"Well, believe it, buster," she announced bitterly. "I'd had enough of his philandering to last me a lifetime; and if I ever marry again, which will prove I'm as deranged as you are, hubby-number-two had better have his life insurance paid up if he decides to stray. A divorce is too damned expensive, both emotionally and monetarily."

Silver Thorn caught the offending digit, which Nikki was still stabbing at him, and held it gently aside. "This is allowed in your time?" he asked. "You make it sound as if divorcing one's mate is most common."

"It's all too common," she admitted. "Readily procured by those who can afford it, and costs a bloody fortune. However, who am I to complain? If it weren't available, I'd probably still be stuck with that skirt-chasing swine. That, or I'd have murdered him by now and be sitting in prison stamping out license plates."

"It occurs to me that I have yet to ask you how far into the future you live. What year do you come from, Neeake?"

"It's 1996, as if you didn't already know," she retorted irritably, jerking her finger out of his grasp and plopping back down by the fire.

His jaw fell in astonishment as he swiftly calculated the time difference. "By the stars! That is nearly two hundred years hence!"

"For a primitive, your math is very good, Silver Thorn, or whatever your real name is," she jeered, "but this charade of yours is getting tiresome. It's a bit like trying to converse with Dr. Jekyll and Mr. Hyde."

"I am not acquainted with these men," he replied vaguely, his mind already on more important matters. His eyes shone with excitement as he leaned forward and said, "Tell me what has occurred in the many decades between your time and mine. What has become of my people?"

For reasons she couldn't fully fathom, and didn't truly want to delve into too deeply, Nikki felt herself being drawn into Silver Thorn's time-travel make-believe. Perhaps it was the intensity in those compelling silver eyes. Perhaps it was the teacher in her, that urge to impart information to a particularly enthused student. Whatever the motivation, she found herself answering his query.

"First off, you joined forces with the wrong side. The Americans beat the British in the War of 1812 and never really had any further problems with them. In fact, they have since become fast allies."

"And what of my people?" he wanted to know.

"After Tecumseh was killed in October of 1813, at the Battle of the Thames in Ontario, the fire went out of their will to fight. The Shawnee . . ."

"Halt!" Silver Thorn stared at her in dismay. "My brother is to die?" he rasped, his voice quaking. "In but four moons more, Tecumseh will walk with the Spirits?"

Nikki winced. Silver Thorn's shock and sorrow were so evident, so . . . real! "I'm sorry. It was callous of me to break it to you so bluntly."

"What of Tenskwatawa, and the others?"

She continued. "The remainder of Tecumseh's warriors returned for a time to Fort Malden, on the Detroit River, then migrated west. Many Shawnee left Ohio then, or soon thereafter, seeking new lands across the Mississippi. Only a few bands stayed on. Those at Lewistown and Hog Creek and Wapakoneta were the last to leave, forced out by the United States government in 1932. They were relocated to government-allotted lands in Kansas and Oklahoma, to places called reservations, with land so poor and desolate that white people had no wish to settle there.

"As you should already know, the Prophet fast lost all his credibility after falsely predicting victory for the Shawnee at Tippicanoe in late 1811. Few of your people would listen to him afterward, let alone follow him on a path to destruction. After Tecumseh, the one man they were willing to follow, right or wrong, was killed, all the Shawnee sought was peace. If I recall correctly, the Prophet died on a Kansas reservation, a drunken, lonely old man, though he lived well into his sixties, I believe."

Silver Thorn shook his head mournfully. "Tenskwatawa is ever ruled by whiskey. It comes as no surprise that it will be his downfall until his death." He sighed, deep and long, focusing sad eyes upon her. "I should have known it would gain me more sorrow than gladness to ask the Spirits to reveal the future. Your Aesop, in a fable, said it thus: 'We would often be sorry if our wishes were gratified.' He was correct."

Nikki nodded in commiseration. "In my day, the adage is, 'Be careful what you wish for, because you just might get it.' "

"I must consider all you have related to me," he stated. "Perhaps there is yet a way to change what is to happen, to save Tecumseh and my people."

"Silver Thorn, you can't rewrite history. What must be, will be. Also, as much as I regret being the bearer of bad news, I really have to go now." She rose and stepped toward her small pile of belongings.

"Your clothing is not yet dry," he pointed out.

"Even if it were, it would only get wet again," she countered, indicating the rain that still fell outside the cave. "I won't melt, and my car heater works well. So, if you'll excuse me and turn your back, I'll get dressed and leave you to your solitary contemplations."

"No."

"No to what? No, I won't melt? No, you won't turn your back and afford me my privacy?"

"No, you cannot leave. I may have further need of your knowledge. Moreover, though I summoned you here, I know not how to send you back from whence you came."

"Now look, fella. I'm not staying. I've played along with you as far as I'm going to. More than was wise, no doubt, but then I've never had to deal with a schizophrenic psychopath before."

As she spoke, she decided to forego dressing and edged toward the cave entrance. She'd run stark-staring naked through a briar patch if she had to, if that's what it took to escape this lunatic. Any moment now, he might turn violent. Better embarrassed than dead any old day of the week!

She was four feet from the entrance, a mere yard from possible freedom, when Silver Thorn raised his arms toward the roof of the cave and issued what appeared to be a loud command in a strange language Nikki assumed was Shawnee. Suddenly, the earth beneath her began to quake, as did the walls and ceiling. Nikki lost her balance and fell to the floor. She huddled, paralyzed by fear, as the rumbling sound grew to a roar. Between one instant and the next, a large portion of the roof came crashing down, missing Nikki by a hair's breadth.

Dust choked her. For long moments, she couldn't see. Couldn't breathe. Couldn't move. When the air finally began to clear, Nikki lay gasping for breath. At length, she screwed up the courage to open her eyes and was immediately dismayed at the sight before them. The entrance to the cave was totally blocked by several huge boulders and a multitude of slightly smaller rocks. Only a slim section across the top, perhaps a foot-and-a-half deep, had not been filled.

"Oh, God!" she whimpered, hysteria sprouting full-blown. "We're trapped! I'm entombed with a maniac! I'm going to die! I don't want to die!"

Four

"Cease that wailing and calm yourself, Neeake!" Silver Thorn commanded brusquely. "You are not harmed, nor shall you be. When the time comes for us to leave, I shall remove the rocks as easily as I put them there. I promise. This is merely the simplest measure to prevent you from attempting to flee before I am ready to let you go."

If the man had sprouted horns and a tail, Nikki couldn't have been more stunned. "You . . . you?" she stuttered, indicating the rockslide. "No. In a million years, you'll never convince me you had anything to do with that. It was an accident. An earthquake or something. One of those odd coincidences."

Silver Thorn shrugged. "Believe what you want, little goose."

She frowned up at him. "Even if you were responsible for the cave-in, don't you think it's a rather drastic move?"

"Perhaps. Were you not so provoked, I might have chosen to place you in a dream state; but I was not certain of success, given your state of mind."

"Well, gee! Why ever should I be upset?" she mocked. Levering herself into a sitting position, she swiped at the chalky dust layering her face and limbs. "I've only been abducted by a crackpot actor who believes he's an Indian from another century, lugged around like a sack of dirty laundry, and now I'm likely to die of starvation . . . but only if I'm fortunate enough to live that long!"

She stood and faced him squarely, more furious than frightened now. "Okay, hotshot! You say you can get us out of here. Prove it. Twitch your nose or your toes or your fingers and move those rocks if it's so blasted easy!"

He met her glare calmly. "When I deem the time appropriate, I shall do so, and not before. My powers are not at your disposal, Neeake. Nor are they for your amusement."

"Well, guess what, sweetcheeks? I'm not in the least amused!" she railed. "In fact, I'm damned mad!"

Nikki had never attacked another human being, not even her ex-husband when she was most angry at him. But without a moment's thought to the consequences, she launched herself at Silver Thorn, her fingers curled into talons and aimed at his throat.

Taken by surprise, Silver Thorn was knocked off balance. Together, they tumbled to the dirt floor, landing with Nikki astraddle him and shrieking like a banshee. First, she attempted to choke him; and when that didn't offer the desired results, she pummeled him with her fists, cursing like a sailor all the while. When he caught one wrist and held it at bay, she changed tactics and aimed her sharp claws at his face.

"It's all your fault!" she screamed. "You and your asinine delusions!" Her nails missed his eye by a quarter inch, raking a long furrow across his cheek. "You belong in the cracker factory in a rubber room and a straitjacket!"

He snagged the second wrist and pushed her arms down to her sides, even with her waist. "Enough!" he demanded sharply. "Your anger, though not unfounded, will serve you no good."

"I don't actually give a rat's butt!" she spat back, her eyes shooting lavender flames past the veil of dark hair that had escaped the barrette and fallen into her face. Her chest heaved in rage and from the effort she was expending as she continued to struggle against his superior strength.

It was a futile attempt, ending with Nikki's elbows propped firmly on Silver Thorn's ribcage. They lay staring into each other's eyes, their bodies aligned from head to thigh. With each harsh breath she took, the tips of Nikki's scantily covered breasts brushed Silver Thorn's muscled chest. Her response was purely carnal and not at all in accord with any conscious will as she felt her nipples tighten into pert buds. A reflexive quiver shot through her.

Silver Thorn's eyes widened. His nostrils flared slightly, as if catching the scent of her borning desire. His body answered hers, lusty male to beckoning female.

As Nikki felt his arousal grow, nudging her through her flimsy bikini panties, she became aware of another disturbing reality. In their skirmish, Silver Thorn's blanket had come dislodged and hers had been lost when she'd lunged at him. He was now lying totally nude, and fully stimulated, beneath her, while she wore only two skimpy pieces of nylon and lace that shielded next to nothing from his view . . . or his touch.

A blush licked her face and torso, painting them with heat. "I . . . I've heard it said that anger can be a potent aphrodisiac, but this is ridiculous!" she stammered. "I don't know you. I don't trust you any farther than I could throw you. A minute ago, I wanted to rip your head off and cram it down your throat!"

Silver Thorn had the audacity to grin up at her, white teeth flashing. " 'The lady doth protest too much, me-thinks,' " he quoted. "I am also reminded that there is more than one means to tame a shrew."

"Stow the Shakespeare, Thorn," she warned with a glare. "It won't cut any ice with me."

"Ice?" he repeated drolly. "You are all but ablaze, my wild goose. And what of *my* 'spear,' which is, indeed, 'shaking' for want of access to your most hidden heat?"

His manhood nudged her again, this time quite deliberately. "Shall I bury it inside you as we both wish?"

Nikki swallowed hard. "You're not long on the preliminary getting-acquainted routine, are you?"

"You require wooing?" he queried, still amused, though his eyes now glowed with sensual fire. "In what manner shall I court you, Neeake?"

"Flowers and candy would be a nice change of pace," she suggested smartly, stalling for time, hoping that their mutual lust, which was still churning between them, would dissipate as quickly as it had surfaced. *Let him try to gather a bouquet and a box of chocolate cherries inside this stone fortress!*

Her thoughts were curtailed as Silver Thorn, in a voice as thick and dark as fudge, said, "What need have you of flowers when your eyes are the color of the blossoms which grow in the meadow in spring and your mouth is like a wild summer rose?" As he spoke, his lips reached for hers, gently and leisurely sampling their texture and taste.

Nikki's pulse raced. When his mouth retreated, she felt absurdly bereft.

"Your flesh is as soft as the petals of the rose," he continued in a mesmerizing purr, his lips now seeking her throat, "and as sweet as the sugar from the maple tree."

His mouth trailed a damp path down her chest and caressed the swell of one breast. Chill bumps rose on her skin; her nipples budded tighter. Drawing her upward, Silver Thorn's tongue traced her areola with his tongue, chafing it through the gauzy fabric of her bra.

Nikki instinctively drew in a sharp breath. Her breasts burgeoned, pressing insistently against the confining garment, seeking his touch more fully. His teeth grazed the peak, and she bit back a moan of intense desire.

"What is this harness you wear?" he murmured. "And how does it release?"

"You're in charge of this seduction," she groaned, contrary even in the face of rapidly rising frustration. "You figure it out."

Capturing her wrists in one hand, he raised them over her head, out from between their bodies. With his free hand, he fumbled with the intricacies of her bra for mere seconds before his own patience wore thin. Still unable to disengage it, he simply yanked at the cups, drawing them down until her breasts sprang free. The elastic and cloth, stretched to the limit, pressed her breasts upward and inward, securing them firmly for his avid perusal.

"You spoke of candy," he rasped, his silver gaze sweeping the offering displayed before him. "The fruit I now behold is more tempting than any other treat. Tasty *pacanu* and ripe red berries perched atop plump *usketomake*. There is no more appealing morsel, no more succulent delight than these."

His palm cupped her left breast. His callused thumb rasped over the crest.

Nikki quivered, her breath catching. "Berries . . . and what?" she whispered.

A devilish smile arched his lips. "*Usketomake*. Melons. Firm, juicy melons." His tongue lashed out to swipe a long wet line along the curve of her breast. "And *pacanu*. Savory brown nuts." He caught her nipple between his teeth, nipping lightly.

A keen thrill shot through her. Her toes curled. Her bones felt as if they were melting.

"Shall I woo you further? Taste of you more deeply?" he taunted softly.

"Maybe . . . . just a nibble or two," she conceded weakly.

He had her panting in a matter of seconds as he toyed with the pouting peak as a cat would tease a mouse, batting at it with his tongue, rolling it between his teeth, licking, sipping. Then, quite suddenly, he changed tactics and drew her breast fully into his warm, moist mouth, suckling with such force that Nikki felt the pull clear through her. Her womb echoed each magnetic tug, as he suckled deeply, time and again. Her blood turned to liquid fire, pulsing loudly in her ears, pooling in her belly, anointing her body in a balmy dew and making it throb in places she'd almost forgotten existed.

By the time he'd lavished the same thorough attention on her right breast, the crotch of her undies were wet and she was whimpering incoherently. When Silver Thorn swiftly altered their positions, placing Nikki on her back beneath him, she barely registered the change—until she felt his tongue prodding at her through her damp panties.

Nikki's initial response was one of pleasurable anticipation. It had been three years since she'd last enjoyed a rousing romp. No, more accurately, it had been three years since her divorce and closer to four since she'd had satisfactory sex, and even then it hadn't been much to shout about. By that point, her husband had been putting his best efforts to practice elsewhere, outside their marriage.

Still, she couldn't remember a time with Scott, even at the start of their relationship, when their lovemaking had been this hot! This titillating! Eliciting such primal, wanton need that it was almost frightening in its intensity. This was akin to living out one of those alien movies, discovering a stranger had invaded her mind and now abided in her body . . . someone she didn't know lurked there, just below her skin, waiting to emerge at the most inappropriate moment.

His tongue licked intimately at her, and she shivered, wanting him more than she recalled ever wanting anything. Her resolve wavered, but only for a moment. "No!" she gasped out. "Stop! You can't . . . we can't!"

His dark head rose from between her legs, his silky hair brushing her bare thighs. Still seething with passion, his gaze snared hers. "What is it, Neeake? Why do you wish me to cease? It is not as if you were an untried maiden, untaught in the ways of joining."

"I'm not a whore, either," she countered stiffly, though conversing with the man through the gap between her knees didn't exactly lend a whole lot of credibility to her statement. "Whether you choose to believe me or not, I've never made love with anyone but my husband. I don't make a habit of sharing my body with strangers."

"That is good, but there is no shame in what we do here, Neeake. I will have no contempt for you afterward."

"Hah!" she snorted with dark humor. "What woman hasn't heard that line from a man? 'Sure, baby, I'll respect you in the morning.' And the check's in the mail, and . . .'"

"Is it fair that you judge me by other men you have known?" he interrupted. "Any more than it would be for me to judge you by the same measure?"

"No," she admitted, feeling chastised despite herself, "but there are more important considerations here. Like AIDS, for instance."

"AIDS?" he mused.

"Yes, AIDS, as in Acquired Immunodeficiency Syndrome. As in, you catch it, you die. As in, transmitted by unprotected sex, among other ways. And don't you dare try to tell me you don't know what I'm talking about!"

"I am aware of sicknesses which are given to others through mating," he acknowledged somberly. "My people were free of such maladies before the white man brought them to us. One such is known as the French disease and has been known to bring about madness if it progresses sufficiently, but I know of none that cause death."

"You're speaking of venereal diseases that can be controlled or eliminated by medicine. There is no cure for AIDS, and I'd rather be safe than sorry." When he made no immediate response, she added forcefully, "In other words, buster, playtime is over. Let me up."

"You do not have this AIDS, then, and fear getting it," he concluded.

She tried, unsuccessfully, to press her legs together, only to have him nudge them farther apart. "Look, Tonto, I'm not a blasted wishbone! Do you think you could leave my joints intact? Better yet, go hump a . . ."

Again, he interrupted her. "I am not that easily deterred. I require an answer, please."

"No, I do not have AIDS!" she warranted, thoroughly exasperated. "No thanks to my husband's wandering ways," she added dryly. "I've been tested, and I'm squeaky clean. Can you say the same?"

Somewhat to her surprise, Silver Thorn nodded. "I, too, am free of disease. Are your fears now eased, little one?"

She shook her head. "Not at all. I'd feel a darn sight more secure if you'd get off me and forget the whole idea of further intimacy between us. Can't we just shake hands and go back to our corners? Or to our opposite sides of the fire, in this case?"

He chose to ignore the stated options and changed the subject entirely. "Do you know that your private parts remind me of an ear of corn?" he remarked, his hand stroking over her belly, and then lower.

"What?" she squeaked, taken totally off guard.

His fingers crept beneath the elastic into the nest of dark curls between her legs. "It is so," he told her, his voice deceptively calm while his eyes danced with mischief. "Your hair here is soft and fine, like cornsilk. And like the husk that covers and protects the corn within, you also have a shield guarding your womanly essence and the tender kernel hiding there." His eyes held hers as his fingers deftly parted the concealing folds and delved unerringly to that tiny button of flesh that governed her desire.

Nikki lurched beneath his touch, already craving more. In the small portion of her brain that was still functioning logically through the rising tide of need, she could not quite believe what was happening. This man . . . this maniac . . . had but to speak, and she was virtually seduced—his to command, like a puppet ruled by a puppeteer. A look from those crystalline silver eyes, and she was practically mesmerized. And a touch . . . God, a mere touch was like being branded with lightning!

"Let me taste of you, Neeake," he murmured, "that I might sip the sweet nectar buried within."

Though she said not a word, her body answered for her. The taut muscles in her thighs relaxed, allowing him free access. When he tugged her panties down, she lifted her hips to aid him. And when his head lowered in quest of the prize, she sighed and tilted her pelvis in search of his mouth.

Then, all thought was beyond her grasp as he sipped and suckled and sent her spiraling. Precisely when he released her wrists, she could not have said, but next she knew she was clutching his head to her, weaving her fingers through the black satin of his hair, pulling him up and over her as she offered herself to him and met him halfway. They rode the wind, soaring higher with each thrust of his body into hers, until they burst through the sun and it splintered into thousands of shimmering shards.

Nikki had always thought of herself as a sexually educated person. She was well read and, for a while at least, had led a healthy, supposedly normal lovelife. Foreplay was nothing new, though there were some things Scott had wanted to try that she'd considered kinky and declined outright. She'd even achieved climax on a regular basis, something which some women never experienced. But she'd never climaxed like this!

If anyone had tried to tell her it could be, or should be, like this, she would have called that person a liar. Or at the least, a gullible fool. A climax of such magnitude only occurred in movies and romance novels, not in real life. Bells did not really chime. Alarms did not sound. Celestial bodies did not fall from the heavens. All that was fantastic bunk!

Oh, but now Nikki knew better, and if she wanted to tell someone else how profound it was, she doubted she could find words to adequately describe what had just happened to her. She had honestly thought she might die from it, that her heart would simply explode in her chest. The pleasure was so intense, it bordered on pain. And at the end, the nearest thing she could compare it to were accounts of near-death encounters, with bright light and a sensation of flying, of spinning through space, her soul apart from her body.

In the aftermath of the most glorious, overwhelming experience of her life, Nikki lay stunned and breathless, basking in the lingering glow, savoring the ebbing reverberations that vibrated through every love-sated cell. At this moment, she was sure that nothing could destroy her sense of well-being. Nothing could pierce the rosy haze enveloping her.

Until she heard Silver Thorn's gravelly voice intone wonderingly, "In all my days, I have never lost myself with any woman as I did with you just now, Neeake. Always before, I have been aware of my body and its every action. This is the first time I have planted my seed within a woman's womb, but I know without doubt that this is what I have done today and that it was meant to be. Though we come from different worlds, different times, and I am as yet unsure how our joint venture will proceed or end, of this I am certain. Together, you and I have just spawned a son, Neeake."

Five

Nikki bolted upright, inadvertently ramming her forehead into Silver Thorn's face. As he moved hastily aside, clutching at his throbbing nose, she gaped at him in dumbfounded outrage. "I'm still trying to decide if you're insane or simply stupid. At this point, it's a toss-up or I'd probably kill you for spouting such nonsense and expecting me to believe it!"

"It is true, little goose," he assured her seriously, pressing his fingers to his bridge and testing the bone to see if it were still intact. "My seed is taking root in your body as we speak."

"I sincerely hope not! The last thing I need is to be impregnated by a half-strung yo-yo! Lord only knows what the poor child would turn out like!"

Silver Thorn sighed. "The choice is not yours. Nor was it mine. This was fore-ordained by the Spirits. Written in the stars long before you or I were born."

"Well, unwrite it!" she shot back, suddenly next to tears.

"I cannot. What is done, is done."

"Prophetic last words. After our little discussion about AIDS and disease, didn't it even occur to you to use a condom?"

"What is a condom?"

Nikki screwed up her face and let loose an irate shriek. "A rubber, you dumb son-of-a-buick! A prophylactic! A device to deter the spread of disease and impede conception."

"Ah, a sheath!" Silver Thorn concluded at last.

"Well! Light dawns on marblehead!" she quipped sarcastically. "Will wonders never cease?"

"You need not be so scornful, woman," he informed her. "Among my people, it is often the women who tend to such matters."

Nikki glared at him. "Don't try to pass the buck, Romeo. I've been divorced for three years and, for all intents and purposes, out of circulation. Therefore, I had no reason to go on the pill or otherwise take preventative measures. And I certainly didn't foresee this bizarre escapade."

He gave a sage nod. "It is fortunate that you no longer have another husband or I could not take you to wife."

Nikki clamped a hand to her head, feeling distinctly disoriented. "I wonder if this is what Alice felt like when she fell down the rabbit hole?" she muttered.

"Are you not well?" Silver Thorn inquired with concern.

Nikki groaned. "I'm not actually sure. I can't seem to make up my mind whether to laugh, cry, or toss my cookies."

"Perhaps you should lie down," he suggested.

Nikki nodded lethargically and put up no resistance as Silver Thorn led her to his pallet and lay her down on it. "Yes," she agreed numbly. "I need a nap. A nice, long nap. Like Rip Van Winkle. And when I wake up, this will all have been a dream, and I'll be back in my own bed, in my own house, in my own time . . . and you won't exist at all." She yawned and smiled up him drowsily. "Won't that be lovely?"

As was her habit, Nikki woke slowly and reluctantly. Loathe to leave her snug nest, she tucked her legs up and wriggled her nose deeper into the blanket. She sniffed

once. Then again, and frowned. Since when did Downy
smell like wet horse? Or had Her Nibs, that ornery An-
gora-with-an-attitude, buried a dead mouse in the bed?

Nikki cocked one bleary eye open, sure she would find
the blasted cat sitting there smirking at her. Instead, her
gaze centered on Silver Thorn, sitting cross-legged before
the waning fire, staring into the diminishing flames.

"Oh, Lord!" Nikki groaned prayerfully. "What did I do
to deserve this? Aren't regular nightmares bad enough? Do
they have to come in re-runs and sequels now?"

Silver Thorn did not look up from his contemplation of
the fire, nor did he direct any comment toward her.

"Say, shouldn't you add some more wood to the fire?"
she suggested. "And while you're at it, how about a couple
of thick, juicy steaks? I missed lunch, and I'm starving."

Still Silver Thorn made no response, verbally or otherwise.

Nikki glowered at him. "What's this? The silent treatment? Isn't that the typical male! He gets the goodies, then
ignores you."

Silver Thorn didn't twitch as much as a muscle. He just
sat there, silent and unmoving, like some frozen mummy,
and suddenly his utter stillness struck Nikki as incredibly
odd.

She rose, clutching the blanket around her, and approached him cautiously. "Yo! Tonto! You didn't go and
die on me, did you?" She leaned closer and noted that his
eyes were open, but unfocused. At least they hadn't rolled
to the back of his head, as she'd heard a dead person's
did.

"Hey! Hi, ho, Silver! Wake up and smell the coffee!"
she called out, snapping her fingers in front of his nose.
He just sat and stared, as if turned to stone. "Geez!" she
murmured, rubbing at the goose bumps now peppering her
arms. "This is spooky!"

Nikki squatted next to him, trying to gear herself for

what she knew she must do next. "So help me God, Thorn. If you're just messing around to scare me, I'm going to make you regret it." Tentatively, she reached out and touched his arm. To her vast relief, it was warm. She heaved a sigh.

"So far, so good," she told herself. Her hand moved to his chest, and she felt the heavy, rhythmic beat of his heart. "Okay, you're alive. So what's going on here? Did some evil genie sneak in here and put a spell on you?"

Then, as her own words sank in, the truth dawned on her. "You're in a trance, aren't you? I'll be darned! You did mention a dream-vision earlier. That's what this is all about! You're in some type of self-induced hypnotic state . . . and I'm out of here!"

Realizing that this was her best chance to escape, Nikki wasted little time. She yanked her clothes on, swung into her backpack, and charged the hill of rocks at the cave entrance. She managed to get a third of the way up before the rocks gave way beneath her feet, sending her skidding down again. Catching her breath and reviewing the situation, she attacked the blockade more slowly the second time, but to little avail. For every step forward, the pile shifted, sending her backward two strides. All she gained was a lot of unwanted exercise, a scraped palm, and two broken fingernails. And the rocks were still blocking her exit.

"Drat! I'll never get anywhere this way," she admitted to herself. "I'm just wearing myself out and getting nowhere! There's got to be another way."

There was. Her gaze swung to the back of the cave, toward the rear tunnel. Was that an alternate route out? Was that why Silver Thorn had not been troubled when the rockslide had blocked the forward entrance?

She eyed the murky hollow with trepidation. Did she dare even think about it, let alone try it? What if she got lost and wandered around in there forever?

"Coward!" she berated herself. "How bad can it be? You toured the other caves, and nothing happened. You've got a flashlight in your pack with a fresh battery. Besides, you have to go to the restroom anyway. Just walk a few steps inside, and take a look."

And watch for snakes and sudden drop-offs, her 'self' suggested in reply.

"There weren't snakes or perilous pits in the other caves," she contended. "There were even lights and an air ventilation system."

So go for it, her alter ego said. *And call me when you find the light switch*!

"Good grief! Here I am arguing with myself—and I called Silver Thorn bonkers!"

Nikki fished out her flashlight and tested it to make sure it was operating properly. Gathering all the courage she could muster, she walked to the tunnel and peered carefully inside. Though gloomy, it was dry, and the floor appeared fairly wide and level. Best of all, it wasn't crawling with insects and nothing with teeth, claws, or fangs leapt out at her.

"Why not just scare yourself to death, Nikki?" she grumbled. "You've got to stop watching all those late-night horror flicks!" Sucking in a deep breath, she stepped forward. Immediately inside the passageway, she stopped and listened.

So, what are you waiting for, dummy? her psyche sneered. *Or did you expect a trap door to fall shut behind you, like a scene from* Raiders of the Lost Ark? *If you're real lucky, maybe you'll run into Harrison Ford and the two of you can have a mad fling in here.*

"Mad being the operative word. Not only am I talking to myself, I'm answering myself, too."

There was no light switch. Nor did the glow from her flashlight reveal any hint of wiring or string of bulbs, as in the caves she'd visited previously. Swallowing her inner fears, Nikki forced herself to start walking. A few yards along, she found a slight indentation in the wall, an adequate if not choice spot to relieve herself. After juggling the flashlight, her britches, and her own shaking anatomy—no mean feat for someone who could rarely walk and chew gum at the same time—she concluded the task and continued onward.

The passageway took numerous twists and turns before branching off at several points. It was only after she'd traversed what seemed like miles that Nikki realized she should have been more consistent in her choice of paths, either always veering right or only left. That, or she should have found a way to mark her trail in the event her escape route turned out to be a dead end. Of course, the ideal situation would have provided a detailed map and a competent tour guide.

A short time later, Nikki stopped to check her watch and estimated she'd been walking for approximately forty minutes. The corridor was narrower here and seemed to be slanting steadily downward. She debated whether to retreat and try an alternate path or forge ahead. Deciding to go back a ways, she turned around. When she did so, her backpack snagged an outcropping on the wall, throwing her off balance. Nikki went sprawling. The flashlight flew from her hand. It bounced several times, throwing eerie patterns of light and shadow along the rock, then abruptly went out.

The sudden darkness was absolute, blacker than anything Nikki had ever encountered. It was like being struck blind. She'd heard the expression about not being able to see your hand before your face. Now she was experiencing it personally, and it was truly terrifying. And totally disorienting. She knew she was kneeling on the floor of the cave. She could feel the grit beneath her palms. When she reached out, her fingers brushed the walls on either side of her. Yet, even knowing this, feeling it, there was a strange sensation of not being able to distinguish up from down or forward from backward.

Someone whimpered, and only after she'd jumped in fright did Nikki recognize the sound as her own voice. She fought to retain her wits. Intellectually, she knew the flashlight was mere yards away. She could find it, she assured herself. All she had to do was stay calm and in control and crawl along the path and feel for it.

But the moment she moved, Nikki lost her sense of equilibrium once more. The dizziness hit her with such force that she was nauseous. It was several long minutes before she could try again. And yet again. Creeping forward inch by inch, feeling her way like a sightless snail.

When at last her seeking fingers touched the cool cylinder, it was only to knock it further down the path from her. A sob of frustration lodged in her throat. She began the search again. Slowly. Carefully. But she could not locate the flashlight. Thinking she might somehow have passed it, she scooted backward. Then forward. Until finally she became so disoriented she wasn't sure which direction was which—and still the light, her sole salvation, eluded her.

Trapped in a world of eternal darkness, Nikki lost her grasp of logic and succumbed to the panic gnawing at her. Her screams of horror reverberated through the stony canyons of the cave like multiple ripples in a pond, returning to assault her own ears. Her imagination began to play tricks on her mind and body. Her skin began to tingle as if a thousand spiders were swarming over it. She slapped at them, raking her own flesh with her nails, trying to rid herself of them. At one point, she swore she heard a gruff noise akin to a low growl. Then she felt something large and furry brush her face, something rough and wet swipe across her chin, but when she swatted frantically at it, she touched nothing but her own tear-stained cheek.

Nearly mindless with terror, deaf to all but the clamor

of her own screams and frenzied heartbeats, Nikki did not hear Silver Thorn calling to her until he was almost upon her. So strong was her panic that her brain failed to register the fact that she could actually see, until Silver Thorn stood directly in front of her, his face reflected in the glow of his torch.

She reached for him, her arms scratched and bleeding as she held them out to him. "Thorn! Thorn! Hold me! Save me!"

He bent and enfolded her in his embrace, trembling nearly as badly as she. "I have you, Neeake. You are safe."

"No! There's some animal in here! I know it! It . . . it touched me!"

"Do not fear. It was only Macate, my cat. My animal spirit-guide. He is the one who led me to you just now."

Silver Thorn shifted, the better to lift her into his arms, and Nikki's anxiety returned full force. "No! Don't leave me! I couldn't bear being alone in the dark again!"

"I go nowhere without you," he crooned. Cradling her close, he said softly, "If your hand is steady enough to hold the firebrand without setting both of us ablaze, I will carry you."

As her panic receded, reason quickly reinstated itself. "I dropped my flashlight. If you can find it for me, it will be safer to handle."

His gaze caught the glint of the metal tube. He retrieved it and handed it to her. "Is this what you seek?"

"Yes. I just hope it still works."

Nikki flipped the switch, which had apparently been knocked into the *off* position when she'd dropped it, and a welcome ray of light streamed from the lens.

Though no less surprised than he'd been when she'd lit the cigarette lighter, Silver Thorn accepted this new curiosity with more aplomb. "More of your magic from the future?" he assumed inquisitively.

She nodded. Flashlight in hand to light their way, she

looped her arms securely about his neck. "Yes, but it's not infallible and it will never replace sunlight. Take me out of here, Silver Thorn. Please. I need to see the sky, to breathe fresh air, to be in a place where there are no walls bearing down on me."

"Twice now, you have fled from me, and twice you have become lost and courted disaster." Silver Thorn studied Nikki, his expression somber. "Have you at last learned the danger of such reckless behavior?"

They were sitting on the ledge outside the cave entrance. The storm had passed, leaving behind the washed-clean smell of damp grass and earth. Nikki sucked in another gulp of rain-freshened air.

"Yes," she replied shakily. Fast on the heels of her fright in the tunnel, Nikki had received another pair of shocks, and she hadn't sufficiently recovered from any of them.

Upon reaching the rockslide blocking the entrance, Silver Thorn had intoned a Shawnee chant; and before Nikki's disbelieving gaze, the entire pile of rocks had tumbled away from the opening and down the hillside. She still wasn't sure *how* he'd done it, but she'd witnessed the startling phenomenon with her own two eyes.

Dumbfounded, she'd scarcely regained her power of speech when a large, streak of gray fur dashed past them. For a mere heartbeat, the beast stopped on the ledge and stared back at her with feral, gold eyes. If Silver Thorn had not still been carrying her, Nikki would surely have crumbled to the floor in a mass of quivering, rattling bones.

"That . . . That's a lynx!" she'd shrieked.

"Hah-háh. Yes, the *peshewa,* the wildcat I mentioned to you. I call him Macate, for his pelt is the color of gunpowder."

"But . . . but . . . they're practically extinct, aren't they, at least in the United States? I think they still exist in the wilds of Canada, but not around here."

"I am saddened to hear that these creatures no longer roam our forests in your time. There must be many changes from this day to yours. I would hear of these things from you, Neeake, when you have rested and collected your thoughts."

"You may have a long wait," she'd informed him glibly. "At least until I finish my nervous breakdown."

Now, as they sat outside the cave, Nikki was comfortably nestled in Silver Thorn's lap—yet another first for her. She'd never snuggled up with a man in a breechcloth before. Maybe next year, she'd vacation in Scotland and have a fling with a guy in a kilt!

As they watched the setting sun paint the western sky in shades of red and violet, he said, "I must have your solemn oath that you will never again attempt to flee from me, Neeake. You are carrying our son in your body, and I wish no peril to befall either of you."

"You can't know that," she contended. "Even with the newest test kits, it would be impossible to detect pregnancy this early. And without amniocentesis or a sonogram, it's anyone's guess if a fetus is male or female."

"I know that my son grows within you at this very moment."

"Prove it, here and now, and you have my promise that I'll stop running away," she offered, confident there was no way he could present evidence to support his incredulous claim.

Silver Thorn's cocky smile shook her certainty. Without another word, he slipped his hand inside the waistband of her jeans and rested his palm low on her belly. For several seconds, nothing happened. And then she felt it. A quickening deep inside, the lightest of flutters.

"It's just nerves," she assured him, and herself. "Just a nervous twitch, a muscle spasm, maybe."

No sooner were the words spoken, than she felt it again. That ticklish little shimmer. Only this time, it generated bands of heat that spread outward in warm spirals.

A feeling that could only be termed *maternal* coursed through her, bringing tears to her eyes. Nikki loved children. She'd always wanted one of her own. Even after her divorce from Scott, she'd often wished they'd had a child, though it would have meant hassling with her ex over custody and visitation privileges. Now, if she dared believe it, Silver Thorn was telling her that she had, at long last, conceived. But did she dare to hope that her dearest desire was coming true, simply because this man said it was so? He obviously needed psychiatric help in the worst way. And after today, she most likely did, too.

."Wishful thinking," she concluded. "The power of suggestion. You planted the idea in my mind, and my body is simply responding to it."

"Look at your belly, Neeake, and tell me what you see," Silver Thorn advised. "You require proof. I give it to you."

"I see my jeans," she sallied.

"Beneath the trousers, woman. On your bare flesh."

She eyed him skeptically. "Are you sure this isn't just a sneaky little maneuver to get into my pants again?"

He said nothing, waiting patiently for her to do as he'd said.

"Okay. I'll play along." She unzipped her denims and hiked the material down, along with the top elastic of her panties.

Her eyes widened. Her jaw dropped. There, as plain as day, was a bright blue imprint, similar to a tattoo, in the shape of an arrow.

Nikki grabbed Silver Thorn's hand, turning it over to inspect his palm and fingers. There were no traces of ink, no markings like those on her stomach, no concealed rubber stamp.

"How?" she wondered aloud.

"It is the sign you demanded," he told her frankly. His clear, crystal gaze captured hers, compelling her to believe. "The child will be born in the Moon of the Crow, and in honor of that bird of words and wisdom, our son shall be named Sage."

Six

Nikki gave a lamenting groan and directed a look of helpless resignation across the fire at Silver Thorn. "Does it bother you at all to know that I have the most compelling urge to curl up in a corner and start sucking my thumb!"

He sent her that grin again—that beguiling, bewitching, totally exasperating grin that immediately took ten years off his face and made him look like a handsome "thirty-something" devil with mischief up his sleeve. "Perhaps it is the child in you," he quipped wryly, nodding toward her stomach.

"Oh-ho! And aren't we the witty one?" she bantered back.

Silver Thorn continued mixing water with the dried mixture he'd poured from a leather pouch. "What are you doing?" she asked with just a hint of sarcasm. "Whipping up another magic potion?"

He laughed. "Nothing so mystical, little goose. I am preparing our meal."

Nikki eyed the grayish gruel and wrinkled her nose in disgust. "That's our dinner? It looks like moldy oatmeal."

"On the morrow, I will check my snares, and we will have fresh meat. Perhaps a fat squirrel or rabbit. For now, the *takuwah-nepi* will serve to fill our bellies."

"Taco what?" she questioned.

"*Takuwah-nepi*. Breadwater, made of cornmeal and

dried berries. It is very nourishing, and not at all unpleasant in taste," he assured her, slapping the mixture into patties and setting them on the hot rocks ringing the fire. "Once it has baked on the rocks, it will be more appealing to your eye."

"I doubt that," she debated. "Besides, if you'd said something earlier, I could have saved you the trouble. I have a sack lunch in my backpack."

"You have brought food with you from your time?" he inquired curiously. "I would be most interested to see how it survived the passage from your time to mine."

"Yeah, well don't get too excited," she warned him. She retrieved her knapsack and started rooting through it. "I only brought a ham sandwich, a bag of chips, two pieces of fruit, and a couple of drinks. After sitting around all day, everything is probably either stale or soggy. I just hope nothing's spoiled. A rousing case of food poisoning is all I'd need to top off my day."

She pulled out an insulated lunch bag, opened it, and removed the foil-wrapped sandwich. As she unwrapped it, Silver Thorn seemed more interested in the foil that the food.

"What manner of cloth is that?" he asked. "I have been to supper at the Galloway house, where they have fine linen squares called napkins, but I have never seen any so bright and shiny."

"This isn't linen. It's not even cloth. It's aluminum foil," she told him, too hungry to argue with him now about this crazy time-travel tale. She divided the sandwich and handed him half of it. "I hope you like chopped ham and cheese."

Silver Thorn peeled back the puffy upper bun and peered at it and the sandwich. "Fat bread," he noted. "What is the yellow paint?"

"Honey mustard," she replied thickly, having just taken a bite of her own portion. "It's good. Try it."

After sniffing it, Silver Thorn tasted the sandwich. He chewed, and nodded. "Good," he agreed.

From the sack, Nikki retrieved a small bag of potato chips. She poured some into her lap and tossed the rest to Silver Thorn. "If I'd known I was going to share my lunch, I'd have bought another sandwich and a larger bag of chips."

"These are called *chips*?" He held one up and studied it. "Do they ripen like this?"

Nikki giggled. "No, goofy! They're made of potatoes, sliced thin and fried in oil."

Again, he nodded. "Then I will try one, despite its disagreeable name."

"What's so awful about calling it a *chip*?" she wanted to know.

His brow rose questioningly. "Have you never heard of deer chips? Elk chips? Cow chips?"

Nikki's face contorted as she caught his meaning. "Ooh, yuck! Gross!"

"Precisely."

Just the thought made Nikki want to rinse out her mouth. Delving into her sack, she withdrew a can of Diet Coke and a small carton of pineapple-orange juice. "Which one do you want?" she offered.

Silver Thorn frowned at the objects in her hands. "What are these?"

Nikki rolled her eyes and strove for patience, an asset she tapped often in her capacity as a teacher. "This," she said, holding up the white-and-gold can, "is caffeine-free Diet Coke in a tab-top can. And this," she elaborated, lifting the second container, "is pineapple-orange juice, all natural with no sugar added, in a waxed-paper box."

"What is the *calf* Coke made of?" he inquired.

"Beats me," she countered with a shrug. "Coke syrup and carbonation and a bunch of other ingredients I wouldn't recognize if I bothered to read the label. I will tell you that my brother once used it to clean the corrosion from his battery terminals. As much of this stuff as I drink, I'm surprised I still have a stomach lining, but what can I say? I crave my cola!"

"And the other drink? It is of some type of apple?"

"Pineapple. A tropical fruit grown in the Hawaiian Islands. And oranges. You are familiar with oranges, aren't you?" she added cynically.

"I have tasted the orange," he admitted, accepting the fruit drink from her and puzzling over how to open it. "The Galloway family received some at the holiday they call Christmas."

The surname rang a bell buried in Nikki's memory bank. "The Galloways? As in Rebecca Galloway and family?"

"Hah-háh. Yes. You know of them?"

"I've read of them," Nikki corrected. "In history books. Tecumseh courted Rebecca, didn't he?" Seeing his problem with the juice box, Nikki took it, opened it, and handed it back to him.

"Five years past, Tecumseh thought to marry her and relieve our sister, Tecumapese, of the burden of rearing his two sons, but Rebecca would have him only if Tecumseh would embrace the ways of her people. This my brother could not do, so they parted company. Tecumseh has since devoted himself to forming his confederacy."

"I've always wondered what might have happened if Rebecca and Tecumseh had married," Nikki mused. "Would he have given up his quest for an alliance of Indians against the whites? Would his views have leaned more toward peace?"

Silver Thorn, who had been glutting himself on the juice, stopped in mid-gulp. "You may have just given me a solution to my dilemma," he announced. "Tomorrow we shall ride to the Galloway farm. I have not visited in many moons, but I know they still live there. If Rebecca can be swayed, there may yet be a chance to save my brother from his destiny."

"You're putting me on," Nikki remarked. "Even if she really were living nearby, what makes you think you could convince her to change her mind after all this time?"

"There is always a possibility that she regrets her earlier decision. Also, she and her family are not only friends to Tecumseh, but to our sister and to me. It is Rebecca's father, James, who lends me his books to read."

"The classics?" she guessed. "Shakespeare?" Nikki baited the trap slyly. "And where did you learn to read?"

Silver Thorn evaded it with ease. "Blue Jacket taught me."

"Blue Jacket?" Nikki exclaimed in awe, drawn into his fantasy despite herself. "The white boy adopted by the Shawnee, who grew up to be a famous chief?"

"The same."

"Now *there* is a man I'd like to meet someday," Nikki commented.

The look on Silver Thorn's face plainly showed he was not pleased that Nikki, after mocking him, would show such enthusiasm for meeting another man, even one as fine as Blue Jacket. "You arrive three years late for that, Neeake."

"Rats! Is he already dead?" she inquired.

Silver Thorn nodded. After a moment's pause, he said, "Neeake, it is not our custom to speak openly of those who have journeyed to the afterworld. It is my error to have mentioned him to you, but please do not question me further about him."

Nikki was taken aback, both at the sincere regret in Silver Thorn's voice at the death of his friend and at her unintentional gaffe. "I apologize, Silver Thorn. I didn't mean to hurt you by dredging up sad memories."

She changed the subject. "You say Tecumseh has two sons. I assume, then, that he also has a wife. Won't Rebecca balk at the idea of sharing him with another woman? As far as that goes, is it acceptable for a Shawnee man to have more than one wife?"

"It is allowed, though not all men do so, and Tecumseh has no wife now. He divorced his first wife, who bore his first son. She returned to her own village, and Tecumapese, our sister, took over the babe's care."

"Why did Tecumseh divorce her? Did she burn his bacon or something?" Nikki jeered, faking a look of horror.

Silver Thorn leaned closer, matching her look for look. "She was a scold, constantly discontent and complaining, never giving the poor man a moment's peace. Much like you could be, I imagine, if I were to give you full rein."

"He divorced her for that?" Nikki squawked. "What kind of wimp was he, anyway?"

"Wimp? What is a wimp?"

"Your big bad brother, evidently. In other words, a sissy, a pantywaist, a weak man."

"This Tecumseh is not," Silver Thorn declared adamantly. "Nor am I, as you will soon learn. And though I teased you, the true reason he divorced Monetohse is that she did not mother their son properly. She wanted naught to do with the infant. Thus, Tecumseh was able to invoke a long-standing Shawnee law and retain possession of his son, who would normally have gone to live with his mother."

"He's lucky then, because even in modern times it's hard to prove incompetency and most judges tend to award the mother custody of the children," Nikki commented. "But you mentioned another son. Is Mona-whoever his mother, too?"

"No. Tecumseh wed again, an older woman who bore him Naytha-way-nah and then succumbed to childbed fever. That was ten-and-seven years ago, and Tecumseh has not, in all the years since, found a woman other than Rebecca with whom he wishes to marry."

"So his sons are young men by now," Nikki calculated. Another question popped into her head. "What about the women of the tribe? Do they take more than one husband?"

Silver Thorn was shocked. "Never. She who would suggest such a disgraceful notion would surely be banned!"

"Oh, so it's the old double standard, is it?" Nikki said, her feminist hackles rising. "It's okay for a man to fool around, but let a woman try it and she's immediately labeled a slut. A man can have his cake and eat it, too, but a woman is expected not only to bake the damned dessert, but to serve it to her lord and master on a silver tray! Is that close enough to the truth?" she railed.

"Not at all," he responded. "Shawnee men and women are equals in most matters. While there is a natural division of labor, with heavier tasks allotted to the male, it is not uncommon for a man to assume his wife's duties or for a woman to perform those most usual to a man. It is customary that a husband is not condemned for seeking the company of another woman while a wife is readily denounced for the same. Still, in most matters, their authority and responsibilities, both in the home and tribal affairs, are equally shared and their opinions mutually respected."

"Is that why you're not married? You can't stand the idea of sharing control with a woman?" she needled. Then, as the thought gelled, she exclaimed softly. "Or maybe you are! Lord in heaven, it never even dawned on me that you could be married, that at your age the average man already has a wife and two-point-five children! While I admit you're not what anyone, by any stretch of the imagination, would consider *average,* I think you owe me the truth. Are you now, or have you ever been, married?"

"I was joined with another when I was young," he confessed. "She was the only daughter of my father's most honored friend."

"Are you still married?" Nikki awaited his answer anxiously.

Silver Thorn shook his head. "She, too, is gone, many years now. We had been wed but a short while when our camp was visited by disease. Measles. So common to the white man, but so lethal to the Shawnee."

"Do you have children?"

"I have already said that you are the only woman with whom I have sown my seed. I have no other wives or offspring."

Tired of discussing his past relationships, Silver Thorn switched topics. "I have eaten of your repast. Now, you must eat of mine."

After having inadvertently committed several social blunders in succession, Nikki could hardly refuse. Reluctantly, she accepted the corncake he handed her and nibbled tentatively at it. Surprisingly, it wasn't as bland as she had expected. "Not bad," she told him. "Not bad at all. If you can make this taste good, I can hardly wait to see what you do with a steak or a roast or maybe a turkey."

He chuckled. "I cannot be wife and husband all at once, Neeake, though I shall help you with many daily chores."

Nikki sighed. "Look, pal, I like you. Really, I do. And I can't deny the sexual chemistry between us, but let's not rush things. If you're really serious, we'll see about getting you some good psychiatric help and play the rest by ear, okay? Besides, I'm not quite ready to buy into the wife routine again. Once burned, twice shy, and all that. So just hang loose, and maybe in a year or so, if you've responded well to treatment, I'll accept your proposal and agree to marry you."

He eyed her curiously. "Do you not understand, Neeake? By sharing this feast and joining our bodies we are already wed. You are my wife and I your husband, bound by the laws of our people."

She stared at him, aghast, but rallied quickly. *"Your* people, Silver Thorn. Not mine."

"Our people," he corrected firmly, his eyes glinting like burnished steel. "You, by your own words, share our blood and our ancestry. Therefore, in this time, you must also abide by Shawnee custom and rules."

"When pigs fly!" she countered haughtily.

"That should not be too difficult a feat for me to accomplish," he responded with a cocksure smirk. "Will morning be soon enough, *wife,* for me to make pigs fly for you?"

"Oh, sure!" she exclaimed, throwing up her hands in defeat. "Silly me! I forgot! I'm dealing with a man who can literally move mountains, who can transport humans and objects through time and space, who can implant his sperm at will and designate the sex of his child—all without breaking a sweat! Flying pigs should be a breeze for you!"

She heaved an exasperated sigh. "Holy Moses, Thorn! If we're supposed to be equally matched, tell me how in sweet hell I'm supposed to compete with that!"

He reached for her, tugging her around the fire and into his arms. "You have your own power, Neeake. Woman's magic, potent enough to bring a strong man to his knees." His lips sought hers, caressing softly and persuasively. "Shall I let you test it on me once more?"

"Aw, heck!" she muttered, her mouth melting beneath his, her hands already delving into his sleek black hair. "Why not? *In for a penny; in for pound.* What is it about you that turns me on so . . . you handsome, crazy, horny hunk?"

Seven

"Get a grip, Neeake!" Silver Thorn exclaimed.

Nikki swiped her sopping hair from her eyes and glared up at him, her expression both accusing and triumphant. "Aha! If that isn't modern slang, I don't know what is! I knew you'd slip up sooner or later and give yourself away!"

"Stop spouting nonsense and do as I say, woman. Reach out and grab hold of the *olagashe,* the canoe!"

"For crap sake, Thorn! I'm sitting in a foot and a half of water! I'm not likely to drown unless I start breathing through my rear end!"

Silver Thorn tossed the armful of gear on the bank and waded quickly into the river. "The canoe," he repeated irritably as he flung himself forward and arrested the floating craft, "was drifting away, as were the paddles."

"Well! How nice of you to be concerned for my welfare!" she huffed. "And I fail to see what you're so ticked about. I'm the one who took a dunking."

He righted the canoe and pulled it back to shore, casting her a peevish glance as he passed her. "You needed a good dousing after crawling through the bowels of the cave on your hands and knees. However, you could have avoided getting wet if you had not lunged into the canoe like a stampeding cow."

Enraged, Nikki reached out, snagged the heel of his moccasin, and yanked. A split second later, with a mighty splash, Silver Thorn landed on his backside beside her. Propping himself on his elbows, he shook the water from his black mane, sending the spray in all directions.

Before he could utter a word, Nikki was snarling at him. "Call me a cow again, and see how fast one of those oars connects with your thick skull, buster!"

"I did not call you a cow," he argued. "I merely compared your clumsiness to one."

"Semantics!" she countered. "Furthermore, if you'd bothered to instruct me on the proper way to board that floating booby trap, we might both be dry right now."

He rose to his feet and extended a helping hand toward her. "It did not occur to me that you would not know this, Neeake."

She accepted his aid, her disposition only slightly improved. "For your information, I was not a Girl Scout and I never attended Camp Wishy-Washy, or whatever."

"*Oui-sah, oui-i-si*?" He spoke precisely, trying to mimic her enunciation. "You have young female scouts lodged in this place of Good Head?"

Nikki stared at him, her puzzlement momentarily as great as his.

"I think I misinterpret," he concluded. "Is your English word not the same as our Shawnee word *oui-sah*, which means either good or great? Is this not Good Head then, but perhaps Camp Great Head when imparted by your tongue?"

"Lord, I hope not!" Nikki burst out laughing as the risqué side of his unintentional double entendre struck her funnybone. "Especially when it comes to those little darlings selling all those cookies to millions of Americans each year! And, in case you're wondering, *my* tongue doesn't grant such *generous* favors either, at least not on the first date."

His face was a study of confusion. "What is so amusing? Explain, please."

"No way, José," she intoned playfully. "You're not luring me into another one of those intimate exchanges now. We don't have time for more 'show and tell.' Later, if you're a very good boy, maybe I'll give you a 'brief' demonstration."

Nikki went into gales of giggles again at her own glib pun, and it was some time before Silver Thorn managed to bundle her, their possessions, and himself into the canoe and set off at last.

The morning was made-to-order, the sky a cloudless blue canopy above them. A light, balmy breeze played over the sun-dappled water. Birds sang, frogs chirped, squirrels chattered as they chased from tree to tree; butterflies flitted about in gay abandon. It was all so picturesque, Nature at her finest.

As Nikki's clothes began to dry and she began to appreciate the beauty surrounding them, her mood mellowed accordingly. When Silver Thorn pointed out a fawn and its mother drinking at the edge of the creek, she was thoroughly enthralled.

"Despite our bumpy start, I'm glad I came along with you today, Thorn," she said. She missed the measuring glance he threw back at her from his place in the front of the craft. "Between classes and grading homework papers and the numerous other tasks that make up my routine, it's rare that I get an opportunity to just kick back and really enjoy the wonders of the world around me."

She trailed a hand lazily through the water at the side of the canoe. "This is much better than one of those crowded, noisy tours—even if my guide *is* rowing with one oar," she added impishly.

"I am aware of the implication, Neeake," he informed her dryly. "That is an old jest, one the white man learned from us."

"Explain to me, then, why we aren't going in circles."

He chuckled. "Because I know how to ply my paddle,

little goose. Which would be good for you to keep upper-most in mind."

"Spousal battering is against the law," she informed him confidently.

"Perhaps in your era," he allowed, "but in mine, when a wife needs correction it is her husband's duty to dispense it."

She let that issue rest as she drank in the sight of him, so strong and straight and handsome. He was decked out in full Shawnee regalia this morning, complete with silver wrist and arm bands, a breechcloth ornately decorated with quill embroidery, and the requisite "spirit" bag hanging from a cord around his neck. He also sported the "magic" amulet, and a quilled hair disc. A silver ear cuff dangled from his left earlobe, not detracting one whit from his blatant masculinity. Rather, it only served to enhance it, somehow.

"How long will it take to reach our destination?" she asked some time later.

"We will be on the river for most of the day."

"The whole day? We'll stop somewhere to eat and stretch our legs and use the bathroom, won't we?"

"Bathroom?" he queried.

"Oh, come on! Quit jacking me around," she grumbled. "The restroom. With a toilet and sink. The potty. The place you go when you have to pee."

"The Galloways have a building behind their house for that purpose. It has a quarter moon cut into the door."

"An outhouse?" Nikki squealed. "You've got to be kidding!"

"They consider it a necessity," Silver Thorn went on, "but I fail to understand why they close themselves into that tiny, stinking room when they could as easily relieve themselves outdoors, behind a tree or bush if they require privacy."

"Ri. .i. .ight," Nikki intoned incredulously, dragging the

syllable out the way her students often did when they didn't believe what they'd been told. "So where are we eating lunch? Is there a riverside Mickey D's?"

"When we are hungry, we will stop for our meal. If I catch the fish, can you prepare it?"

"Sure," she countered with a saccharin smile, "if you can conjure up an outboard motor. Nothing fancy, mind you, just something fast and reliable."

It was dusk when they secured the canoe to the dock at the edge of the Galloways' front yard. Nikki was bone-tired, queasy, sweaty, and peppered with mosquito bites. In contrast, Silver Thorn appeared as fresh as morning dew.

As he helped his itching bride alight from the rocking canoe, Silver Thorn said, "If you would have applied the bear grease I offered you, you would not be scratching now."

"Oh, pu . . . leeze!" she griped. "I was nauseous enough without inhaling that obnoxious stench."

"And what put your stomach awry?"

"All right, rub it in! So the fish was a little underdone. I've never tried to make sushi before. Besides, I don't think the fish made me sick. More likely, it was that five-mile hike we took through the wilderness in the noonday heat. You didn't tell me we were going to have to walk part of the way."

"You did not ask," he parried. "And you have little to complain of, for I bore the canoe while you carried only your back sack."

"Backpack," she corrected wearily, her teacher's reflex kicking in automatically.

"Before I take you to meet my friends, we must do something to correct your appearance."

"Ah, geez! Stroke my ego, why don't you! Tell you what, sweetcheeks. Why don't I just dash down to the nearest beauty parlor, get a wash and set and a manicure, and dig out my war paint?"

This brought him to immediate attention. "You have war paint in your bag?"

"What woman doesn't?" she replied indignantly.

"Do you also have more clothing? Your shirt with the writing and your men's trousers are most improper attire."

"Sorry, Charlie. Wrong tuna. If I'd had extra clothes, would I have been huddled in a blanket and my skivvies all yesterday afternoon? Of course, I could always wear my birthday suit," she taunted. "Would that be more appropriate?"

"What is . . ."

"Oh, hell! Talking to you is like trying to converse with a Martian! A person's birthday suit is his skin, you dunce! Naked skin! Just what you were born with, and nothing else covering you!"

Silver Thorn was more than astounded; he was perturbed. "You propose to meet the Galloways wearing nothing?" he thundered.

"Hey! You're the one who doesn't like my T-shirt and jeans!" she pointed out.

"I suppose there is no help for it," he admitted. Then, "Could you wear your blanket-coat over the shirt?"

"Blanket-coat? Oh, my sweater! Sure." Nikki dug the garment out of the top of her bag and quickly donned it.

At the sound of approaching footsteps, Silver Thorn murmured. "Our host approaches. I have but one parcel of advice, Neeake. Do not mention where you come from or how you came here. These people will not understand."

"Neither do I," she groused.

"Who's there?" James Galloway called out.

" 'Tis I, Silver Thorn."

A second later, the farmer emerged from the darkness and thrust out his hand in welcome. "It's been too long since you last visited us, my friend. Who is this young fellow with you?"

"Neeake is not a lad, James. She is my wife."

"Oh, I beg your pardon, ma'am. My eyes must be failing me to make such a mistake."

Nikki forced a smile. "No, apology needed, Mr. Galloway. Silver Thorn thinks I look like a boy in these clothes, too."

Silver Thorn rushed to explain. "Neeake's clothes were all lost . . . in a mishap. We were able only to secure these garments for her."

"Well, we'll fix that soon enough," Galloway claimed. "I'm sure my wife can find something more adequate. If her dresses are the wrong size, Rebecca left a few behind."

"Rebecca is not here?" Thorn inquired. Realizing how abrupt that sounded, he added, "Neeake was looking forward to meeting her since they are of much the same age."

"Becky has gone East for a time," James said. As if reluctant to pursue that vein, he turned and led the way up the slight incline to the house. "Come. Mrs. Galloway will be wondering who is here and what became of us. We don't want to worry her."

As they stepped into the house, Nikki felt as if she'd just entered the Twilight Zone. That or she truly had stepped back two centuries in time.

To the left of the hallway, which appeared to run the length of the house, front to back, they entered what could only be termed a *parlor*. Oil lanterns and candles were placed strategically around the room, the only sources of light as near as Nikki could tell at first glance. A huge stone fireplace dominated one wall; but as the evening was warm, it was unlit. On the mantel sat a pendulum clock, the old key-wound type. The furniture, though not crude, was of an older handmade style, including what was probably a horsehair sofa. The backs and arms of the couch and the tops of the few tables were adorned with stiffly starched crocheted doilies. A large braided rug covered the plank floor. There were no electrical appliances in view. No television. No radio. No telephone.

On either side of the fireplace and along the wall nearest Nikki, shelves had been built. They were crammed with at least three or four hundred hardbound books, with nary a paperback among them. A quick scan of the titles and the authors within range of reading sent Nikki's eyebrows soaring. Homer's *Iliad, The Canterbury Tales* by Chaucer, *Don Quixote, Pilgrim's Progress;* poetry by Robert Burns and Wordsworth; works by Goldsmith, Dante, Fielding, Plato, Wesley, and Milton; and volume upon volume of Shakespeare, in leather-bound, gold-leaf editions. And that was only a small portion of an assortment designed to make a book collector's heart do flip-flops!

All in all, Nikki was in a state of stupefaction, matched only by the stunned, what-do-I-say look on Mrs. Galloway's face as they were introduced to each other. Again, Silver Thorn explained their predicament concerning Nikki's strange attire; and frontier courtesy being what it was, Nikki was immediately shepherded away beneath Mrs. Galloway's benevolent wing.

"You poor dear," she sympathized. "Imagine being married, torn away from your home, and losing your worldly goods all in the space of a few days. But don't you fret. We'll have you straightened around in no time. Have you eaten supper yet? I have some leftover beans and cornbread on the sideboard. It won't take a moment to heat it up."

The older woman rattled on, barely giving Nikki a chance to get a word in edgewise. Evidently she missed having her daughter around and was very enthused at having another female with whom to converse.

In short order, Nikki had been supplied with three hand-me-down dresses and an assortment of homespun underwear and left alone to change into her new clothes. She cleaned up as best she could, using the old-fashioned washbasin, lye soap, and linens her hostess had thoughtfully provided. Then she sat down at the antique dressing table—or what *should* have been an antique under normal circumstances.

She began working the tangles from her hair, employing the brush mechanically as her mind struggled to analyze the compounding mystery of the past two days. Disregarding her encroaching panic, she methodically reviewed the various aspects of the enigma and the possibilities they presented.

First, she could have fallen, hit her head, and now be dreaming or in a coma. After all, the most brilliant doctors were as yet unsure precisely what went on in a person's brain in that catatonic state. Still, as useful and tidy an explanation as it would be, this theory just didn't ring true somehow. Surely, even intravenous drugs couldn't induce hallucinations this wild, and Nikki's imagination had certainly never run to these extremes before.

Next scenario: The park had devised a new, unadvertised adventure for the tourists, something like virtual reality but on a grander scale, and Silver Thorn and the Galloways were simply actors playing their parts, with Nikki as the unsuspecting guinea pig. However, if that were the case, a lot of money had been spent recreating this frontier illusion, complete with props and stunts, and the creator of this elaborate hoax deserved to be shot. Better yet, he should be made to endure his own set of calamities. Let him get abducted, lost in a dark cave, made to believe he was losing his mind, and see how he liked it.

But, wait. There was a big snag in the fabric of this concept. In this day and age, what actor would risk life and limb by making love to a strange woman? And what tourist, upon discovering the ruse, would hesitate to initiate the biggest lawsuit on record? The charges would be innumerable. Kidnapping. False representation. Endangerment. Mental cruelty. Rape. Rape? Well, maybe involuntary seduction, if there was such a thing. Certainly, they should be cited for scaring a person witless!

Conjecture number three. Either she or Silver Thorn was crazy. Possibly both of them were. If not, they were sure headed on the right track.

Last, but not least, and perhaps the most conceivable at this point—Silver Thorn really had sucked her back into a prior era. For two days, Nikki hadn't seen a speck of evidence to refute his claim. On the contrary, everything seemed to support it.

In the past thirty-six hours and approximately forty miles of actual travel, she had yet to see one utility pole or wire, one bridge, one road, or car or store. What she had seen was unblemished nature, a forest that seemed to stretch forever—and a house, as well as its goods and inhabitants, that might well hail from a previous century. Upon further reflection, Nikki realized that—though she had failed to recognize it earlier—the river, the air, the whole environment seemed cleaner, unpolluted. In fact, she could not recall having spotted a single piece of litter anywhere or one solitary jet trail marring the sky. She'd heard no planes, trains, or mechanical noises—only the sounds of nature.

Then, there was Silver Thorn himself. The man was definitely not your average blue-or-white-collar yuppie. His manner of speech, his dress, the way he moved, his entire demeanor was decidedly out of the norm. As were those inexplicable stunts he'd pulled—inciting that tremor, and later removing those huge rocks, as if by magic! And that trick of the blue imprint on her belly, which no amount of scrubbing had removed, and his prediction that she was pregnant with their son. Talk about eerie!

Could it be that all this was real? That Silver Thorn actually was a Shawnee shaman and Tecumseh's brother? That he wasn't a lunatic and she wasn't losing her mind?

That she was sitting in 1813 in the home of the historically documented Galloways?

And if it were true, what about her own life back in 1996? Had she disappeared from there or was she somehow living a dual existence, with one foot in the past and one foot in the future? If she had vanished from her own time, body and all, had she been missed yet? Were her parents and brothers worried sick about her? Searching in vain?

Would she ever get back? Was there a way for Silver Thorn to return her to her own time? In the meanwhile, who would keep her bills paid up? Would her friend Sheree continue to feed Her Nibs and water Nikki's plants and collect her mail? How long would the school board wait before hiring someone else to teach her class in the fall? What would happen to her house? Her car? Her cat? Her . . . life? What if she were stuck here forever?

Eight

"Did the willow bark tea not ease the ache in your head, Neeake?" Lying close beside her, Silver Thorn addressed her in the darkened bedroom. She'd suspected he, too, was still awake.

"I took two aspirin, and my head is fine; it's my brain that needs repair," she replied.

"Why can you not sleep?" he asked. "I know that you are weary."

"For one thing I miss my queen-size bed. For another, I always thought a feather bed would be like sleeping on a big, fluffy cloud. I never figured it might be the size of a miniature marshmallow and much too soft for comfort."

"I, too, am accustomed to sleeping on a harder surface," he agreed. "Now, tell me the real cause of your restlessness."

She rolled over to face him though he was little more than a warm shadow in the dark. For several seconds she was silent. Then, in a small voice, she said, "Is it possible to send me back to my own time, Silver Thorn?"

"Ah, so you acknowledge at last that all I have told you is true?"

"I don't know. Maybe." She sighed. "I suppose so."

"And will you now cease calling me crazy?"

"I'll consider it, if you answer my question."

"I do not know if it is possible for you to return, Neeake. Until you appeared, I was not certain I could successfully summon a messenger from the future. Therefore, it was not important to know if the deed could be reversed. It could take much time to discover the proper means to transport you back again."

"How long, approximately?" she pressed.

"This I cannot answer. I first called upon the Spirits for guidance in this matter three winters past; and though I persisted, my efforts did not produce results until *wo lah ko*, yesterday, when you finally appeared."

"Three winters?" she shrilled. "As in three years?"

His fingers rose to her lips. "Hush, wife. You do not want to awaken the Galloways, and the walls inside this house are as thin as parchment."

"Silver Thorn!" she whispered anxiously. "I can't be gone from my life, my world, for three years! For that matter, three weeks would be far too long. I have family and friends who will be frantic not knowing where I've disappeared to. I have bills to pay, a house, a mortgage, a job. My library card and my driver's license are due to expire soon!" she added nonsensically.

"You also have a husband here," he reminded her, not unkindly. "And in the spring, you will have a son. The Spirits have willed it so, or it would not be. Should you not consider these things when you speak of leaving? You belong to me now, and I to you, and the child to both of us. Would you leave me and your baby behind? Or take my son far from my reach? If it were possible, do you imagine that I would allow this?"

Again Nikki was struck dumb. "I . . . I guess I'm having a little trouble digesting everything at once. What's real, what isn't. The notion of being pregnant is new to me. Amid all the other considerations and confusion, it momentarily slipped my mind. Not that I wouldn't love to have a child. It's been a dream of mine for several years. It's just that here, now, it just all seems so unbelievable . . . so incredible."

"It will not seem so when your belly is as big as a pumpkin and our son is thumping on your ribs like a big-footed rabbit," he predicted with droll satisfaction. "Then you will have no doubt that you are soon to be a mother."

"I can only imagine what that must feel like," she murmured. "As for the rest of this fantastic phenomenon, it literally scares the hell out of me. I feel as if I'm up to my neck in quicksand."

"As you said, this I can only imagine. But you need not be frightened, Neeake. Until I cease to draw breath, I will care for you and protect you from harm."

She was still for so long that he wondered if she'd fallen asleep at last. Then she spoke in a weepy whisper. "Silver Thorn, will you hold me, please? Just hold me? I feel so . . . lost!"

He gathered her tenderly into his arms, cradling her head on his broad chest. Her hot tears scalded his skin as she wept silently. His fingers stroked her hair soothingly. "You are not lost, my little bird," he promised. "I have found you."

The next morning, James Galloway offered them a ride in his wagon as far as Dayton. "We can haul your canoe in the back, and you can put in on the Miami and head north from there."

"Are you sure, James?" Silver Thorn inquired. "I do not want to take you away from your day's work on the farm when Neeake and I can walk the distance."

For herself, Nikki held her breath and prayed she wouldn't have to trek almost fifteen miles on foot through the wilderness. She could have jumped for joy when Galloway replied gallantly, "It's no trouble. I need to make a supply run one day this week anyhow, and it may as well be today."

By wagon, bumping along the rutted road at a snail's

pace, the trip took four hours. As they neared town, Nikki was astonished at the contrast between what she knew as Dayton, Ohio, and what constituted the city in 1813. Though she knew better, she somehow still expected to find high-rise buildings dominating a city of nearly two-hundred-thousand residents. Instead, she spied a small valley community of perhaps a few hundred people. In place of crowded thoroughfares and interstate highways was a handful of narrow streets. Gone were the sprawling suburbs, the bustling shopping malls, the car lots, and industries.

On the bright side, however, there were no smelly exhaust fumes, no haze of smog, no barrage of billboards cluttering the landscape, and no roar of engines or blaring horns.

Skirting the southern edge of the town, Galloway directed the wagon along a lane leading down to the Great Miami River. "Aren't we going into town?" Neeake questioned.

"That might not be wise for you and Silver Thorn," the farmer responded. "The whites and the Indians aren't on real good terms these days, what with the war and all. It's best to avoid any confrontations."

He and Silver Thorn unloaded the canoe from the wagon bed, and within minutes they were ready to cast off. The two men shook hands. "You take care now," Galloway said. "Watch out for scalawags, and try to steer clear of the military. Some of those young soldiers are fresh from the East and eager to collect scalps. They don't know a peaceful Indian from a turnip and couldn't care less."

Silver Thorn nodded. "We are headed north and will soon be away from your white villages."

"Good. If you see Tecumseh, give him my regards and tell him he's always welcome at the homestead, whether Becky is there or not."

"I will relay your greeting," Silver Thorn vowed.

"Thank you for your hospitality, James, and for saving us a long walk today. My bride is not yet used to such lengthy excursions."

Galloway hesitated, then said, "Silver Thorn, I don't mean to poke my nose into your affairs, but should you be taking her north with you? You know how your brother and his followers feel about whites these days, and it's plain by the way she looks and talks that she's not an Indian. She can stay with us while you're gone, if you'd like."

"No. Neeake is my wife, and where I go she goes also; but I thank you for your kind offer."

Nikki stepped forward. "Don't worry, Mr. Galloway. I am part Shawnee, so perhaps they will accept me more readily than you think." She dug into the side pocket of her backpack and pulled out a folded five-dollar bill, holding it out to him. "Please accept this in payment for the clothing and convey my gratitude again to your lovely wife."

With Silver Thorn's help, Nikki managed to board the canoe without mishap. They pushed off, with a final wave of farewell.

James Galloway stood on the bank and watched as they glided swiftly into the distance. Only as Galloway turned to leave did he recall the money Nikki had pressed into his hand. Paper currency, usually issued by individual banks or by the state, was often next to worthless here on the frontier, but he hadn't wanted to hurt her feelings. Unfolding it, he gave it a cursory glance. Then, taking a closer look, his brow furrowed in confusion. The bill, with a stated value of five dollars, displayed the portrait of a gaunt bearded man Galloway had never heard of. His name, printed below his image, was Lincoln. On the back of the bill was a painting of a huge, pillared building called the Lincoln Memorial. Upon closer inspection of

the front of the note, Galloway gasped. The date, in minuscule but clear print, read 1993!

"How peculiar!" he wondered in bewilderment. "First
her strange clothing, and now this fake currency! What
manner of female is Silver Thorn tangled up with?"

Though Nikki understood from the conversation between Mr. Galloway and Silver Thorn that this section of
the country was sparsely settled, she'd still expected to see
some signs of habitation along the riverside just north of
Dayton, if only the sporadic cabin or two. When she mentioned the lack of such to Silver Thorn, he explained.

"The settlers have learned that it does little good to
build too near the river, for it floods badly in the spring.
Those who have tried have lost their cabins, their livestock,
even their lives to the Great Miami."

Perhaps twenty miles upstream, though it was hard for
her to properly estimate the distance, they did pass a tiny
settlement. Silver Thorn told her it was called Washington.
"That's odd," she said. "I don't recall a town down this
way by that name."

The puzzle was solved nearly an hour later, when Silver
Thorn directed the canoe to shore. Instead of disembarking
immediately, he simply sat and stared at the surrounding
landscape, a pensive look on his face.

"What is it?" Nikki asked softly. "Why do you look so
sad?"

"This was once my home for a time, as was Chillicothe
before it."

"Oh. Your village was here?"

He nodded. "The one called Lower Piqua."

She blinked in surprise. "Piqua? I've been here . . .
there! Oh, for heaven's sake! That town we passed, the one
you called Washington, is known as Piqua in my time.

That's why I couldn't place it before. They renamed it, in honor of the village you had here."

He shrugged and offered a bleak smile. "Then perhaps it was named well. Piqua, in our tongue, means *a man formed out of the ashes*, as told in the accounts of the creation of the Piqua band."

"Truly?" Nikki was fascinated. "Just like the Christian version of creation?"

"Similar to the tale in your Bible."

To her surprise, he pushed the canoe back into the current and headed the craft northward again.

"Aren't we going to camp here?" she asked. "It will be dark soon."

"I do not want to camp so near a white settlement," he told her. "We will go on, to the place where the Miami joins with the Loramie."

"I'm familiar with that name, too. There's a fort there, isn't there? And a Lake Loramie?"

"There is a fort some distance up the Loramie River. We will pass close to it tomorrow. But I know of no lake."

"No matter. It's probably one of those small lakes which was formed later, by damming the river. I think that's how they created Indian Lake, too, but I'm not certain. I do know that Lake Saint Mary's is totally man-made, and supposedly the largest in the state."

"Perhaps this is so, with your Saint Mary's Lake. But there is a place, centered between the village of Wapakoneta and the Mad River, near the origin of the Great Miami, which we call Indian Lake."

"Really?" Nikki scanned her mental map, trying to recall the area more distinctly. "I'll be darned. It's got to be the same place. Well, I'll have to remember this. It will be an interesting topic to discuss with my students when I get back since Indian Lake is practically in their own backyard."

This sparked his interest even more. "You come from the region of Indian Lake? In your time, you live near it?"

"About fifteen miles away, actually, and about seven miles north of Wapak. It just so happens that I live in a township known as Shawnee and I teach at Shawnee School. Both were named after your tribe, of course."

Silver Thorn took a minute to digest this information. "So, though you claim the Shawnee no longer live here in your day, we are not forgotten altogether."

"Not at all," she agreed. "I suppose everything comes full circle, if you wait long enough. In 1996, we're quite proud that the Indians lived in our locale. There are schools and towns and lakes and all sorts of things named after various tribes such as the Shawnee, the Ottawa, the Miami, and others I can't recall right off hand. They . . . you . . . have become an honored part of our heritage and history."

"I wonder if it is worth being driven from your land merely to be honored and remembered in later history?" he submitted with bitter irony. His face twisted into a grim mask, the pain and anger raw in his eyes. "To my mind, it is too great a price for too little recompense. A grievous cost, to be paid with the blood and tears and pride of my people."

"I'm sorry, Silver Thorn," she offered for lack of anything more comforting to say.

"It is your loss also," he reminded her. "But perhaps, when we reach Wapakoneta and speak with Chief Black Hoof, he will offer wise council and hope. Perhaps, together, we can devise a way to alter our fate."

"We're going to Wapak?" she exclaimed. "Is that where you're taking me? My gosh! That's practically home to me! Some of my friends live there!"

"Were I you, I would survey the village with a new eye, Neeake," he recommended dourly. "See it as it is now, to the Shawnee, and equate it to the place in your time. Then,

when you have done this, tell me which is better, your
village or mine."

That night they set up camp near the river and made
their bed beneath a canopy of stars. Dressed only in her
bikini panties and her T-shirt in lieu of a nightgown, Nikki
lay snuggled next to Silver Thorn, a small bouquet of wild
violets resting near her head. Silver Thorn had picked them
for her, poetically comparing them to her eyes. He'd also
gently removed a large splinter from her finger and kissed
it well again. Her fearsome Shawnee was really such a
sweetheart beneath his well-muscled, sometimes-gruff ex-
terior.

Staring up at the sky above, she remarked reflectively,
"This is really weird, to look up at the sky and know that,
at this precise moment, these same stars are shining down
on my home, another century and a half away. It just
doesn't seem feasible, reasonable, or otherwise sane. Do
you realize that, in my time, I've passed this very spot
dozens of times on my way from home to Dayton and
back? Interstate 75 would be about a mile east of here;
and if I were lying in this exact place in 1996, I'd be able
to hear the hum of traffic and see the headlights of the
trucks and cars on the highway. It's enough to boggle one's
mind."

"You keep mentioning this car, but I cannot understand
what it must be."

She shifted in his arms, burrowing her head against his
shoulder. "A car," she repeated, wondering how to explain
it to him when practically nothing mechanical existed in
his world. "It's a vehicle, somewhat like a wagon or buggy
with a cover on top. It has windows in the front and sides
so you can ride in the snow or rain and not get wet, yet
you can still see where you are going. In place of horses
pulling it, it has a gasoline-powered engine. I suppose the

best analogy would be to say that it's pushed along by a metal team of horses and that it is capable of great speed, the likes of which you can only imagine. I can't explain it any better than that. You'd simply have to see one to fully understand."

"One sits on it?" he asked.

"In it," she corrected. "Depending on the size and model, it can have one or more cushioned seats. The driver controls it by means of a steering wheel, a gas pedal, a brake, and other assorted devices."

"How fast does it travel?"

"Well, just to give you a proper perspective, we could drive from here to Wapakoneta in half an hour or less and not really be hurrying."

Her head dropped from his shoulder with a thump as he rose partially and rolled toward her. "Surely you adorn the truth and think to make a fool of me," he scoffed.

"I am telling you the absolute truth," she insisted. Rubbing the back of her head with one hand, she pushed him back down with the other and resumed her comfortable position. "You know, it strikes me that you might have been wiser to come to my time instead of summoning me to yours. Then you could have witnessed firsthand all the marvelous inventions and advancements of my day."

"Speak to me of these wonders, for other than your cars, all I have learned of the future are the misfortunes of my people and my land."

"Oh, Thorn!" she sighed. "I didn't mean to paint such a bleak picture. The Shawnee did not fare as well as others, I grant you; but for Americans as a whole, life is much more convenient in the twentieth century. We have all types of modern technology that make our lives and our work easier and more pleasant. There are machines to wash and dry our clothing and to cook our meals. We have refrigerators and freezers to keep food from spoiling. We have electric power supplied directly to our homes and furnaces to heat them in winter and air conditioning to cool them in summer. You don't have to go outdoors to go to the bathroom or to get water; the plumbing is indoors."

He turned to her with a disgusted grimace. "You relieve yourself inside your *wigewa*? Is this also where you sleep and eat and take shelter?"

"Yes, but it's not as unsanitary as it sounds. Our houses have many rooms, and the bathroom is just one of them. In it we wash and shower our bodies and brush our teeth. There are pipes that carry away the waste water and such to an outer location. And the kitchen, where food is prepared and eaten, is separate from the bathroom, though it, too, has indoor water and drains."

He shook his head in utter disbelief. "This still does not make good sense to me, Neeake, to cleanse your mouth and body in the same place you relieve yourself."

His comment, the way he voiced it, had Nikki wrinkling her own nose in revulsion. "You know, I've never really thought about it, but you're absolutely right. Yuck! My toothbrush can't hang half a foot from the toilet. When . . . if I get home, I'm going to start brushing my teeth in the kitchen. Speaking of which, the apples Mrs. Galloway sent with us sufficed as a satisfactory dentifrice today, but I really need something more adequate for cleaning my teeth on a daily basis."

"When next we pass a dogwood tree, we will gather a few tender twigs. When chewed and rubbed on your teeth and mouth, they serve the same purpose as your toothbrush."

"Really?" Nikki was surprised and impressed at his resourcefulness. "I suppose I'm so used to dashing down to the supermarket or drugstore for all these necessities that I've forgotten that the Indians and pioneers had all sorts of natural remedies and solutions at hand. Actually, I've heard that many of our modern medicines have their foundation in old-time herbs and roots."

"You have good medicine in your time?" he asked.

"Yes. Children are now inoculated to prevent them from contracting chicken pox and measles and mumps. Scientists have found cures for many plagues and ailments and made great strides toward eliminating others. There are many lifesaving operations and machines. Unfortunately, for every cure, it seems there arises another new disease, more terrible and drug-resistant than the last."

"Such as this AIDS," he assumed.

She nodded. "That and cancer and Alzheimer's. The list goes on and on."

"And still you claim your world is preferable?" he questioned.

"Well, it's a darned sight more convenient, at any rate," she countered. "I don't have to shoot my meat and skin it. Other people raise the animals and slaughter them. The average person simple hops in his car and drives to the supermarket to buy food already cut and packaged. Then there are marvelous inventions such as the telephone, with which a person can communicate with someone else who is miles away."

"That is nothing so new," he informed her with a superior expression. "My people have done this for many lifetimes. One requires only a shiny object to reflect the sun, and a signal can be sent to another, who can then relay the message on, if need be."

"And what do you do on a cloudy day?" she mocked.

"A signal can be sent by means of smoke or flaming arrow."

"And at night or if it rains?" she persisted.

"A drum signal can be sent or a trained dove or falcon can deliver a vital message."

"But how can that work? I thought you didn't have a written language."

"Words are not formed only with scribbled letters, Neeake. Since the beginning of all creation, man has used images and signs to convey his thoughts. On skins or walls or drawn in the dust, they have served him well enough. I know that you are an educated female. I, too, have learned your written language. But do not surmise any man witless simply because he cannot read or write your tongue. In his mind, he may be many times more clever than you; and if he be your enemy, it could prove fatal to dismiss him so lightly."

Nikki mulled this over. "Okay, Solomon, I concede the point to you, though reluctantly. Education is a major part of my life. I am a teacher, after all. However, I can see how I might appear a bit arrogant now and then."

His teeth flashed white in the darkness as he grinned at her. "It is a fault you must strive to overcome. A wife must never put herself above her husband."

"Hey! I thought you said Shawnee men and women are equals. I'm not about to walk ten paces behind you, Thorn, so you can just forget any ideas you have along those lines."

"So your shirt suggests. And I would not require that of you. Your place is beside me . . . or better still, under me," he added, his smile radiating devilment.

As he pulled her beneath him, covering her with his hard, warm body, she murmured, "Thorn! You're insatiable!"

Her comment was more compliment than complaint, and they both knew it. A long while later, relaxed and replete, she admitted drowsily, "I might mosey along behind you once in a while. You do have a cute set of buns back there. Much nicer than the guy on my shirt."

She missed the bright blush that flooded his face. She wouldn't have believed it if she'd seen it.

Nine

"Good God, Thorn! They're shooting at us!" Nikki screamed. Twisting around, she stared in shock at the two soldiers standing on the bank. Her stunned mind watched in disbelief as they hurried to reload their rifles. Behind them, more soldiers were streaming down the hill from Fort Loramie.

"Neeake! Get down into the bottom of the canoe!" Silver Thorn commanded. The rhythm of his strokes increased as he applied to his paddle all the power and speed he could summon, hastening them away from their enemy.

"A fat lot of good that would do!" she hollered back. Grabbing the other paddle, she thrust it into the water on the opposite side of the canoe and began to mimic Silver Thorn's actions as best she could. Though clumsy, her strokes added extra impetus to their flight. Within seconds, though it seemed much longer to her, they rounded a slight bend in the river, and were out of sight of the soldiers.

Still Silver Thorn did not slow his actions, but continued the rapid tempo. Thoroughly shaken, Nikki struggled to keep pace. What must have been a quarter hour later, Silver Thorn finally slowed. Nikki, her arms feeling like aching lead weights, followed suit.

"Thank you, Lord! Thank you!" she panted. "I thought we were goners for sure, didn't you, Thorn?"

As he guided the craft toward shore, Silver Thorn issued only a grunt in reply.

"What did those trigger-happy asses think they were doing?" she fumed. "We didn't do anything to provoke them."

"Come. Hurry," he told her. "We must hide." In his haste, the usually agile Shawnee nearly fell from the canoe. Quickly, he grabbed the prow and began pulling it to shore.

"You think they'll come after us?" she asked, tumbling out after him and lending what little aid she could.

"Yes. They, too, have canoes," he supplied tersely. "Even now, they may be close."

This frightening thought kicked Nikki into overdrive. Fast on his heels, she thrashed through the underbrush lining the bank. Perhaps a hundred yards inland, surrounded by dense forest and out of sight of anyone cruising the river, Silver Thorn lowered the canoe and dropped to the ground.

Nikki plopped down next to him, gasping for breath. "Are we safe now, do you suppose?" she wheezed.

Again she received only a grunt for reply. Silver Thorn was tearing at a buckskin bag with his teeth, trying to open it. His face, dripping in perspiration, was twisted into a grimace.

"Here, let me help," Nikki offered.

A leather thong attached the pouch to the waistband of his breechcloth. Intending to release it, she reached forward—then stopped and stared in mounting horror at the gaping red hole in Silver Thorn's side. Blood gushed from it, streaking his belly, his legs, and pooling on the ground.

"You've been shot!" she exclaimed faintly. "My God, Thorn! You've been shot!"

"The medicine bag," he groaned. "Inside. The white powder. Quickly."

The pain and urgency in his voice snapped her out of her stupor. Jerking the pouch open, she dug several packets out of it. "Which is it?" she blurted, thrusting them all in front of his face.

He selected one and ripped it open, lapping at the contents with his tongue. Then he slumped down again, clutching at his side with both hands.

Momentarily flustered, Nikki promptly recovered her wits. Yanking up her skirt, she tore a strip of material from her petticoat. Wadding it into a ball, she nudged Silver Thorn's hands away, pressed the cloth to his wound, and placed his hands over it again. "Hold that tight, until I can get another piece to tie it in place."

Quickly, her hands trembling all the while, she ripped off another lengthy ribbon of fabric and bound it around his waist as gently and firmly as possible. That done, she sank back on her heels and gazed helplessly at him, at a loss for what more to do.

His eyes were closed, his face pale and rigid and drenched with perspiration. His lips were drawn, his teeth tightly clenched, his labored breath hissing between them.

"Tell me how to help you, Thorn," she pleaded. "I don't know what else to do."

His only response was to open his eyes and stare blankly at her, his pupils so dilated that she could scarcely see the silver outer rims. His lids drifted shut again.

For several more minutes, Nikki sat watching him, grappling to keep the panic at bay. As was a long-established habit of hers in times of stress, she began to reason aloud. "Okay, we've bound the wound. Hopefully, the pressure will stop the bleeding. There is no antiseptic, so we can only pray that infection doesn't set in, which it probably will, especially if the bullet is still in there. For that matter, I don't even know if they use bullets in this day and age, but I suppose they load some sort of lead missile in those blasted guns. Either way, I don't know the first thing about removing it and would probably do more harm than good if I tried."

Upon raising her hands to brush her hair from her brow, she noted the blood streaking them. Silver Thorn's blood. His life's essence, so much of it, staining her flesh as well as his. Tears sprang to her eyes.

"Thorn?" she whimpered, her gaze seeking his face once more, fearful of what she might find. "You're not going to die and leave me here alone, are you? You can't do that. You hear me? You can't just yank a girl from her century to yours, give her a child, and up and die. It's just not right! Not to mention damned rude!"

"I would not be that impolite, little bird," he murmured.

Weak with relief at hearing his voice, though he had yet to open his eyes again, she sobbed out, "You'd better not. This baby is going to need a father. I'm not into the single-parent scene, you know."

"Fear not, Neeake. Today is not my time to die or I would have foreseen it, as my father and eldest brother did before me."

"Sure, but what about tomorrow or the next day? You've lost an awful lot of blood, Thorn, and infection could set in. We've got to get you some help, quickly. If we were in my world, I could flag down a motorist or boater, have them call 911, and rush you to a hospital. Here, I don't know how to help you."

"You have done well by binding my wound," he told her. "The powder is calming the pain. Soon we can go on, but it would be wise to cover our tracks from the river and the trail of blood I have left. Can you do that, little one?"

"Yes."

He instructed her how to go about it. "Select a leafy branch from amid a thick bush. Remove it well back to the main stem from a spot where the adjoining branches will spring back to hide its absence. Use it to brush away our footprints. Also, attempt to repair the most obvious damage we have made to the plants and spread loose leaves and pine needles over any evidence of our passing which you cannot brush away. Above all, use speed and caution and abandon your efforts if you see or hear any sign of soldiers."

She nodded. "Got it. Is there anything you need before I start?"

"My bow and quiver, and a sip from the water flask. If it is safe, you can refill the flask at the river. If not, we will use what remains sparingly until more can be obtained."

She located a suitable branch a few yards away and snipped it off with Silver Thorn's knife. As she started to backtrack, he called after her. "If the soldiers come, you must flee for your life. Run as fast and as far as you can. Save yourself and our child first, and worry not about me."

She turned and fixed him with a level, if tear-blotched, look. "I will not save my own hide at the expense of yours. We're in this together, sink or swim, as you have reminded me time and again." She waved the frond at him in a jaunty salute. "So, as Schwarzenegger so aptly put it, 'I'll be back.' "

Her appointed task wasn't nearly as fast or easy as it always looked in the movies. By the time she was done, her dress clung to her in sweaty patches, and where it didn't, she was a mass of fresh scratches and welts. Dirt was ground into her knees and beneath her fingernails, and her hair was a snarled mess.

"If my friends could see me now, they wouldn't believe it!" she puffed, throwing herself down beside Silver Thorn. "I seriously doubt my own mother would recognize me."

While she'd been gone, Silver Thorn had propped himself into a sitting position against a tree trunk. His hand rose to stroke the damp hair from her temple. "You are beautiful to me, my pet," he assured her.

His compliment went a long way toward restoring her flagging energy. "How are you feeling?" she inquired. She peered at the make-shift bandage. Though spotted, it was not soaked through with blood. "Has the bleeding stopped?"

"For now, I believe. Rest for a moment, then we must seek more adequate cover. We are too near the river and the fort."

"Then we'd better find someplace to stash the canoe," she added. "You'll be lucky if you can walk, let alone lug that puppy through the woods."

His smile eased her fears, reassuring her that his demise was not immediately imminent. "What would you suggest, my sassy goose?"

"Well, at the risk of sounding even more impertinent, it would be lovely if you could make it, and us, invisible. Heck, if you can transport someone from the future and make pigs fly, invisibility should be a snap."

His answering chuckle ended in a moan. "Please, do not make me laugh. The powder is powerful, but it has not yet taken full effect."

"What's in that potion, anyway? What is its purpose?"

"Extracted from the fruit of a tree, it suspends pain. Though a wound be deep or a limb removed, with it a man will not suffer."

"But he can still bleed to death," she surmised.

"Yes, but he will not die in agony."

"I've heard similar stories about people who are so hopped up on drugs that they can be shot several times and not appear to feel it. This one guy on the evening news actually kept coming, literally charging the police, until he fell dead at their feet. The coroner later claimed he couldn't have had two drops of blood left in his body, but he was still moving. Apparently the opiate he took was comparable to what you're describing, but it's still hard for me to fathom."

"Yet, becoming as a ghost, unable to be seen, is not?" he queried.

"I suppose it's a matter of degree and what's most imperative. So, can you make us invisible or not?"

"At another time, perhaps, but it would take too long and too much concentration just now, and my mind is becoming muddled with the pain dust. However, if we disguise the canoe well enough, it will serve the same purpose."

"You mean cover it with brush or something?"

Silver Thorn nodded.

"And I suppose, given your delicate condition, that's going to be my job." Nikki shoved herself to her feet. "Okay, but once you're well, you owe me big time, Thorn."

With him directing her actions, she soon had the craft resembling a fallen log. "So far, so good," she commented, eyeing her accomplishment with a critical eye. "So, what about us? What do we do? Stick our arms in the air and make like a couple of trees?" She struck a demonstrative stance.

He laughed outright, with no sign of discomfort. "No, my amusing wife. We leave this site and hide elsewhere, in the event your efforts are in vain. Come. Help me rise that we may be on our way."

Evidently, though he no longer felt pain, his muscles were still weak. With her aid, he made it to his feet and teetered precariously for a moment before gaining his balance. After donning her backpack and handing him his bow to use as a cane, Nikki wedged herself beneath his arm, on his good side, to lend her support. "All right, let's see how far we can get without breaking your wound open again. But I'm warning you, if you start bleeding heavily again, we're going to stop and take our chances."

"Yes, *Nee ke yah*," he replied placidly, grinning at her. His words sounded just different enough from the pronunciation of her name to make her wary. "What did you call me?" she inquired suspiciously.

"I called you *my mother*," he stated unrepentantly. "She, too, is small in stature, but possesses a domineering nature."

Nikki offered a wry smile. "A woman after my own heart. I can't wait to meet her. I'll bet she could tell me some hair-raising tales about your childhood escapades."

"Someday I will take you to visit with her," Silver Thorn promised. "Presently, she and others of our tribe have gone to live with our brothers, the Cherokee, away from the madness of this war into which Tecumseh has drawn us."

Nikki wasn't about to add to his misery by informing him that his mother would not be safe there, either. If she were still living with the Cherokee in a few years, she would undoubtedly be among those marched forcibly along what had become known in the annals of American history as the Trail of Tears. Many, young and old alike, would fall along the way, dying of fatigue and starvation.

Later, when Silver Thorn recovered from his injury, Nikki would tell him, and maybe he could warn his mother and convince her to relocate elsewhere. Perhaps to Canada or somewhere out West. At present, he had enough to worry about.

As they stumbled along, Nikki dragged the branch behind them, but she doubted she was erasing all evidence of their route. Just when she thought surely it would be safe to stop, that it was doubtful they were being pursued after all, she heard the distinctive howl of a hunting hound. Her eyes widened, meeting Silver Thorn's.

He voiced her thoughts. "Dogs. They have brought dogs to track us. Had I suspected they would do so, we would have stayed on the river, where they could not follow our scent."

"If we'd done that, you'd be dead by now for lack of

attention to your wound," she pointed out. "You'd have
bled dry trying to paddle that canoe, and I couldn't have
managed it on my own, so don't blame yourself. Personally, I'd rather have you alive; but if we want to stay that
way, we'd better come up with another plan real fast."

As a team, they scanned the immediate area, noting no
handy place to hide. Then, Silver Thorn glanced upward.
"I will go on and draw them away from you. This tree
will provide sufficient concealment if you climb high
enough into the branches. I do not believe they will think
to look there. Even should the dogs pause, they will catch
my scent and follow it."

Nikki shook her head, negating his proposal. "Nothing
doing. Whither thou goest, and all that. If I can hide there,
so can you. Most people never see what's right in front of
them, let alone bother to look up, so we should both be
safe as long as we're quiet."

"You forget the dogs and their keen noses, Neeake. They
will stop and point out our shelter to the soldiers."

"If we're lucky, they'll be miles ahead of their masters.
Maybe we can chase them off before the men catch up."
Nikki grabbed his arm and tugged at it. "Come on, Thorn.
Move it. The time for hesitation has passed. Either you
climb up there with me or we both make a run for it, and
I can't see either of us eluding capture that way."

"I doubt I have the strength," he argued. "But you do."

"Damn straight!" she countered stubbornly. "If I have
to, I'll haul you up there by the nape of your neck, inch
by blasted inch; but one way or another your butt is going
up that blasted tree!"

It must have been adrenaline that endowed them the extra surge they needed. Nikki could account for no other
explanation. Somehow, pulling and tugging and boosting
one another, she and Silver Thorn hoisted themselves into
the tree, climbing high into the thick screen of leaves—and
not a moment too soon. Below them, so far that it made

Nikki dizzy to watch, a trio of hounds bounded from the brush.

Noses to the ground, the dogs scurried to and fro and ran circles around the base of the tree. Then, of one accord, they began to leap up and down on the trunk, pushing and shoving and baying at the top of their lungs—their insistent howling a signal that they'd trapped their quarry.

Nikki's nerves, already frayed, went haywire. She clung to the narrow limb, trembling so hard that the leaves surrounding her shook and rattled. It was fortunate that Silver Thorn was perched on a separate branch, which she had not set quivering, or he would never have succeeded in stringing his bow. However, just as he took aim at the dogs and was about to release the arrow, four armed soldiers burst onto the scene.

Without brushing so much as a leaf, Silver Thorn melted back amid the foliage. Mutely, he motioned for Nikki to be still. Though she tried, tiny whimpers echoed in her throat. She could only hope they could not be heard from below.

"Whatcha got, boy?" one soldier called to his hound. "Did ya tree somethin', fella?"

"By gum, I think they have," a second man said.

"Yeah, more'n likely a 'coon," the third fellow contributed. "That dog o' your'n is 'bout worthless as tits on a boar hog, Luke."

"He's a sight smarter than yours," Luke countered. "Least mine don't chase his own tail the day long."

"Pipe down, you two," the fourth soldier ordered. "I thought I heard something rustling around up there." He peered upward, squinting against the sun.

His friends did likewise. "Danged if I see anything," one said.

Lady Luck chose that moment to awaken from her nap. Chattering angrily, a fat fox squirrel leapt onto a lower branch, noisily berating them all for intruding on his territory.

"See?" the dissenter scoffed. "Told ya it weren't nothin' to get all het up about. Nothin' but a bushy-tailed varmint."

"Looks like supper to me," Luke claimed, raising his rifle to his shoulder. "Bet I kin get 'im with one shot."

Some distance above, Nikki stifled a scream. Fortunately, the squirrel was still chattering loudly enough to cover the small sound which emerged. From her vantage point, it looked as if the soldier were aiming straight at her, and it amazed her that he could fail to see her. Then again, with her dark dress and hair, she blended in with the bark, which could now prove a calamity instead of a blessing.

Luke had the hammer back and his finger on the trigger when, out of nowhere, a large, furry beast came streaking past the hunting party. It dashed between Luke's legs, knocking him off balance, and bolted into another clump of bushes. The dogs, their attention diverted from their original prey, gave chase.

Luke tumbled to the ground, his gun flying from his hands and landing several feet away. The weapon hit hard, discharging its load on impact.

"Shee-it!" Luke's buddy exclaimed. "Did you see that? That were a blamed wildcat, or my name ain't Tom Clancy. Fergit that scrawny squirrel. We got better game now, lads."

"Tom, quit yammerin' on. We got bigger trouble. Luke's been shot."

"Shot?" Tom echoed stupidly. "He shot hisself?"

Several yards overhead, Nikki was nearly faint with relief. Until hearing that Luke had been shot, she hadn't been sure she or Silver Thorn hadn't been. Pumped full of painkiller, Thorn probably wouldn't have felt it. For herself, she'd heard tales of people getting wounded and being

too much in shock to register the pain immediately. She
was overjoyed to discover that this was not the case. Moreover, she was stunned to realize that she felt not an ounce
of sympathy for poor Luke, now bleeding like a stuck pig.

"C'mon! We got to get him back to the fort," one of
the men said.

"What about those Injuns?" Tom wanted to know.

"Jesus, Tom! What you got for brains, boy?" another
man exploded. "Yer ma must've hatched you on a stump!
Forget the Injuns. Most likely, they're halfway to Canada
by now, and Luke here needs a doc right fast!"

Within minutes, they were gone, thrashing through the
brush, carrying their fallen comrade with them.

"We should wait to make certain there are no more soldiers coming before we leave our safe refuge," Silver
Thorn suggested quietly.

"That . . . that's fine with m . . . me," Nikki stammered. "I couldn't move now if my life depended on it.
My legs have turned to Jell-o, and my arms seem to be
glued to this limb. You may just have to leave me here to
rot."

"What goes up, must go down," he misquoted.

"Don't bet on it. Unless I just let go and drop like a
stone, which may be my only recourse."

"You mis-value your own courage, woman."

"It took full-fledged panic to get me this far off the
ground. I've climbed my share of trees in my younger
years, but never this high up. It may take a bomb to get
me down again."

He delivered the necessary missile effortlessly as he
said, "I will require your assistance to make the descent
myself. My wound is bleeding anew."

That's all it took—an admission from this strong, caring
man that he needed her help, and the knowledge that without it he could die. Nikki sighed, long and deep, knowing
that no matter how shaky and scared she was, no matter

what it took to accomplish it, she would somehow get them both safely on the ground again.

She inched toward him, muttering, "I'll bet Jane never had this problem with Tarzan."

Ten

They were back on the river, headed northeast. Nikki had bound Silver Thorn's wound with fresh dressings. At his further instruction, she had first sprinkled another chalky substance from his medicine bag on it and packed it with moss. All this seemed rather primitive to her, but she'd seen the miraculous effects of the painkiller he'd taken earlier and had to trust that these archaic remedies would work just as well.

She was concerned, however, that the added exertion of paddling the canoe was aggravating his wound and sapping his energies. Even with Nikki manning the second oar, she could see the strain taking its toll on him, but nothing she said would deter him. He was determined to get them further into Indian territory. Already they had put many miles between themselves and Ft. Loramie. No other forts now lay between them and Chief Black Hoof's village.

It was late afternoon when they reached the end of the river. Or perhaps its source; Nikki was not sure which. Either way, the result was the same. The river had ended; and according to Silver Thorn, they would now have to portage across the marshy expanse for a few miles before encountering the Auglaize River and continuing on to Wapakoneta.

Traversing dry land would have been one thing; trudging through this bog was another, requiring much more energy. "We'll never make it," she told him. "Even if I could carry the canoe, you're much too weak to walk that distance in this mire. We'll have to camp here and continue on in the morning when you've rested."

"No. We must go on," he insisted.

"Damn it, Thorn!" she shouted. "Don't be so frigging stubborn! Even with that magic powder of yours, you're not Superman!"

He ignored her and bent to lift the canoe onto his shoulders. The weight of it sent him crashing to his knees. The craft fell to one side, but Silver Thorn remained as he was, head bent, shoulders stooped, his breath coming in labored gasps.

Disregarding the muck, Nikki knelt before him. As his eyes met hers, she noted their glassy appearance. His copper skin, even more flushed now, was taut and dry. Despite the heat of the day, not a drop of perspiration dotted his flesh.

Reaching out her hand, she tested the temperature of his forehead. "Great Scott! You're burning up! Why didn't you say something earlier? I've got a bottle of aspirin in my purse. It's a modern medication to reduce pain and fever, though I doubt it will do much for the infection, which is more than likely the underlying cause."

"That is why we must hasten to reach Black Hoof's village," he reiterated. "There, you will be safe and I can obtain proper care. Should the fever render me unaware, my people will watch over you until I am well again."

She could not refute his reasoning. In view of his rapidly worsening condition, getting him aid was more imperative by the moment. "Okay, if you can manage to place one foot in front of the other and not fall on your face, I'll manhandle the canoe somehow. It's too big for me to carry, but I suppose I can drag it along without damaging it too much. God knows, the ground is soft enough that it shouldn't hurt it."

Stubborn didn't begin to describe this man of hers. He

insisted on pulling his own weight—and the front end of
the canoe. As much as Nikki hated to admit it, even to
herself, she could not have managed it on her own. It was
a supreme effort simply to trudge through the swampy
sludge. Though she'd removed her Nikes and looped the
tied laces around her neck, the mud sucked at her bare
feet, making every step twice as hard as the last.

Only once did Silver Thorn expend the energy to speak,
and only to issue a dire warning. "Watch for snakes,
Neeake."

That short statement sent shivers rippling up her backbone. He would tell her this after she'd removed her shoes!
"What kind of snakes?"

"Water moccasins and rattlesnakes. The others are harmless."

Nikki was fairly certain she could recognize a rattler if
she spotted one, and maybe a water moccasin, but she had
to ask, "What do I do if I see one?"

"Stop and stand perfectly still until it has passed. If you
do not move or make enough noise to vibrate the ground,
it will disregard you and go on its way."

"Right," she replied on a gulp. "No problem. If I do
see one, I'll probably faint anyway, so you won't have to
worry about me screaming or dashing around like a nit-
wit."

It was slow going, and what amounted to approximately
three miles took them three hours to negotiate, but at long
last the Auglaize River was in sight. By now, Silver Thorn
was barely coherent, and Nikki figured it would fall primarily to her to navigate the craft to the village. But first
she had to know which direction led there.

She was about to ask Silver Thorn what course to take
when another canoe, bearing two Indians, sailed into view.
They steered directly toward her and Silver Thorn. Her
heart in her throat, Nikki could scarcely squeak out,

"Thorn. Tell me you know these two Indians bearing down on us and that they're friendly."

Her message got through his muddled brain, for Silver Thorn raised his head and peered at the men approaching them. "Fear not. They are friends, from Black Hoof's band."

As they drew closer, Nikki saw a large lump of furs resting in the center of the canoe between the two men. Apparently, they had been trapping animals for their pelts. Then the furry hump moved, raised its head to display two huge tufted ears, and leveled a golden gaze in her direction. "Thorn! That's the lynx, isn't it? The same one you claimed was your pet."

"Macate," he confirmed, rasping out the lone word.

"But . . . how? How did it get here? All the way from the caves?" Nikki was utterly flabbergasted. Then another astounding thought came to her. "It was him at the tree, wasn't it? He tripped that soldier and saved our lives."

Silver Thorn grunted what she assumed was an assent.

"Holy Neds! This is getting weirder and weirder!"

The men beached their craft and hurried forward. A quick interchange, conducted entirely in Shawnee, ensued. Then one of the men hoisted Silver Thorn's canoe on his shoulders and carried it the rest of the way to the river. The second fellow, bracing Silver Thorn against him, shepherded Nikki along behind.

Just before he passed out, Silver Thorn murmured, "I have told them you are my wife. They will not harm you. Behave yourself, Neeake."

As if she had any other choice! Upon reaching Wapakoneta, Silver Thorn was hustled into a wigewa, followed immediately by several men and women whom Nikki could only hope were the Shawnee equivalent of surgeons and nurses. Though she tried to impress upon them that

she was Silver Thorn's wife, and therefore should be allowed to remain at his side, they turned deaf ears to her
pleas. She was left to sit outside the entrance to the
wigewa until finally a woman approached her and gestured
for Nikki to accompany her.

To Nikki's surprise and delight, the woman spoke broken but understandable English. When Nikki repeated her
wish to stay with Silver Thorn, the woman told her, "I
have much sympathy for your desire to be with your husband, but you must allow the medicine men to tend to
him. Your man is very sick, and it will take all their skills
to make him well. Later, when he is mending, you may
sit with him and care for him, but for now you must not
be in the way."

The woman led Nikki to another wigewa a short distance away. "This is the wigewa of Mona Kahwee, Silver
Thorn. Here you will find mats and blankets and all you
need. If you require anything more, you need only ask and
it will be provided for you." She gestured inside the bark-
covered structure. "Please. You are weary and must rest or
you will sicken and not be fit to tend your husband when
he wants you. After a while, I will bring you food, but
first you must rest."

She turned to leave, and Nikki called after her, "Wait.
I would like to wash first."

The woman nodded. "I will bring water and cloths. Tomorrow, you may bathe more better in the river, but for
now just a fast rub, yes?"

Nikki offered her an exhausted smile. "Yes, thank
you . . ." She paused, not knowing the woman's name.
"My name is Nikki, or Neeake, as Silver Thorn says it."

"I am called Konah Wiskeelotha, Snow Bird," the
woman supplied. Before Nikki could respond, she was
gone.

Nikki stared after her, all but paralyzed with shock. Now
she knew why the woman seemed so familiar to her, al-

though she knew they'd never before met. Konah was the spitting image of Nikki's Grandma Swan in her younger days. Nikki had seen photos of her grandmother as a young woman and had marvelled over how pretty she was. She recalled how Grandma had laughed and told Nikki that her own grandmother had claimed that Grandma favored their Shawnee ancestress, a woman by the name of Kona Whiskey Lota, as near as they could pronounce it.

Kona Whiskey Lota? Konah Wiskeelotha? It was simply too much of a coincidence to ignore! Turning, Nikki stumbled into the wigewa on rubbery legs and fumbled her way to a bench. For long minutes, she sat there in a daze, contemplating the idea that she'd just been introduced to her own great grandmother, seven generations removed! A grandmother who couldn't be more than thirty-five if she were a day! Who was slim and lovely and a mere five years or so older than Nikki!

And if Nikki were stunned, how would Konah react if Nikki were to present this bizarre theory to her? But how could she? How did one find the words to explain? After all, you just couldn't say, "Oh, by the way, I'm your great, great, great, great, great granddaughter," and expect the woman to believe you were anything but a nutcase!

Oh, but it was tempting to try! If only in order to feel connected to someone else in this historic era. Someone other than Silver Thorn. Someone of her own flesh and blood. To have a sense of family again, of roots, of belonging and caring and sharing that went beyond sex and that man-woman kind of love. Maybe then she wouldn't miss her twentieth century family so badly. Wouldn't feel quite so lost in this world so removed from her own.

Three days later, Nikki still hadn't worked up the nerve to say anything to Konah about their relationship. Konah and the other women of the tribe had readily accepted her into their midst, though it was plain they considered Nikki incredibly ignorant about ordinary, everyday affairs— everything from wifely duties to general day-to-day living. They excused her ignorance for the most part, however— since it was apparent from her unusual violet eyes that Nikki was at least partially white—and tried to instruct her in their way of doing things.

By now, she could at least start a fire and bake those little cornpone cakes that Silver Thorn had made for her that first night they'd met. Of course, when no one was looking, Nikki cheated and used her cigarette lighter to ignite the pine chips; but for a gal who normally nuked her meals in a microwave, she wasn't faring too badly.

Another blessing was the local bathing pool, which had been formed by damming a small offshoot of the river. Nikki's hair, her body, and her clothing were now clean of grit and grime. She was especially grateful for something the women called a soap plant, which served as a remarkably effective shampoo and creme rinse. For the first time in days, her hair was free of tangles, hanging shiny and smooth down her back. Konah had even trimmed the ends for her, marveling over Nikki's cuticle scissors.

It was particularly hard for Nikki to hold her tongue concerning the link in their lineage when she met the rest of Konah's immediate family. Konah was married and had three small children, two boys and a girl, one of whom had to be a main branch of Nikki's family tree. Konah's mother lived with another tribe, further north, as did her older sister and brother, but her younger sister, Melassa, also resided in Wapak. Melassa, whose name meant sugar or molasses, also had a husband, a son, and was pregnant with her second child.

After meeting them all and feeling an instantaneous affinity toward them, Nikki yearned to disclose their mutual kinship. Only her certainty that they would think she was insane and no doubt reject her and her equally crazy notion kept her silent.

Meanwhile, when she wasn't spending time with Konah, Nikki was now permitted to sit at Silver Thorn's bedside in the medicine lodge. Though he was still unconscious, his fever had finally broken after raging for three nights and days. He slept peacefully now, no longer thrashing and ranting deliriously, and could wake at any moment. Nikki wanted to be there when he did.

His wound had been cleaned and treated for infection, and the bullet removed. With the dressing changed every few hours and fresh medicines applied, it was beginning to show signs that it would heal with no serious complications. For this alone, Nikki was eternally thankful. Her greatest fear had been that gangrene would set in, or some equally fatal contamination.

It occurred to Nikki, as she sat praying fervently for Silver Thorn's recovery, that her feelings for this man had changed immensely in the past few days. What had begun as antagonism had quickly metamorphosed into much more affectionate emotions. Now her feelings ran more toward respect, admiration, genuine liking and concern, not to mention lust and a few others she wasn't sure she could categorize.

By the end of their first day together, she'd known she needn't fear him, which was fortunate since she'd fallen into his arms like a sex-starved spinster. The handsome devil certainly had more than his fair share of charisma! By the end of the second day, she'd accepted that he wasn't a delusional lunatic, that he really had zapped her into 1813. But what she felt now was more than mere desire, more than feeling safe with him. And it wasn't just awe over the strange and mysterious powers he possessed. Or the knowledge, and hence the apprehension, that he might be the only person capable of transporting her back into her own time—that if he should die, she'd be stuck here alone.

Thinking back, Nikki wondered if her emotions had begun a turnaround when he'd so bluntly announced that she'd conceived his child. Though she had yet to develop any physical signs or symptoms of pregnancy, other than that blue design on her belly that still wouldn't wash off, she found herself believing him. Mostly because he was so sincere in his declaration. Or maybe because she wanted to believe it so badly. A child of her own would be such a wondrous gift, her dearest wish come true. Especially his child.

If she'd deliberately set out to find the perfect father, she couldn't have selected a man with finer attributes than Silver Thorn's. Sure he was stubborn to a fault, with a wide vein of arrogance and a formidable temper when he wished to display it, but he was also one of the kindest, most honest men she'd ever met. He possessed a strength that went beyond bone and muscle to the depths of his inner being. Intertwined with that strength was an ingrained tenderness that Nikki couldn't help but admire. Many of the men she'd met previously had been so intent on proving their machismo that they considered any exhibition of tenderness a sign of weakness. Those few of her acquaintance who had shown a gentler side, had also been somewhat wimpy.

But Silver Thorn—well, Silver Thorn had it all, everything Nikki had always wanted to find in a mate. He was strong enough to be tender. He was intelligent, patient for the most part, caring, forthright, protective, extremely handsome, and had a marvelously wicked sense of humor. All admirable qualities. Furthermore, he found her equally attractive, which certainly added bonus points to his side of the scoreboard. Not only didn't he mind her being a little plump, he truly seemed to find it appealing. Additionally, he admired her mind as well as her body. A rare and wise man, indeed, one who commanded respect.

Beyond and above all that, he'd rescued her when she'd been lost in the cave and had been ready to forfeit his own safety for hers when the soldiers had been chasing them. If that weren't chivalry at its highest, Nikki didn't know what was. Loyalty on that level was hard to come by these days . . . or those days . . . or whatever.

That wasn't to say the man was perfect or that she wasn't still a tad miffed at him for setting her down in the middle of this mind-boggling mess; but after having come to better know and appreciate him this past week, she'd found that his assets far outweighed his liabilities. Who could help but like a man who gave you wildflowers and compared them to the color of your eyes? Or to adore him when he was down on his knees removing a splinter from your hand with such gentleness?

In the past week, Nikki had shared more of herself with Silver Thorn—her needs, her opinions, her aspirations, her whole mind and body—than she had with any man she'd known, including her ex-husband, her father, and her brothers. In fast order, he'd become her lover, her protector, her husband, and her friend. He'd made her laugh, cry, and scream with exasperation. He'd also shown her a passion she'd never dreamed existed.

Now he was lying here, unconscious and battling infection. Her wounded hero. And here she sat, praying for his recovery and trying to judge just how deeply she cared for him. No doubt they were beyond the "casual-lovers" stage, or that age-old marriage-of-convenience thing. The question was, did all this caring, this sharing, add up to more than she'd bargained for?

Had she, somewhere along the route from animosity to friendship, actually gone and fallen in love with him? Was that why the worry that he might die had filled her with such terror? Why, after such short acquaintance, she was already so comfortable with him—and yet more excited just to be near him that she could recall ever being with anyone else? Why the thought of sharing his life and bearing his children made her dizzy with delight? Was this giddy, butterflies-in-her-stomach, all-consuming yearning actually love? The kind of love she'd searched for and been missing until now?

Nikki couldn't help but laugh, at herself and at the hand Fate had dealt her. "My timing always did leave something to be desired, but this is downright ludicrous!" she muttered, shaking her head at the irony of it all.

"What amuses you so, my wife?" Silver Thorn had at last emerged from his sleep and was gazing at her with curious silver eyes.

Nikki leaned forward to place her hand gently over his heart, all her newly acknowledged emotions spilling out amid joyous tears. "Nothing all that monumental, my darling. Just that I'm the only woman I know who had to travel two centuries, and an entire civilization away, to fall in love with her own husband."

Eleven

Silver Thorn, though tremendously elated, took Nikki's declaration of love much more calmly than he did the revelation that she'd met her great grandmother of seven generations past. The look on his face when she related that Konah was her great-great-great-great-great grandmother was so stunned, so absolutely priceless, that Nikki regretted not having the foresight to dig her camera out of her backpack and capture his expression on film.

"I know," she told her dumbfounded mate. "It's enough to blow your mind, isn't it? Not everybody gets a chance to meet a long-deceased ancestor face to face and in the flesh."

"I never would have thought it possible," he declared, profoundly staggered by her tidings. "When I thought of bringing someone from the future, I contemplated only what information I could gleam from him. Never did I conceive the prospect that he and his forbearers would encounter each another. Neeake, this must be very strange for you. I am sorry if it has caused you any distress, for truly the idea of this happening never came into my mind."

"I know that," she allowed. "You had higher goals than instigating a family reunion. It's been eerier than anything, meeting Konah and seeing her as only a few years older than I am—and even spookier being introduced to her children. I'm the great granddaughter, several lifetimes into the future, of one of those kids. But here and now I'm older than they are and expecting a baby of my own, yet another offspring of the old family tree. I'm telling you, Thorn, this is getting deep!"

"We must speak to Black Hoof about this matter and seek his advice on whether you should tell Konah of this," Silver Thorn proposed. "He is Konah's uncle, and will know what is best."

Nikki gaped at him. "Thorn, if we tell the chief about my relationship to Konah, we'll have to tell him the rest of this bizarre tale as well. How you summoned me from my time to yours. The whole ball of wax."

Silver Thorn nodded. "It has always been my intention to do so, Neeake. Black Hoof is a very wise and respected leader. He has lived nearly ninety winters and seen much that cannot be explained by reason but must be accepted by faith. I suspect that our account will be no great shock, though it will be of interest to him."

"All right, it's your game. Play it the way you see fit," she replied with a shrug. Then something else Silver Thorn had said finally registered. "Wait. You said Black Hoof is Konah's uncle. Do you mean he's her actual uncle or is he just a close friend of the family? I swear, the way you people use familial terms so loosely is awfully confusing. As I understand it, when you say *brother*, you can mean anyone from your real brother to a cousin to a comrade. Sisters are nieces and grandmothers are any old woman . . ."

Nikki paused, then let loose a wry laugh. "And who the hell am I to talk? Before this is all over, I'll probably be my own daughter, twice reincarnated! Just tell me one thing. Are you related to Black Hoof in any way? Because I'd like to know if I'm married to my own cousin or nephew or whatever. Of course, it probably doesn't matter at this point. The bloodlines are so thinned out, or were when I was born in 1966 anyway, that our children stand a fair chance of being normal. I think."

Silver Thorn just shook his head and laughed at her. "Set your muddled mind at ease, Neeake. You and I are not bound by any blood except by that of our son. However, our union is just as sacred and our bonds to each other are those of mutual faith and love."

At that, hope blossomed in Nikki's heart. "You said mutual love. Can I take that to mean that you love me, too?"

A gentle smile lit his eyes and curved his lips. "Of course, Neeake. I have loved you since that moment when you first begged me not to kill you and then had the courage to give me your hand in trust. I knew then that we were meant to be mated. It was writ . . . ."

"I know," she interrupted, her face radiant with joy. "It was written in the stars. Fate. Destiny. Kismet."

"Kiss your et?" he queried confusedly.

She giggled, her eyes dancing with glee. "Sweetheart, you'll kiss a lot more than that in the next fifty years or more, so you'd better rest up while you can. Once you're well again, I intend to wear you out."

Meeting Black Hoof was akin to greeting royalty, at least in Nikki's book. For all his advanced years, the elderly Shawnee chief had a regal bearing about him. Tall and thin, with the lines of age and experience etched into his face, he held himself erect and proud. In mind as well as body, he was as fit as a much younger man.

Alone in Black Hoof's wigewa, Silver Thorn and Nikki recounted their adventures to him. Then they sat silent before him, awaiting the chief's response. After mulling it over for several long, tense minutes, Black Hoof speared them with a censuring look, one directed primarily toward Silver Thorn, as the instigator of the fiasco.

"This comes as no great surprise. I knew it would come to this one day," Black Hoof said. "You and your two brothers have ever courted disaster with your chicanery;

and though you commenced this latest scheme with noble motives, you have now wreaked havoc on this young woman's life. We can only hope you have not also disrupted the delicate balance of her world and of ours with your impulsiveness."

Black Hoof raised his hands before him, palms up, then dropped them again to his knees with a sigh. "Ah, but what is done is done, for better or worse. Now we must consider those things we can control. Perhaps, as you have suggested, this, too, was meant to happen for some reason beyond our understanding. The Spirits may be trying to guide us through you and your young wife."

The elderly chief turned to Nikki. "What have you to say of all this? Are you content to remain here as Silver Thorn's mate?"

"Yes, sir, though I must admit that I miss the many conveniences of my life in the twentieth century. And I miss my family and friends. My parents and brothers, most of all."

Black Hoof nodded. "It would be strange if you did not; but from what you two have told me, it would appear that you have family here also. Konah, her husband and children, Melassa, and me. As well as this young buck," he added, gesturing toward Silver Thorn, "and the child you have conceived."

Nikki's eyes went wide, and not merely at hearing her middle-aged husband described as a *young buck*. "You?" she exclaimed softly. "I'm related to you, too?"

Black Hoof nodded once more. "If you are of Konah's blood, then you are of mine as well. You may call me *Grandfather*—or *Uncle*, if you prefer."

"Thank you. I'm honored," she declared sincerely. She shook her head in wonder. "I am still having trouble crediting all this. Yet you believed it instantly and don't seem at all incredulous."

The old chief chuckled. "I have known Silver Thorn

and his brothers almost from the hour of their birth. I knew them when they were first testing their powers, and I have seen them at their best and at their worst. Nothing any of the three could do would truly shock me, though this has come near to doing so."

"I wished only to look into the years ahead, my chief," Silver Thorn put in mildly. "That we might see the future of our people, the better to guide them."

"And what have you seen but tragedy?" Black Hoof countered. "Has this made you any wiser for the knowledge it brings, or any happier?"

"It has made me even more firm in the belief that the Shawnee must quit this war with the Shemanese. That it is not wise to follow the course Tecumseh has set for us. As I have told Neeake, if we can convince Tecumseh to abandon this fight, perhaps there is yet hope to save him and our people from needless disaster."

"Many of us do not follow him now, and yet he persists," Black Hoof pointed out.

"True, but if more of the people cease to align themselves with him, he will have no fighting force. And without warriors, there can be no battle," Silver Thorn argued. "We must convince more of our people to forsake Tecumseh's cause. If we embrace peace with the Americans now, perhaps all will not be lost."

Again, Black Hoof turned his attention to Nikki. "What say you of this, Niece? You are the messenger summoned from the future. Have you any wisdom to impart?"

"I wish I did," Neeake said with a discouraged sigh. "But I just don't know what to think anymore. It's always been my belief that, though you can change the future, you cannot change history. Of course, I never thought it would be possible to find myself suddenly whisked into the past and viewing my old life far into the future. Perhaps it is possible to change history, just as I now know it is possible to travel from one time into another. However,

I also believe that not just anyone is capable of accomplishing this. If it can be done at all, it will be done by someone with extraordinary powers."

"Such as your husband," Black Hoof suggested.

"Or Tecumseh," Nikki added. "Perhaps only he is capable of rewriting his own chapter in history, of altering his own destiny and that of his followers."

"A provocative thought," Black Hoof conceded. "And perhaps it will take someone just as skilled as he to sway Tecumseh." His attention swung to Silver Thorn. "I will think on this and ask the Spirits for guidance. While we are waiting for the answer, it would do no harm to call some of our people here for a council. As you have suggested, the fewer who follow him, the fewer to fight."

"And lose," Nikki appended.

Black Hoof shook his head, sadness dimming his eyes. "No, my innocent. All get blamed for the deeds of a few. That is the way of life and of war, whether we speak of the Shawnee, the British, or the Americans. One side must win; the other must lose. Those who lose pay the penalty which those who win impart. It has been thus since the dawn of civilization, and will be so until the last man draws his final breath on this, our Mother Earth."

Word went out immediately to other tribes and bands. While they waited and Black Hoof contemplated, the chief made time for several talks with his new niece. He was as fascinated with her revelations of life in the late nineteen hundreds as Silver Thorn was. He asked her countless questions about the miraculous inventions, even though he was appalled at some things she told him. Nikki demonstrated her "firestick," as Silver Thorn had dubbed her cigarette lighter. Black Hoof was so enthralled with it that she offered it to him as a gift.

He accepted eagerly. "But you may borrow it when you

need it. I hear you are not adept at starting your lodge fire," he teased.

There were a lot of things Nikki was not adept at in this antiquated society. Trying to cook a meal over an open fire in a cast-iron kettle or on a spit or to bake muffins on a hot rock was highly exasperating. She simply couldn't get the hang of correctly judging heights, distances, cooking times, and temperatures.

"Boy, this makes me appreciate my old oven!" she declared, eyeing in dismay the half-done, half-charred loaf of bread before her. "Its thermostat regulator might not have been right on the money, but it was a darn sight better than this! And I'd give my right arm for my trusty microwave."

"You speak in riddles again, Neeake," Silver Thorn commented, though he didn't look any more enthused about eating her *burnt offering* than Nikki did. He was recovering from his wound, slowly but surely, and was now able to stay in his own wigewa with Nikki.

"Never mind," she grumbled. "Just wishful thinking on my part. Even if I had my modern kitchen appliances, they wouldn't do me a diddley darn bit of good without electricity. And don't ask me to explain that one, either."

"Why not?"

"Because it's like trying to tell a stranger about rock and roll," she quipped. "Besides, I don't want to get into a long-winded discussion about kites and keys and lightning, okay?"

Silver Thorn eyed her curiously. "You are in a surly mood this day."

"No kidding, Sherlock. Is this the first you've noticed that women sometimes get a little bent out of shape? Didn't your first wife ever gripe at you or get PMS?

"PMS?"

Nikki squeezed her eyes shut and muttered a quick prayer for patience, a commodity in short supply for her these days. "Premenstrual tension," she snapped. "That week or so prior to having her monthly bleeding. Most women tend to get a little bitchy then."

"Yes," Silver Thorn said. "But you cannot claim that excuse now, can you?"

His superior tone grated. Nikki stuck out her tongue at him. "Everybody likes a little ass; nobody likes a smart one. Moreover, I've never been pregnant before. Maybe getting grouchy is part of it, along with the sore boobs."

"Boobs?"

"These suckers!" Nikki leaned forward, cupping her breasts in her palms and almost shoving them in his face.

"Ah! Suckers!" Silver Thorn's face lit up. "A fitting term for them, indeed."

Nikki groaned. "I give up!"

"Then I win?" he teased. "Good. I claim these *suckers* as my prize." With a swiftness that belied his injury, he flipped Nikki onto her back next to the fire and proceeded to unbutton the top of her dress.

As his mouth clamped over her turgid, tender nipple, Nikki groaned again, this time in pleasure. "You know what, Thorn? You're dumb like a fox. Sometimes I could swear you know precisely what I'm talking about and just bait me deliberately, for the sport of it."

He raised his head long enough to seek her other breast. "It is good then that we both enjoy this sport, is it not?"

"Practice makes perfect, so they claim," she grated out, passion making speech nearly impossible as he laved the second nipple with his tongue. "But we can't. . . . Your side . . . you shouldn't. . . ."

He came up for breath once more and gave her a wolfish, toothpaste-ad grin. "There are more ways than one to skin a rabbit, wife. And, my Neeake, more than one way to cook a wild goose."

* * *

While he was healing, Silver Thorn worked on small projects around the wigewa such as braiding a leather horse halter and restringing his bow. For days now, he'd been etching and polishing a round metal object. When Nikki questioned him about it, he shrugged off her queries, usually by changing the subject. On this day, he called her over to him.

"Hold out your arm," he told her, indicating her left one.

She did as he requested. "What's this all about?"

He slipped a wristband over her hand and into place. "This is my gift to you, my wife, a sign to you and to others that I hold you in high esteem and close to my heart."

Nikki gazed first at him, then at the band on her wrist. Surprise and delight registered on her face. "Thorn! This is what you've been working on these past days. It's beautiful!"

Indeed, it was wrought of silver, polished to a brilliant sheen, and intricately engraved with flowers and geese. "Is . . . is this your equivalent of a wedding band? In my culture, when a couple marry, they usually exchange wedding rings, small ones that fit on one's finger."

"If by that they are giving a token of their love, then yes, this is my wedding band to you," he replied solemnly.

She sank to her knees and crawled into his arms, her own linking around his neck. "I'll treasure it always, Thorn. My only regret is that I have nothing of like value to give to you in return, to show you and the world how very much I adore you."

"You have given me your heart and soon you will give me a son. That is worth much more to me than any band of silver."

"Then it is made of silver?" she asked. "I thought so, but I can't imagine where you would get such precious metal around here. As far as I know, silver has never been mined in Ohio. Do you trade for it with another tribe, perhaps to the west?"

"No, my curious goose. There is a place perhaps two days' ride from here where the Shawnee have always found silver, for longer than I have years."

"Wow! Imagine that! And the white men know nothing about it?"

"It is a secret among the Shawnee. None among us will ever reveal the source. Just as we will never tell any white man from where comes our special pain powder."

"The one you took when you got shot? The one that has an effect similar to opium?"

"Yes, but it is not from the flower that yields the white man's opium. Nor does it make one develop a need for it, as does opium, though it is more potent."

"I recall you said something about the powder being made from the fruit of some tree. How is it, then, that the frontiersmen and settlers haven't discovered its marvelous potential?"

"Because they think the product of this tree is poisonous, more lethal than the bite of a snake," he informed her with a sly smile. "Which it is, if not properly prepared from the fruit and flowers."

"This is just a wild guess, mind you, but did the Shawnee help to perpetuate this fear the Americans have of the yield of this particular tree?"

Silver Thorn grinned widely. "As your President Washington would say, 'I cannot tell a lie.'"

"I wonder if this tree still grows in the area in my time," she mused.

"One day soon, when I am more fully healed, I will walk with you into the forest and show this tree to you," he promised. "I, too, would want to know if the tree still grows in your era, and perhaps you can tell me if the white man ever discovered its true usefulness."

He cuddled her closer, nibbling erotically on her earlobe

and sending quivers skating through her. "For now, enough of this talk. Would you not prefer to demonstrate to me how much you like your gift?"

In turn, she laved his ear with her tongue, laughing softly as he shivered. "I would. I shall."

She did.

Twelve

"You missed a few plump ones on that last bush." Silver Thorn pointed. "There, to the left."

He and Nikki were down by the river. He was resting on the bank, watching as she picked summer berries. Those, at least, she didn't have to cook, so there was little chance of her ruining them.

Nikki cast him a telling glance as she ripped another berry off its stem. "Big whoop!" she declared. "Who do I look like, anyway? Juan Valdez?" She lobbed the fruit at him, hitting him in the chest with it.

He retrieved the mushy tidbit and popped it into his mouth. "Who is Juan Valdez?"

"He's this little Colombian coffee-bean farmer, who takes his donkey into the mountains and picks every swinging coffee bean all by himself, just at the peak of flavor," Nikki intoned mockingly. "Now, unless you want to pick these berries yourself or at least provide me with a danged donkey other than your sweet braying self, stick a sock in it."

"But the more I tease you, the more berries you throw my way," he told her playfully.

"Which is why my basket is only half full," she retorted.

She strolled over and plopped herself next him on the grass. "Lands, it's hot!" She lifted an arm and tugged the wrist-length sleeves of her dress away from her armpit. "I'm wringing wet! You know, if you'd bothered to give me a little forewarning before whisking me backward in time, I could have packed an antiperspirant-deodorant in my purse. About midafternoon, I'm going to be as ripe as a three-day road-kill."

"It would help if you would remove all that cloth from your arms," he suggested.

"You wouldn't mind if I ripped off the sleeves?" she asked. "You didn't like my other clothes, so I thought maybe it would be a little immodest, according to the standards of your era."

"Not for the Shawnee," he informed her. "Have you not noticed that our women's garments do not cover their arms? In winter, yes, but not in summer." Unsheathing his knife, he offered, "I will aid in ridding you of your discomfort, if you wish."

"Please do, before I melt into a stinking puddle!" she exclaimed gratefully. "If you can just help loosen the seams near the shoulder, we can rip the sleeves off without too much damage to the dress."

"Why do white women need to cover their bodies from neck to heel?"

Nikki shrugged. "Presumably, because their stupid husbands don't want other men seeing their bare flesh. Or perhaps it's the only way to keep their skin from being exposed to the sun. Lily-white complexions were prized in the old days, and maybe they had the right idea after all. In my day, we dress much more comfortably, but we also risk skin cancer, which has become increasingly prevalent. But you can give me a cool pair of shorts and a camisole any old day instead of this."

"You could ask Konah to show you how to make a dress of doeskin."

She wrinkled her nose thoughtfully. "I'll consider it, but I have a hunch this cotton is cooler, not to mention easier to launder. If I ditch the petticoats, it would be better yet."

"Why do you not?" he asked.

She grinned at him. "Because at the first hint of a breeze, my nipples would show."

He shook his head. "No, only the form of them, as your breasts do already. They would still be clothed."

Nikki glanced heavenward. "Thank you, Lord, for such a wise and understanding husband. At least this one has some common sense."

They sat for a time, enjoying the breeze wafting in from the water. Looking out over the landscape, Nikki said, "Sitting here, I can almost picture in my mind where I would be in my own time. This tree might be one that still stands beside the river. Behind us, Blackhoof Bridge would span the Auglaize, and there, at the crest of the slope, would be a line of stores and shops along Blackhoof Street, with their back doors and parking lots facing the river. I figure the spot where the Council Lodge stands now, is approximately the location of the new antique mall or maybe the bank; and just about where that tall shrub is, would be the old dime store. It's vacant now, but in the early eighteen hundreds there was a mill there, built and run by the Quakers and used by both white settlers and Indians to grind their flour."

"Perhaps your history is again mistaken," Silver Thorn put in. "We are now in the early years of that century, and there is nothing built here by the white men, Neeake."

"There will be, in just a few years. Probably as soon as this war is over. You mark my words, Thorn. It will happen."

"The beginning of the end," he said sadly.

"No, just its inevitable progression," Nikki corrected softly. "The beginning was long ago, at Jamestown and Plymouth, when the first pilgrims stepped ashore. I've always thought the Indians should have greased that damned rock at Plymouth and let them all slide into the ocean."

Having read the history in James Galloway's books, Silver Thorn was inclined to agree with Nikki's assessment.

Still, he couldn't help but laugh at the way she chose to express it. "I am beginning to suspect that my life before you arrived was very dull compared to what it will be from this day forth."

She raised her palms in a gesture of innocence and smiled guilelessly. "What can I tell you? You asked for it; you got it."

There were numerous other differences between the Wapakoneta of her time and his. For one, life was so much simpler here. Children under six or seven years of age ran about naked, their sturdy nut-brown bodies sun-kissed from head to toe. There was an easy order to the day. When the sun rose, so did the Shawnee. When it set, villagers retired to their wigewas, enjoyed their meal and a few hours with their families, and went to sleep. In the hours between, they performed their various chores, visited back and forth, and often found time to play—adults and children alike.

Much as Silver Thorn had said, the work was shared by one and all. Despite what some history books had claimed, the Indian women were not relegated to a slave-like status while their men lazed around being catered to the day long. The men hunted, but so did some of the women. Many baited their own snares. What a person caught, he skinned—be it fish, fowl, or beast. Often, the men prepared the meat, salting and drying it in long strips.

Hides were scraped and softened and smoked, and again both sexes were engaged in the process. A man or woman might skillfully cut and sew it, mostly depending on what was to be made of the skin. If it were destined to be a knife sheath or a quiver or the covering for a saddle, the men usually took charge. If the hide were to become a garment, most often the women would sew it.

Crops, already planted and sprouting, were tended. Here, even the children were useful at pulling weeds. Nikki was amazed at the variety of cultivated plants. Not only were there tender shoots of corn poking through the soil, but pumpkins, squash, a type of bean, melons, and turnips. Even wild onions had been transplanted to a location more convenient to the village. At harvest time, every able-bodied Shawnee would help reap the produce, gathering and preserving all they could to hold them through the long winter months.

Another thing peculiar to the village, versus Nikki's modern time, was the lack of noise—or perhaps, more aptly, the difference between the sounds of the two centuries. Children still laughed and squealed and cried, of course. But they didn't whiz by on skateboards, boom boxes blaring from their shoulders. In place of horns and squealing tires, Nikki was more apt to hear the snort and stamp of a horse. When the wind kicked up, it whistled through pines and tree boughs, but did not whine through power lines. In the wigewa, there was only the crackle of the fire, no hum of electric appliances, no constant chatter from radios or televisions, no phones ringing.

"Egad! I can actually hear myself think, for once," Nikki marveled. "I just hope the peace and quiet doesn't start to drive me up a wall after awhile."

"Which reminds me," Silver Thorn said. "The birch strips I cut earlier in the spring should now be dried and ready to use. As soon as I am able, we will tear down these old wigewa walls and replace them with fresh ones."

"Say what?" she queried. "We, as in you and I, are going to replace the walls? Why? They look perfectly fine to me. A little smoke-cured, but nothing a good coat of paint wouldn't fix."

He chuckled. "Oh, Neeake, you do have much to learn of our ways. Fresh birch smells good and will repel rain better. It will also discourage mosquitos and other insects. Are you not the one who is constantly mewling about such things and checking your hair for lice?"

"Well, why didn't you say so sooner?" she griped. "If I'd known that, I would have reshingled the blamed thing myself."

It was after midnight, in the wee hours of the morning, when Silver Thorn grumbled, "Woman, why is it you cannot settle down so that we may both rest? Trying to sleep with you this night is like lying next to a sack full of mating chipmunks!"

"I can't help it!" Nikki whined. "I *itch!* All over, as if I've been bitten by a thousand mosquitos or bedbugs or something! God knows this wigewa is probably full of them. I swear, I'm going to burn this pest-ridden hut down tomorrow. I'll sleep in the open, in the rain if I have to, until we can erect a new one with that fresh birch."

Silver Thorn sighed. "Neeake, we have burned birch in our fire, and that is sufficient to drive away all the bugs you worry about. I have seen none and have not heard one mosquito all evening."

"That doesn't mean squat!" she retorted. "It's a known scientific fact that only the male mosquito makes that irritating droning noise, and he doesn't bite. The female is the one who sneaks up on you without a sound and nabs you." She scratched fervently again, raking her nails over her arms.

"If you would just lie still and think of something more pleasant," he suggested, "the itch would most likely go away."

Through grated teeth, she snarled, "Darn it, Thorn, it is not my imagination! I can feel the blasted bumps on my skin!"

He said nothing, but rose and chose a piece of birch bark from the woodpile. Twisting it into a torch, he held it to the coals until it flared into flame. "Let me see your arms, Neeake," he said. "Perhaps then we can solve this problem and get to sleep."

The moment he saw the blisters, he could have kicked himself for making light of her misery. For her part, upon seeing them, Nikki wished they had been insect bites. "Oh, no! Look at this! I'm covered with poison ivy!"

"My poor pet!" Thorn exclaimed in commiseration. "No wonder you are so uncomfortable. We must put a balm on it immediately." So saying, he located his herb pouch and rummaged through it.

"I hope you have something better than calamine lotion in there," Nikki challenged. "And I hope you really enjoyed those berries I picked for you, since I'd almost bet that's where I got into the poison ivy."

Silver Thorn returned with a leather packet and hunched down beside her. "Lie down, and I will apply this to the blisters."

"What is it?" she questioned warily.

"A salve made from a forest plant. You may know it as a woods lily, one James Galloway calls Solomon's Seal for the six-pointed star beneath the stem."

He spread the cream onto her skin, rubbing some in and leaving a generous overcoating. Not only were her arms and hands blotched with the rash, but big patches were erupting on her legs, neck, chest, and back. There was even a spot starting on her chin.

The balm was cool and soothing and brought a measure of relief almost instantly. "Oh, thank you!" she sighed. "That feels so good . . . so very good."

"You must cease your scratching, for it will only worsen the malady," he told her.

"I know. I've had this before. But it's so hard not to scratch. Would you tell a dog not to scratch at a flea?"

"You are not a dog and should have more control." Finished with her front side, he flipped her onto her stomach. "However, if you cannot govern your own actions, I can bind your hands in cloth, though it would actually do little to remedy matters."

Nikki cranked her head around to glare at him. "I am not a child, and I do not need a pair of mittens."

In the process of smearing the lotion on her bottom, Silver Thorn gave her a gentle whack with the palm of his hand. "Then lie still and behave yourself." He dropped a dollop on her back and smoothed it across her shoulders, massaging her tense muscles as he went. "Tomorrow we will gather more cures for you. Had it occurred to me that you were sensitive to the ivy, we could have prevented it beforehand."

"How?" The word emerged on a grunt of pleasure as he kneaded her back and buttocks.

"The juice of the No-Touch flower can bathe away the sap of the ivy. If you wash with it, the blisters do not appear."

"Mmmn. That's nice. Don't stop." Nikki was now in a cataleptic state of bliss.

His hands worked their way down her thighs, her calves, to the arches of her feet. His thumb prodded, wringing another grateful groan from her. Lulled nearly to sleep, she smiled as she felt him kiss her toe.

"If you keep that up, you're gonna get poison ivy on your tongue," she warned drowsily.

She heard the laughter in his voice as he replied softly, "More likely, I will experience an eruption of a different sort on another part of my body entirely. But that can wait until another time. Sleep now, little goose, and fly on the wings of sweet dreams."

For the next four days, Nikki went around looking like a badly speckled pup. Her sole consolation was that, as long as she used the lotions Silver Thorn had prepared for her, the itching was greatly reduced. In fact, his herbal remedies worked far better than those she would normally have purchased at a pharmacy. In light of this, she had to concede that perhaps there *was* something to great grandma's chicken-soup cure after all.

Moreover, as they'd walked through the woods collecting plants and roots for his cache, she'd been astounded when Silver Thorn had pointed out the source of his opium-like powder.

"Jumpin' Jehoshaphat! I can't believe it! These trees grow all over the state! Not in any great abundance, but we do have them. Actually, there's one growing just down the road from my dad's farm. My brothers and I used to collect the nuts and string them for necklaces. And those *are* nuts, Thorn. When you said fruit, I thought you meant something like an apple or berry."

He shrugged. "Nuts. Fruit. Regardless, they cannot be eaten."

"Damn straight! From the time we were old enough to walk, my parents warned us how lethal they are. Pretty, but poisonous."

"Then your learned doctors have not yet discovered its hidden powers? They have remained a secret, as the Shawnee intended?"

Nikki gave an energetic nod. "Believe me, if our scientists knew what they'd overlooked, they'd be beside themselves. Especially when it's been right under their noses all the while. They'd pay big bucks to discover something of this magnitude.

"No amount of deerskin would be worth revealing this long-held secret."

"Deerskin? I was speaking of money. Dollars."

"Do you not trade in pelts and skins?"

"That went out with the bustle, sweetheart," she said with a grin. "Buying and selling is now done with printed money and coins. Not to mention credit cards, loans, and a multitude of other methods. However, your way certainly has its merits. I can only imagine how it could frustrate the IRS!" she added on a hoot of laughter.

"What is this IRS?" he asked curiously.

Nikki's nose wrinkled as if she'd just gotten a whiff of something rotten. "Officially, it's the Internal Revenue Service, the government division that collects federal taxes on a person's yearly wages. Of course, every working man and woman believes they collect far more than is fair. I've heard the IRS referred to as the *Infernal* Revenue Service often enough to know that a few thousand citizens would like to throw another tea party in Boston Harbor."

"If the citizens are that discontent, why have they not?" he wanted to know. "It appears to have worked well the first time."

Respect for him gleamed from her eyes. "I sometimes forget how well educated you are. I see you have read accounts of early American history.

"But to answer your question, Americans gripe a lot, but they can also be notoriously disorganized. We hold elections, and somehow the representatives who have promised to help repair the ills of Congress rarely remember to do so once they are voted into office. Some of them give it an honest try; but on the whole they're in the minority, so nothing ever really improves much.

"But there's always hope for next year, the next champion-of-the-people, and so forth. Someday, the public will create enough of a stink that the government won't be able to ignore the people's issues any longer; but in order for that to happen, we first need a strong, influential leader who can really shake things up in Washington. Someone with the courage of George Washington, the honesty of Abe Lincoln, the fortitude of a Roosevelt, and the charisma of John Kennedy."

An ironic thought struck her. "If Tecumseh weren't so misguided, he'd be exactly what America needs in 1996!"

Thirteen

Konah, when informed of her relationship to Nikki, greeted the staggering news with a simplistic acceptance that Nikki envied. Konah was also genuinely delighted.

"Welcome, granddaughter," she said, as she drew Nikki into her embrace. Then Konah giggled. "That sounds so odd when you are of my same age, does it not?"

"It will definitely take some getting used to," Nikki agreed. "You don't seem terribly surprised or upset about this, or maybe you don't really believe it."

Konah's dark eyes twinkled. "Knowing your husband, I believe. Since I was a child, I have been amazed at the ability he and Tecumseh have to make strange and wonderful things occur."

"What about the Prophet? Isn't he, too, something of a magician?"

Konah shook her head. "Compared to his brothers, he is but a pretender, a common prankster. I think it is his jealousy of his more talented brothers that makes Tenskwatawa so hateful and ugly."

"From all I have heard of him, if he would divert his energies to better use, he might also be capable of great deeds," Nikki proposed.

Konah shrugged. "Perhaps, but I doubt it."

"Tell me about Silver Thorn and some of the unusual feats he has accomplished," Nikki urged.

Konah smiled and complied. "Once, when his canoe

was floating away, I saw him make the river run backward, the better to retrieve it."

Nikki chuckled. "Why that stinker! That trick would certainly have come in handy a couple of times on our trip up here, if he'd only chosen to employ it. What else has he done?"

Konah thought a moment. "He and my husband were out hunting two summers past and surprised a mother bear with her cubs. The bear gave chase. Knowing they could not out-run her, Skotai Kitehi and Silver Thorn climbed into a tree, hoping the bear would not follow. When the bear stood beneath them roaring and clawing at them, Silver Thorn called to her. Fire Heart swears that when the bear looked into Silver Thorn's eyes, she turned as tame as a river turtle. Calmly, she went back to her cubs, and the two hunters went on their way, unharmed."

Nikki gnawed her lip thoughtfully. "I wonder if bears can be hypnotized," she mused. At Konah's questioning look, she clarified, "Put in a trance."

Again Konah gave a nonchalant shrug. "With Silver Thorn, anything is possible."

"Amen!" Nikki breathed. "Living with him is like standing on the brink of a cliff, knowing a stiff breeze could come along at any minute and knock you off. It's fascinating, but at the same time, it's nerve-wracking."

Konah was extremely curious about Nikki's previous life and family. The two women spent many hours happily trading tales. Also, as women tended to do everywhere and in every age, they talked about wifely concerns. Raising children. Cooking, cleaning, keeping their husbands satisfied. Health and hygiene.

The latter led Nikki to confide, "You don't know how lucky you are to have such sparse body hair, Konah. I wish I'd inherited that trait, as well as some others. Unfortunately, along with my violet eyes, I also acquired a few undesirable genes from my mother's side of the family."

She hiked up her skirt and poked out a leg. "See? Right now, I'd give my eyeteeth for a razor. I've been here over two weeks now, and my legs are so hairy I'm starting to feel like an ape. If I don't find a way to shave them soon, I might as well begin braiding them."

Konah wrinkled her nose and laughed. "Horse-blanket legs. The better to keep your husband warm at night," she teased.

"Go ahead and laugh, but I'll bet if you had this problem it wouldn't be so funny."

"How did you rid yourself of this terrible affliction before?" Konah asked, assuming feigned gravity. Her twitching lips gave lie to her somberness.

"Shaving, plucking, waxing. You name it."

"This shaving scrapes the hair off, yes?"

Nikki nodded. "Plucking is better, but only if you use a device similar to an electric razor that pulls many hairs out at once. Otherwise, you could spend a month of Sundays tweezing your legs one strand at a time."

"And waxing?" Konah inquired.

"You smear wax over your legs, or upper lip for that matter, let it cool and tear it off. It literally rips the hair off. Painful, but effective."

"Why do you not try the wax here, then? Or is bees' wax not the same as you use?"

Nikki's face lit up as she hugged Konah hard. "You're a genius! Why didn't I think of that?"

Konah laughed and affected a superior attitude, her nose in the air. "Because I am the grandmother. Besides, everyone knows the Snow Bird is smarter than the Wild Goose."

* * *

Having Konah and Melassa to confide in was wonderful. It was Melassa who told Nikki what to expect as her pregnancy advanced. She and Konah both instructed her on which foods to avoid, how best to counter morning sickness, and what balm to use on her breasts and tummy to prevent stretch marks.

They also taught Nikki more about their daily life and the varied tasks she must learn. Along with cooking, herbal cures, and caring for the crops came Nikki's first sewing project. She watched queasily as Konah demonstrated how to scrape the deer hides and stretch and soften them with a mixture of brains and liver.

When they were soft and pliable, all hair and matter removed from them, Konah turned the skins over to Nikki. "Now they are ready for you to smoke them on the frame I showed you how to erect over your fire. Use the fresh white cedar Turtle gathered for you, and the leather will become light cream or tan in color. Then you can cut and sew it into clothing."

Along with the hides, she handed Nikki a pile of rawhide strips to be used in place of thread and three needles made of fishbone. "When you are done, you can decorate it with dyed porcupine quills in any design you choose." She indicated her own blouse. "Very pretty, yes?"

Nikki had to agree, for Konah's top was quite ornate. "Yes, very beautiful. I only hope I can do half as well. Are you sure I shouldn't start with something easier than a shirt for Silver Thorn, though? Like maybe a nice, flat, rectangular breechcloth? I never was any great shakes in home-ec class."

"If you use an old shirt for a pattern, you will do fine," Konah assured her. "Fortunately, your man has reached his full growth, unlike my sons, Turtle and Red Pipe, who are growing faster than the weeds in the corn patch."

Clamping her hands over Nikki's shoulders, Konah gave

her a light push in the direction of Silver Thorn's wigewa. "Go, now. Make your husband proud of his new wife."

Nikki tried, but Murphy's Law seemed to be working overtime. The fire filled the wigewa with smoke, making her cough and her eyes smart. Only then did she recall Konah saying she should dig a separate firepit outside over which to smoke the hides. To make things worse, the frame she'd fashioned from green willow branches was much more flimsy than the one Konah had made. The ties kept wanting to come undone, and the whole structure would list and droop, no matter how carefully she placed it over the fire. The hides didn't have a mind to stay put, either, and kept sliding off onto the dirt floor. At one point, the entire frame collapsed onto the smoking wood, charring the leather before Nikki could rescue it from the coals.

After several unsuccessful attempts, Nikki said, "To heck with it!" Holding the scorched skin up and viewing it with a critical eyes, she decided, "Better whole than holey. Another hour or so wouldn't really change the color much anyway, I don't suppose. Besides, if it sucked in as much smoke as I have, I think we can call it done."

Next came the challenge of marking and cutting the hide. Using an old shirt of Silver Thorn's as a pattern and a piece of charred wood in lieu of tailor's chalk, Nikki set to work. After the end of her stick broke for the fourth time, Nikki tossed it aside. Digging into her purse, she located her eyeliner in her cosmetic case and did much better. Soon she had the pieces outlined.

Her next problem was trying to cut them out. In Nikki's inexperienced hands, the knife-like instrument Konah had given her was unwieldy, and she gouged a few holes in the skins before discovering a technique that would work for her. By scoring the material several times over, she wore a line thin enough that her cuticle scissors would cut it, though raggedly. Both scissors and hides were worse for wear when she finished.

"So, a little fringe along the edges will be decorative," she rationalized. "No harm done."

This decided, she enlarged on the idea, making the uneven strands longer. Only when she set about trying to sew the front to the back did she realize that she'd barely left herself enough material to work with and Silver Thorn's new shirt might be just a bit snug.

"Oh, well, he's probably lost a little weight during his recuperation," she told herself. "And since this is more of a tunic, really, with no sleeves, that should automatically allow for more freedom of movement."

Sewing modern materials with needle and thread was much easier than poking through buckskin with a fishbone and thick leather strands. In the end, Nikki resorted to punching holes in the hide with the point of her knife, and then jabbing the fishbone through in whipstitch fashion. The end result was a bit rough, the stitches uneven, and the fringe somewhat irregular; but for her first attempt, Nikki didn't think it was half bad.

"Besides, this is a summer shirt and a few gaps in the stitching will just let the air flow through better," she concluded.

Konah tried to be diplomatic when she saw the finished product. "You will do better the next time, I am sure. At least your seams appear tight enough to hold together."

"I tried my best," Nikki announced with a pout.

"I am sure Silver Thorn will appreciate your effort," Konah said. "Still, I would not spend much time applying the quillwork. A simple design would be best, I am thinking."

Flexing her blistered, pricked-to-bleeding fingers, Nikki agreed. She chose to appliqué a single thunderbird on the front. For the next three days, she labored diligently. The final product more resembled a lame duck with unbalanced wings and an offset eye, but Nikki was satisfied.

"Heck! If it's good enough for Picasso, it's good enough for me, and for Silver Thorn."

If Silver Thorn had to bite his tongue to keep from laughing, he hid it well. Moreover, he agreed to wear his new shirt the very next day. "I am going on a short hunt with the other men," he told her. "We must have meat for our guests when they arrive from the other villages for the council."

"Are you well enough?" she questioned, her concern obvious.

"I would not go if I were not," he assured her. "You will not be afraid to stay here by yourself for just one day, will you?"

"No. I'll miss you and I'll worry about you, but I won't be scared. I won't set foot out of the village; and if I have any problems, Konah and her family can bail me out, I'm sure. You'll be back before dark, won't you?"

"Most likely. Do not worry, little goose. I will return to you safely. And I will bring more hides for you to sew," he added with a crooked grin.

She forced a smile. "Yippy-skippy! I can hardly wait!"

Early the following evening, Nikki was making rabbit stew with dandelion greens and cornbread, determined that she would not ruin this meal. She was stirring the unappealing mess in the kettle, trying to convince herself that it would taste better than it looked, when Silver Thorn charged into the wigewa.

"Woman, you are in trouble!" he roared.

Startled, Nikki's head jerked up. The sight before her made her jaw drop open and her eyes pop wide. Silver Thorn's face was beet red, his expression as ominous as storm clouds. But it wasn't this that held Nikki in a mute state of disbelief. It was his new shirt. Where just this morning it had hung nearly to his hips, the hem now rode just beneath his pectoral muscles, with a crooked line of fringe dangling across his upper stomach. The material that had draped over his shoulders onto his upper arms was now drawn nearly to his neck. And the center-slit opening at the throat was drawn firmly to his windpipe. The bright blue thunderbird now appeared to be trying to strangle him with deformed wings.

Torn between laughter and dismay, Nikki finally found her tongue. "What have you done to your shirt?" she shrieked.

"What have I done?" he thundered. He turned the question back to her. "What have *you* done? Did Konah not instruct you to smoke the hides before using them?"

"I . . . I did!" she claimed. "Well, I tried, but . . ."

"Apparently you did not try hard enough, or long enough," he interjected angrily. "Had you done it properly, it would not have shrunk the moment I got it wet!"

"And how did you get it wet?" she countered.

"I slipped on a rock while crossing the river. That in itself caused me little concern until my own shirt began to choke the life out of me!"

Nikki could hold it no longer. Laughter erupted from her, sending her rocking back on her heels. Once started, she could not stop. Within seconds she was howling, tears of mirth streaking her face.

Silver Thorn's voice boomed. "I fail to see the humor, wife. Because of you, my friends have enjoyed tormenting me the day long."

Weak with laughter, she lamely waved a hand at him. "Don't . . . don't have a cow, for crying out loud! A little humility now and then is good for the soul, especially for someone as arrogant as you can be."

"Are you saying you did this purposely, to humiliate me before my fellow Shawnee?"

He was incredulous, which only seemed to make his silver eyes bulge all the more. Seeing this, Nikki went into fresh gales of glee. Her sides were aching by the time she caught her breath again. She looked up at him, towering over her, impatiently awaiting her reply.

"I did not do it on purpose, Thorn, though I might have been tempted if I'd thought of it. You needed to be brought down a peg or two, if only to make you realize that you are merely human and not a god, despite your almighty powers. This time, however, it was an honest mistake."

His face eased somewhat, though the frown remained. "One which I trust will not be repeated," he warned.

"I'll give it my best shot," she vowed. Holding up her hand, palm toward him, she added impishly, "Honest Injun!" Once again she dissolved into giggles.

Her laughter, even though directed toward him, was contagious. His mouth, though he deliberately tried to keep it stern, began to quirk at the corner. Reluctantly, it blossomed into a smirk, and then a full-blown smile. "Blast you for a witch, Neeake!" he chuckled. "I should beat you. I should . . ."

"You should thank me for reminding you not to take yourself so seriously. A man who is able to laugh at himself is one who will be loved by all."

He sat down next to her and reached out a hand to ruffle her hair. "I care not if no one loves me but you."

"I do love you," she said, wiping the joyous tears from her face. "I do, and I didn't mean to laugh so hard, but . . . but you should see yourself!"

He grinned back at her. "I suppose I do look the fool."

Nikki had a sudden inspiration. "Wait! Before you take that ridiculous shirt off, I'm going to get a picture of this!"

She scooted to the rear of the wigewa and rummaged through her backpack. "This is a Polaroid camera," she said, holding it out for him to see. "With it, I can catch your image on a special piece of paper, almost like an instant painting. It's called a photograph."

She flipped open the camera and pointed it at him. An

expression approximating fear flashed across his face. Immediately, she was contrite, knowing she should have explained more fully. "It's all right, Thorn. It doesn't hurt. It doesn't do anything bad. I know in some cultures they believe that taking someone's picture steals their soul, but believe me when I tell you that it doesn't. This will simply produce a likeness of you."

"I will trust you concerning this," he stated tensely, as if trying to convince himself.

"You do that," she said, offering him a conspiratorial wink. She looked around and decided that there was sufficient light in the wigewa for the camera to operate properly with the flash. "Okay, sweetheart, stand up, so we can get the full view. And smile."

He stood, his muscles rigid and his smile as stiff as cardboard. "Loosen up," she commanded. "Relax. You look like one of those cigar-store Indians carved out of wood. Except I'm sure none of them would be caught dead in an outfit that ludicrous!"

He tried, with little result. "Say cheese," she suggested.

"Why?" he queried.

"Because it's supposed to make you look like you're smiling naturally," she replied.

"Cheese."

Nikki sighed. "That's even worse. Now you look as if you've just bitten into a sour grape. Let's try something else. Say money."

"Money."

"Your lips still look funny, like they're stretched back over your teeth and stuck there. Say sexy."

Still no success.

Nikki paused. Then she smiled. "Repeat after me. The big black bug bit the big black bear."

"This is foolishness."

"Do it anyway, to please me. Say it as fast as you can."

"The big black blug blit the blig black bear." Silver Thorn

frowned. "No, that is not right." He tried again. "The blig black bug bit the blig back blair." He shook his head, as if wondering whose tongue was suddenly in his mouth.

She giggled. "Once more," she urged. She readied the camera.

He concentrated and deliberately slowed his speech. "The big black bear bit the big black bug. There!" he crowed. "I did it!"

She captured his triumphant smile. The flashbulb startled him momentarily and he flinched, but only after the shutter had closed.

"See? It didn't hurt a bit," she comforted. With a whir, the camera spit out the photo. "Here," she invited, patting the spot beside her. "Come and watch what happens next."

Warily, he did as she asked. Apprehension quickly turned to awe as he watched his image appear on the black paper. "This is truly wondrous!" he exclaimed, taking the picture from her. As excited as a child, he pointed at it. "This is me! As I appear in Mrs. Galloway's mirror or on the surface of the river when it is calm!" He turned the snapshot over to inspect the reverse side of it and seemed disappointed to find nothing there.

"What is it?" she asked curiously.

"Why did it not paint the back of me?" he questioned.

Nikki laughed. "Because only the front of you was facing the camera," she explained. "If you want a picture of your backside, you'll have to turn around."

This time he posed eagerly, glancing back at her over his shoulder with a broad grin.

"Lord, I've created a monster!" she claimed. "A real ham! I only wish your breechcloth had shrunk, too, so we could capture *all* of your dimples on film!"

Once again, their dinner was burnt.

Fourteen

It became Nikki's habit to "air dry" following her daily bath. Fortunately, with her olive complexion, she'd never had to worry much about getting sunburnt. Also, since no one in her family, most especially on her father's side, had ever been diagnosed with skin cancer, Nikki weighed her risks as minimal and thanked God for her Shawnee heritage and coloring. Still, her natural skin tone was much lighter than that of the other Shawnee, and she figured a good tan would put her more on a par with the rest of them.

She was sunbathing alone, sans clothes, in a private glade near the edge of the pool, when Silver Thorn discovered her there. "Konah told me I might find you here, but she neglected to warn me of the delights in store for me when I did. What are you doing, just lying there in the sun, Neeake? Are you ill or too weak to dress and return to the wigewa?"

She propped herself up on an elbow and tugged her sunglasses off her head onto her nose, the better to see him in the bright glare of day. "I'm perfectly healthy; and if you tell me I look pale, I'm going to hit you. I've worked very hard to acquire this tan."

He sat down beside her on the blanket she'd spread out on the ground. "But why?" he questioned.

"Because I'm tired of being the only paleface in the

crowd. It makes me feel like an outsider, as if I don't really belong."

"That is absurd. You are my wife. You are kin to Konah and Black Hoof. There is no one who would dare claim that you do not belong here. Has anyone made you feel unwelcome?"

"No, but my eyes are the wrong color and my skin is too light. While I can't do anything to change the color of my eyes, I can at least darken my skin this way." She leaned toward him as if to emphasize her need. "I want to fit in here, Thorn. I don't want to feel set apart by my differences."

"But your differences are what make you special, little goose," he pointed out. "As far as the color of your eyes is concerned, my eyes are also unlike those of my Shawnee friends and relatives. Even Tecumseh has eyes of a lighter hue, with brown and gold and other colors mixed together. Our Mandan brothers to the west often have eyes of gray or blue, and some have white hair in their youth. Many tribes have skin lighter or darker than the Shawnee, with more red or yellow cast, yet all are our brothers. All are made by the same Creator."

"Yes, but I'm part white," she countered. "In a way, that makes me feel like some poor relative, someone to be pitied and accepted here only on grace."

"You are not alone, Neeake. Others of our number also carry white blood, but they are not despised any more than you. Still others were born white before coming to join us and being adopted into the tribe. Many, such as Blue Jacket, have risen to become great leaders."

"Okay, you've stressed your point. Maybe I am being a little silly, but I still think a nice, even tan is to my favor. And I hope our child inherits your coloring instead of mine, right down to your fascinating silver eyes."

"Is that why you have covered your eyes with those strange silver spectacles?" he wanted to know. "James Galloway has similar ones, though his are smaller and have clear centers. He uses them to see better when he reads."

Nikki removed the mirrored, aviator-style sunglasses and handed them to him for his inspection. "These are sunglasses. The lenses are tinted to protect one's eyes from the glare of the sun. I use them only in the sun since I don't need prescription lenses to enhance my vision. I admit mine aren't very stylish these days, but I prefer them to some of the other shapes."

Silver Thorn turned them over, examining the frames, and held them up to squint through the lenses.

"Go ahead, try them on," she urged. "Slip the side pieces over your ears and slide them onto your nose."

The one-size-fits-all frames with their large, mirrored lenses fit Silver Thorn perfectly. As he played with them, tilting his head this way and that and peering over the top to compare the difference, Nikki clamped a hand to her bare breast, which was suddenly beating double time. She felt ridiculously like a teenage groupie, enthralled with a rock idol. With his cinnamon skin and his straight, Greek-god nose, he rivaled any film star for simple, straightforward, sex appeal.

"Eat your heart out, Tom Cruise," she murmured.

"What?" He turned toward her, smiling, and Nikki caught her breath.

"You are the most incredibly handsome creature God ever fashioned," she rasped out, her voice husky with desire. "Not to mention compassionate, loving, and sensual. Sometimes I can hardly believe my luck, that someone as ordinary as I could attract someone as marvelous as you. What kept you single all these years, Thorn? Back home, you'd be beating the women off with a stick just to have a moment's peace!"

He plucked the glasses off and tossed them aside. As he leaned over her, his mouth hovered above hers. "I was waiting for you, my love, and you are far from ordinary.

You are lovely and beguiling, most especially dressed as you are now, in nothing but a smile and the kiss of the sun."

"I'd rather have your kiss," she whispered, twining her arms around his neck and drawing him nearer still.

"And so you shall," he promised on a raspy growl that sent shivers of anticipation shimmering through her.

Their coming together was wild. Primal. Needy. A thing of feral lust, with little concern for preliminaries. All teeth and claws and urgency. When it was done, they lay together, panting, still reeling from the fierce onslaught of their passion.

"I've died and gone to heaven," Nikki sighed. "I have no bones. You melted them all."

Silver Thorn mustered a chuckle. "Perhaps we will have to crawl back to the wigewa."

"If we wait until dark, we won't even have to dress first," she suggested.

"Just remind me to collect my breechcloth from the bushes," he added.

She blinked at him, perplexed. "What's it doing in the bushes? I thought you were wearing it."

He laughed. "I was, until you tore it off me and tossed it to the winds. I am left with nothing but the thong around my waist."

"Not to worry," she assured him, mischief dancing in her eyes. "I hear thong bikinis are quite the rage on the Riviera this year."

Two days later, Silver Thorn again came upon Nikki when she least expected it, but this time she was sitting beneath a huge old oak tree in a clearing not far from the village—and she was crying. Instantly alarmed, he raced to her side.

"Neeake, what is it? Have you hurt yourself? Has some-one else hurt you?"

With her head bent, she waved both hands at him in a gesture he could not understand. All he could do was wait for her to gather a measure of composure. Her lashes were glistening with teardrops when she finally raised sorrowful eyes to his. "I'm not hurt," she gulped. "At least not physi-cally. I'm just a little homesick, and heartsick. I miss my family back home."

Silver Thorn lowered himself to the ground and pulled her into his lap, cuddling her close to his heart. "That is to be expected, love."

"Yes, but I didn't expect it to be this bad!" she wailed, clutching at him. "I'm a grown woman, and I've lived on my own for years; but right now I feel like a little girl and I want my mommy and daddy so much! I want to tell Mom about you, and about our baby. I want to go shop-ping with her for baby furniture and maternity clothes and tiny blue blankets. She and Dad would be so thrilled. Dad would be out buying miniature baseball bats and advance tickets to the Reds game for his new grandson. By Christ-mas he'd be knee-deep in sawdust in his workshop, making a rocking horse for him.

"Right now, Dad probably wonders where I am and why I didn't get home in time for Father's Day. Why I at least didn't bother to send a card or call if I couldn't make it home. July Fourth is just around the corner; and if they don't already suspect something is dreadfully wrong, they certainly will by then. The whole family gets together every Fourth. My brothers and their families, aunts, uncles, cousins. We all gather at Mom and Dad's farm for a huge picnic. Everyone brings food, and we set up games in the yard and play croquet and volleyball and touch football. After dark, we set off fireworks and sing patriotic songs and celebrate Independence Day in grand style. It's won-derful.

"But this year I won't be there to join in the fun. And I imagine my absence will dampen their enthusiasm as well. They've probably got the state police out looking for me. Maybe they've even found my car by now, in the parking lot at the caves. They're probably searching the woods and the caves and dragging the river, expecting the worst but still hoping I'll turn up alive and unharmed.

"Oh, Thorn! It must be horrible for them! If there were just some way I could let them know that I'm all right. To give them that much comfort, at least. Can't you, with all your mystical powers, devise a means of contacting them somehow? Or maybe you could send me home, for just a few days, just long enough to visit and explain to them, then bring me back here."

He stroked her hair, his own heart aching for her. "I do not know if it is possible to send a message to your family, but I will strive to find a way. As for sending you home again, I would not want to attempt it, Neeake. The danger could be too great, for you and for our child, who would travel with you. Might not such a journey harm our son? Moreover, I do not know how to send you back to your same time. What if I tried and misjudged and sent you to another year? How would I find you again or you me? No, my love. Better you should ask me to give you the moon than to send you from me with such risk."

Nikki hiccuped, trying to stem her tears. "I don't want to risk losing you either," she told him. "But it's so hard, knowing how they must be worrying. This isn't like missing my refrigerator or Monday Night Football. This is my family we're talking about. People I love, who love me."

"I know, Neeake. I am sorry for your pain." Then, as if to divert her attention to a more pleasant topic, he inquired softly, "You miss football?"

She nodded and gave a shaky laugh. "Silly, isn't it? My brothers used to play when they were in high school, and I'd go to all their games with Mom and Dad."

"Did you not play?"

"Only at home, with the boys and the other kids. At school, the girls had softball and basketball teams of their own, but no football; and we weren't allowed to play on the boys' team."

"Here, the women play against the men," he told her.

She pulled back and gave him an incredulous look. "You play football? Here?"

"Yes, but only in the spring and early summer. It is our way of asking the Spirits to bring the rain for the newly planted crops. In midsummer, we cease the games, for too much rain then would be bad for the growing season. At this time the corn and beans need the sun to ripen them for the harvest. A game is planned soon, during the time of the council meeting. Our guests will be invited to join us in this, and in the dancing afterward."

"Football? And dancing, too?" The sadness left her face, replaced by delight. "It sounds like fun."

"First the council, which is a serious matter, and then the pleasure. Do not be surprised if Black Hoof requires you to stand and speak to the assembly of chiefs. As our eminent messenger from the future, your words could bear much weight in their decisions."

"Would they listen to a woman?" she queried skeptically.

"If they can be made to believe that the Spirits have truly sent you to us, they will be eager to hear you tell what is to befall our people, and perhaps heed your warnings."

"I hope so, but I still don't hold out much hope for the future of the tribes. What will be, will be, regardless of our puny efforts to change history."

Silver Thorn agreed. "As the Spirits will it, so it shall come to pass. Yet we must try, for Tecumseh's sake."

He rose, pushing her up with him. "Enough of this

dreary talk. The day is too fair for it, and the council meet is not yet. I searched you out to see if you would like to ride with me."

"In the canoe?" she asked.

"On horseback," he clarified. "For the safety of the babe, we will not go far and will keep an easy pace."

"Uh, I have to tell you that I haven't ridden in years, not since I was a young girl. Even then, my mount was just a short-legged pony Dad had bought for us kids. I'm not sure I can still sit astride without falling off, especially without a saddle."

"Do you not want to ride?" he asked.

"I'd love to!" she declared. "I'm just warning you that I'll probably be a little clumsy at it."

"The mare you will ride is very gentle," he assured her. "Also, I have anticipated your need for a saddle and have borrowed one for you."

Nikki nearly danced with enthusiasm. She grabbed his arm, tugging at him. "Well, then, what are we waiting for? Time's wasting!"

Upon seeing the pretty little gray mare she was to ride, Nikki was doubly delighted. "She's a beauty. I hope her owner doesn't mind my riding her."

Silver Thorn shook his head. "I think not, since she belongs to you. She is a gift from your uncle, Chief Black Hoof."

"A gift?" Nikki echoed. "Oh, my lands! I must find a special way to thank him for such a generous present."

"Perhaps you could sew him a shirt like the one you made for me," Silver Thorn suggested as he boosted her into the saddle.

"Very funny!" Nikki wriggled into a comfortable position on the oddly fashioned wooden saddle, thickly padded with a furred cougar pelt and decorated with the cat's actual claws. As she took up the reins, she asked, "Does the mare have a name?"

Silver Thorn mounted his own horse. "In your English, she would be called Misting."

Nikki glanced over at him with a whimsical expression. "Did you say Misting or Mustang? I've always wanted a Mustang convertible with four on the floor, but this isn't precisely what I had in mind."

Her mare whinnied and shook her head. Silver Thorn laughed. "Misting would appreciate it if you would refrain from making jokes of her name."

Nikki's brow rose. "Oh, you understand *horse*, do you?" she said, recalling Konah's tale of the mother bear. "How many other animal languages do you speak?"

"All of them," he countered blithely, kneeing his horse into a walk.

Nikki followed suit, riding alongside. Her eyes sparkled with impish delight. "How interesting. Can you demonstrate a few for me? Perhaps the next time you're whispering sweet nothings in my ear?"

His answering smile was as mischievous as hers. "Which would you prefer? Which would you consider the most ardent? Perhaps the cougar? Or the goose? Or the wolf, who takes but one mate?"

"Later, maybe. First, I want to be romanced in muskrat talk," she replied with a giggle. "Ever since I first heard a song called 'Muskrat Love,' with all those intriguing trills and squeals, I've been dying of curiosity to know what those two little creatures could be saying to one another."

His grin grew. "A fitting choice," he agreed. "And since you are such an inquisitive goose, someday soon you must allow me to demonstrate how porcupines couple."

She laughed and urged. "Tell me, how *do* they do it? Very carefully, I would guess."

He shook his head. "My lips are sealed. Some things are better experienced than explained."

For the next hour and more, Nikki's head was reeling with odd impressions, as she tried to imagine just how porcupines actually *did* mate.

Fifteen

They were returning to the village, riding along the river trail, when they came upon a clearing and what appeared to be a white man. He was an odd-looking fellow, barefoot and dressed in what looked like old flour sacks, with a tin pot on his head. He was kneeling on the ground, where he had dug a small hole. As Nikki and Silver Thorn approached, they saw him drop something from his hand into the hole and push the dirt back into place.

Something about the man's unique appearance and apparel niggled at Nikki's brain, suggesting she should know this man, but for the life of her she could not place how or why. It hit her as Silver Thorn raised a hand in greeting and called out, "John Chapman, my old friend! What are you planting here? More apple trees?"

The man rose to his feet, a broad smile on his weatherworn face. "Silver Thorn, you scamp! I was hoping to run into you again."

Nikki was elated, and more than a little awed. "As I live and breathe!" she exclaimed. "It's Johnny Appleseed!"

John tipped his makeshift hat. "Yes, ma'am. I see you've heard of me."

"Who hasn't?" she marveled. "Why, you're a legend!"

Shy by nature, Chapman actually blushed at her compliment. Silver Thorn took pity on him. "This is my wife, Neeake. Her tongue, though truthful, often runs off with her."

John chuckled as Nikki threw Silver Thorn a mock glare.

"Are you headed for the village?" Silver Thorn asked him.

"I'd thought I might," John said with a nod. "Just for a short visit, of course."

"You are always welcome, for as long as you will stay," Thorn told him. "Come. Gather your things, and you can ride with us. Neeake and I can ride double."

Chapman shook his head. "You go on ahead. I want to get this plot planted before dark. I'll be along later, and I'll bring a couple of potatoes for the cooking pot. Don't want to be a burdensome guest, you know."

"Potatoes?" Nikki's mouth started watering at the thought. "You've got real, honest-to-goodness potatoes? Not just some wild root that looks like one?"

Silver Thorn scowled at her. "Neeake, where are your manners?" he reproved.

It was her turn to turn red. "I'm sorry. That was terribly impolite of me, Mr. Chapman. My only excuse is that it's been weeks since I've had so much as a skinny French fry."

"French fry?" Silver Thorn echoed.

"It's a kind of fried potato, sliced in long strips, but not as thin as hash browns," she tried to explain.

"Hash browns?" John queried. He looked to Silver Thorn for further clarification.

Silver Thorn shrugged. "Whatever they are, they will be hash blacks when Neeake is done with them. But fear not, my friend, she has not poisoned me yet. Better yet, when Konah hears you are coming, perhaps she will volunteer to prepare our meal."

"Maybe she'd like to cook all of yours from now on," Nikki suggested with a sour look.

John glanced from her to Silver Thorn. "Uh-oh. I think you've made her mad, and I sure wouldn't want to be in your moccasins right now."

Nikki offered him a genuine smile. "Mr. Chapman, you are still welcome for supper, whether Konah cooks it or I do. And don't worry about Silver Thorn. He has riled my temper before and lived to tell of it. Besides, I don't get mad; I get even. Moreover, in all fairness, my revenge is only directed at the person responsible. In this case, my beloved husband, whose mouth often runs away with him, too. So please, don't let our silly little domestic difference of opinion keep you away. We'll be thrilled to have you visit with us."

"Yes, John," Silver Thorn concurred. On a wink, he added, "Please do bring those potatoes. Perhaps they will help soften her heart toward me."

"Don't bet on it, buster," Nikki muttered darkly.

Silver Thorn's eyebrow rose as he cocked his head in consideration. "Then again, perhaps they will not. Ah, well, such are the trials of marriage. Come, Neeake, we must let John get back to his planting."

Silver Thorn turned his mount toward the village. Nikki followed, fuming silently.

John watched them go. Before they were out of earshot, he heard Silver Thorn say to her, "Would you care to hear how a muskrat would compliment your beauty?"

"I'd rather hear Mr. Muskrat squeal with his tail in a trap!" she shot back.

"Can I tempt you with porcupine caresses?" Silver Thorn suggested.

"Well . . . maybe," she hedged.

They left Johnny standing there, shaking his head at their odd conversation. "Married folk make no sense at all sometimes."

Once having unearthed her camera, Nikki wanted to take pictures of everything and everyone, most especially her new family members and friends. Like Silver Thorn, many of them were skeptical and frightened of her "magic paint box," as they came to call it. But once assured that it would not harm them, they posed graciously.

Nikki photographed Konah and Melassa as they scraped skins, as they labored in the fields, as they splashed in the bathing pool. She snapped Silver Thorn and Fire Heart indulging in a game of Indian dice. The children were her favorite subjects. She caught them at play—frolicking like pups in the sunshine, giggling as they caught raindrops on their tongues, chasing through flowered meadows, or looking so precious and innocent as they slept.

She even managed to capture the elusive and shy Johnny "Appleseed" Chapman on film when he was unaware. Naturally, he was busy planting his apple seeds at the time.

Though Chief Black Hoof balked at first, he finally consented to having his photo taken. However, it was he who warned Nikki, in the presence of her husband, to exercise caution with her camera.

"There are those who would make much of this magic paint box and your use of it. They would deem it evil, simply to suit their own sinister purposes. Beware, lest they label you a witch, Neeake, and seek to burn you at the stake."

"He speaks of my brother, the Prophet," Silver Thorn elaborated. "Tenskwatawa held himself in high esteem, far above other mortals, and as a judge of them. His followers were just as zealous as he, and the entire band of them are responsible for the deaths of many good people."

"I know. I've read how they went around arresting or killing dissenters, those who refused to join Tecumseh or spoke against his ideals. But I thought all that was done with after the Prophet disobeyed Tecumseh's orders and instigated that misguided battle at Tippicanoe—which, if memory serves me, the Indians lost in late 1811."

"This is true," Silver Thorn agreed. "After the disaster Tenskwatawa made of Tecumseh's grand plans for a uniting of the tribes, Tecumseh thrust him away, disclaiming him as our brother. To this day, Tecumseh will not speak Tenskwatawa's name, nor will he consider forgiving him. Tenskwatawa is as dead to Tecumseh and to many of the Shawnee. He showed himself to be a false prophet, and is now disgraced and ridiculed by most of the tribes."

"As well he should be, the murderous little charlatan!" Nikki claimed adamantly. "However, that being the case, I fail to see what I have to fear from him."

Black Hoof took it upon himself to explain. "Tenskwatawa angered many people, but he also roused their fears of witches in their midst, and later of false prophets. You, my dear niece, with your strange devices and your predictions from the future would seem the embodiment of both. This could be very dangerous for you, most especially if Tenskwatawa should somehow again gain favor. For your own well-being, you must exercise caution. It is the lowly wren, which draws less attention to itself, that often will outlive the strutting pheasant."

Nikki was confused. "If you wish me to be discreet, then why do you want me to speak to the council?"

"The council will be a meeting of chiefs, leaders I respect and trust. They must hear from your own lips what your history says will befall our people if Tecumseh is not persuaded against the British. Most of these men, like me, are not involved in this war between the whites, but they hold much sway, not only upon their own bands but upon others they claim as friends. Just as Tecumseh is aware, uniting the people to one cause is important. You, Neeake, can be the cord which binds them together, and as one they might convert Tecumseh to peace."

The council convened four days later, but Indians from the other villages began arriving in advance of the meeting. New, temporary wigewas went up faster than Nikki could keep count. With friends and relatives exchanging greetings, visiting and eating together, it was like a huge family reunion.

Konah had no qualms about introducing Nikki as her granddaughter, just as Black Hoof didn't hesitate to tell one and all that she was his grand-niece and the acclaimed messenger from the future. Neither of them suggested that she amuse the newcomers with any of the items she'd brought with her from her own time, and Nikki was inclined to agree. While they were open to the idea that she was a visitor from a coming era, being confronted with her small bits of modern technology might really freak them out. As it was, she was walking a fine line between praise and prejudice, and she certainly didn't want to do anything to tip the scales out of her favor.

By the time she was due to speak to the assembly of chiefs, Nikki was more nervous than if she'd been called up before the school superintendent and the board of education. In preparation for the event, Silver Thorn and Black Hoof had carefully coached her on the proper etiquette for such a gathering, telling her what to do and say—and what not to. Konah presented Nikki with a traditional doeskin dress and moccasins for the occasion. Nikki had rehearsed her speech until she could recite it in her sleep, and still she felt like Marie Antoinette on her way to the guillotine.

She recalled the age-old suggestion that a speaker, while envisioning himself as fully clothed, should envision the members of his audience as naked. When she related this to Silver Thorn, he deduced, "This is supposed to make you feel superior, and thus more confident?"

"Yes, but in this instance, I don't think it will have the desired calming effect. Most likely, I'd just get the giggles and insult everyone, which is the worst thing I could do."

"You are making this more difficult than need be," he told her "Think of yourself as their teacher, and them as your students."

Nikki thought about his suggestion, then grinned. "That will work, as long as I can keep from imagining them in high-top sneakers and Dead Frog T-shirts. The earrings won't throw me, since many of the boys in my class sport small studs. Those you Shawnee wear are much more elaborate, however."

"Dead Frog T-shirts?" he echoed.

She laughed. "Don't ask. You'd have to see it to believe it."

During the first part of the meeting, Nikki sat quietly, trying to be as inconspicuous as possible. When the calumet filled with sacred tobacco was passed around, she was not expected to partake, which was fortunate since she was sure she would choke on the smoke and make a complete fool of herself. Each of the ten attendees then rose and gave a short oration, conducted primarily in Shawnee. As Silver Thorn explained to her, this was normal opening protocol for all councils. Finally, Nikki was introduced to the assembly.

Nikki had found a pack of chewing gum in her purse. As a prelude to her talk, and as a gesture of goodwill, she passed the sticks out. Feeling much like a magician at his first major performance, Nikki watched as the chiefs warily unwrapped the sticks of gum and, following her example, popped them into their mouths and began to chew. Caution instantly turned to delight. With nods all around, they exclaimed over the mint-sweet treat.

Having gotten their attention, Nikki launched into her prepared dialogue. Silver Thorn stood by, to interpret her words for those few who did not understand English.

"My brothers, my fathers, my grandfathers: Silver Thorn summoned me from the future to tell you what is to become of our people. What I must relay saddens me greatly, for in the time to come, the Americans will claim this land for their own and all tribes will be forced to move from their homes to new locations west of the Great Mississippi

River. Regardless of Tecumseh's efforts, there will be no stopping them.

"In this war between the British and the Americans, Tecumseh has unwittingly chosen to align himself and his followers with the wrong side, mistakenly assuming that they will win. The British will soon leave these shores, never to return. They will not be here to pay the price for the American victory or to offer their protection to you. Those of you who seek peace with the Americans now, who do not follow Tecumseh's route of war, may fare better, though I cannot promise that this will be so. Who can say if, once a people's destiny is written on the wind, it may be altered or not? But to align yourselves with a losing cause will surely bring bitter retribution. Would it not be better to form a favorable bond with those who will win this battle that they would recall our good intentions?

"Therefore, I beseech you. Speak with your tribes. Warn your people against aligning themselves with the British or Tecumseh's warriors. Also, if you can sway others away from his side before it is too late for them, I implore you to do so, for their own sakes as well as yours."

Nikki paused. Her expression was even more solemn as she continued. "The tide has already begun to turn in this war. Now the British and Tecumseh will taste defeat, while the Americans will taste of victory. Soon will come a great battle in Canada. There, if he cannot be persuaded to abandon his cause, Tecumseh and many of his warriors will fall. Tecumseh's death will signal the demise of his alliance."

She looked at each of the chiefs in turn. "I do not wish for this to happen, to see so many brave men spill their blood in the waging of a war which is not truly theirs. But if Tecumseh does not turn back now, I can see no way to prevent this loss of life, this waste of courage. If any among you can sway your fellows, or they Tecumseh, I beg you to try. Perhaps the worst of the tragedy may yet be averted. I can only hope that what is recorded of this time in history may yet be rewritten."

At the end of her oration, Nikki resumed her seat. Amid the resulting silence, she fought not to fidget.

At last, Peahchaete, the Shawnee chief from the Hog Creek band, spoke. "Your words are persuasive, but how can we know that they are true?"

Chief Black Hoof, who was the principal chief of all the Shawnee and Peahchaete's superior in rank, straightened. His back became as rigid as a post and his face stern with censure. "Do you dare to question my niece's honor, Peahchaete? I should cut your tongue from your mouth for such insolence."

Afraid he would do just that, Nikki strove to intervene. "I am sure he meant no disrespect, Uncle. Peahchaete is a prudent man, I suspect, and requires more convincing. Only a fool would not question such distressing and alarming news when presented by a stranger."

"Is this so, Peahchaete?" Black Hoof demanded.

Peahchaete gave a brusque nod. "Yes, my chief. I seek to know more of how Neeake came to be here and from whence she came. How do we know that Silver Thorn, while trying to summon a revealer of truth, did not conjure instead a ghost? Is she truly your niece—or a clever pretender?"

"So now it is my skill you question," Silver Thorn put in angrily. "Peahchaete, take care. You are treading shaky ground."

Yet another chief now inserted his concerns. "While your powers are renowned, Silver Thorn, so are those of your brother. Both you and Tecumseh have repeatedly demonstrated your immense might. Now, by bringing Neeake here, you have presented us with a dilemma. Whom do we believe? You? Or Tecumseh, who has also performed miraculous feats and claims to know what is best for our people? How do we choose between you?"

"He has a valid argument, husband," Nikki said. "If you will permit me, I will offer more evidence in our favor. I'm sure we can settle this to everyone's satisfaction and without needless animosity. After all, we are gathered here in an effort to promote peace, not violence, are we not?"

To her relief, everyone seemed agreeable to her suggestion. They all settled back and waited expectantly.

Nikki hoped she hadn't just painted herself and Silver Thorn into a corner. She'd opened her big mouth. Now it was time to put up or shut up. "Okay, fellas," she muttered under her breath. "It's showtime."

Removing her digital watch, she held it out for all of them to see. "This is a timepiece," she explained. "Right now, it shows the present hour, the minute, and the seconds which are fast passing. However, when I push this button, it displays the date. The month, the day, and the year. As Silver Thorn can verify, according to the white man's calendar, this year is 1813. I hail from the year 1996, a hundred-and-eighty-three years into the future. Now, who among you can read the white man's numbers?"

Two of the chiefs indicated that they could. Nikki handed the watch over to the nearest of them. "Push that small button on the side and tell me what numbers appear on the front."

The man swelled with pride at having been selected to perform this task. Poking at the prescribed knob, he squinted at the face. "A six stands alone, then a three and an aught as a pair. Last, I see a one, two nines, and a six all together."

Nikki nodded. "The six stands for the sixth month, June. Silver Thorn tells me that you call it the Moon When the Hot Weather Begins. The three and the zero combined make up the number thirty, which is the final day of the month. The last four digits represent the year, in this case the year from which I came. Nineteen hundred and ninety-six."

Several of the chiefs readily accepted her explanation and the verification of the date by their fellow leader. A few still doubted. "What else can you show us?" one asked. "This timepiece is interesting, but perhaps you are able to change the numbers to any you desire to have it display."

"Smart cookie!" she declared softly. "Okay, let's try something else." From the pocket of her dress, she produced her calculator. "This device adds numbers and gives the sum very quickly. I will match its answers against any of yours—and do it in the blink of an eye." She demonstrated by adding a column of numbers, subtotaling, then dividing by four and displaying the total, all within seconds.

Those watching accepted her challenge and began shouting out numbers to her. A couple of the men, attempting to stump her, computed lengthy mathematical calculations of their own, and only after reaching their own conclusion did they offer up the problem to her. For the next few minutes, Nikki's fingers flew over the calculator buttons. Again and again, her tiny device spit out the correct answer, in a fraction of the time it took to do so by ordinary means. Inevitably, however, there came the moment she'd dreaded—when her total differed with that of one of the chiefs. While the others watched, she and he both recalculated. In the end, hers proved to be correct, and she heaved a silent sigh of relief that she hadn't pressed a wrong button.

"You still present us with nothing but numbers," another man protested. "Show us something different from the realm of the future, something uncommon to our time."

Black Hoof handed her the cigarette lighter. Feeling ridiculously like a cross between a Tupperware demonstrator and a circus hawkster and hoping her uncle hadn't used up the butane, Nikki flicked her Bic. This time, all present were properly awed. They exclaimed in amazement over her "firestick," each of them wanting his turn at making it light. When she produced her flashlight, their reaction to her "torch with no flame" was much the same.

At length, Black Hoof called them to order. "Having seen for yourselves the marvels of her world, what say you now, my chiefs? Do you believe or nay?"

As one body, they were sufficiently convinced. After conferring with Black Hoof and Silver Thorn, lest her dates be wrong, Nikki issued a prediction of her own. "Any day now, General Harrison of the American Army will contact you, wanting to parley. He seeks to assure himself that you will all remain peaceful."

Black Hoof cast an eagle eye upon his underlings. "I trust that you will ease his mind on this matter," he said solemnly. "I also trust that you will heed my niece's warnings and act upon them without delay."

As it happened, there was no time for argument, or for further discussion, for at that moment a runner entered the lodge to announce the imminent arrival of General William Henry Harrison of the United States Army.

Sixteen

According to Shawnee tradition, this was the last day the football ceremony could be performed. General Harrison, or no General Harrison, this important Shawnee ritual would go on as planned. So Chief Black Hoof decreed.

Though not pleased at the postponement of his impromptu peace conference, Harrison was at the same time relieved to learn that the Indians had gathered at Wapakoneta for nonviolent purposes rather than to conduct a war meeting. He was further appeased when Black Hoof invited him to stay and observe the ceremonies. Additionally, the general would have the opportunity to speak with Johnny Chapman, who often kept the U.S. military informed concerning Indian plans to attack white settlements. Though not actually employed as an army scout or spy, Chapman was a loyal American who felt it his duty to warn his fellow countrymen of impending danger. Over the years, he had saved countless lives, never asking anything in return.

Nikki, with her tan, her dark hair, and her new doeskin dress, blended well with the other villagers. She was confident that, as long as Harrison and the members of his entourage didn't get close enough to notice her eyes, they would never suspect she hadn't been born and raised in the tribe. Even if they did, the oddity could be explained by letting him assume she had a white ancestor in her background, which was not all that rare, actually. Many frontiersmen had taken Indian wives in the years since Ohio had first begun to be settled. Moreover, none of the Shawnee were going to spill the beans to a white man about their Mystical Messenger from the Future.

Still, knowing what she did, Harrison presented quite a temptation to Nikki. Of all of them, she was the only one who knew what the coming years would hold for this man—that he would someday become President of the United States, if only for a month before he contracted pneumonia and died. She'd never been this close to a President before, except when Ronald Reagan had made a stop in Allen County during his campaign and she'd gotten to shake his hand at the airport.

Of course, at that time Reagan hadn't been President yet. He'd merely been the Republican candidate. Harrison, on the other hand, was a sure bet, which made Nikki feel oddly akin to a gypsy fortuneteller who'd misplaced her crystal ball. How she wished she could march right up to Harrison and blurt out everything she knew about him— things the man himself didn't even suspect yet!

It was a shame she couldn't do just that, but caution dictated otherwise. However, when no one was paying heed, she did find the opportunity to snap Harrison's picture when he was standing with Black Hoof outside the council lodge. Immediately afterward, she stashed her camera in her backpack in the wigewa, counting herself fortunate that no one, most especially Silver Thorn, had caught her taking such a stupid risk.

As the time for the football game approached, Nikki's fascination found a new target. Much to her surprise, Silver Thorn had no objections to her playing with the rest of the women. She'd thought he would claim that the game was too rough, that in her delicate condition she should not participate.

When she broached the subject, he told her simply, "I

foresee no danger to you or the child or I would forbid it."

Nikki batted her lashes at him in an exaggerated way and clasped a hand over her heart. "Gee, I forgot I was married to a soothsayer. Sorry, darling. I should have known you would already have divined the whole affair. So tell me, who is going to win today, the men or the women?"

"The men, naturally," he replied with a wink.

"Did you *see* this or is it just wishful thinking?"

"I need no prophesy for my prediction. We men have the advantage of added strength, speed, and height. Moreover, the women have won only one of the last ten games between us."

"Yes, but that was before they invited me to join their team," she reminded him with a smug grin. "I'm a football enthusiast from way back, and I know all the best moves, the strategic plays. Brains can win out over brawn any day of the week."

"Would you care to wager on that?" he proposed.

"I already have," she informed him. "I bet my tube of coral lipstick against Fire Heart's silver hoop earring, and my breath mints and hand cream against Black Hoof's hair disc, the one with the eagle feather dangling from it. My uncle was hoping to get my flashlight, but we Scots are shrewd negotiators. I learned from the best—my mom. Given the opportunity, I believe she could have talked Jack Benny out of his violin."

Silver Thorn didn't bother to ask who Jack Benny was. He was much more interested in contracting a wager with his wife. His eyes glittered like twin stars as he leaned closer and said, "I would make you a more interesting offer, little goose."

"Oh, yeah? Like what?" she asked with a flirtatious toss of her head.

"You have shown me the pictures of your family that

you keep in your handbag. I am particularly fond of the one of you as a baby, lying naked on that white pelt. If you will teach me how to use your camera, I would have a picture of you that way again."

She shot him what would have been an innocent look, if not for the teasing gleam in her eyes. "Gosh, I don't know, Thorn. I'm not into pornography. Besides, I've grown a bit since then and you don't have a white pelt, do you?"

His grin was devilish. "No, but the bear fur would serve well, do you not agree?"

"I suppose it might," she hedged, "but what would you do with the photo if you had it? You don't have a gym locker to tape it in, and I wouldn't want it hanging someplace where everybody and his brother might see it."

He agreed adamantly. "Most assuredly not! This is a private matter between husband and wife. No one would ever set eyes upon it but me, for I would keep it safe within my spirit bag." He touched the small leather pouch which hung from a cord around his neck.

Nikki eyed the pouch curiously. "What else do you keep in there?"

"My special charms, those objects which the Spirits have directed me to keep with me always for protection against illness and enemies. The contents are personal, known only to me, as is our way. That is all I can tell you, Neeake, for I would not anger the Spirits by revealing these items to you; and you must promise that you will respect my privacy and never look upon them."

She frowned. "I'm as inquisitive as the next gal, but I'm not a snoop. And I certainly wouldn't want you to do anything that goes against your religious beliefs. If it's that sacred to you, you have my word. I'll never so much as peek into that little magic bag of yours."

He nodded, accepting her pledge. "We have strayed from our original discussion."

"The wager. Okay, I know what you want, but what are you willing to match for a picture of me, butt-naked on a bear rug?"

That roguish grin was back in place. "Would you care for a saddle of your own?" he offered.

Nikki shook her head. "I don't think so. In a few months I'll be too fat to ride."

"Perhaps a silver neck band or a pair of hoops for your ears?" he suggested.

"Save that idea for our first anniversary," she told him.

"What then?" he queried. "What would you consider a fair recompense?"

Her smile was as naughty as his. "I'd accept the same thing. A picture of you, posed nude on that bear rug. My own personal memento, if you will."

His brow rose. "And where would you secure it, wife? You have no spirit bag."

"Maybe I'll make one for myself," she informed him blithely. "Surely, in such an equal society, that custom is not reserved solely for men. Can't women have one, too?"

"Some do," he conceded. "Those who received guidance from the Spirits."

"And how does one go about contacting the Spirits for this counsel?" she pressed. "Do they go on a vision quest and fast and pray? I've read of young men doing that in other tribes."

"As do we," he said. "However, there is no need to journey afar. The Spirits are all around us, Neeake. They are in the trees and the rocks and the beasts. In everything you see and touch. Among them is the Spirit meant especially for you, that closest to your soul. You need only open your mind to it, with a pure heart and body, and the Spirits will commune with you."

"Meditation," she concluded. "Freeing your mind of all else so that you are more receptive and in tune with nature."

"The body must be cleansed as well, inside and out," he reminded her. "One cannot entreat the Spirits and be unclean in any way."

"So we're back to fasting, I assume." Nikki wrinkled her nose. "Not that the notion is foreign to me. God knows, I've tried every diet on the market, though they didn't do much good in the long run. My willpower always wavers in the face of chocolate, I'm afraid. Still, I'd be willing to give it a fair shot. It would only be temporary starvation, unlike some of the regimens I've been on. When can I try it?"

"Whenever you wish, little one. I will prepare a sweat lodge for you."

"How long will that take?"

"Half a day, at most. Just long enough to erect it, heat the rocks, and purify it with herbs."

"Wait. Will all this fasting and sweating be bad for the baby?"

"I foresee no problem."

"Great! But don't start building it until tomorrow or the day after. We've got a football game to play today, and the dances tonight. And I want time to collect my wager from you afterward. Besides, it will be more peaceful around here once the others return to their own villages. I'll be better able to concentrate properly then, and there will be less chance that someone will interrupt my meditation."

Nikki was surprised at how similar the Shawnee football game was to those to which she was accustomed. The field was only three-quarters the length of a regulation football field, seventy-five yards rather than a hundred, but there were goal posts at either end, just like back home—and the basic objective of the game was the same: to score a goal by kicking or carrying the ball across the opposing goal line. However, in this instance, the ball had to go between the goal posts, which were set only three feet apart. Each goal counted as one point, and the first team to score twelve would become the winner.

The ball was made of rawhide stuffed with deer hair, but it was round and small, just slightly larger than a tennis ball. Also, the rules for the two teams were different. The men were only allowed to kick the ball while the women could pick it up and carry it, which served to even the odds somewhat. Here, old and young alike were invited to participate on both teams. Grabbing, tackling, and stealing the ball were permitted, though Silver Thorn assured Nikki that the men took care not to be unnecessarily rough with the women, just as all were mindful not to hit the children or elderly players too hard.

"That's good to know," she said, "especially since there is a noticeable lack of helmets and mouth guards and shoulder pads for protection. I'm just glad we'll all be wearing moccasins instead of cleated shoes. Those babies would really kill your bare ankles. Talk about bumps and bruises and cracked shins!"

"Many of the players wrap their lower legs in *metetawawa*, hide leggings," he informed her. "I will secure a pair for you, if you wish."

Nikki gave a vigorous nod. "I wish, and some elbow pads might not be amiss, either. It's been a long time since I've played, but I'm sure I recall many a scraped knee and scabbed elbow in earlier games with my brothers. I even wound up with a black eye once, when Jack's knee got in my way as I was scoring a touchdown. I wouldn't have minded so badly, but that was just a week before my junior prom—an important dance at school," she clarified. "I had a heck of a time trying to disguise the bruise with makeup so the colors wouldn't clash with my gown."

* * *

Rather than a coin toss, the game began when a mediator tossed the ball into the air at center field. Naturally, the men, being taller and able to jump higher, gained first control of the ball. But not for long. Amid a flurry of thrashing feet, one of the women kicked the ball into the hands of a teammate, and the rush was on. She lobbed it to another, who tossed it to another, who promptly threw it into the hands of the opposing team.

That's when Nikki realized that boos and hisses were not exclusive to modern-day ballgames. Neither, it seemed, were those little victory dances players were prone to perform on scoring. When the men's team scored first, the fellow who kicked the ball through the goal posts did a respectable imitation of any number of pro players Nikki could have named, hooting and kicking up his heels in a veritable jig.

It didn't take Nikki long to realize that there were far fewer rules in Shawnee football. Forward, lateral, and even backward passes and kicks were perfectly acceptable. There were no delays, no huddles, no time-outs, and the substitution system was chaotic at best. She noticed that whenever anyone tired, he took himself out of the game for a rest period and came back whenever it suited him. Others joined in whenever they took the notion to do so or quit altogether in the midst of play. The only problem in that was trying to convince the other players not to tackle you as you departed the field.

What the game lacked in order was made up for in enthusiasm. Over grunts and groans and collisions, a great deal of laughter could be heard. Those on the sidelines cheered on their favorites, and those on the field encouraged their teammates, screamed at their opponents, and generally had the time of their lives. Good-natured ribbing was a highlight of the game. Nikki didn't even have to understand the language to decipher most of it. She knew, when she pulled her elbow out of one man's stomach, exactly what his complaint was. Just as the fellow who pushed her face-first into the dirt readily understood her hand gesture and facial expression as he helped her to her feet.

After about an hour, the men were leading six to two. Nikki knew something had to be done quickly. She also suspected that organization of any sort would be an improvement. With no apparent rules against it and with Konah's help, she began conducting quick huddles on the sidelines. Surprisingly, the women caught on immediately, with little debate over strategy. Under Nikki's direction, with competent input from the other women, plays were decided and put into action. Soon the tide began to turn as the women scored the next three goals consecutively. Of course, it didn't take the men long to figure out what was happening, and they were quick to initiate their own tactical sessions. That was when Nikki decided that, if all was fair in love and war, the time was ripe for the women to declare all-out war.

As their self-appointed coach, she directed her troops. "Everyone needs to pick one man on the field and find a way to stop him, whether he has the ball or not. Those of you who are, er, *bigger*, should oppose the biggest men. Tiny women team up against the smaller men. Fastest against fastest, tall against tall, short against short. We need a front line of defense ready to trip any men who cross their path, most especially the one with the ball. Turtle Dove, you have a good throwing arm, and Konah, you're good at catching. The two of you should work together. Sweet Water, you're the fastest runner, so you stand downfield to receive the ball and run for the end zone."

Nikki turned to a huge woman who was built like a linebacker, right down to the space between her two front teeth. "You have a special task. Position yourself in front of our goal line and stay there. Don't let anyone or anything past you, most especially the ball. Squat. Sit. Spread out your skirts or lie flat on the ground. Do whatever it takes, but stop that ball."

The woman gave Nikki a gap-toothed smile and nodded eagerly.

"Okay, girls, pass the word to the others, and let's give 'em hell! Get out there and gouge some eyes! Kick some butt! Scrape some shins! Squash 'em like bugs!"

Nikki's pep talk had great impact. The women charged onto the field, revved-up and smelling blood. A number of them kicked off their moccasins, not just for better traction but to add sharp toenails to their small cache of weapons. Even the youngsters found added motivation. They rushed into the fray, shrieking like a pack of hyenas and butting like little rams.

Some of the women squared off against their own husbands, regardless of the contrast in their sizes, which Nikki at first thought was a mistake—until she caught on to their devious maneuvers. These women knew their husbands' weak spots better than anyone else. One poor fellow was obviously so ticklish that once his wife got her fingers into his ribs, he was as helpless as a newborn kitten. Another woman had only to blow in her mate's ear, and he stopped dead in his tracks to stare at her with a stupefied grin.

Taking her cue from them, Nikki zeroed in on Silver Thorn. As they came face to face, she winked at him and gave a saucy little shimmy that sent Silver Thorn's eyebrows rising. Because his attention was on her and not the ball, it sailed right past him—about the same time Nikki sidled up and wound her leg around his—and tripped him. He toppled onto his back like a felled oak. Nikki followed him down, planting her knee atop his solar plexus while the tip of her moccasin rested at his groin.

Silver Thorn made an aborted attempt to roll her off of him, stopping when Nikki nudged his lower anatomy warningly with her toe. "Don't even think about it, big boy," she cautioned with a smug smile. "Try it, and the term *football* is going to take on a whole new meaning."

"Woman, you do not play fairly," he complained, his glower all for show.

"No kidding," she retorted smartly. Seated astride his upper thigh, she ground her pelvis against him. The result was predictable and immediate.

Silver Thorn stifled a groan.

Nikki grinned.

The crowd roared. The women had just scored another touchdown and the game was now tied at nine-nine.

Though the men attempted similar tactics, it didn't work nearly as well. Twenty minutes later, Sweet Water sprinted through the goal posts to score the winning run. The game ended with the women ahead by one point. They straggled off the field, tired and smeared with dirt and sweat and grass stains, but triumphant.

Nikki sauntered over to Silver Thorn. Her tongue snaked out to lick at her lips, and she saw his eyes darken with desire. She gave a low, wicked chuckle. "Sweetheart, you are going to look sooo *fine* on that bearskin rug!"

Seventeen

After the rigors of the football game, Nikki wasn't sure she would have the energy to participate in the dancing that evening. To her surprise, after sipping a sweet concoction Konah offered her, assuring her that it would do nothing to harm the baby, Nikki felt remarkably revived.

She joined the other women in assembling the feast, which would be eaten all through the night. Roasted meats, an assortment of steamed tubers, corn cakes, and beans constituted the main fare. There were dessert dishes and candies, most of them made of varieties of berries, molasses, and honey. Beverages ranged from plain water to different types of juices and teas—flavored from fruits, leaves, and bark—to a potent fermented brew which Nikki assumed was comparable to corn liquor.

"That's all this world needs," she commented to Konah. "A bunch of Indians drunk on their ears. And you say the dancing lasts all night? Does the last man standing get some sort of prize?"

Konah laughed. "No, but he probably should. Do not fret, granddaughter. Our men will not consume so much that they will become unruly, especially with the general and his men here. Black Hoof would see them staked over anthills if they dared do anything that foolish."

Nikki had managed to brush most of the dirt off her dress and neatly French braid her hair. In honor of the occasion, she even applied a modicum of eye shadow, mascara, and lipstick. After weeks of toting wood, tending fires, pulling weeds, and gathering foodstuff, her fingernails were a mess. A quick manicure and a coat of pink polish helped disguise much of the damage.

Upon seeing her, Konah and Melassa declared that they, too, wished to paint their nails and faces. Word soon spread; and before she knew it, Nikki found herself in the role of beautician as two dozen exuberant women argued and haggled over her meager supply of makeup.

"Good grief!" she declared. "Now I know what those poor clerks feel like at a super-clearance sale!"

She quickly adopted her teacher's tone in an attempt to restore order. "Ladies, please! Let's not quarrel and pull at each other! If you will all just sit down and be patient, everyone will have an equal opportunity to use the cosmetics. However, a little goes a long way, and I would suggest that you allow me to help you. Your husbands might object to wives who resemble a troop of circus clowns."

Using Konah as a model, Nikki demonstrated how to apply the cosmetics. She then paired the women off. "You will be partners, each helping the other with her makeup and hair. I will supervise." Dividing her few shades of shadow, nail enamel, gloss, and lipstick, she doled them out with a droll admonition. "Share nicely, ladies, or none of you will get to play with my goodies again."

Between offering advice to the others, she French-braided Konah's hair while a couple of the women carefully watched the procedure so they could learn to do it. Melassa decided she wanted the front of her hair fringed into bangs on her forehead. Another had Nikki help arrange her hair into an intricate twist, anchoring it to the back of her head with a silver comb so ornate that Nikki was stunned by the workmanship. It rivaled any she might have found at an exclusive jewelry shop in her own day and time.

As she made the rounds, allotting a spritz of her travel-sized hair spray where needed, she studied her students with a critical eye. The final results weren't too bad at all, and the women were as pleased as punch as they admired themselves in Nikki's small hand mirror. A dab of musk cologne for each, and they proudly scampered off—*hot to trot*, as Nikki phrased it—to glean compliments from their unsuspecting spouses. For her part, Nikki hoped the husbands would not be upset with their new and improved wives—or with her for instigating the make-overs. She certainly didn't want to be the cause of any marital disputes, caused by a dab of paint here and there.

She needn't have worried. The men seemed quite enchanted with the new look their wives presented. Most particularly, however, they were intrigued by the sensual fragrance wafting from them. Though not normally so demonstrative in public, Nikki spotted many a man sniffing at his mate's neck or wrist, just as Silver Thorn was at hers. "You smell wonderful," he told her. "Good enough to eat."

While she relished the compliment, Nikki couldn't help but giggle. "You wouldn't say that if you knew what they use to create the cologne."

His brow arched in silent question.

"Skunk glands," she informed him baldly. "I don't know the precise procedure, but I do know that perfumes are made from the musk obtained from the testicles of certain animals, skunks among them."

"You are jesting," he claimed.

She shook her head. "I'm perfectly serious."

"How can this be? No skunk ever smelled this good. Even I, with all my powers, could not endow him with such a sweet scent."

His expression was a blend of confusion, disbelief, and outrage, and Nikki had to chuckle. "As I said, I don't know how they do it, only that they do." She gave him a consoling pat on the shoulder. "Don't try to analyze it, darling. Simply enjoy it."

He scowled. "It would be much easier to do so if I could delete from my mind the thought that while I am smelling your neck, I might as well have my nose stuck up the ass-end of a skunk."

Nikki was pleased to discover that, while some of the evening's dances were solely for groups of men or for women only, most included both males and females. In some, the steps were relatively simple. Others were more complicated. Several reminded her of dances she'd learned as a young child, with certain variations, of course. One highly resembled the *bunny hop*. Another was remarkably similar to the *hokey-pokey*. A third imitated a game of *crack-the-whip*. Many were a form of line-dancing. They varied from slow and sedate to fast and furious, following the beat of the drum and the commands of the head dancer. Sometimes the dancers lined up as couples and danced beside each other. In others, they aligned face-to-face, often with one of the pair dancing backward.

Of those performed by only the women, including herself, Nikki favored the Dove Dance. Of the "couples" numbers in which she and Silver Thorn joined, she liked the Stirrup Dance—so named because the woman would loop her arm about the neck of the man and place her near foot atop his, using it as a sort of stirrup. Then, united in this awkward, three-legged position, they would follow a counterclockwise pattern around the dance area, stopping on cue to twirl in a circle. With so many pairs mismatched in height or weight, it was hilarious fun. Many a couple toppled over, others tripping on them and falling into a heap. There was much good-natured joking and giggling and horseplay.

Of all the dances, Nikki's absolute favorite was one she

did not participate in, due to the intricacy involved. It was the Swan Dance, performed so beautifully and with such grace that it brought tears to her eyes as she watched. No ballet team could have displayed more elegance than these Shawnee dancers with their sweeping, flowing movements. Then and there, Nikki vowed that she would have Konah teach her the steps and that she would practice them faithfully so that she might take part in the Swan Dance at the next ceremonial meet.

At around two o'clock in the morning, the ceremonial drum was retired, but the dancers kept going, accompanied alternately by singers, flutes, and rattles made from turtle shells. Unable to keep her eyes open, Nikki napped sporadically, her head nestled against Silver Thorn's shoulder. Every now and then, he would leave her, once to bring a blanket from their wigewa and a few times to join in the dances. Finally, as the rising sun was tinting the sky in pale hues of pink and gold, the drummer returned, signalling the closing dance. Appropriately, it was called the Morning Dance and could only be performed if the dancing had continued throughout the night.

Silver Thorn tugged Nikki to her feet. "Come, love. Join me in the final dance."

"But I dozed off," she said with a yawn. "Doesn't that disqualify me?"

"No. Others have also slept. It is not required that all stay awake, only that enough do so that the dances can proceed."

"Oh, okay." She wobbled along beside him, positive that without his support she would have fallen on her face. She stopped and stood shaking one leg and foot. "Danged things fell asleep," she grumbled.

She wondered that she somehow made it through that last dance, stumbling and shuffling along like a big rag doll. At the end, there was a great outcry of the people in celebration for having successfully concluded the ritual.

Weary but glad, they straggled off to their wigewas and their beds.

Nikki rolled over in her sleep and threw out one arm in search of her husband. Her hand met only the roughly woven blanket, cool enough to tell her that Silver Thorn had risen some time before. She blinked sleepily and rose on her elbow to look around. He was not in the wigewa. She wondered where he might be. Perhaps out riding or maybe he'd decided to start building the sweat lodge.

For a moment she debated going back to sleep, but a glance at her watch told her it was past noon. If she didn't get up now, she would have a hard time getting to sleep tonight. She rubbed her eyes, and her hands came away blackened with mascara. "Twenty-four-hour mascara my foot!" she groused. "Only if you don't mind walking around looking like an idiot!"

Nikki wasn't the only one. Once she'd dressed, she joined the other women at the bathing pool. Each of them was busily scrubbing the dark rings from around her eyes. Altogether, they looked like an entire pack of exhausted raccoons.

"Sorry, ladies," Nikki apologized. "I would have warned you what to expect, but this is a new brand and it's not supposed to smear."

A couple of the women turned to glare at her. At least Nikki thought they did, but it was hard to tell if they were really peeved or if it were just an optical illusion due to their black-streaked faces. She was unlacing the front of her dress, preparatory to her morning bath, when Melassa stopped her.

"No, Neeake. We are not bathing today, not with the soldiers at the village. Wet your cloth and wash your face and hands, but do not disrobe. We cannot be certain that one or more of them is not lurking nearby, spying on us. Nor would it be wise to wander about on your own today. Always be in the company of others, the larger the group the better."

Though it shouldn't have been, Melassa's sound advice came as something of a start to Nikki. Here, surrounded by family and friends, Nikki had forgotten the need to be cautious. This wasn't something she was used to in her everyday life, coming as she did from an average, middle-class family. In her world, she was an American woman who, though not ashamed of her Indian heritage, passed for white. But here, she was Shawnee. In her time, her government was not at war with any other country. Here, at least part of her tribe was at war with the United States. Distrust flourished and danger abounded between the white Americans and the native tribes.

Shaken anew, Nikki washed quickly and returned to the village in the company of the other women. With every step, she caught herself listening for the snap of a twig beneath a booted foot, probing the shadows along the wooded path with wary eyes. By the time they reached the village proper, her nerves were taut and her tongue laden with the sharp, unfamiliar tang of fear.

The meeting between Harrison and the chiefs lasted until late afternoon. Outside the council lodge, life went on with as much normality as possible, with some modifications. Today, the women did not go to the fields to hoe and weed the crops. They kept their children near, rather than letting them have the run of the village. The men who were not in the conference did not go hunting or fishing as they might have otherwise. Traps were left temporarily unattended while the men gathered in groups to play dice or talk or just to work on small projects.

Nikki noted that a number of the men were casually restringing their bows, feathering arrows, honing hunting knives, even cleaning guns—their weapons ever at hand. Just in case. It dawned on her that it was little wonder so many history books portrayed the Indian male as lazy. To the heedless eye, these Shawnee men must appear so as they laughed and gossiped and gambled the day away. But beneath the laughter lay keen vigilance. Beneath that relaxed facade, they were intensely alert. Watchful. Ready. Waiting.

While Silver Thorn was in the meeting, Nikki visited with Konah and Melassa and the children. Her female relatives were unusually quiet, their faces drawn in tight lines, as Nikki knew hers must be. Every few minutes one of them would glance toward the council lodge with a worried expression. Just as often, someone would exhale heavily, as if weary of holding her breath. After three hours of fruitless waiting, Nikki had endured enough of the strained silence and the sighs.

"This is ridiculous! I don't know why we're all so tense. We're scaring ourselves silly for no good reason, don't you think? Surely Silver Thorn would have warned us if he'd had any premonition of danger. Besides, from everything I've read about him, General Harrison is a good and honorable man, unlike some of his fellow leaders."

Beside her, Konah gave a mute shrug.

Across from them, Melassa clutched her swollen stomach in a protective gesture toward her unborn babe. "I hope you are right, Neeake."

"Nothing happened yesterday. Or last night, for that matter," Nikki hastened to say.

"We did not sleep. We were awake and attentive," Konah pointed out.

"No more than we are now," Nikki countered.

Her comment was met with more sighs and silence. Nikki went back to nervously drumming her fingers on her knee. In the two years since she'd quit smoking, she'd never wanted a cigarette more than she did now.

At long last, Harrison and the others exited the lodge. As the villagers watched, the conferees shook hands all around. The general's smile was matched by the chiefs, and a collective wave of relief swept the camp. It was going to be all right after all. At least this time, with this army commander, with these tribal leaders. Tomorrow or next month, it might turn out differently; but for now the truce would stand between the Americans and this peaceful body of Shawnee Indians who had chosen not to align themselves with Tecumseh.

Nikki could have jumped for joy. She could have hugged each and every one of the chiefs. Her faith in Silver Thorn and his ability to predict danger, at least in this instance, had not been pinned on thin air. And her faith in General Harrison had not been misplaced. It seemed he truly was the just and fair man depicted in her history texts.

On a sudden impulse, Nikki leapt to her feet and ran to her wigewa. From her purse, she took her ballpoint pen and a scrap of paper. Quickly, she scribbled a short note. It read:

General Harrison,
Enclosed with this note, you will find a pen. It is a novel invention, one of a kind. There are no others like it. The ink is already inside, in a tube. You need not fill it, and I regret to say that you cannot do so when it eventually runs dry. To use it, simply depress the small button on the back end. This will allow the point to appear at the other end. Press the point to the paper and write. If you use this pen prudently, perhaps there will still be ink in it when you become President of the United States. It pleases me greatly to think of you signing an important document with this gift—this small token of my esteem.

Sincerely,
A Friend

Shaking with excitement, Nikki dashed from the wigewa before she lost her nerve. With an outward nonchalance that scarcely disguised her pounding heart, she sauntered to the area where the general's horse was already being saddled. His saddlebags sat on the ground nearby. On the pretense of tripping over them, Nikki slipped the pen and the note inside the leather flap and went calmly on her way.

Only afterward did she recall that the pen was one she had picked up at the opening of a new bank branch. What would Harrison think when he read the words *Fifth-Third Bank* on it? Heaven knew, she'd been confused at the name when she'd first heard it. It still sounded odd to her. Fifth-third? Was that a fifth of a third or the fifth third in a row or what? She imagined the poor general puzzling over the strange inscription for years to come.

Eighteen

By the following day, Silver Thorn had the sweat lodge set up for Nikki. Much to her surprise and relief, starvation really wasn't a prerequisite. She did eat breakfast, albeit a light one. This being her first *sweating*, she wasn't sure how her body would react to the new experience, and she certainly didn't want to risk becoming either faint from a complete lack of nourishment or nauseous as a result of eating too much. Also, where a man might have worn just a breechcloth or gone naked into the lodge, Nikki chose to wear her T-shirt, which was long, soft, and loose enough not to be binding.

Silver Thorn had heated the rocks, doused them with water, and left a large pot and dipper inside for further use. He had also sprinkled the hot rocks with sage and cedar needles, and when Nikki entered the lodge, she was immediately enveloped in a cloud of scented steam. "This is wonderful!" she declared. "Hot as Hell, but much more fragrant. My sinuses are going to love this, I can tell!"

Just behind her, Silver Thorn entered the lodge and secured the entrance flap from the inside. As a spiritual leader, he often joined others in such purification rites, and now he was prepared to lead his wife through hers. He would act not only as her guide through the ritual, but also as interpreter if she received the vision she sought.

Now he told her, "The cedar is used to aid in the purification of our minds and bodies. The sage, which represents the powers of Creation and the mysteries of our world, is an offering to the Spirits. It brings our minds and bodies closer to the Great Creator. Within the lodge, the four essential elements of life are all represented. The rocks symbolize Mother Earth, from which we are formed. The fire embodies the sun and its heat, which is also in our bodies. The air is the essence of our being, as is the water, upon which our bodies thrive. Nature and mortal, both formed of air and water, earth and heat, brought into perfect harmony."

He directed her to sit with her back propped against a low, padded backrest which resembled one of those squat beach chairs she'd seen people use and took a place for himself across from her. "Close your eyes and let yourself relax. Breathe deeply and let the herbs calm your inner self as the heat seeps into your body. Allow your mind to drift wherever it so desires."

"What if I fall asleep?" she asked.

"Then rest well and dream sweet and know that I watch over you."

She smiled and settled herself more comfortably against the backrest. At first the heavy, sultry heat was oppressing. She wondered vaguely why they'd even needed to erect the sweat lodge since the early July weather nearly imitated the temperature and humidity in here. Perspiration began to pour out of her, quickly plastering her cotton T-shirt to her. It ran in rivulets down her sides, between her breasts and her legs, over her forehead, making her hair lie wet upon her skull.

She imagined herself on a sandy beach, basking in the hot sun. The still air was moist and redolent with tropical spices and flowers. There was the soft thrum of a guitar in the background, the occasional hiss of the waves against the shore. Lazy contentment stole over her, robbing her of the will to move or even to think. She floated with it, steeping herself in the welcome lethargy. With each breath, she eased closer to slumber. Colors wafted across her closed lids, bright broken pieces of a kaleidoscope waiting to fall into place. She observed them with passive interest, wondering what picture they would finally form.

Across from her, while Silver Thorn watched and waited, he quietly chanted a song to the Spirits, asking them to direct Neeake's dreams. Periodically, he reached out to dip water onto the rocks, eliciting a hiss of fresh, aromatic steam. Soon, Neeake's limbs lay limp. Her head lolled. Her breathing slowed.

When he saw her eyes begin to dart back and forth beneath her lids, he knew she had begun to dream. Softly, lest he disturb her and cause the dream to flee, he murmured, "Tell me what you see, Neeake."

When she spoke, her words were slow and wispy, as if coming from a long distance. "I see a pink flower. A rose, I think, about a third unfurled from its bud. There is a silver thorn on the stem. And . . ."

Silver Thorn waited.

"There is another type of plant growing around the rose, or through it somehow. Sort of a grayish-green color. It seems somehow to be entwined with the rose."

Again she paused. Then she smiled.

"What?" he prompted. "What else?"

"A butterfly. The most beautiful butterfly I've ever seen. It's similar to others I've seen; but instead of being black with orange or yellow, this one is sort of bronze with turquoise markings, with almost an iridescent quality about it. Ooh! How precious! It just landed on the rose, and it's sitting there fluttering its wings, just resting and preening in the sunshine."

Neeake was silent after that, and Silver Thorn knew that the dream had ended, at least for the present. She slept for a short time more, then awoke feeling sluggish and very thirsty.

"Come. The sweating is done for now," he told her.

"Does that mean I'm as pure as the driven snow?" she inquired, offering him a weary grin.

"It means your mind is melting into silliness," he countered. He swept her into his arms and carried her from the lodge.

"Where to now, oh, mighty warrior?" she quipped, lying limp against his chest. She barely had the energy to loop her arms around his neck.

"To the pool."

It took a moment for her steam-steeped brain to absorb that statement, and by then they were more than halfway along the path to the pool. "That sounds refreshing," she murmured.

It was actually more of a shock, albeit an invigorating one. With no preliminary splashing or sprinkling, Silver Thorn waded waist-deep into the water and then simply opened his arms and dropped her. To Nikki's overheated body, the tepid water felt like ice, so great was the contrast between it and her skin. Her yelp of surprise sent a froth of bubbles rising to the surface, followed immediately by an irate Nikki.

"You beast!" she screeched, flipping her dripping hair from her face. "You did that on purpose!"

He didn't bother to deny it. "It is part of the ritual, Neeake. I explained that to you earlier."

The immediate shock was already passing, as was her anger. Actually, the water felt wonderfully refreshing now that she was beginning to adjust to it. "I must have forgotten," she admitted. "It was just so startling after becoming so relaxed."

For her quest, Nikki had chosen a peaceful place where the river ran through a meadow. There, in the shade beneath a leafy elm, surrounded by wildflowers, she tossed sage to the four winds and then seated herself in the cool grass. "Okay, now what do I do?"

"Just sit and wait," he replied. "And listen. Let yourself become one with the earth and the sky and all of nature."

"Should I close my eyes again?"

"Only if you wish." Silver Thorn backed away. "I will be nearby, guarding against intruders. If you need me, call out."

Left on her own to commune with nature, Nikki felt slightly ridiculous—like some throwback from the sixties hippie era. All she lacked were a few strands of beads, a joint, and a wreath of flowers for her hair. What she *needed* was a good romance novel to help her pass the time. Of course, that might have directed her mind and emotions toward another type of "nature" altogether, so it was probably better that she didn't have a book available.

She tried concentrating on the beauty surrounding her. The grass was a vivid green with a pungency all its own. The earth, not yet parched by the hot summer sun, still held that wondrous moist smell. A light breeze was blowing in from across the river, gently rustling the leaves and the flowers, creating its own form of air-conditioning. The meadow was brimming with wildflowers, their colors mingling into a tangled rainbow, their combined fragrance more alluring than the finest perfume.

Above her, birds sang happily in the trees and chased each other through the blue skies. From all around her came the sights and sounds of nature at work and at play. Bees hummed busily, dragonflies darted through the air, graceful butterflies flitted from flower to flower. From some distance away, she heard the rat-tat-tat of a woodpecker and the sharp chirrup of a squirrel—or maybe a chipmunk.

A field mouse scurried past Nikki's foot, eliciting a gasp from her as she hastily tucked her legs up and her shirt more closely about her legs. The mouse dashed off through the grass; and as she watched it warily, Nikki was rewarded by the sight of three rabbits, one adult and two youngsters, quietly munching grass nearby. No doubt they'd been there for some time, so successfully camouflaged that she simply hadn't noticed them. She watched them, totally intrigued with the way their little noses twitched as they chewed and the way their ears seemed to pivot like ever-alert antennae, searching out sounds from every direction.

Past the leaves and spreading limbs, Nikki surveyed a few puffy clouds, ever changing their shape as they drifted slowly through the heavens. Even as a child, she'd loved to watch them, to see what shapes they would assume from one minute to the next—first a dragon, then a clown face, a feather, a castle, a dog begging for a treat.

How long she sat, pleasantly absorbed in this serene activity, she didn't know. The change came so gradually that she didn't realize it was happening until she found herself caught up in the midst of it. In a way, it was similar to a daydream, for on some level she was still perfectly aware of all that was going on around her. Yet, at the same time, she was being drawn into a kind of illusion. It wove itself around her like one of those surround-screen productions with multi-audio and visual capabilities or a virtual reality experience.

Yes, it was like viewing a movie, even while you became a part of it. She watched in awe as she saw herself, or at least an image of herself, strolling along the riverbank. Then, as often happens in dreams, she found herself transformed into a goose. So real did it seem, that she could feel herself fluff her wings—or the goose fluff hers. When the goose waddled down to the bank and slid into the river, Nikki could feel the coolness of the water, the way it slid smoothly along her lower body as she paddled around. The sun was warm, the water sparkling. Every so often, the goose would duck her head beneath the surface to pluck at weeds and vegetation, her dinner.

Suddenly, as a cloud obscured the sun for a mere moment, a squirrel set up a racket in a nearby tree, chirping madly. The goose stiffened and jerked her head around as if searching for danger. A menacing shadow swept the earth. With a squawk, the goose hurried from the water. Not nearly as graceful on land, she half-hobbled, half-flapped her way toward a clump of bushes a short distance away. The shadow, now identifiable as that of a large, predatory bird, swirled silently overhead. All the while, the squirrel sounded the alarm, dashing excitedly from tree to tree, from limb to limb, seeming to scream, "Run and hide! Run and hide!"

The branches of the bush, though laden with long, sharp thorns, parted easily for the goose, closing behind her to encase her in their protective cover. Nikki—the goose—hastily flung herself over her nest and the four eggs within it, one of which was already crazed, showing signs that the gosling within would soon make his entrance into the world. Lying there, hissing softly, quivering violently, the adult female was fully prepared to forfeit her own life in the defense of her young.

The hawk dived downward, taking aim on the bush where the goose hid. His big body, talons extended, brushed the upper leaves as he swooped by, but the thorns held him at bay. Twice more he arced from the sky, and twice more he was pricked and thwarted in his attempt to reach the nest. Meanwhile, the feisty squirrel darted to and fro, creating considerable racket and distraction. On his last pass, again failing to gain entrance past the thorns, the frustrated hawk turned his attack on the squirrel, but the furry little animal nimbly escaped by circling the tree trunk and darting into a small hollow. Finally, the hawk gave up and flew away.

Even as the vision faded, Nikki felt shaken, as if she, along with the goose—or perhaps in her place—had just had a very narrow escape. Her breathing was harsh and erratic, her pulse racing, her skin clammy despite the heat of the day.

"Oh, wow!" she exclaimed softly. "What a trip! If those Hollywood producers could find a way to recreate something as real as this for mass audiences, they'd be dancing on air!"

No longer relaxed, Nikki figured she was not receptive to further visions. Rising, she went in search of her husband. He met her at the edge of the meadow. Extending his hand to her, he said, "Come. You can reveal your vision to me as we walk."

"How do you know I even had one?" she inquired.

His silver eyes glinted knowingly. "Tell me what you saw."

She related everything she'd seen, and everything she'd felt. "I think I was the goose," she said at the end of her tale. "I have no idea who the hawk or the squirrel were supposed to be. Do you?"

"The squirrel spoke to you, warning you of danger. He is your spirit guide."

Nikki arched an eyebrow at him. "That itsy-bitsy animal? How is it that you get a big bad lynx and I get a measly squirrel?"

Silver Thorn shrugged and grinned. "Perhaps because you already have me to protect you. I was the thorn bush in which you and our children hid. The squirrel warned you and tried to lure the danger away. I shielded you from harm."

"And the eggs were our children?" she queried.

Silver Thorn nodded.

"Uh . . . is there any significance to the fact that there were four eggs in the nest?"

Again he nodded.

She nudged him with her elbow. "Hey! Don't clam up on me now, old chum. Explain."

"I would interpret that to mean that you and I will have four children."

"Not all at once, I hope!" she exclaimed, wide-eyed. "Triplets like you and your brothers would be enough of a handful, but four?"

"If you have related it correctly, only one of the eggs was preparing to hatch. Therefore, I would assume that a single child will be born first. Our son. For the rest, I cannot determine."

"Okay, I'll buy that for now."

Suddenly she remembered something that she'd almost missed seeing in her dream. "I just recalled something strange. As I was hiding in the bush, covering the nest, I looked up and saw the hawk circling overhead, preparing to dive. But that's not all. Beyond him, I saw tall buildings in the background, like those in a city."

At this, Silver Thorn frowned. "You are certain? It was not just clouds you saw? Or hills?"

Nikki shook her head. "They were buildings, of steel and concrete, just like back home. What do you suppose that means?"

"I must think on this," he admitted, "for it is not clear to me at this time."

"And the hawk?" she pressed. "Is this a particular enemy or simply representative of any and all peril?"

"My impression is that he signifies all danger which might arise in the future."

"What about my other dream? The one I had in the sweat lodge? Does it mean anything?"

"In it, you were the rose, and I the thorn. The sage, the other plant in your dream, was our firstborn son."

"And the butterfly? Don't tell me that flighty little thing, which couldn't harm a flea, is supposed to be another one of my spirit guides."

He laughed. "No, Neeake, but it is your special symbol—your charm, if you will—meant to bring peace and beauty into your life. It also represents the changes you will encounter along life's path. The rose, too, is your personal emblem."

"Wait a minute. I'm getting confused. In both dreams you were the thorn, while it would have made more sense if you were a gander in the last one. After all, whoever heard of a goose mating with a thorn? Moreover, I was a goose in one vision and a rose in the other. I don't understand."

"We are not meant to immediately understand everything shown to us. Often, certain portions of our dreams become clear to us only as time passes," he explained. "Perhaps the goose embodies the devoted mate and the maternal part of you, while the rose denotes the delicate, lovely, feminine person you are."

"Delicate? Me?" she scoffed. "Darling, that's sweet of you, but your interpretation is way off base. There is nothing dainty about me, and probably never will be. But I'm glad that you consider me lovely, in spite of it."

He didn't argue with her assessment, but merely shook his head and said, "One day you will see yourself as I and others do. Until then, nothing I can say will convince you otherwise."

They returned to the sweat lodge. Silver Thorn had explained to her that it was customary to sweat both before and afterward. "I can't say I'm looking forward to a second round of this," she told him. "I'm already hot and sweaty. Besides, I'm getting cranky, probably because I haven't eaten much."

"The time will pass quickly," he assured her. "By then Konah will have our meal prepared and you can eat your fill."

"Konah is fixing our supper?" Nikki commented. "How nice of her, of you, to think of it."

"I am a very thoughtful husband," he replied smugly.

"For which I expect just reward from my appreciative mate."

"I'm sure." Nikki chuckled. "You're also modest to a fault, my dear."

Silver Thorn sprinkled fresh herbs and water on the hot rocks. Steam billowed up in fragrant clouds. "No one will disturb us," he assured her. "It is quite safe for you to remove your shirt if you wish." So saying, he removed and discarded his loincloth before seating himself next to her, cross-legged and unconcernedly nude. Nikki, feeling decidedly overdressed for the occasion, shrugged out of her T-shirt.

Within minutes, she was feeling lethargic, almost as if she'd been drugged. Pearls of perspiration misted her flesh. Through heavy lids, she noted that Silver Thorn's bronze flesh had taken on a similar sheen. A languorous desire stole through her, heating her in an altogether different way. That Silver Thorn was responding in a similar manner was clear by the molten gleam in his eyes, making them shimmer like mercury—not to mention his bold erection, which he took no steps to hide.

Rather, he reached a finger out to trace a droplet of moisture as it tracked across her breast. Her nipple peaked, begging his attention. He answered the silent call, leaning forward to lap at the dimpled crest with his tongue.

Fire streaked through her. "Should we be doing this?" she asked on a moan. "I mean, is it proper? Here? Now?"

"The ritual is complete. We may do as we please," he answered in a passion-roughened voice. "Just now, it pleases me to please you."

"Likewise, I'm sure," she breathed huskily. Then his mouth closed over her breast, and she could speak no more.

Still suckling, he pressed forward, urging her onto her back. Her arms drifted upward, her fingers twining through his midnight hair, anchoring his head to her. Her back arched as she offered herself more fully into his embrace.

He took his time, laving her breast thoroughly before ministering equally to its twin—lapping the dew from the pert peaks, the pearlescent mounds, the velvety undersides, the valley between them. His hands glided lovingly over her torso as if relearning every curve, every bend and dip. He cupped one breast in his palm, studying its form, testing the texture and malleability with tongue and sweat-slick fingers.

"So soft," he murmured. "So sleek. Like moist clay ready to be molded by a potter's hand."

"Yes," she answered in a whisper. "By your hand." Her own hands sought his shoulders, measuring their breadth, then slipped to his chest, revelling in the contour of taut muscle overlying bone. She inhaled deeply, drinking in his musky, male scent. "If I were a master sculptor and tried for a hundred years, I could not hope to duplicate your magnificent masculine beauty. So hard, so finely honed, so flawlessly fashioned."

They adored one another with their eyes, their mouths, their hands—stroking each other to the pinnacle of passion, twining and twisting like two slippery otters. As he slid into her tight, slick warmth, he groaned at the pleasure. She fit him so perfectly, held him so firmly.

Nikki arched to meet him, welcoming his fierce thrusts. He filled her so completely, and yet she clung to him, craving more. Her head thrown back, teeth gritted, her nails clawing at his back, she whimpered helplessly, "If I live forever, I'll never get enough of you."

As if taking her words literally, he braced her hips in his hands, lifting her, laying her legs over his shoulders—driving into her more deeply, powerfully, as if to stamp his indelible mark on her innermost being—branding her heart, soul, and body with his. Pushed over the edge, they joined in a shattering all-consuming climax. Their glad cries reverberated in the sultry air, dwindling into soft sighs in the enveloping mist.

Lying sheltered in his loving arms, replete and secure, Nikki suddenly shivered. Out of nowhere came a terrible fear that their love was too perfect, too wonderful, and that something awful was bound to happen—something destined to part them. So strong, so frightening was this feeling that she cried out aloud, "No!"

Silver Thorn was alarmed, especially when he noted how pale her face had turned. "What is wrong?" he demanded.

She shivered again and clutched him tightly to her in an attempt to regain that warm sense of security. "It was probably nothing," she claimed, denying the lingering fear. "My grandmother would say that a goose just walked across my grave, I guess. It gave me the willies, that's all. An unreasonable sensation of dread, as if something bad is going to happen to destroy our happiness."

He held her near, raising her face to his. "Rest assured, my dearest heart, that I will quell any and all peril that might threaten our life together," he pledged somberly. "Nothing but death will ever come between us, and even then I will find a means to be with you."

Nineteen

A month went by with nothing calamitous occurring, and Nikki began to breathe easier. She chalked her strange feeling of pending disaster up to the after-effects of the *sweating*. "Too much steam on the brain," she joked.

The only other consequence was that her visit to the sweat lodge seemed to have precipitated frequent bouts of morning sickness. Nikki calculated that she'd now missed two full menstrual periods, this being the first of August, and if she truly had conceived that first time she and Silver Thorn had made love, she was two months along in her pregnancy. Surprisingly, though her breasts were tender and brimming over the cups of her bra, she now had to fasten her bra on the inner hooks. Before, she'd always had to use the outer hooks or the lower band was simply too binding against her ribcage. Even her panties seemed awfully loose, though the elastic in the waist didn't appear to be losing its stretch.

Curious about this oddity, Nikki dug out her jeans and tried them on. Much to her wonder, they were so loose they barely stayed up, hanging low on her hips. The waist was at least two inches too large, and the legs and rear sections bagged terribly, rather than fitting snugly the way they used to.

It took a few seconds for the pieces of the puzzle to fall together, but when they did Nikki let out a whoop of delight. Whether it was her current diet or the added exercise she was getting these days or a combination of factors, one thing was clear: She had lost weight—and inches! At that moment, she would have traded her left elbow for a full-length mirror . . . a measuring tape . . . a pair of scales . . . something—anything—that would reveal exactly how many pounds she'd lost and let her view the results for herself.

On the heels of delight came the disheartening thought that, though she probably weighed less and looked better than she had in five years, it was only temporary. She was pregnant and would no doubt regain every ounce and then some in the next few months. Not that she wasn't looking forward to having a child at long last; but drat it all, why did Mother Nature have to tease her like this?

Her bad humor carried over, dimming the joy of the moment, and she found herself bemoaning the fact that her new, trim condition was to be so short-lived. To which, Silver Thorn replied calmly, "You put too much importance on being thin. That is not the most vital facet of life, Neeake."

"Easy for you to say," she retorted waspishly. "You probably haven't been chubby since you lost your baby fat."

He leveled an impatient look at her. "If you had a choice, which I assure you that you do not, would you rather be skinny or have our baby?"

"The baby, of course. I just wish I could enjoy being thin for a while longer."

"Then kindly cease your whining and enjoy it while it lasts," he told her. "Or are you one of those people who are not happy unless they have something about which to complain?"

"Well, excuuuuse me!" she snapped back. "At least I have an excuse. Everyone knows that when a woman is pregnant her hormones change and she has mood swings. If I'm getting on your nerves, you have no one to blame but yourself. You're the one who was so hot to get into my britches and share your sperm. Given that and an old adage—now that you've married in haste, you may repent in leisure, buster."

Despite the moodiness and the morning sickness, Nikki felt healthier than she had in years. She was eating better, sleeping better, and her muscle tone was improving daily. Junk food was just a pleasant memory, though there were times when she would have mugged someone for a Coke or a Snickers bar—if there had been anyone to mug for one.

She was somewhat concerned that she might not be getting the amount of calcium she needed in her diet, however, particularly now that she was pregnant, since fresh milk was basically non-existent in the village. When she expressed this concern to Konah, the woman assured her that healthy children were the rule rather than the exception among the Shawnee.

"Yes, but calcium is very important so the baby will have strong bones and teeth and so that I will have a nutritious supply of breast milk for him. I've never been pregnant before, but I've been around my brothers' wives long enough to know that much."

"I do not know this word *calcium,*" Konah said. "But I am sure that fish and meats, beans and greens, offer some of this, do they not?"

"Yes, but cow's milk or goat's milk supplies more. So do eggs and spinach."

Konah nodded "Eggs are good. We can collect turtle eggs for you, and maybe some fish eggs. Too bad it is too late for the eggs from the birds and the ducks."

Nikki grimaced. "Call me plebeian, but I've never cared much for caviar, thank you. The turtle eggs don't sound too awful, though."

"We must also boil some bone soup for you," Konah said. "Like makes like, you know. If you want strong bones for your babe, you eat the bone of a strong animal."

Nikki looked skeptical, but Konah was undeterred. "You listen to your grandmother, girl. You, with all your fancy ideas from the future, do not know everything. We have lived upon this earth since time began, and we are still here to tell of it."

Only one other aspect of her pregnancy really worried Nikki, and that was not having a physician to monitor her condition, her progress, and to be on hand when she went into labor. Additionally, there was the fact that she would deliver her child in the lodge instead of a nice sanitary hospital with all those modern sterile instruments, nurses to attend to her and the baby, and drugs to make the delivery as painless as possible. She was, quite naturally, afraid that something might go wrong, and here there would be no natal care unit or specialists to correct any unforeseen problem that might develop. She tried telling herself that women had been having perfectly healthy babies without these amenities for centuries, but she still worried.

Moreover, more than anything else, more than at any other time she could recall, Nikki desperately wanted her mother. Konah realized this and tried as best she could to fill that role, and though Nikki appreciated her efforts, it just wasn't the same. *Mom* was something—someone—special, with red hair and violet eyes and the scent of White Linen wafting about her. *Mom* was warm, wonderful, and had a wacky sense of humor that seemed to strike at the oddest times. Only Mom's arms could soothe everything from teenage angst to the pain of a broken ankle. And now, just when Nikki needed her the most, she was miles and literally years out of reach.

With this uppermost in her mind, Nikki was thrilled

when Silver Thorn told her he had an idea of a way she could try to let her family know that she was well.

"Is there some place near their home that you might recognize, even now?" he inquired.

After considering a moment, Nikki replied, "There is a small river, more of a creek really, on the farm. I think I could locate it, with your help. It branches off the Auglaize River. Nor far from where the two meet, the creek crosses Dad's property near the farmhouse. It runs through a couple of the fields he plants."

"Is there a particular landmark somewhere near? A large hill, perhaps, or a strange configuration in the river?"

"That creek curves like a dog's hind leg," she told him. Suddenly her eyes brightened. "There is one thing. When the boys and I were children, we had a certain tree down by the river that we liked to climb. It's a huge old oak with branches that curve nearly to the ground. Dad always griped about the way the tree stood out from the river into the field, making him have to cut a wide swath around it when he planted. For years, he threatened to cut it down, but the trunk was a good seven feet across and the root system would have been a nightmare to dig out, so he let it stand.

"But this spring, after the wheat was already up, we had an awful windstorm. If it weren't an actual tornado, it was the next best thing. It ripped that old oak out of the ground, roots and all. Dad said that when it fell, every window in the house rattled. He estimates that tree was around two hundred years old. If he's right, that same tree should be in that same spot right now, even if it's only a sapling."

Silver Thorn nodded. "And it is still there now, in your time, though the wind felled it."

"At least for now, I guess," Nikki said. "Where it's situated, Dad can't get to it until he harvests the wheat." She paused as something occurred to her. "Oh, dear! This is

August, and he probably took the wheat off about two or three weeks ago. Still, summer is a busy time of year and he has other crops and fields to farm, so I doubt he's gotten out there to cut the oak into firewood yet. But he will soon, I'm sure."

"Then time is of the essence," Silver Thorn concluded. "Neeake, I am thinking that if you were to write a letter to your family and leave it there at the tree, your father might find it in his time as you found the amulet. I cannot promise that it will be so, but we could try."

Nikki's face lit up. "Oh, Thorn! That would be so marvelous, if it did work! At least then they'd know that I'm okay and not worry anymore. How would we do it—tie the note to a branch if we can find the right tree?"

"No. In a hundred and eighty-three years time, it would surely blow away or the birds would pick it apart or someone in another year would remove it before your father. But if we were to bury it near the base of the tree where the roots are, wrapped with thick deerhide, perhaps it would withstand the rigors of time. Then, it would remain safely hidden until the tree fell, exposing the roots and the ground beneath it."

"And the package," she deduced. "Thorn, that's brilliant!"

"If it works," he reminded her.

"Yes, but it's certainly worth a try!" She launched herself into his arms. "Oh, thank you! This is going to make me feel so much better! When are we going? How soon can we leave?"

"There is more I have not told you," he stated, setting her apart from him a space, his expression serious. "Our journey is to be twofold. While you have been missing your family, I have been worried about Tecumseh. It distresses me greatly that in two moons I have yet to devise a means to change his fate, though I have spent long days and nights contemplating this problem. If, as you say, he is to die in another two moons, something must be done soon. I must go to him, Neeake, and tell him what I have learned from you and try to convince him to get out of this war now, before it is too late for him. It may be the only way to save him since I can see no other solution."

"We're going to Detroit?" she asked. "That's where he is now, isn't he?"

"I have heard that he is near there or perhaps across the river at Fort Malden."

"But . . . but that's British-held territory," Nikki said with a disturbed frown. "And the war has been raging steadily in the northern section of the state. How can we ride right through the middle of a battlefield?"

"We will not," he told her. "I am taking you only as far as Peahchaete's village on the Hog Creek, which is but a morning's distance from here. We will bury your message to your parents, and then I will continue north alone. You may either remain at Hog Creek or return here to await me. Peahchaete will see that you are escorted safely."

"No." Her look was as firm as her tone of voice. "I will not remain behind and worry myself sick. If you are going in search of Tecumseh, then so am I. All the way to the arctic circle, if necessary."

"It is too dangerous," he said. "You must think of the babe."

"It's not any more dangerous for me than it is for you," she pointed out. "If you insist on trying to get yourself killed, then I'm going to be right there beside you. We're in this together, Thorn, through thick and thin."

He scowled at her and stated flatly, "I forbid it."

Three little words. That's all it took, and Nikki felt her hackles rise. She met him, toe to toe and nose to nose. "If it's war you're looking for, you don't have to go all that far to find it," she informed him tersely. The light of battle shone like violet flames in her eyes. "In case you misunderstood, let me clarify my position. I may be your wife, but I am also my own woman, with a mind and a will of my own. If I want to do something, I'll do it. I don't require your permission. Furthermore, I do not take kindly to being ordered around, especially when you do it in such an arrogant manner."

Silver Thorn's face could have been carved of rock. "You forget, woman. You are in my time now, not yours. Here, a wife obeys her husband."

She stood her ground. "Well, guess what?" she intoned sassily. "I brought a little bit of women's liberation with me when I came. It's part and parcel of my personality, and there's not a damn thing you can do about it. So stick that in your peace pipe and smoke it!"

"Do you wish to send the message to your parents or not?" His tone implied that if she did, she would abide by his restrictions.

"Yes."

"Then I will take you as far as Hog Creek with me and no farther. Nor will I discuss this with you again."

"We'll see about that. But for now, we'll put it on the back burner."

He nodded stiffly. "Go write your note and pack what you will need. We leave at dawn."

"By land or by sea?" she quipped.

"By canoe."

She offered him a snide smile. "Then I'll be sure to bring my deck shoes," she said haughtily. "Soggy moccasins are the pits!"

The canoe trip the next morning was short and silent. Both Nikki and Silver Thorn were still miffed with each other, their differences far from settled between them. However, once they reached their destination, Nikki's excitement overrode her anger. She gazed at the little Shawnee village with a sense of awe.

"My God! I know exactly where I am!" she exclaimed. "In my time, this is a small shopping mall with a grocery store and a pharmacy. And over here," she waved her hand to a spot to her right, "would stand one of my favorite places. McDonald's. If I close my eyes and concentrate really hard, I swear I can almost smell cheeseburgers and French fries and Egg McMuffins! We should be standing in the middle of Shawnee Road, and the school where I teach is only about a mile away. And a couple of bends of the river to the northeast is where they'll build the oil refinery. Of course, if you really want the truth, I don't miss seeing those smokestacks and that big orange flame. The stench could be terrible, and there always seemed to be a murky cloud of pollution overhanging the area."

After greeting the chief and informing him of their mission, they borrowed a couple of horses and set out on a trail that led from the Hog Creek settlement to the newly established Fort Amanda. Again, Nikki was overcome with a sense of familiarity. "You can't know how many times I've driven this same route in my car. Though it's paved, it's still called Fort Amanda Road in my day. However, Hog Creek is more politely known as the Ottawa River."

They were perhaps halfway to their destination, with Nikki becoming more excited by the minute, when a small party of Indians suddenly emerged from the cover of the trees on either side of the trail. With no forewarning, Nikki and Silver Thorn found themselves surrounded and held at gunpoint by eight fierce-looking warriors, all decked out in warpaint.

What should have been a tremendous scream somehow got stuck in Nikki's throat and emerged as a tiny, panicked yelp. Beside her, Silver Thorn motioned for her to remain quiet. After assessing the situation and their adversaries with a measuring glare, he turned his attention to one particular man who appeared to be the leader. For several seconds no one spoke, the prolonged silence tearing at Nikki's jangled nerves.

At last, Silver Thorn broke the stalemate, and Nikki nearly fell off her horse as she heard him say, "What mischief are you up to now, Tenskwatawa? Or should I still address you as the Prophet, brother?"

Twenty

Nikki stared in dismay at the man known as the Prophet. Though she'd seen portraits of him, they really hadn't done him justice. Short, dumpy, and disfigured, he was much more loathsome in person. A good part of his ugliness was due to a childhood accident that had caused the loss of his right eye, leaving a puckered scar across a portion of his face. Disregarding his outer maiming, however, there was also a sinister mien about him that seemed to emanate from the man himself. His reply to Silver Thorn's query was proof of this.

"I want the woman, Silver Thorn," Prophet announced. "She is evil. She must die."

Nikki forgot how to breathe.

"Neeake is my wife. She is not yours to take," Silver Thorn replied brusquely.

"She is a witch. She must burn," Prophet declared loudly.

Nikki's heart stammered in her chest.

Thorn's eyes spat silver flames. "You are a thousand times more wicked than she will ever be, Tenskwatawa. Yet you live on to spread your lies and evil. Perhaps Tecumseh would have done well to have killed you rather than merely renounce you. And to think I pitied you when he did so!"

Prophet's malevolent laugh sent shivers through Nikki. "Keep your pity, brother. Hand over the woman."

"Not as long as I draw breath," Silver Thorn challenged.

Nikki strangled on a gasp as Prophet leveled his rifle at Silver Thorn's chest. "That can be easily remedied," the man hissed.

Silver Thorn's gaze narrowed in warning. "Take care, brother. My powers are not feigned as yours are. I could strike you down in the blink of an eye."

"But you would not," Prophet sneered. "Of the three of us, you are the weakest. You could not kill another of your own blood."

"Do not wager your life on it," Thorn advised him somberly. "In defense of my wife, I would do it most gladly."

Prophet's confidence wavered visibly for a mere second. Then he rallied. "You may slay me, but my men will also slay you and your white witch. You cannot battle all of us at once."

"Again, I would not stake my life on rash assumptions, Brother. Even were your men to kill me, I would see you dead first, and several more with you."

It was a standoff, one both men contemplated seriously. After a moment's thought, Prophet proclaimed, "Then you shall accompany us as well, Silver Thorn, and we will present our case before Tecumseh. Let him be the judge as to which of us is right."

"Ah, it comes clear at last," Thorn said mockingly. "This is your way of trying to get back into Tecumseh's good graces. Present him with a witch. Tell him she is trying to harm his cause. And he is so grateful that he forgives your many past transgressions."

Prophet shrugged, not bothering to deny Thorn's allegations. Nor did he back down, however, or order his men to lower their arms.

"Fine. Have it as you will," Silver Thorn announced calmly.

Nikki nearly swallowed her tongue. Prophet's shaggy

brows rose in surprise at Thorn's sudden capitulation. Both waited breathlessly as Silver Thorn began to speak again.

"Neeake and I will go with you to Tecumseh's camp. Had you inquired, you would have known that this was our ultimate destination. However, be forewarned. If any harm befalls my wife along the way, be I dead or alive, I will personally rip out your throat and feed your wretched carcass to the wolves. You, dear brother, and your fellow villains will serve only as our unworthy escorts. Do not mistake yourselves as anything more important.

"Now," he added, "I suggest that we return to Peahchaete's village to return these horses we have borrowed and retrieve our canoe. The river will provide faster travel. Moreover, the chief is expecting Neeake and me to stay the evening and will suspect that something is wrong if we fail to appear."

"We will go with you to get your canoe," Prophet agreed. "But do not think that I fear what that old man will think. He is leaning over his grave and presents no threat to anyone."

Silver Thorn had managed to gain a slim thread of control, for which Nikki was thankful. She hoped he knew what he was doing, that there were some way in which he could dominate his brother's actions or at least limit them. Her previous fervor for going north with Silver Thorn had waned drastically in the past few minutes, shattered in the face of reality.

When they reached the Hog Creek settlement, Peahchaete was irate that Tenskwatawa had dared to accost his guests. Still, there was little he could do to remedy the situation beyond verbally castigating the Prophet. The village was small, populated in large part by older citizens, with few warriors willing to stand up against the Prophet and his men.

"You dishonor yourself," Peahchaete railed. "How dare you accost Chief Black Hoof's niece? Be sure that I will send runners to Wapakoneta immediately to inform him of your vile actions, Tenskwatawa."

Peahchaete's words took the Prophet by surprise. "This woman . . . this witch is Black Hoof's niece?"

Silver Thorn smirked. "It would seem that your white witch is Shawnee after all. See what trouble you bring upon yourself with your hasty plotting? First you cause the downfall of Tecumseh's confederation and now you try to abduct our high chief's niece. When will you learn to look before you leap, brother?"

"It matters not who she is, only that she is an evil sorceress," Tenskwatawa blustered. "This changes nothing. We leave for Tecumseh's camp immediately."

Silver Thorn ignored the directive. "I should also tell you that Neeake is our illustrious messenger from the future, sent to us by the Spirits. To offend her is to invite the wrath of the Spirits upon yourself."

"So you would have me believe, Silver Thorn," the Prophet scoffed. "It is a chance I am willing to take to see justice served."

"You wouldn't know justice if it bit you on the butt!" Nikki put in, surprising everyone with her sudden rebuttal. The primary shock had worn off at last, and her natural spunk was returning. She faced her brother-in-law squarely, meeting him look for contemptuous look. "My mission here is one of vast importance to the entire tribe, yet you want to take your petty accusations to your older brother just to weasel back into his favor. Has it occurred to you at all that Tecumseh is in the middle of a war and will not appreciate your untimely interference?"

"Who are you to question my actions?" the Prophet shouted, leaning toward her in a threatening manner. "You are a mere woman."

She glared back at him. "That's your first mistake, buster. Do yourself a favor and make it your last." While the men had been occupied with their discussion, Nikki had surreptitiously dug into her backpack and located her pepper spray. Now she drew it forth and pointed it at Tenskwatawa. "Back off, Tenski. Get out of my face and my space or I'll blast you with this and make you cry like the big baby you truly are."

He eyed the minuscule canister in her hand and dared to laugh. "What harm can you do with that?" he jeered. "I spit on your puny lies."

His lips were still puckered to execute his threat when she depressed the lever. Her aim was off. Rather than squirting him in the eyes as she'd intended, the spray hit him in the nose and lower face, but it was enough to do the job. In the next instant, Tenskwatawa was hopping around, clawing at his face and screaming in pain while the others looked on in amazement.

"*Skotai! Skotai!*" he shrieked. "Fire! Fire! My face is on fire!" Meanwhile, his swiping at the spray had smeared it across more of his skin and onto his hands.

One of his cohorts ran for water while the others looked on in helpless fascination. Two of the fellows had the presence of mind to keep their weapons pointed toward Nikki and Silver Thorn, however, which prevented either of them from leaving the scene. One of the men took a step toward her, and Nikki raised her pepper gun again.

"Do it, turkey. Make my day," she told him.

The man retreated, but only a couple of paces. The look on his face clearly showed that he hoped he was now out of range of her strange weapon.

Silver Thorn leaned close and murmured, "What did you spray on him that burns so?"

"They call it pepper spray. To tell you the truth, this is the first time I've used it. I had no idea it would work this well."

"Will it wash off?"

"Not easily or quickly, or so they claim. It's not supposed to cause any permanent damage. It's mainly a deterrent against attackers. But I think it takes awhile to wear off."

By this time, tears were running down Tenskwatawa's blistering cheeks, just as Nikki had predicted. Chief Peahchaete was duly impressed. "You possess strong magic, Neeake. It is good."

"Yes, but not good enough, I'm afraid," she told him. She nodded toward the Prophet's henchmen, who were still on guard.

She directed a whispered inquiry to her husband. "Do you have any super tricks up your sleeve, darling? Or are we still obliged to travel to Tecumseh's camp with these yahoos?"

"We will go," he replied tersely. "I must speak with Tecumseh; and if I left you behind now, I would worry that Tenskwatawa would continue his efforts to harm you. Far better that we keep him within our sight than have him sneaking up from behind us."

"A valid point," she concurred. "Never turn your back on a rabid animal."

"I do not think you need fear that these scoundrels will accost you on the way," Peahchaete put in. "They will keep a fair distance between themselves and your small but mighty heat-shooter. As a further safeguard, I will send three of my braves with you. I will notify your uncle as well. Black Hoof will most likely send warriors to your defense."

"Thank you, Chief Peahchaete," Nikki said. "We appreciate your kind efforts."

"Your assistance will not go unrewarded," Silver Thorn added.

Their attention was diverted as Tenskwatawa, having endured the agony as long as he could, made a mad, wailing dash toward the river. A loud splash and wild thrashing followed.

Nikki, Silver Thorn, and the chief shared a laugh.

"That should keep him occupied for a while," Nikki commented blithely. She hooked an arm through each of theirs, grinning up at them. "Shall we dine, gentlemen? I'm positively starved!"

Tenskwatawa was sufficiently recovered by late that afternoon to embark on the journey. His face and hands were red and puffy, and his chest was streaked with vivid welts where the spray had dripped on it, but he was in a rush to leave. Nikki figured he wanted to be gone before Black Hoof could receive Peahchaete's message and send reinforcements.

"It will be fine," Silver Thorn assured her as he helped her into the canoe. "Tenskwatawa knows that Black Hoof's warriors will be close behind. My brother is impulsive, but he is not entirely witless. He knows that Black Hoof, unlike Tecumseh, would not hesitate to kill him."

In all, there were four canoes in their party. Tenskwatawa's men rode in the lead and rearmost canoes, with Nikki, Silver Thorn, and the three braves from Hog Creek sandwiched in the middle. One of the village braves, a man named Fish Spear took the rear position in Silver Thorn's canoe to help with the paddling and thus speed the journey along since Nikki's proficiency was fledgling at best.

At a normal pace, the journey would have taken three or four days, with regular stops during the day and the nights spent camped ashore. This was not to be a leisurely trip. At the brisk pace they were traveling, allotting the bare minimum for rest, Silver Thorn estimated they would reach the southern shore of Lake Erie in two days or less. Neither he nor his brother were inclined to dawdle, each having his own reasons for wanting to reach Tecumseh as soon as possible.

For the first few hours, Nikki was merely restless. After

the sun set, twilight turning the river as dark as ink, she became very tense. "How can you navigate when you can't see where we're going?" she asked anxiously. "What if we hit a rock or a submerged log or something?"

"I can see well enough," Silver Thorn assured her. "The moon is on the rise, and we know the river and its hazards well."

"You must have eaten a lot more carrots than I did," she mumbled. "To me, it's as dark out here as the inside of Hogan's goat! Are we going to stop anytime soon?"

"We will most likely continue on for a few hours yet."

"I can't wait that long," she told him. "You men may have bladders the size of a moose, but I have to piddle."

They made a stop soon thereafter, primarily for her benefit. Tenskwatawa was none too thrilled at the delay; and when Nikki headed for the bushes, he started to follow, though several paces behind. Silver Thorn stepped into his brother's path, cutting him off, just as Nikki turned around to confront them. With her flashlight in one hand and her pepper spray in the other, she announced loudly, "Thorn, you'd better tell Randy Rabbit and his buddies that if any of them come skulking around after me, they'll get a good dose of my pepper spray in a very private area. Not only will it wilt their . . . uh . . . ardor, it could very well make it fall completely off."

Predictably, no one came anywhere near her after that dire warning—not even when they made a three-hour layover around two in the morning for a too-brief sleep. They were on the river again after a quick breakfast, during which Tenskwatawa griped incessantly because the "squaw" refused to cook for them.

To which, Nikki replied irritably, "Stuff it, Buffalo Belly. I only work for union wages."

It was a long, tiring trip. Fortunately, though the sky was overcast, it didn't rain. Again they stopped briefly during the night, after silently slipping past Fort Meigs; and by midmorning of the third day, they were nearing the area where Tecumseh was rumored to be camped.

They knew they were in the right vicinity when they began to pass sentries, who announced their arrival with a series of bird calls and varied signals. By the time they reached the campsite, Tecumseh and twenty of his warriors were stationed on the riverbank to greet them, fully armed and scowling. Tecumseh stepped forward, leveled his rifle at The Prophet's head and, in a voice like thunder, commanded, "Tell me how you dare show your face before me again. Then tell me why I shouldn't shoot you."

"Because I bring you the white witch who is turning your people against you," Tenskwatawa whined.

"Because he's not worth the price of a bullet," Silver Thorn offered disdainfully.

"Because he's stupid beyond belief?" Nikki added. "Besides, history says he is to live a long and miserable life."

At this, Tecumseh's gaze turned toward her. "Are you this white witch of whom he speaks?"

Under the scrutiny of those intense hazel eyes, Nikki had to fight not to squirm. Fortunately, her voice was stable and her own gaze unwavering when she spoke. "I am your sister-in-law, Silver Thorn's wife, and Black Hoof's niece."

"She is not a witch, Tecumseh. She is Shawnee," Silver Thorn put in. "Tenskwatawa is simply up to his old tricks."

Tecumseh waved him to silence, his attention still directed at Nikki. "And do you speak against me, as is claimed?" he pressed.

Nikki drew a deep breath. "I speak against your involvement with the British in this war, but not against you. I have seen what the future holds for you and the Shawnee, and I would change it if possible. That is why Silver Thorn summoned me from the future."

Tecumseh nodded. "I would hear more of this." He

waded into the shallows and offered his hand to help her disembark. "Come. We will talk."

Their hands touched, and Tecumseh gave a start. His eyes widened. "You are carrying Silver Thorn's child," he stated softly.

"Yes," Nikki admitted, "your nephew. It is our wish that you live to see him born."

Twenty-one

Tecumseh led Silver Thorn and Nikki to his lodge. The Prophet and his men were directed to another lodge, where they would be kept under guard. Tecumseh didn't trust Tenskwatawa not to stir up more mischief if left on his own to wander around the camp.

Silver Thorn led the discussion by telling Tecumseh how he had bid the Spirits to send him a messenger from the future and of Nikki's appearance with the amulet. He told of the strange and wondrous items she'd brought with her from her time and much of what she'd revealed of her world.

"She is no witch, Tecumseh. She is the messenger I summoned, and she knows what will happen with this war and with our people. If we cannot change it, disaster is sure to come."

Next, Nikki related all she could remember about the war, its progress, and its eventual outcome—citing places and battles and dates with an accuracy the men found uncanny. Then, as gently as she could, she broke the worst of her news to Tecumseh.

"Unless you quit this war, my history states that you are destined to die soon in what will be known as the Battle of the Thames, along a river of the same name in Canada. There, on the fifth day of October, minutes into the battle, the British will surrender to the American forces, leaving you and your Indian troops to fight alone.

You will be slain; and with no one left to lead them, your troops will disperse and return to their homes.

"The Americans will go on to win the war against the British. The British will return to England; and in a few years time, all Ohio tribes will be forced to leave their homes and move to lands west of the Mississippi River. Poor lands, that will grow little and sustain few. Reservation lands, allotted by the American government, with no vast forests and abundant game, where the Shawnee will no longer be masters of their own lives.

"This fate also awaits other tribes, even those in the South. The Creeks. The Seminoles. The Cherokee will be driven like cattle across the miles to a reservation in Oklahoma. Many will not survive the long, hard journey. So many will perish that the journey will thereafter be known as the Trail of Tears. The future for the Indian tribes is very bleak. Some tribes will vanish from the earth altogether, while others will be greatly reduced in number. Yet, somehow, they will carry on, despite poverty and hunger and disease. But it will never be the same as it is now."

Again, Silver Thorn took up the appeal. "Tecumseh, when I called upon the Spirits, I never thought I would learn of such disaster for our people. Nor did I think to learn that you would soon be taken from us. It is my hope that, by revealing this to us through Neeake, the Spirits are giving us a chance to alter the course of destiny for us all. I implore you, brother. Withdraw from this war now. Help us to avoid this tragic end. Save yourself and our people while there is yet hope."

Tecumseh closed his eyes on a deep sigh. When he opened them again, they were bleak. "It is too late, Silver Thorn. I have spoken to my followers. I have told them that I feel this war is lost. That there is no need to pursue it further. Many took my words to heart and have already left. For that, I am glad. The others will not hear me. They have pledged to stay and fight until the end, and they wish me to stay and lead them in it. They are right. I cannot abandon them, as much as I would wish to end this now. I must stay, no matter the cost."

"No!" Silver Thorn could not sit still and allow his brother to resign himself so easily to his own death. His eyes flashed angrily. "Curse you, Tecumseh! Where is your fight? Your fire? Your will? Can you not see that by acting now you may save entire tribes? By going on with this, you are knowingly condemning them and yourself. Is this what you planned when you devised your great confederation of tribes? I think not!"

"The confederation is lost as well, but a bright dream that faded away too soon," Tecumseh pointed out unnecessarily. "Tenskwatawa saw to that, blast his detestable hide. If ever there were an opportunity for the Indian to prevail over the white man, this was it, and his rash actions destroyed it before it could be properly born. For that, I will never forgive him."

"Hate him to your dying breath, then," Silver Thorn concurred. "But hate him hard and long. Not for so short a span. Tecumseh, you are too great a leader to abandon us now. Give yourself and the people enough time to recover and to reconsider. Build the dream anew. Without Tenskwatawa to sabotage your best efforts, you may succeed beyond your wildest expectations. Your confederation may yet breathe new life and prosper, and our people with it."

"No. It took twenty years to prepare the uniting of the tribes before. I am too old and too tired to start again."

"That's a heap of buffalo dung, brother. You and I were born at the same time, and I am not near ready to give up on life. With Neeake at my side and my son on the way, I am eager to meet the challenge of each new day. So should you be."

"I am glad for you, Silver Thorn. I wish you well. But

I haven't the heart to attempt it anew. There are no challenges that interest me any longer."

"Truly?" Silver Thorn's brow rose in question. "That is too bad, for I was about to propose one to you. One which I thought would hold enormous appeal for you."

Tecumseh waved his hand indifferently, but gestured for Silver Thorn to continue.

"I propose that the two of us engage in a contest of powers. We will select seven men to act as impartial judges. If I win the match, you will withdraw from the war. What you choose to do with your life afterward will be up to you. If you win, I will accept the inevitable and never speak again of this matter."

Tecumseh sat silent and thoughtful for several minutes. At last he said, "If I accept your challenge, there is one thing more I would have from you, Silver Thorn. Should I win, I would have your pledge that you will remove my body from the battlefield before the soldiers can mutilate it. Bury me covertly and in honor and keep my grave a secret from all who would plunder it, that my spirit might rest in peace."

"You have my solemn vow," Silver Thorn said somberly. "However, I do not plan to lose this contest. If I have my way, that pledge may not be fulfilled for many years to come."

The competition was to take place the next day, which gave the men a short time to rest up and prepare themselves mentally and physically for the challenge. Word of the contest spread like wildfire; and before long, everyone was placing bets on which of the brothers would win.

Tenskwatawa was among those who claimed Tecumseh would triumph. Now released from temporary custody, though under supervision, he was quick to involve himself in the betting. At the same time, he took advantage of the opportunity to spread his volatile opinions about Nikki.

"That brownnosing little weasel!" Nikki fumed. "For two cents, I'd teach that vile little rumor-monger a lesson!"

"You have done that, I believe, with your pepper spray," Silver Thorn reminded her.

"Evidently the message didn't stick very long. Your brother must have a short attention span."

Delving into her backpack, she came up with her camera and headed toward the group of men in whose midst the Prophet now stood, spreading his lies to anyone and everyone who would listen.

Silver Thorn grabbed her by the arm, halting her progress. "What are your intentions, my little hothead?"

"If I'm going to wear the name, then by God I'll play the game. I'm going to steal Tenskwatawa's soul."

"Is that not throwing more fuel on the fire?" he inquired quietly. "Only a few are likely to believe him now. But if you offer them proof in favor of his accusations, then many more will think you truly are a witch. Do not let Tenskwatawa make you act rashly, Neeake. While all the warriors know that Tecumseh does not condone the killing of women, children, or unarmed men, they possess a deeply seeded fear of sorcery that could well override their chief's edict. Do not aggravate what could soon become a sensitive situation."

"I'm not the one trying to incite a riot!" Nikki stated heatedly. Still, even through her anger she saw the wisdom of Silver Thorn's reasoning. "Okay," she agreed. "I'll try to ignore him for now. But it won't be easy."

A warrior approached them with a message for Thorn. While everyone's attention was diverted from her, Nikki furtively snapped off a quick shot of Tenskwatawa with her Polaroid and stuffed the photo into her pocket. Who could tell how or when it might come in handy?

* * *

Nikki awoke the next morning to find her husband preparing for the bout with his brother. Nikki watched silently, intrigued at this new facet of her husband, of which she'd heretofore only gotten the smallest glimpse. Silver Thorn was chanting in Shawnee, evidently calling upon certain Spirits for their blessing, their help, or both. That, or he was conjuring up a spell. As he did so, he was smearing some sort of goop on his face, his torso, and arms. Since he had his back to her, Nikki could only see bits and pieces of what he was doing, but she viewed enough to surmise that he was applying what amounted to war paint. At frequent intervals, he would stop, touch his medicine bag prayerfully, and then continue.

He finished the ritual and turned toward her at last. Nikki could not sustain the gasp that rose to her lips. Had she not known who he was, she would never have recognized him, so different did he look—just as a circus clown in full makeup would not resemble the same man he was without it. The entire front of Silver Thorn's body, including his face, was now blue. A vivid blue. On his chest, in black, was an artistic rendering of a thunderbird. Black lightning bolts adorned his cheeks, streaking outward from high on his nose to his lower jaw. Matching designs flowed from shoulders to wrists and were again duplicated on his legs. He looked all warrior now, proud and fierce and ready to do battle with his foe . . .

. . . until he smiled, his teeth gleaming out at her from that blue face. Nikki couldn't help it. She burst out laughing. "Omigod!" she giggled. "You look like a cross between a Mighty Power Ranger and a giant Smurf!"

He frowned at her, not quite sure what to make of her comment. "I am not certain, but I think I would rather be a powerful ranger than a smurf, whatever that is."

"I take it back. On second thought, you look like my mother giving herself a facial!" Nikki whooped gleefully.

"I can tell you are allotting this the solemnity it merits," he chided.

Nikki sobered, suddenly reminded of the import of today's contest. "I'm sorry, Thorn. You are correct. It is not a laughing matter. And I must admit, now that I'm becoming more accustomed to it, that you do look rather dashing and fearsome. That is, I suppose, your intent. To intimidate your opponent."

"That, and to honor the Spirits as they bestow upon me their might and magic. I shall need all the aid they can grant me today if I hope to defeat Tecumseh."

"I have faith in you, Thorn," she told him honestly. "Even he, at his most powerful, did not bring forth a messenger from the future. Only you performed that impossible feat."

Tecumseh, too, had enhanced his image for the event. In keeping with his personal symbol, the panther, Tecumseh's body was painted entirely black, except for his chest. It was stark white, with a black panther's head in bold relief. Also white were the tips of his fingers decorated so that they resembled a cat's claws. His teeth gleamed from his darkened face like sharp animal fangs. Truly, he did look savage.

Tecumseh greeted his guests and informed Nikki that he had arranged for one of his trusted lieutenants to watch over her during the contest. "Unfortunately, Tenskwatawa has inflamed a few of the more superstitious members of the tribe. I will feel better knowing that you are well guarded while Silver Thorn and I are otherwise occupied."

The meet was to take place in a large, tree-ringed clearing not far from the camp. Tecumseh's lieutenant led Nikki to a place near the panel of judges where she would have an unrestricted view of the proceedings. Already, the clearing was girded by excited spectators, among them Tenskwatawa and his cohorts.

The pounding of a drum announced the start of the match, as well as signaling the crowd to silence. Everyone seemed to respect that the two contestants would need immense concentration in order to summon their vast powers. So quiet did they become that Nikki could hear the leaves rustling in the trees many yards away.

There were to be five individual divisions to the contest, each comprised of a pair of feats, one by each of the participants. Each segment would be judged apart from the others. The first man to win three of the five bouts would be declared the winner. A painted stone, tossed into the air, constituted the equivalent of a coin toss. Tecumseh won and elected to go first.

He walked to the center of the clearing, raised his arms high, and began to chant. As one, the crowd held its breath. They did not have to wait long. Within the span of a minute, a dozen huge trees encircling the makeshift arena toppled in succession, all at spaced intervals.

The onlookers murmured in wonder, nodding their heads in hushed approval.

Then Silver Thorn stepped forward. He stood with his eyes closed and his arms held slightly away from his sides, palms out, as if in prayer. He held this stance as all twelve trees raised and replanted themselves in the very spots from which they fell.

The throng exclaimed softly in unison. Nikki gaped in mute awe. The judges awarded the first bout to Silver Thorn.

As winner of the initial event, Silver Thorn was obliged to perform first in the second. Quickly, he made a few motions with his hands, as if gathering or calling something. Within seconds, the clearing was literally crawling with grasshoppers.

Immediately, Tecumseh took his place. Almost instantly, a legion of frogs appeared, feasting on the grasshoppers.

In the midst of this, Tenskwatawa decided to inject a bit of his own magic, a trick many had seen him do before, but this time on a grander scale. With a yell, he threw down his walking stick. As it struck the ground, it was transformed into a nest of writhing rattlesnakes. The snakes slithered off into the mass of frogs and bugs, striking randomly. Suddenly the rattlers regrouped and headed en masse toward Nikki. Before anyone could do anything to stop them, they had formed a circle around her and her befuddled guard and were coiling to strike.

Nikki's heart thudded violently, sending blood pounding into her brain. Her vision began to dim, and she feared she was about to faint. To do so would be disastrous, for she would surely fall across the line of venomous snakes, riling them even more.

From a distance, past the tinny ringing in her ears and the fearful rattling of the snakes, she heard Silver Thorn say, "Do not move, Neeake. I will take care of it. All will be well."

Abruptly, the snakes were gone, dispatched by Silver Thorn. Nikki slumped into Silver Thorn's arms, barely aware of Tecumseh dispensing with the frogs and insects. Silver Thorn handed Nikki into her guard's care once more and, with a wrathful countenance that had Nikki wincing, turned toward Tenskwatawa.

"As soon as I have finished this contest with Tecumseh, I shall kill you, brother," he announced direly. "Prepare your soul for judgment."

"No," Tecumseh countered. "He shall die at my hand. Had I done it before, he would not have been alive to threaten your wife."

Tenskwatawa's gaze swiveled from one irate brother to the other. He cowered visibly and his voice quavered as he claimed, "I wouldn't have hurt her. I meant only to frighten her."

"You lie. Your tongue is as forked as that of your

snakes," Silver Thorn declared. He raised his hand and pointed it at Tenskwatawa. A bolt of light flew from his finger; and before the startled audience, the Prophet promptly froze into a short, plump, pillar of salt.

An instant later, he transformed again, this time into a stone statue.

Silver Thorn whirled on his oldest brother. "Tecumseh!" he roared. "Do not meddle with my magic!"

Tecumseh laughed. "I am merely improving upon it, brother."

Silver Thorn grunted, pointed his finger again, and Tenskwatawa reverted to salt.

Then to rock.

Back to salt.

"Enough already!" Nikki exclaimed, cutting short their battle for supremacy over Tenskwatawa's fate. "If you just want to put him on hold until the contest is done, then install him in a stockade for safekeeping and be done with it, please. You can argue over his final fate later."

Evidently both men accepted her suggestion at the same time. Tenskwatawa, looking totally dazed, returned to his normal state. A rock barricade mounted swiftly around him, stone by stone, as Silver Thorn and Tecumseh worked in tandem to erect it.

"Blasted show-offs!" Nikki muttered. "They're worse than a couple of toddlers."

Beside her, the lieutenant chuckled in agreement.

The judges' long delayed decision gave the second match to Tecumseh, who began the third segment of the competition in spectacular fashion. As he spun slowly around, his hand outstretched, the leaves of the trees assumed their brilliant autumn colors. A breeze sent them swirling to the ground in a vibrant display, much to the delight of those watching.

As if to.compliment his brother's feat and expand upon it, Silver Thorn promptly produced a miniature snowstorm.

The onlookers, granted this brief but wondrous reprieve from the stifling August heat, were thoroughly enchanted.

So were the judges, and Silver Thorn won this round handily.

As his next accomplishment, Silver Thorn produced three ponds, fully stocked with fish that leaped playfully in the water. In the center of each pool, a water spout danced in the sun, creating a trio of dazzling rainbows. It was like watching a fairy tale come to life.

Not to be outdone, Tecumseh sent a shower of glowing embers raining down upon the pools. As they hit the water, they flared into tall flames, which then frolicked atop the surface in a fiery ballet. Shortly, Tecumseh doused the flames and presented the crowd and the judges with fried fish.

Predictably, the fourth match was his, and the contest was now tied at two apiece. Which only lent added import to the final sequence.

Tecumseh took center stage, his face set in determined lines, his expression that of intense concentration. He stood stiffly, his hands clenched, for several minutes while the others waited in tense anticipation. With a loud shout, Tecumseh fell to his knees. As his fists pounded the ground, the earth swelled and began to tremble.

Cries rose up from everyone as the ground rolled beneath their feet and they toppled into heaps. The earth groaned and cracked, bucking and swaying in ever-mounting waves. As suddenly as it had begun, the quaking ceased. The earth pulled itself together again, healing its gaping wounds. The stunned assembly, first speechless with awe, cheered enthusiastically. Any who had doubted, now believed without reservation that this great Shawnee leader was, indeed, capable of producing earthquakes.

As shaken as the rest, Nikki wondered how Silver Thorn could ever top this astonishing achievement. Yet he had to if he hoped to save his beloved brother's life.

As Silver Thorn took his place in the center of the circle, the air fairly hummed with suspense. Arms upraised, his face turned toward the heavens, Silver Thorn spun on his heel—around and around, faster and faster, until he was but a blur. From outside the circle, over the tops of the trees, clouds began to boil forth. The wind began to howl and blow from all directions at once. Then, before their dumbfounded eyes, four separate tornadoes swept down from the clouds, swirling and weaving in place. Still suspended some distance above the earth, they suddenly swept forward, meeting directly over Silver Thorn's head to combine into one gigantic twister. Slowly, as if savoring its intended victim, it lowered over its creator's body, swallowing him in its spinning, grasping mouth.

Nikki's cry of dismay was echoed by alarmed gasps all around. The same thought reverberated through everyone's mind. Surely, Silver Thorn was dead. No one could withstand being caught up in such a seething tempest.

Distraught, numb with disbelief, Nikki could only stare at the spot where the cyclone still spun. Even as she watched, it dissipated and—miracle of miracles—Silver Thorn emerged as hale and whole as ever!

The throng gaped and roared in amazement. Nikki could stand still no longer. She ran as fast as her legs could carry her and threw herself into her husband's open arms.

"You fool!" she sobbed. "You big, reckless fool! Were you trying to kill yourself?" She didn't give him time to answer. "Are you all right?"

"I am unscathed, woman, but for the fact that you are choking me to death," he teased gently.

She thumped him on the back with her fist, her tears wetting his bare shoulder. "Don't you ever scare me like that again! I nearly died of fright!"

He hugged her tightly. "Would it help to know that I love you?"

"Oh, Thorn! I love you, too!" she wailed. "Too much to ever survive losing you."

Twenty-two

Silver Thorn could not believe it. Neither could Nikki or many others who had watched the two brothers perform their duel of powers. Silver Thorn had done his best. He'd been magnificent, especially with that last feat. He'd been sure the contest was his—relieved and glad that Tecumseh would now abandon the British and perhaps live to a ripe old age. But for some undefinable reason, the judges had decided to call the final meet a tie, which rendered the entire contest merely an exercise in futility. Also, since Tecumseh was satisfied with the verdict, neither he nor the judges would sanction Silver Thorn's request for one final, deciding bout. The ruling would stand as it was, a draw between these two sublimely skilled men.

Which meant that Tecumseh would go on fighting, until his death. And that Silver Thorn was free to keep plaguing him to stop. It also meant that, in order to do so, Silver Thorn would have to remain at Tecumseh's side, also involving himself in the war and its inherent dangers.

That presented yet another problem. While Silver Thorn was perfectly willing to risk his own neck to save his brother's, he was not willing to risk Neeake's as well, or that of their child. Nor could he leave her behind or feel comfortable returning her to Wapakoneta to the care of her uncle and other relatives. Not since Tenskwatawa had escaped his stone stockade.

Evidently, when Tecumseh had created the earthquake,

the stones and earth forming the prison had shifted, far enough and just long enough for Tenskwatawa to wriggle to freedom. Then Tecumseh had restored the earth to normal, and all had seemed as it was. In the excitement of the moment, no one had noticed the Prophet fleeing, no one except his comrades. They, too, had fled the village, and heaven only knew where they had gone.

To add to the confusion, eight warriors from Black Hoof's village had arrived just after the competition. Their mission was to rescue Neeake and Silver Thorn and to bring Tenskwatawa back to Wapakoneta to stand trial. Half of them immediately went in search of the missing Prophet. The other four remained in camp to help guard Neeake and provide additional escort for her and Silver Thorn on their return trip to Wapakoneta.

Silver Thorn wasn't sure they would be returning to the village, however. He'd already concluded that, while Tenskwatawa was on the loose and undoubtedly bent on revenge, he could not leave Neeake where his evil brother could find her. Nor could he keep her with him if he meant to follow Tecumseh. Which left but one logical alternative. He must send her back to her home, to her own time, at least until he could resolve these pressing issues that would require all his attention for the next few months.

Neeake was not going to like being parted from him, he knew. Likely, she would throw a fit to rival the witch she was purported to be. But it must be done—soon. And the sooner he informed her of his decision, the better.

Silver Thorn found Nikki in the lodge rifling through her purse. She looked up with a disgruntled expression and waved a bit of paper at him. "Look what I just found. Lottery tickets! Wouldn't it be ironic if I were holding the winning numbers to an eight-million-dollar prize and have absolutely no way to collect it? Talk about lousy luck! Maybe I should include them with that letter to my parents.

That way, if they really are worth anything, Mom and Dad could claim the money." Her face grew more concerned. "In all the recent confusion, I forgot we never got to send my message to my parents. Is there any way we can go back there soon? I'm afraid if we wait too long, Dad will have the tree cut and cleared and our plan will go to ruin. I may never have another chance like this."

"There is no need," he informed her flatly. "You can present your explanation to them personally as soon as we can arrange it."

Her frown deepened. "What? What are you talking about, Thorn? How?"

"I am sending you back, Neeake, back to your time, if it is possible to do so. There are several ways that might work. We shall begin trying them immediately."

The color drained from her face, and for several seconds all she could do was stare at him in stupefaction. She felt as if she'd just been slammed in the chest with a sledge-hammer. Was this cold, stiff stranger the same man who just a few hours ago had told her he loved her? And now, suddenly, he was stating very matter-of-factly that he was sending her away? "Wh . . . why?" she stammered. "You're coming with me, aren't you?"

"No. I cannot. I must stay until this matter with Tecumseh is resolved, one way or another. If the worst comes to pass, I have pledged to bury him. I cannot leave here until my obligations to him are fulfilled. Also, I must see to the welfare of my mother and sister. As I have told you, they are now with the Cherokee. After what you have told us of this Trail of Tears, I must take them to a more secure place. If Tecumseh is not here to care for them, then I must make certain that they will be properly looked after, that they have all that is sufficient for their needs."

"I understand that. It is what any responsible son would do, but what has that got to do with sending me back to my era? Why can't I stay here and go with you? Or wait for you at Wapak? Or . . . or maybe you've just decided you don't want me anymore," she suggested. She gulped back a sob, but the tears still rose to her eyes, making them shimmer like violet pools. "Is that it, Thorn? You've had your fun, and now you're tired of me?"

He dropped to his knees before her, his expression now as miserable as hers, and took her face in his hands. "Never. You are my one love, my only love. It rends my heart to think of being separated from you, if only for a short while."

"Then . . . then why? Explain to me why you want me to go."

"Because I cannot devote myself to you and to Tecumseh at the same time, my pet. I cannot. . . . I will not place you in the path of danger any more than necessary. Tecumseh is determined to continue on his course of destruction. The battlefield, the center of a war, is no safe place for you and our babe."

Nikki nodded, the action sending two fat tears coursing down her cheeks. "I understand that much, but why can't I go back to Wapak and stay there with Black Hoof and Konah? In two months, at most, you will have fulfilled your pledge to Tecumseh. Then you can come and get me and we'll go together to find your mother. I'm looking forward to meeting her, anyway. We'll escort them to Texas, where some of the others have already gone. Or to Mexico. I recall that the Indians who relocated there were accepted much more readily and lived better lives than those who remained in the United States. You and I could live there, too. I wouldn't mind, as long as we could be together."

"It will be a long way to travel, but if they will live in more comfort there, it will be worth the journey. But this is yet another matter I must attend to alone, Neeake. Even taken slowly, with all the proper provisions, it will be an arduous venture, strewn with all manner of possible perils.

You could be great with child by the time we reach the end of the journey. It would be too hazardous, too hard on you."

"Then let me stay with Konah. I'll wait for you, Thorn, for as long as it takes."

He shook his head regretfully. "Even there, I fear you would not be safe. Tenskwatawa would know where to find you, and he would know that I was not there to protect you. He would not hesitate to try some evil scheme, and the next time he might succeed. I cannot take that risk. Nor can you. We must safeguard our child."

Nikki clutched at his arm, her face earnest as she peered into his eyes. "You speak of risks. Isn't it just as much of a risk to me and the baby to chance sending us back to my own time? Any number of things could go wrong, Thorn. I could end up in another year and be completely out of my element, with no one to turn to for help. That or I could lose the baby in the transition. Or what if the baby only exists in this time? That by leaving this time and place and entering mine, I found that I was no longer pregnant? If the transfer itself didn't destroy me, that certainly would. I want this baby, Thorn. If we're weighing gambles, that has some pretty high stakes, too."

"If I were forced to choose between you and our son, I would choose that you live, Neeake," he informed her somberly. His eyes reflected the depth of his own distress. "I hope. . . . I believe that you can travel to your era without harm to either of you. Contrarily, if you stay here, there is every likelihood that Tenskwatawa will kill you both, if only to spite me."

"What if I refuse to go?" she suggested stubbornly.

"The choice is not yours to make," he informed her, his gentle tone softening the blunt statement somewhat.

"What do you mean? That you can send me back whether I wish to go or not?" she inquired, stunned at the prospect.

"I believe so," he replied. "After all, did I not summon you here without consulting your wishes? However, I do not wish to part from you with anger between us, my love."

"Well, I don't want to part from you at all," she countered.

"Nor do I. A day without you will seem a year."

She gave a forlorn laugh. "Easy for you. As for me, a minute away from you will amount to approximately one-hundred-and-eighty-three years, give or take a few weeks. That's an awfully long time to ask a woman to wait for you, Thorn. Especially when there is no guarantee that she'll ever see you again." Her words ended on a harsh sob.

"I'll come for you, my lovely wife," he vowed. "If I must use my last breath, the final drop of blood in my body, I will come for you."

She blinked up at him through tear-misted lashes. "You'll come for me? Does that mean that you will attempt to come to my world? Wouldn't it be simpler just to call me back to you? Thorn, you don't even know if it's possible for you to travel from this time to mine."

"I found a way to bring you here, did I not? I shall find a means to come to you. I would not have you return here only to have Tenskwatawa resume his attempts to harm you. In your world, you and the baby will be safe from him, and I will join you there as soon as I possibly can."

"Thorn, dangers lurk in my world, too. Possibly more so than here. Everyday, hundreds of people are mugged, beaten, robbed, killed. Who can say if I would be safer here or there?"

"But you will be with your family, with your parents and brothers who will surely look after you. You will be in a world that is familiar to you, and near your mother, which will be of much comfort as you near the time to give birth."

"I'd rather be with you. Especially then. In either place."

He nodded. "If all goes well, I will be with you to welcome our child into the world. However, I think I would rather come to you and try living in your time, to experience the many wonders you have described to me, than to continue living on in mine after all you have told me is to transpire. My life here, as I have known it, will no longer exist."

Nikki made yet another attempt to sway him. "It's not all microwave ovens and automobiles and modern marvels. While I'll admit that the conveniences are wonderful, we have plenty of problems with which to contend." She ticked a few examples off on her fingers. "We have crime, corruption, pollution, the drug problem, gang wars, disease, hunger, poverty, racial prejudice, teen suicides, discord among nations and religions, the nuclear threat, natural and manmade disasters of immense proportions. All in all, sometimes I think the world is going to Hell in a handbasket with the Devil holding the handle."

Silver Thorn's smile was as bleak as hers. "Has it not been thus since the dawn of time?" he asked softly. "Does not each age have its own distinctive problems?"

"Then let me stay in yours," she implored, her heart in her eyes. "At least we'll be assured of facing our difficulties together. I don't want to live in a world without you in it, Thorn. You're my life. You're every breath I take, every prayer I've ever prayed. If you send me away, I'm afraid we'll never find each other again. And without you, I'll die a little more each day."

"As will I, little goose. But it must be done." He drew her close to his heart, cherishing the feel of her in his arms. "Do you feel that?" he asked after a moment. "Our hearts beat as one. That is how I shall find you again, my sweet. I need only search for the missing half of myself."

Twenty-three

Neither of them slept much that night. Knowing it could very well be their last together, they made sweet tender love, rested briefly, and indulged their passions again. And again. It was as if they could not get enough of one another. Even in those short interludes of respite, they clung tightly to each other. Each kiss, each touch, every lingering caress was an expression of their deep, abiding love. A treasure to be hoarded against the long, dark days ahead.

All too soon, dawn lit the eastern sky. "It is time, Neeake," he told her.

She clung to him, holding him at her side. "Not yet. Please. Not yet. Give us a few more days together." Tears clogged her throat, preventing further speech.

Gently, but firmly, Silver Thorn disentangled her arms from around his neck. He kissed her lightly, tasting the tears on her lips. Then he rose, leaving her alone on the mat. "I am not sure I have the spell determined correctly as yet," he said, offering the only bit of hope he could without backing down from his decision. "Perhaps it will work, and perhaps not. We will not know until we try."

Nikki sniffled and swiped at her cheeks, drying them with her hand. "All right," she conceded wearily. "Let me get my things together. Or do you want me to leave them here? All except for my driver's license and my keys, of course, and some money. I'll need those to get home from the park, if that's where I find myself once you do succeed in sending me away."

He picked up on the anger lacing her last statement, and the sadness. Experiencing both himself, he could not fault her for venting her feelings, even though they were primarily directed at him. Just now, it was probable that she saw him as the sole villain, not another victim like herself.

"Take your possessions. Pack them in your back sack, as you did before."

She graced him with a sneer. "Sorry. I guess you don't want any reminders of me left behind for your next *wife* to find, do you?"

Before he gave any real thought to the move, his hand shot out to grasp her arm and swing her around to face him. "You are right. I will need no reminders of you, Neeake. But not for the reasons you claim. I need none, for you have carved your image into my mind, your name into my heart, your very essence into my soul. I could not erase you from them if I lived five lifetimes."

He hauled her against him and kissed her once more—hard. Then he left her to pack, waiting for her outside the wigewa, where he wouldn't be tempted to touch her again or to delay their parting.

Nikki could barely see for the tears streaming down her face. She dressed hurriedly and stuffed the rest of her things haphazardly into her backpack. Then she had to unpack half of it to find her purse, and a tissue so she could wipe her nose. Hurt, anger, sorrow, rebellion. All this and more boiled around inside her until she could scarcely function. Her head throbbed; her hands shook, and she felt more than a little nauseous.

As she was cramming her things into her purse once more, her wallet fell out and flipped open to the photo compartment. Her own image stared up at her from its plastic casing—not a studio portrait, but a snapshot of

Nikki sitting on her bed at home, with her cat in her lap. Sheree, a fellow teacher and Nikki's best friend, had snapped the photo just a few weeks ago.

Impulsively Nikki ripped the picture from her wallet. "You won't heed my wishes, Thorn, so why should I give a tinker's damn about yours?" she murmured defiantly. "You're going to have at least one reminder of me, whether you want it or not." With that, she shoved the photo into the leather pouch Silver Thorn used as a traveling bag. Her small act of rebellion didn't make her any happier, but it did help to release some of her anger. She joined him outside, feeling slightly less hateful, though still bitter.

Silver Thorn was extremely frustrated. Nikki's nerves were shot. All day, he had been experimenting with various ways to send her home. Each had failed. He'd tried having her dress exactly as she'd been upon her arrival. He'd revised the incantations several times. He even attempted to "re-empower" the special amulet that had brought her to him at the start. Nothing worked. Still, each time Silver Thorn was ready to try again, he and Nikki became tense with anxious anticipation that this would be their last moment together in his world.

By the end of the day, Nikki was emotionally drained. Silver Thorn was baffled and annoyed, but not enough to end the project.

"We shall try again tomorrow," he grumbled.

"It's no use," Nikki told him irritably. "You're whistling into the wind, Thorn, and turning me into a basket case in the process. Can't we just give it up and go back to Wapak?"

She was hoping that, if he would agree, Black Hoof and Konah could talk some sense into him. Such was her reasoning when she added, "Maybe there the transferral will work. After all, I'm familiar with that area."

He mulled this over for several minutes and, to her surprise, agreed. "Yes, perhaps that is what is wrong. We shall return to Hog Creek tomorrow, for that is the place where you live in your modern time. If that fails also, we will go on to Wapakoneta."

Three days later, after a hasty departure from Tecumseh's camp and another swift journey by canoe, Nikki and Silver Thorn once again found themselves traversing the Fort Amanda Trail in search of her family's farm. This time, however, they were accompanied by warriors from both Peahchaete's and Black Hoof's bands. Locating the precise spot along the river was not as easy as Nikki had thought. Most of the present land was still densely wooded, whereas in her day it had been cleared for cultivation. Just as she was about to give up and give in to Silver Thorn's demands that they choose any place that seemed near enough to effect the time transference, she spotted something familiar.

"There!" she exclaimed excitedly. "See that big rock in the middle of the creek? We always wondered how it came to be there, one huge boulder all by itself with no others around it. We used to speculate that maybe it was the remains of a meteorite."

She led the way with confidence. "I know where I am now."

Within minutes she had located a small oak tree set apart from the others along the riverbank. "This has got to be it. It's far enough from the creek to stand out into the field, and you can see the rock from here at about the right angle."

Nikki knelt and started to scoop a hole in the earth.

"What are you doing?" Silver Thorn inquired.

"I'm going to bury my message to Mom and Dad, as we planned before," she told him. "That way, if you don't succeed in sending me back, they might still know what happened to me."

"I will succeed," he declared determinedly.

"Not if I have anything to say about it," she mumbled.

He helped her bury the missive, and they got on about the business of transporting her to her own era. Again, nothing happened. Despite repeated attempts and amid much grousing and griping, Nikki's feet remained firmly planted in 1813.

While Silver Thorn's mood soured, Nikki's improved. With each failed attempt, hope blossomed that she would not be parted from Silver Thorn after all—at least not by nearly two hundred years. "Has it occurred to you that maybe I'm not meant to return to my own time?" she suggested mildly. "That the Spirits aren't answering your request because they want me to stay here?"

Silver Thorn speared her with a disgruntled look. "We will try again at Wapakoneta."

And so they did. With no better results. Here, however, Nikki had reinforcements of her own to help argue her case.

Black Hoof offered to assign a half dozen of his best warriors to guard her. Likewise, Konah said, "Neeake can stay in our lodge where she will be within our sight day and night. With all of us to watch over her, surely no harm will befall her."

Silver Thorn remained unconvinced. "You do not know the depth of Tenskwatawa's madness. I fear he would do anything, risk everything, to wreak his twisted vengeance and to prove himself more powerful than any other living mortal. To do so, he must eliminate his rivals, even those persons he mistakenly deems a threat to himself. That includes Neeake and my son, as well as me and Tecumseh and any other man or woman who would get in the way of his ambitions. I would not put you all in peril to protect what is mine to defend. By sending Neeake back to her own time, I put her out of his reach and no one else is placed in danger."

That put another slant on the matter, one which Nikki had not heretofore considered. While she still didn't want to leave, neither did she want to put anyone else's life in jeopardy.

"So, what do we do?" she asked dispiritedly. "Just keep trying? For how long, Thorn? I know you are impatient to return to Tecumseh's camp and resume your efforts to save him."

"It has come to me that we might achieve our purpose better if we retreat to the caves. It is there that I performed the rites and contacted the Spirits which brought you to me. The caves have always held a mysterious aura of power. Something mystical lingers there, in the air and the rock, in the cool, quiet depths of the earth."

A shiver ran up Nikki's backbone. "Probably nothing more than a lot of ionized air," she argued, offering a more scientific explanation of the phenomenon of the caves. "It's probably not the caves at all, but the waterfall. As it cascades over the rock, it does something to the surrounding atmosphere. I don't know the precise chemistry of it, but I think it charges the atoms in the air with added energy or some such thing."

"Then we will add this energy to that of the Spirits," he decided. "Perhaps that is what is needed to make the spell work properly."

While she hoped he was wrong in this most recent assumption, Nikki feared he was right. Indeed, there did seem to be something unusual, eerie, maybe even supernatural about the area surrounding the caves. She'd felt it that first morning while touring them. That spooky feeling of walking among ghosts—or spirits. She was very much afraid that, if it were at all possible to send her back to the future, it would happen there.

Thus, Nikki bid a tearful farewell to her new/old family,

her very young grandmothers and grandfathers, great-aunts and uncles and cousins, with a growing certainty that she would never see them again. "Do not weep, granddaughter," Konah told her, giving her a final embrace. "We will meet again, if only in the afterlife. When your time comes to join us there, I will wait for you on the star-path to guide your way."

"The Milky Way," Nikki noted sadly. "I will think of you whenever I see it."

A small party of Black Hoof's warriors escorted them to the caves, which allowed them to travel both day and night to better skirt the areas around the forts and generally expedited the entire trip. They arrived at the caves in half the time it had taken Nikki and Silver Thorn to travel the same distance by themselves. Not wanting their presence to interfere with the great magic Silver Thorn was attempting to perform, the warriors retreated downstream, where they would wait at a designated spot along the river for Silver Thorn to join them when he had accomplished his mission.

Alone once more, Nikki threw her pride to the winds and again begged Silver Thorn to relent. "Please don't do this, Thorn. I love you. I don't want to leave you. I'm dreadfully afraid that if we part now, I'll never see you again. You're having a hard enough time trying to get this spell to work. It could take a miracle to find the right one to bring you to me."

"I will come to you," he said. "Nothing but death can stop me from finding you."

"When? When I'm eighty-two?" she countered. "I don't want to spend my life without you. I've only just found you, damn it!" Hot, stinging tears rolled down her cheeks. "Please, Thorn. Let me stay. I'll do anything else you ask. You can lock me in a cave if you want, someplace

Tenskwatawa will never find me. Just don't send me away from you."

He held her close, feeling her heart beat next to his. Then he kissed her, tasting the salt of her tears on her lips. And on his. "Let me love you just once more before we part."

She raised her face to his "Yes. I need for you to hold me, to love me with all your might. I need one final memory to carry me through until we can be together for always."

Even in August, the grass along the riverbank was lush and green and fragrant. Tiger lilies nodded gracefully beneath a windblown spray from the waterfall. There, the two lovers lay themselves down.

Nikki didn't think Silver Thorn had ever appeared more magnificent than he did now—so strong and proud and handsome. His hair shone in the sunlight like polished onyx; his eyes glittered like stars. He resembled a bronze statue come to life.

But no bloodless statue could have loved her as he did then. Only a man, this man, could hold her so tenderly, so possessively—branding her with his hot kisses, adoring her with every breath, each caress, with whispered words and every beat of his heart.

Her own heart soared with the blessing of their love, even as it broke at the thought of leaving him. Her tears bathed him, and her kisses blotted them away. Through misty eyes, she memorized every cherished feature. With trembling fingertips, she worshiped his warm, hard body. When at length he was poised above her, she whispered, "Come into me, my love. I want to be filled with you so thoroughly that I cannot tell where your body begins or mine ends."

"I will always be one with you, my beloved," he replied huskily. "You are a part of me, and I of you. Time and distance alone can never sever what we share."

He entered her slowly, reverently; their eyes locked as their bodies united. The sweet sensation of being so intimately joined overwhelmed them both. Wrapped in splendor, they rode the winds of passion on wings of ecstasy, losing themselves in a world where nothing or no one else existed.

All too soon, reality intruded. Silently, they rose and dressed. Silver Thorn had to assist her with the buttons on her dress, for Nikki's fingers were shaking too badly to manage them on her own. Then it was time. The moment they both dreaded could be withheld no longer.

Silver Thorn held out his hand to her. "Come," he said solemnly. "Once before, in this very place, I asked you to trust me. I ask it again. Trust me, my love."

Reluctantly, she placed her palm in his. "If you don't come for me, I'll never forgive you." Her words caught on a sob.

He led her to a spot nearer the falls than where she'd appeared originally. When she commented on this, he explained, "The sun and the moon are in different places now than they were before. I am trying to take that into account."

There was a rocky path leading through the water to the base of the falls. He pulled her along behind him, holding tightly to her hand. "Step carefully, little goose. The rocks are slippery."

They stopped at the foot of the cascade, and he handed her the amulet. "When you reach your time, drop the charm into the water. When I see it appear, I will know that you have made it back into your own world without mishap."

"What happens if I forget to drop it? Do I come back here?" she asked almost hopefully.

"If you do not release it, I will not be able to retrieve it so that I may later use it to come to you," he told her somberly. The amulet has been endowed with great powers. Without it I may truly never find you or our son again."

"I'll drop it," she vowed, frightened anew by his dire prediction. "The moment I am in my time, I'll let loose of it."

There, in the mist, with the thunder of the waterfall in their ears and the sun forming a bright rainbow above their heads, he claimed one last kiss. Their lips clung, loath to part, and she felt his agony as well as hers. "The pain in my heart is killing me," she murmured. "I feel as if I'm about to die."

He nodded, his gaze too bright, as if he were holding back tears of his own. Silver eyes held fast to those of violet, and he began to chant. A tingling began within her. He must have felt it through her palm, for he released her hand. When she tried to grab hold again, he shook his head, but let the very tips of his fingers hover just below hers.

Her vision clouded. She wobbled dizzily. She felt herself falling, spinning, as if she were being sucked into the heart of the falls. As she cried out, she heard him call to her as if from a great distance, "Go in joy and love, my dearest heart. And wait for me. I will come."

As Silver Thorn watched, his big heart aching, Neeake faded into the mist. It was if the cascading water swallowed her up, absorbing her into its midst. She was gone. His beloved. His wife. The most wondrous thing in his life. Gone. He blinked hard to no avail. The tears fell. Silver Thorn sank to his knees, his dark head bowed to his chest. There, with the water pounding down around him, he wept—and prayed that he would someday soon be reunited with his wife and child.

Twenty-four

Nikki sputtered and thrashed and finally found her footing. Gasping for air, she clung to the rock at the foot of the falls, waiting for the dizziness to pass. For several seconds, she couldn't even raise her head—didn't really want to. In her heart, she knew what she would find, and she couldn't help wanting to put off reality for just a little while longer.

"Oh, Thorn!" she sobbed. "Oh, Thorn! Why, my darling? Why?"

Over the splash of the falls, a voice called, "Hey, lady! Are you okay? You're not supposed to be out there you know. If the park authorities see you, they'll give you a ticket."

Nikki's head jerked up. She focused blearily toward the riverbank and the direction of the caller. A group of four teenagers, two girls and two boys, lined the bank, all watching her anxiously. "I . . . I'm all right," she croaked. "I got dizzy and I guess I fell in."

"You need some help?" one boy asked. "We can wade out and get you."

Nikki nodded weakly. "Yes. Please."

It was then she remembered the pendant, still clutched tightly in her hand. Slowly, she opened her fingers and let it fall watching as it plunged below the surface. The rush of water caught it immediately, thrusting it against the rock. It hit twice before lodging in a crevice. There it stuck, shimmering up at her through the surging current.

She was still staring at it forlornly when the two boys reached her. "You sure you're okay?" the shorter one questioned. "You didn't hit your head or anything?"

Nikki turned, and mustered a weak smile. "I don't think I did. Nothing hurts." *Except my heart*, she added silently.

"You're lucky you didn't drown," the other teen said. "Especially with that backpack strapped to you."

Nikki nodded. "I just hope it's as waterproof as my nephew claims it is."

With a boy on each side of her, holding her elbows, Nikki waded slowly to shore. There, she sank down on the grassy bank and heaved a weary sigh. "Thanks, fellas. I'll be okay on my own now."

She wanted to be alone, to collect her thoughts, to mourn her loss, to try to figure out if she'd landed in the right place and time. She'd already guessed that she was back in the same park, at the same waterfall. At least she assumed so.

"You sure?" one of the girls questioned. "We can stay with you while the guys go for help. Or we can walk you up to the gift shop, if you want."

"There are rest rooms up there, aren't there?" Nikki recalled.

"Yeah, rest rooms and a snack bar," the second girl said. "You really should get out of that wet dress. Maybe buy a T-shirt or something to change into."

"I have jeans and a shirt in my pack, if they didn't get soaked, too," Nikki told them.

She plucked at the clinging cloth of her gray dress, one Mrs. Galloway had given her, the one Silver Thorn had helped her remove the sleeves from the day she'd been picking berries. Bittersweet memories flooded through her, making tears brim in her eyes. Hastily, she blinked them back. Now was not the time to give in to her misery, not with other people around to wonder and ask questions she wasn't prepared to answer.

She sighed again and pushed herself slowly to her feet. "That rest room and some dry clothes are sounding better by the minute," she admitted. "And I really wouldn't mind it if you'd tag along. I'm still a little wobbly."

"You're not diabetic or anything, are you?" the taller boy asked. "I mean, that dizzy spell and all. I was wondering if you need to take some medication or something."

"No." Nikki gave a slight shake of her head. "Nothing like that. I . . . I think I'm pregnant." Her voice broke. By sheer will, she pulled herself together and added, "I haven't had much to eat today, either. That's probably what made me so shaky. I'll get some juice or something at the snack shop and be just fine."

When they reached the gift shop-snack bar, Nikki thanked her escorts and tried to pay them for their efforts. They refused, saying, "Just chalk it up to our good deed for the week. Robby here is an Eagle Scout. Maybe he'll get a ribbon for it or something."

Nikki nodded. "I hope so. You all deserve a reward for being so kind. You're a great group of kids. I hope your parents and teachers appreciate what they've got."

She waved them on their way, assuring them once more that she could fend for herself now. If only she could make herself believe that blatant lie!

Inside the rest room, Nikki stared at the image reflected back at her in the mirror. God! She looked like a hag! Her dress was sopping. Her hair was straggling in dripping strands around her face. Her eyes were swollen from crying and had dark circles beneath them. Her cheeks were hollow. . . . Wait a minute! Nikki blinked and looked again. No, she wasn't imagining things. Her cheeks were sunken, and she actually had prominent cheekbones again, for the first time in years. And a clean, crisp jawline. And collarbones that showed! And an honest-to-goodness waist-line!

Had she not been so thoroughly miserable, Nikki would have been delighted at the thinner aspects of her new self. But the red eyes told their own tale. As did the sorrow lurking in their violet depths. Her hands drifted from her waist to her stomach, lingering there as she uttered a quick, fervent prayer that she still carried Silver Thorn's baby. That was one of the primary things she would have to determine for her own peace of mind.

But there were others things to tend to more immediately. Quickly, she dug her clothes out of her backpack, grateful to find them dry, and changed into them. The jeans bagged dreadfully, and she had to rig a belt for them by using the lacing from her doeskin dress. Though she'd left her damp panties on, her bra was too wet to wear. Fortunately, the T-shirt was roomy enough to bunch into a knot at her waist and pooch the fabric out to hide the fact that she wore nothing beneath it. Deftly, she replaited her frazzled French braid and started to work on her face. A whisk of blemish cream, a touch of light shadow on her lids, a flick of mascara, and a dab of lip gloss, and she'd done the best she could to prepare herself to face the modern world.

Upon exiting the rest room, Nikki passed the door of the gift shop. Outside was a newspaper rack. Her gaze caught on the date—August 10, 1996. Nikki let out a deep breath. They'd done it! She was back in her own time, on the exact date she had calculated it should be, after having been gone for a little over two months.

Then her eye caught a poster in the shop window, and her breath snagged again, this time in dismay. Her picture, photocopied in black-and-white, stared back at her from the poster, with her name in big block letters and the word "Missing" at the top. A description followed: Twenty-nine years old; teacher; five feet, three-inches; one-hundred-forty pounds; dark hair; violet eyes. Disappeared on or about June 4, 1996. Car found abandoned in parking lot of nature park. Any information, contact sheriff's department immediately.

Nikki gaped at the poster as shock waves rippled through her. Somehow, caught up in her own troubles, she'd momentarily forgotten what her family must be going through. Now it hit her anew, with full force. Her car had been found. She was still missing, after two months. Her parents must be frantic! No . . . by now they must surely think she was dead, abducted and killed by some maniac and buried in some remote ravine or woods.

"Oh, my God!" she gasped. "I've got to let them know I'm alive. I've got to contact them immediately! I've got to get home!"

Her mind in a whirl, Nikki raced for the parking lot, searching for her keys as she ran. Just as quickly, she skidded to a stop. Her car! Her car had been found . . . and probably towed away! She scanned the lot with frenzied haste, trying to remember where she'd parked. There! By that tree with the drooping branches. She'd thought it would provide enough shade that her car wouldn't be so hot when she got back to it. Obviously, someone else had the same idea. A black Oldsmobile was parked where her little red Toyota should have been.

"Damn!" Her shoulders slumped. "Of course, it's gone! They wouldn't just leave it here. But where is it? At home? In an impound lot? Where?"

She had half a mind to call the sheriff's department and ask, when it dawned on her that they'd surely ask where she'd been all this time. And what would she say to that? She could imagine it now. *Well, officer, it's like this. I found this charm, and the next thing I knew I was back in 1813, talking with Tecumseh's brother. One thing led to another. We got married; I got pregnant, and then he sent me back so the Prophet wouldn't kill me.* Oh, yeah! That would go over real big! They'd lock her in a rubber room for the rest of her natural life!

"I've got to think about this," she reasoned aloud. "I can't do anything impulsive or I'll just make things worse, though it's hard to see how they could get much worse than they are now."

Retracing her steps, Nikki hesitated at the door of the snack bar. What if they recognized her? A patron exited, swinging the glass doors wide. Nikki caught her reflection in the glass. It startled her anew to see how thin she appeared compared to the way she'd looked before. Her glance darted to the poster, and she almost laughed. "The least they could have done was give the police a decent picture of me!" she grumbled. No, anyone seeing that picture of a chunky, apple-cheeked teacher would never know that woman and Nikki were one and the same person. Still, just to be certain, Nikki donned her sunglasses before entering the store.

Inside, she bought a Coke and a package of cupcakes and found a chair at a small table near the window. "Okay, kiddo. Think this through," she commanded herself silently. "Fact: You have no transportation. You need transportation. So, whom do you call?"

Her gaze swung to the phone hanging just outside the building, visible through the window. "Not the authorities," she decided. "Not until I can come up with a plausible excuse for a two-month absence and worrying my family to death."

She pondered if she even dared call her parents yet. What if their phone were being tapped? They did that sometimes in the movies when someone had been kidnapped. It was probably a silly notion, but it might be better to exercise caution anyway, just in case. Besides, her mom would go spastic, and Nikki wasn't ready to deal with that yet, anymore than she was ready to deal with the police.

So that left her brothers. Again, Nikki hesitated. As much as she loved them, she didn't trust them not to notify her parents immediately, even if she told them not to. And as soon as her parents knew, so would the authorities. Who, then? Who could she call?

"Sheree!" Her best friend's name leapt into her brain, and Nikki wondered why she hadn't thought of her in the first place. They'd been friends forever. Sheree was loyal, dependable, and a self-admitted sucker for anyone in trouble. She even jokingly referred to herself as a Saint Bernard in disguise. And Sheree could keep a secret when she had to. She'd guarded plenty of Nikki's confidences in the past, just as Nikki had done for her.

Nikki didn't have to call the information operator. She knew Sheree's number by heart. But she did place the call collect. "Please don't let me get that blasted answering machine!" she prayed, waiting for the phone to ring.

Her plea was answered. Sheree picked up on the third ring. "Hello?"

Nikki heard the operator ask Sheree if she would accept a collect call from a Nichole Swan. She also heard Sheree's quick gasp. "Nichole? You're sure, operator? Yes! Yes! I accept!" Then, "Nikki? Nikki? Is that really you?"

"It's me, Sheree. I need . . ."

Sheree interrupted, shrieking into Nikki's ear. "Where are you? Where have you been? God, girl, how could you worry us all like this? Do you know we thought you were dead?"

"Sheree! If you'll just shut up and let me get a word in edgewise, I'll explain."

Sheree quit talking so suddenly, Nikki wondered if they'd been disconnected. "Are you still there?" Nikki queried.

"And waiting with baited breath," came the irate answer.

"First, I haven't been murdered or maimed, thank you

very much for inquiring," Nikki said mockingly. "I can't explain everything on the phone, but I need your help."

"What kind of help, if I'm allowed to ask?" Sheree was obviously still miffed.

"Can you come get me? I'm sort of stranded here without my car."

"Stranded where?"

"At the park. At the caves."

"The same place your car was found?"

"Yes. It's obviously been towed away or something. I have no idea where it is now."

"It's parked in your Dad's barn lot," Sheree informed her. "Nikki? Haven't you called you mom and dad yet? Girl, they're absolutely distraught!"

"I'm sorry, but I can't just yet. And I want your word that you won't call and tell them, either. I don't want them to find out over the phone. I want to tell them what happened in person. In private. Which reminds me. Am I correct in assuming that the police have been looking for me?"

"You bet your sweet butt they have!" Sheree declared heatedly. "There's been a manhunt . . . excuse me, a woman-hunt . . . the likes of which hasn't been seen since that tiger escaped from the circus last summer. Where in God's green acres have you been?"

"Later," Nikki promised. "I just want your promise that you won't notify any of my family or the authorities until we have a chance to talk." At the prolonged silence on the other end of the line, she added, "Please, Sheree? It's vital."

Her friend's sigh was audible. "Okay. I promise."

"Can you come get me right away?" Nikki pressed. "It's two o'clock, and it will take you about two-and-a-half hours to get here. I don't want to hang around here any longer than I have to. Someone might recognize me."

"Are you in trouble?" Sheree asked. "You didn't rob a bank or anything, did you?"

"I'm not in that kind of trouble," Nikki assured her. "But I need a friend right now more than I ever have." Her voice thickened with fresh tears. "Hurry, Sheree. I need you."

"I'm coming," Sheree replied instantly. "You just sit tight."

"There's a gift shop and snack bar just inside the park entrance. I'll wait for you there. But the park closes at sundown, so don't dawdle. And don't get lost. I know you have trouble finding your way out of a paper bag, let alone driving all this way alone."

"I could bring someone with me," Sheree suggested hopefully. "One of your brothers, maybe?"

"No. Come alone. And not a word to anyone."

"Tell me how to get there."

"I don't have a map handy," Nikki reminded her. "Mine was in the glove compartment of my car, which is gone."

"Never mind. I'll get a map of my own. I think I can find it. I rode down there with your parents when you were first declared missing. I . . . I helped search for your body." Now it was Sheree who sounded close to tears.

"Don't cry," Nikki murmured. "I'm here. A bit worse for wear and ragged around the edges, but here. We'll have a good sob session when I see you. Just hurry."

Twenty-five

Sheree slammed the door of the motel room she and Nikki had just rented for the night. "Okay, can the silent mummy act, Nikki," she commanded smartly. "Spill it. From the top, and don't leave anything out."

Twenty minutes later, the petite blonde cuddled her sobbing friend and suggested gently, "Now why don't you tell me the truth, Nikki, instead of feeding me this line of bunk about Indians and the War of 1812? Honey, you know you can tell me anything and I'll understand. Except maybe some tale about being abducted by little green men from Mars. So, what's the real story? Were you kidnapped? Raped? A victim of temporary amnesia? Held captive in the woods by some nutso survivalist?"

Nikki jerked away and glared at her friend. "No!" she exclaimed. "It happened just as I said. I know it's hard to swallow, but it's the honest-to-God's truth."

Sheree patted Nikki's shoulder and sent her a sympathetic smile. "You know, you've been through a lot. You probably need some rest. Lots of rest. Why don't you just lie down and take a little nap? When you wake up, you'll feel loads better."

"Oh, sure!" Nikki scoffed. "I'm supposed to nap while you call the guys with the little white coat that ties up the back! Admit it, Sheree. You think I'm off my rocker!"

Sheree grimaced and shrugged. "I presume you've had a rough couple of months and might not be thinking straight," she hedged. "A lot of people react that way to trauma, so I've heard. They can't admit to reality, so they fabricate some wild tale instead."

"Well, I'm not one of them," Nikki declared angrily. "And I can prove it!"

Sheree merely arched an eyebrow and waited.

"Where do you suppose this came from if I'm making all of this up out of thin air?" Nikki charged. She held out her arm, displaying the engraved silver wristband she still wore. "Silver Thorn gave this to me as a wedding present. It's the same as a wedding band."

"It . . . it's lovely," Sheree offered hesitantly. "Can I get a closer look at it?"

Though reluctant to remove it, Nikki did. She handed it over to her friend, saying, "You won't find any jeweler's markings on it, Sheree, if that's what you're looking for."

Sheree's fair skin reddened with guilt. "Sorry. It is a beautiful band. Very intricate. I like the flowers, but why geese? Why not doves or hummingbirds?"

"Because he made it especially for me. He interpreted my name as Neeake, which in Shawnee means wild goose."

"Uh, huh." Sheree handed back the wristband. "Is that it? The sum total of your proof?"

Nikki's eyes glittered with irritation. "No, Miss Doubting Thomasina. Get a gander at this!" From her backpack, Nikki drew forth her doeskin dress and moccasins.

"Good heavens! What did you do, Nikki? Buy out some western-wear store? That dress must have cost you a pretty penny, even if it is stained in places. And those moccasins look as if they've been worn around the globe at least twice."

Nikki glowered. "Well, Sheree, when you don't have a car, you walk a lot, and they didn't have advanced forms of transportation in 1813. They had horses, canoes, and feet."

Sheree held up her hands in a gesture of peace. "Okay. Don't get your panties in a twist! I was just making an observation."

"Well, observe these, sweetie," Nikki suggested. With a flip of her wrist, she tossed a pile of photographs onto the bedspread next to her friend. Then she sat back against the headboard, arms folded over her chest, and waited.

Sheree thumbed slowly through the pictures. With each one, her expression grew a little more puzzled, a little more unsure. "Good heavens, Nikki! Where did you get these?" she inquired softly.

"I shot most of them myself, with my Polaroid camera. Now do you believe me?"

"I want to," Sheree admitted, confused. She dragged her fingers through her short, stylish bob, for once not even caring that she was mussing it. "I'm trying to. God, Nikki, seeing these, it's hard not to. Tell me about these photos. Where were they taken? Who are the people in them?"

Nikki sorted through the stack. A sad smile curved her lips. "This is Silver Thorn. I made him a shirt out of rawhide and didn't smoke it long enough. When it got wet, it shrank. Lord, but he was mad! Especially when I laughed so hard at the way he looked. After he cooled off, he let me take this picture of him."

"Geez! Look at those muscles!" Sheree exclaimed in open admiration. "No wonder you went ape over him, even if he does look quite a bit older than you."

"He's forty-five," Nikki supplied in answer to her friend's questioning look. "A very fit forty-five."

"I'll say!" Sheree held up another snapshot. "And these people?"

Nikki pointed to the woman on the left. "That's Konah. She's my great-great-great-great-great grandmother. And that's her sister, Melassa, and Konah's two sons and daughter." She indicated another shot, one of an old man with long white hair. "That's Chief Black Hoof. He's my uncle, about six or seven times removed."

"I suppose it's hard to calculate that far back," Sheree allowed weakly. She picked up another photo and studied it with a frown. "This guy in the uniform looks sort of familiar, though I can't begin to guess why."

"Could be you've seen his portrait in a history book somewhere," Nikki suggested. "That's General William Henry Harrison, later to become President of the United States."

"Omigod! You're kidding!" Sheree took a harder, longer look. "You're not kidding, are you?"

Nikki smirked. "Nope. Want to see something else amazing?" She shuffled through the photos till she located one of the most recent of them. "Guess who this is?"

Sheree's eyes widened. "Holy moses! That's Tecumseh, isn't it? The nose, the chin, the eyes are just like those old pictures you've shown me of him."

"Only this isn't an old painting," Nikki reminded her. "This is a Polaroid snapshot with the date imprinted on it."

Sure enough, there in the lower corner was the date the photo had been taken. August 6, 1996. Sheree's mouth gaped.

"I might also point out that if these were snapshots of old portraits or paintings, they would be all cracked with age or show brush marks or old edges. These don't."

"I know," Sheree murmured shakily. "I believe you."

Nikki could sympathize with her shell-shocked friend. "It takes a while to get used to, I know. Give it a minute or two to sink in. Would you like me to get you a drink from the mini-bar?"

Sheree nodded mutely, still staring at the pictures.

Within minutes, Nikki handed Sheree a wine cooler. "Will this do or do you want something stronger?" she asked. "Sorry I can't join you; but as I told you, I'm pregnant. At least, I hope I'm still pregnant."

"What do you mean by that?" Sheree inquired with a frown. "Either you are or you're not. One way or the other. No halfway about it."

"Let me put it this way." Nikki's tone was somber. "I was pregnant in 1813. I'm not sure if I still am in 1996 or if by coming forward to my own time the fetus came with me or just sort of . . . evaporated . . . in the transition."

Sheree grabbed for Nikki's hand. "That . . . that sounds awful! I know how much you've wanted children. If you were pregnant, then, I hope you still are. When will you know for sure?"

Nikki blinked hard, trying to hold back the tears. "Whenever I can get to a drugstore and buy a pregnancy test, I suppose. Maybe we can do that tomorrow morning. Then, depending on what it reads, I'll follow up with a visit to my gynecologist, just to be certain."

Sheree flew off the bed, grabbed up her purse, and headed for the door. "I can't wait that long," she declared. "There's got to be a drugstore still open around here. Do you want to come with me or do you want to stay here?"

Nikki quickly collected her own purse and the room key. "I'm coming. Knowing you, you'll get lost going around the block, and I'll be sitting here wondering if you got caught in the middle of a robbery."

Sheree gave an indignant sniff. "Hah! I made it to the caves to pick you up, didn't I?"

Nikki nodded. "And how many times did you take a wrong turn on the way?" she asked archly. "Scout's honor, Sheree."

Sheree wrinkled her freckled nose. "Only three," she admitted ruefully. "You've got to admit, I am improving."

* * *

Nikki paced the floor and glanced at the dresser for the umpteenth time. She eyed her watch and groaned.

"I know," Sheree commiserated, passing Nikki as she paced past in the opposite direction. "This has got to be the longest twenty minutes on record. You'd think if they can send a man to live on a space station, they could invent a faster pregnancy test, for pity sake!"

"They do, but this one is supposed to be the most accurate," Nikki replied. Then she announced, "Two more minutes."

A minute and a half later, both women were hovering over the test vial, awaiting the results with more anticipation than revelers in Times Square on New Year's Eve.

"Come on. Come on!" Sheree urged anxiously. She poked Nikki. "Quick! Cross your fingers for luck!"

"Can I cross my legs instead?" Nikki joked. "I really have to pee, but I'm not leaving this spot until I see the results."

A cross slowly appeared in the open space, and Sheree grabbed Nikki's arm excitedly. "There!" she squealed. "That means it's positive, doesn't it?"

"I think so," Nikki replied anxiously. "God, Sheree! I can't remember! What did we do with those blasted instructions?"

Sheree was already on her knees, rifling through the trash basket. "Here." She produced the paper with a triumphant wave. Then, before Nikki could snatch it from her, she scanned the writing. A second later, she tossed it into the air and let out a shout. "Yes! Oh, wow! I'm going to be a godmother!"

Nikki sank onto the edge of the bed, weak with relief. This time her tears were those of joy. "Thank You, Lord," she whispered gratefully. "Thank You. Now, if You'll just bring Silver Thorn safely home to me, I'll never ask another thing of You."

* * *

Nikki was so tired. Her body felt as if every ounce of energy had been drained out through her toes. She couldn't seem to keep her eyes open, yet she couldn't sleep, either. Though her mind was a muddle, it wouldn't shut down and let her sleep. She lay in the dark, torturing herself with thoughts of Silver Thorn, her pillow damp with tears.

It was going on two in the morning when Sheree rose from the other twin bed and snapped on the bathroom light. She trudged over to Nikki's side of the motel room, tissue box in hand. "Here. I can't stand to hear you sniffling any longer."

"Tanks," Nikki mumbled, her swollen sinuses making her sound like some old-time movie thug.

Sheree perched on the edge of the bed. "As long as we're both awake, maybe our time would be better spent working out some sort of alibi for you."

Nikki's sudden chortle sounded more like a snort. "Geez, Sheree. You make it sound as if I'm about to hit the Most Wanted list and have my picture put on the post office wall!"

"Got news for you, dumplin'. It's already there, in at least a dozen Ohio counties, anyway. Not to mention all the posters in windows in supermarkets, carry-outs, pharmacies, department stores, bowling alleys . . ."

"Bowling alleys?" Nikki echoed in disgust.

"Yeah." Sheree grinned. "I should also tell you that I took the liberty of writing your name and phone number on some of those men's room walls. Don't be surprised if you get a few dozen phone calls from guys looking for a good time."

Nikki laughed outright. "Drat you, Sheree! You just can't stand to see me bawl, can you?"

"Nope. It makes my sinuses ache just to hear you. Now, about that alibi. Have you thought about what rational explanation you are going to give the police concerning your lengthy absence and lack of communication? Note that I stress the word *rational*, here. Obviously, you can't just blurt out the truth."

"I don't intend to," Nikki admitted. "You and my family are the only ones who will hear the real story. After all, I would like to keep my job."

"Speaking of which, I had to fight tooth and nail to get the superintendent to hire a temp to replace you rather than a full-time replacement like they wanted."

"They hired someone to take my classes?" Nikki didn't know why she was so shocked at this piece of news or why it hurt so much.

"As I said, a temp. As soon as they learn you're alive and kicking, you're back in like Flynn. That is, if you can keep your mouth shut and not blab everything about where you've been and what you've been doing."

Nikki's mind was already racing ahead to other matters. "What about my house? And my utilities? And my car payment? I just realized that I'm a couple of payments in arrears on just about everything. I'll be lucky if they haven't repossessed my refrigerator, food and all."

"That was a god-awful mess, by the way," Sheree told her, mugging a face. "Everything in there looked like a laboratory experiment gone amok by the time I got to tossing it out. Your father managed to get power of attorney, and he's kept your bills paid. Your mom wouldn't have it any other way. She was absolutely convinced you were alive and would turn up again. Talk about blind faith! Your philodendron croaked, but your aloe vera is doing fine and I think your cat is in heat. But then, so were you, so you have no gripe there, have you?"

"I guess not," Nikki agreed shamelessly. "But I have to wonder if I'll still have a job when the school board discovers that I'm pregnant."

"Why should they have anything to say about it?"

Sheree argued. "It's not like you're setting a bad example for your students or anything. After all, you are married . . ." Sheree's mouth made a round "O" as she caught Nikki's drift.

"Precisely. I have no legal marriage certificate, no proof, no visible husband. Nothing. Nix. Nada. Except a bun in the oven."

"We'll get you a ring. You can say your husband has the marriage certificate. He's . . ."

"He's what?" Nikki prompted. "I can't claim to be a widow and have him pop up several weeks later—I hope and pray. I have to make it all seem legitimate, especially since this all happened so suddenly and so mysteriously. So, if my bridegroom isn't on hand, where is he?"

"Out of the country," Sheree blurted. "On business."

"Doing what? Running drugs in Colombia? Acting as director of finance in Cuba? Panning for gold in the Amazon?"

Sheree's blue eyes lit up. "That's it! He can be studying native tribes in the rain forest! Who's to know any different? Then, later, if he doesn't show up, which I'm sure he will," she hastened to add, "you could always claim the headhunters got him."

"Cute, Sheree," Nikki grumbled. "And I suppose you're even willing to spring for the shrunken head I receive in the mail afterward."

Sheree shuddered. "I don't think we have to go that far." She thought for a moment, then said, "Okay, it would be better if he had some sort of employment that keeps him out of contact for long periods of time. That way you wouldn't have to fake having heard from him every time someone asks you. So, where does that lead us? A soldier of fortune? An archaeologist? A spy for the CIA? A . . ."

"Whoa! Back up a minute," Nikki interrupted. "I think I like that archaeologist bit, with maybe an accent on Native American tribes. We're talking remote areas with no phones, no fax, not even regular mail service if we say he's working in Central America somewhere. And when Silver Thorn does appear, he'll be able to converse intelligently on the subject without giving us away. It's perfect!"

"Better yet," Sheree added excitedly, getting into the flow, "if you had him working in Mexico, say the Yucatan for instance, he could have taken you there to see his digs, and that's why you couldn't contact anybody here for the past two months."

"Why Mexico instead of Guatemala or Panama?"

"Because you've been there and can describe it, silly," Sheree reminded her. "Also, you can go to Mexico without a passport. The only thing you need is valid photo I.D. and your birth certificate, both of which I know you carry in your wallet. You have to cover all your bases, Nikki, and the best lies are always the closest to the truth."

"Where do you learn all this outlandish stuff?" Nikki wanted to know.

"You know I've always had this passion for murder mysteries. Not everything of value is learned between the pages of a dusty old history tome or an encyclopedia, Nik. There are other books of worth."

"I stand corrected. All right, Sheree Drew, let's see what we have so far," Nikki suggested. She ticked them off on her fingers as she listed them aloud. "I fell madly in love with an archaeologist at first sight. Probably met him right there at the caves, which would account for leaving my car there. We would have left together in his. We rushed off to Mexico. Got married. Started a family. Couldn't phone home." Nikki paused and frowned. "No, that doesn't play right. I would have called before I left so Mom and Dad wouldn't worry. And I wouldn't have left my car in a public parking lot for that long."

"You tried to phone your parents, but they weren't home, and since they don't have an answering machine you couldn't leave a message," Sheree invented. "You wrote a letter instead, and mailed it from . . ."

Nikki filled in the blank. "From Cancun. But the postal service from Mexico is slow and unreliable, and they never got the letter. In fact," Nikki said thoughtfully, "I don't think they ever did get that postcard I mailed when I vacationed there two years ago. What about my car?"

"You called me, got my answering machine, left a message about your sudden trip, and asked me to retrieve your car for you. Unfortunately, my answering machine went on the blink, and I never got the message."

Nikki's eyes widened in appreciation. "Good grief, Sheree! You're so good at this, it's actually scary!"

Sheree sketched a mock bow. "You can thank me by letting me change the first diaper. Now, we've taken you from being an irresponsible, spoiled brat without a concern for anyone but yourself and transformed you into a love-struck newlywed whose best-meant actions went awry. That should settle a few ruffled feathers among law enforcement officials who have been beating the bushes for your body, the news media who have been milking this case for all it's worth, and certain nameless school officials who are nosier than either of the above. Have we missed anything?"

"Just one or two points," Nikki said. "How did I get to Mexico and back? Someone may check with the airlines."

"Private jet?" Sheree suggested. "And don't forget. I came down today to pick you up at the airport."

"Very good," Nikki approved. "One more thing. My husband has to have a name, and as his wife I need a new surname. Don't you think Silver Thorn sounds a little odd for our times?"

"I could go with Thorn for a last name."

"Yes, but I call him Thorn most of the time as a casual form of addressing him. Wouldn't it sound strange if I tend to refer to my husband by his surname more than his given name? I'm sure I will, if only from habit."

"Then turn it around. Call him Thorn, and refer to yourself as Mrs. Silver from here out."

Nikki tried it out. "Thorn Silver. Mrs. Thorn Silver. Nichole Silver. Sage Silver." She nodded. "I like it. It has sort of a continental ring to it, don't you think?"

"As in North American continent?" Sheree teased. "Yeah. By the way, who is Sage?"

"The baby," Nikki informed her. "Didn't I tell you? Thorn says the we're going to have a son this first time around."

"Nuts! I was hoping it would be a girl. Then you could name her after me."

Nikki shook her head. "If Thorn says its going to be a boy, you'd better bank on it. He's rarely wrong in his predictions."

"Then you have nothing to worry about," Sheree stated, sounding much more confident than she felt. "He'll find a way to get here. Sooner or later."

Nikki took the hand Sheree extended, clasping it hard. "I hope it's sooner. I don't know how long I can go on without him, Sheree. I've never loved like this before. I've never ached like this before. It hurts. It hurts so terribly."

Twenty-six

Nikki perched on the edge of her desk and stared at the neat towers of textbooks stacked against the classroom wall. One-hundred-and-fifty-five history texts ready to be handed out to as many unenthused students. School would be starting in three days, and Nikki had the weekend to rest up for the first-day havoc. No matter how prepared everyone was, or tried to be, the entire first week of a new school year was always chaos.

Thanks in large part to Sheree's bulldog attitude, Nikki had retained her teaching position. Of course, her past teaching record, which was excellent, and her tenure had also helped. And once the furor of her return had died down, everyone had seemed willing to accept Nikki's explanation of how matters had become so complicated and misconstrued.

However, those first few days back home had been tough. Nikki repressed a shudder as she recalled just how difficult it had been for everyone, especially those persons closest to her.

Sheree had been a blessing. On the way home from the caves, she'd remembered that Nikki needed a wedding ring. They'd stopped at a busy Columbus mall, where Nikki was no more than another anonymous Saturday shopper and wouldn't be easily remembered. At a popular chain jewelers, Nikki purchased an attractively engraved wedding band of brushed gold, with no stones, for just under a hundred dollars. It took most of her remaining vacation funds, but she paid cash for it. Her name wasn't even listed on the receipt, on the off chance that someone chose to check out a few details of Nikki's fabricated story.

With that out of the way, Sheree had driven straight to Nikki's parents' farm. They'd arrived at noon, when the Swans were inside eating their midday meal. So as not to startle anyone into a heart attack, Sheree had left Nikki outside while she went in first to break the news of Nikki's return as gently as possible. Within seconds, Nikki's parents and youngest brother were stampeding out the door, enveloping her in eager hugs and exclamations of joy.

Amid all the hurried, necessary explanations came the expected disbelief, followed by stunned acceptance when Nikki presented proof of her incredible adventure and, finally, the agreement that an invented tale of a hasty marriage to an archaeologist was infinitely better than actual fact. Nikki's other two brothers and their wives were promptly informed and included in the family conspiracy.

Their jubilant family reunion was quickly cut short, however. As soon as the local sheriff's office was notified of her return, the Swan farm was bombarded by deputies, detectives, and members of various news media. For hours, the place was a zoo, with everyone trying to talk at once and questions being fired right and left. Finally, it was over, but only temporarily. The next day it began again, with another visit from the detectives—"just to tidy up loose ends." This was followed by another wave of news reporters from more distant corners of the state. Nikki awoke to find her face plastered on the front pages of several newspapers and practically her whole life story revealed to one and all. On top of everything else, there was the school board to deal with, more concerns to address, more pointed questions to field. It was not a comfortable few days.

Then there were financial matters to untangle, the least

of which was getting her cablevision reinstated, which her father had inadvertently forgotten to pay; getting a new, unlisted phone number to alleviate all those annoying calls from reporters and nosy acquaintances; applying for a new driver's license and social security card under her married name; sneaking in a visit to her gynecologist to confirm her pregnancy. By the time she'd waded through all the inquiries and red tape, Nikki felt as if she'd been through the Inquisition and barely emerged with her skin intact. The only consolation was that her doctor had confirmed that Nikki was, indeed, pregnant, that everything appeared to be normal, and she could expect her baby sometime in March—just as Silver Thorn had predicted.

It had been a relief to escape into the hectic-but-normal pre-school routine and deal with the business of preparing for fall classes. At school and in her classroom, Nikki could immerse herself in the relatively trivial problems of class scheduling, missing supplies, outdated textbooks, and tedious teachers' meetings.

But as good as it felt to be getting her life back on track again, her work did not occupy enough of her time or attention to alleviate the loneliness, the nagging worry, or the heartache Nikki lived with daily. The nights were worst of all. She lay awake for long hours, reliving her short time with Silver Thorn, praying for his safety and his prompt arrival, even though she knew it would be weeks before he could even attempt to come to her. When she finally slept, her dreams were haunted by images of him, sometimes so real that she could feel the crisp texture of his hair sliding through her fingers, could smell the scent of his sun-kissed skin, could taste the tempting flavor of his lips on hers. Then she would awaken, alone and longing for him, and soak her pillow with her tears.

Nikki was jerked from her current reverie as Sheree poked her head through the classroom door and hailed, "Hey! Are you ready to call it a day and get out of here?

God knows we'll be spending enough time inside this pile of bricks for the next nine months. We don't need to rush it any more than we have to."

Nikki rose and dug her purse out of the desk drawer. "You're right," she replied snappily. "Let's blow this pop stand, girlfriend!"

"I got you something," Sheree said, presenting Nikki with a small shopping bag. "It's a welcome-home gift. Sorry, but I didn't take time to wrap it."

"You've done enough already," Nikki told her. "You didn't need to buy me anything."

Sheree shrugged. "Too late. Go ahead. Open it."

Nikki did and drew out an oak wedge with a brass plate on the front. Engraved on the shiny surface was her name. Her new name. Mrs. Nichole Silver.

"It's for your desk," Sheree informed her needlessly. "So the kids will remember to address you by your married name instead of your old one."

Nikki hugged her friend. "Thank you. I love it. I just hope Thorn doesn't have a hissy when he finds out I've changed his name around. After all, it is a rather presumptuous thing to do and a person's name is very important, private territory."

"I have a notion he's going to be too busy chasing you around the bedroom to care if you've changed his name to Adolph Hitler," Sheree commented on a laugh. "Besides, if he gives you any guff about it, just inform him that it's a whole lot more convenient and less expensive than to have to change the monogram on all your luggage and linens."

The two friends walked together to the parking lot. "What are your plans for the weekend?" Sheree inquired.

"I thought I'd go out to Mom and Dad's and check the tree tomorrow."

Several days after arriving home, once the excitement had died down, Nikki remembered burying the message to her parents beneath the fallen oak near the river. Not really expecting to find anything, but curious nonetheless, Nikki had walked down to the creek to have a look. To her delight, the leather-bound package was actually there! Worn and dirty, but still intact. Inside, Nikki had found her letter.

Oddly, the lottery tickets she'd also enclosed were nowhere to be found. Their peculiar absence had started Nikki thinking that perhaps Silver Thorn had returned to the tree and removed them for some reason she couldn't readily deduce. Which also led her to believe that if Silver Thorn were to try to contact her prior to attempting his own leap into the future, he would probably leave a message for her at the tree, surmising that she would check the location at least once, if only to look for her own missive. On that assumption, false though it might turn out to be, Nikki had convinced her father not to remove the tree from the spot where it had fallen; and since that day, she'd made regular pilgrimages to check it.

Now, Sheree rolled her eyes and groaned. "Not the tree again! You were just out there two days ago. This is getting ridiculous! Why don't you just pitch a tent and erect a blasted shrine or something?"

"I have to go. Thorn might try to contact me," Nikki insisted stubbornly.

Sheree sighed. "I give up."

"Do you want to drive out with me?" Nikki asked. "Or do you have a date with Dave?"

Sheree was currently interested in one of the deputies she'd met at the Swan farm the day Nikki had first returned home. Dave Dawson had been one of the officers assigned to the case and had accompanied the detectives when they'd arrived to question Nikki. He and Sheree had shared an instantaneous attraction and had been dating steadily since that day. Had Sheree not been her best friend—had she been any one of Nikki's numerous lesser friends, Nikki might have worried that Sheree would inadvertently "spill the beans." But Sheree was that friend in a million Nikki could trust with her life—and her deepest, darkest secrets.

"Dave has to work this weekend," Sheree said. "I was thinking that you and I might do a little shopping. Maybe pick up something for the baby."

Nikki grinned. Sheree was really into her role as godmother-to-be. "Well, I was considering a stop at the paint store," she confessed. "Just to snoop through the wallpaper patterns. If they have something I like, I thought I might order a couple of rolls for the nursery."

"Not without me along, you don't." Sheree was adamant. "No godson of mine is going to sleep in a room with a lot of sappy cartoon characters hovering over him like grinning gargoyles."

"So what did you have in mind?" Nikki teased. "Pictures of yourself, all decked out in wings and a halo, maybe?"

"Why not?" Sheree countered with mock indignation. Then she groaned. "Oh, good grief! Didn't you tell Mr. Hopeful to take a powder?"

Nikki's gaze followed Sheree's. There, leaning against the door of her car, a bouquet of flowers in hand, was the man she'd been dating casually prior to meeting Thorn. Unfortunately, Brian was also a reporter, and just now anyone connected with the media was not high on Nikki's list of people with whom she wanted to associate. In the past two-and-a-half weeks, he'd popped up unexpectedly several times, and Nikki wasn't certain what his motives were. He always seemed friendly enough—sometimes too friendly—and didn't seem at all discouraged by the fact that Nikki was now married to someone else.

Nikki sighed. "Drat! When is he going to take the hint? I've told him as politely as I can that he's a nice guy, but I'm married now, so please buzz off."

"What bugs me is that he's a reporter," Sheree stressed. "I can't help but wonder if he's still sniffing around for another twist to your story for a news article or if he's simply sniffing around your skirts like a bird dog after a piece of quail tail."

"I've tried to tell him that hunting season is over, that this quail, or perhaps more appropriately this *goose*, has already been bagged and to go bark up someone else's tree. Not only am I not available, I'm no longer interested. I'm beginning to wonder why I ever dated him in the first place."

"Apparently he's not getting the message," Sheree retorted dryly. "Seems to me he either needs a hearing aid or a swift kick in the pants."

"He seems to think that as long as Thorn isn't around, I'm still fair game. Maybe if I told him I'm pregnant, he'd take me more seriously," Nikki proposed.

"I thought you didn't want everyone to know that yet, just your family and close friends. If you tell old Brian, you might as well advertise the fact on the Internet."

"I know, but how else am I going to convince him that I don't want him around?"

Sheree smirked. "Tell him you caught some mysterious virus in the Yucatan. That ought to send him running with his tail tucked between his legs."

"And probably get me fired at the same time for exposing my students to some dread disease."

"Not if you say it's only communicable through intimate contact."

Nikki shook her head. "Thanks, but no thanks, Sheree. In no time flat, the whole community would think I had AIDS. I'll just have to find another means of discouraging Brian."

"Yeah," Sheree muttered as they neared the waiting reporter. "Like maybe voodoo. You grab him, and I'll rip out a hank of his hair for the doll."

Nikki had to laugh at the ridiculous suggestion. She was still chuckling when Brian Sanders held out the bouquet to her.

"What has you in such a wonderful mood today, gorgeous?" he inquired. "I haven't heard you laugh like that in some time."

Before Nikki could reply, Sheree piped up. "Gee, that says a lot about the depressing effect you have on people, doesn't it? Sure is a good thing you didn't want to be a comedian."

Brian glowered at the diminutive blonde and offered a smart comeback. "Maybe I'll give ventriloquism a go and let you be the dummy."

"Hey, you two!" Nikki intervened. "Let's not have a donnybrook in the parking lot. The principal frowns on that sort of behavior."

"Sorry," Brian grumbled. "Your little sidekick irritates me." He waved the bouquet Nikki had yet to accept. "These are for you."

Nikki's smile was polite, but cool. "They're lovely, Brian, but I really don't think it's appropriate for a married woman to accept flowers from another man, especially one she used to date. I'm sure you can find someone else who would appreciate them more."

"Probably, but I bought them for you. If you don't take them, they'll just go into the trash."

Sheree could see Nikki wavering. She reached forward and yanked the flowers from Brian's grasp. "In that case, I'll take them," she said. "I was going to visit my grandpa's grave this weekend, and this will save me a trip to the florist."

Appalled at her friend's behavior, but amused as well, Nikki was at a loss. "Uh . . . it was a lovely gesture, anyway, Brian. I've got to go now."

"To do what?" Brian wanted to know. "Wait by the phone for your truant bridegroom to call? Honey, that's no way to spend your time. You need to get out and have some fun. If nothing else, maybe it'll make your new hubby wake up and realize that if he doesn't pay attention to you someone else will."

Nikki went stiff with anger. "Thorn will be here as soon as he can," she replied frostily. "This separation is tough on both of us, but it couldn't be helped. I'm sure he's not enjoying it any more than I am, and I'm certainly not about to abuse his trust in me by painting the town with other men. Now, if you will please get away from my car, I have places to go and things to do."

Sheree grinned. "Why don't we go to the mall, Nik?" she suggested airily. "I hear Sears has a sale on satin sheets. After roughing it in the wilds for so long, I'll bet Thorn would get a charge out of slip-sliding around with you on a set of those."

Nikki blushed. Though she knew Sheree had deliberately made the outrageous statement to irk Brian all the more, in her estimation Sheree was laying it on pretty thick. "First the wallpaper store," she reminded her curtly.

"Yeah." Sheree's eyes lit up, and she sliced a snide look at Brian. "Got to spruce up the old master bedroom. No time to waste." With that parting shot, Sheree sauntered off to her own car.

Nikki sighed. "Look, Brian, I'm sorry about Sheree, but she's right—not very diplomatic, but right. I'm married now; you've simply got to accept that."

"I do," he countered, "But I don't see why you and I can't still go out once in a while. Just for dinner and a movie."

"No. Give it up, Brian. I made my choice."

He gave a mirthless laugh. "Women are famous for changing their minds, aren't they?"

"Not me. I found what I want." Nikki slid into her car and slammed the door, her face tight with repressed anger. She started the car and backed out of the slot, barely missing Brian's foot. Brian rapped on the hood. "See ya around, doll! I don't give up that easily."

Nikki gunned the motor and took great pleasure in watching Brian hastily sidestep as she peeled past him. "Jerk!" She punched the air-conditioning button and flipped the fan on high, hoping the icy air would help cool her temper as well as her temperature. "A couple of lousy dates, and he sticks like super glue! The damned fool thinks he's God's gift to women. Well, I have news for him. Next to Thorn, he's God's idea of a bad joke!"

Twenty-seven

Ohio—1813

Silver Thorn touched the amulet which hung from its cord around his neck. He'd watched anxiously until the pendant had appeared beneath the surface of the water, his relief that Neeake had reached her own time safely tempered by his sorrow at being parted from her. How many times since that day had he asked himself if it had really, truly been necessary to send her away from him? She'd been gone a full moon now, and he felt as if half his heart had been ripped from his chest.

One entire moon, and there had been no sign of Tenskwatawa, though a number of Black Hoof's warriors still searched for him. Perhaps he'd learned his lesson and had ceased his treacherous actions after all. Perhaps he was less a threat than Silver Thorn had thought. Then again, perhaps not. It was not a chance Silver Thorn had been willing to take—not with the life of his wife and child.

But in sending Neeake away from him, had he risked too much too hastily? Would he be able to revise the spell that had brought her to him, to reverse it so that he might join her in her time? He wasn't sure. He prayed that he could, but he wasn't totally certain.

Which was why he'd retraced their path to the tree she'd told him was on her parents' property. It had occurred to him, tardily, that he might need something from her era, some tangible object that had come into Neeake's possession just prior to the time she had first appeared to him. He recalled the lottery tickets she'd buried with the missive to her parents and had hurried to retrieve them before anyone in Neeake's day could do so. Now they rested safely within his spirit bag, alongside the treasured photograph of her which Neeake had left behind for him, awaiting the moment when he could weave them into the spell.

That moment was not yet at hand, however, which was both a blessing and a burden. The same span of days both loomed and plodded, depending on Silver Thorn's mood. When measured by time away from Neeake, it felt endless. When measured by the days left to convince Tecumseh to change his course of action, it was much too short. One moon gone, one left in which to alter Tecumseh's destiny. Was ever a man so torn by his responsibilities—to his wife, his brother, his mother—each needing his attention, each pulling him in a different direction?

"Oh, Neeake, my love." Silver Thorn gave a forlorn sigh. "Be patient, little goose. Be brave. Do not lose faith. Do not forget me. I will move heaven and earth to come to you."

Ohio—1996

Nikki's birthday fell on Labor Day, when the family traditionally gathered at the farm for the last holiday of the summer. This year, they'd combined the customary picnic with a party to celebrate Nikki's birthday, complete with all the standard ribbing about turning thirty. Though not in a party mood, Nikki found she didn't mind their jokes as much as she might have. Much of her former discontent about her age had had to do with the fact that she'd wanted to start a family of her own before she got much older. Being pregnant was a gift in itself.

It still surprised her, when she thought of it, how easily her immediate family had accepted her tale of being whisked back in history. But maybe for them it was easier than most. On her mother's side, there had been stories of Scottish ancestors with "the sight," which was strange in its own right. On her dad's, there was the Shawnee bloodline, which lent itself naturally to the belief. Even Nikki's brothers seemed willing to honor her bizarre experience with more credibility than the average modern person might have, for which she was truly grateful. Now they were all gathered around her, lending their support.

Jack, the oldest and a confessed computer nerd, had driven up from Columbus for the weekend with his wife and children. He was the quintessential yuppie, a stockbroker fast on the rise in his company with all the prerequisites—ambition, intelligence, an impressive house in the suburbs with a mortgage and a swimming pool, a supportive wife and two point three children. He and Mariette were expecting their third child in January and hoping for a girl after having boys the first two times around.

Denny, the second oldest at age thirty-six, was a partner in a small local law firm. He, too, was married, and he and Danielle were the parents of two children, a thirteen-year-old son and a seven-year-old daughter.

Sam, the youngest brother, but still Nikki's senior by three years, was following in their father's footsteps. Farming was in his blood, and he'd majored in agriculture in college. The only bachelor of the brood, and a very eligible one at that, he'd built his own house just a couple of miles down the road from their parents, far enough for privacy but conveniently near for helping the elder Swan with the farming.

"So, how's my favorite sister?" Jack asked, coming up to Nikki and looping his arm around her shoulders.

Nikki grinned. "I'm your only sister," she reminded him.

He chuckled. "That's why you're my favorite. You're one of a kind, thank God. The family couldn't have stood another one like you." His handsome features fell into more serious lines. "Are you getting along okay?"

"I'm coping," Nikki told him. "It's not easy, but I'll get by."

"You look thin," he commented critically. "Are you eating properly?"

Nikki rolled her eyes toward the heavens. "Geez! The first time in years I can look in the mirror and like what I see, and the whole world thinks I'm wasting away! I'm fine, Jack. My appetite isn't what it used to be, but I'm not going to knock it. It might keep me from looking like a total blimp in the next few months. And, yes, I'm drinking my milk and getting all my proper vitamins and nutrients for the baby." She cocked an eyebrow at him. "Do you bug Mari this way? It's a wonder she hasn't landed a frying pan alongside your head."

Mari sauntered up and curled into her husband's side. "I've been tempted," she confessed, having overheard the conversation, "but I don't want to jar his brilliant brain too badly. Let it not be said that I don't know which side of my bread is buttered," she teased.

Sam joined them. "Did you really like my present, Nik?" As handy at carpentry as he was with farming, he'd made her a trellis for the climbing rosebush by her front porch.

"I love it, Sammy."

"I can come by tomorrow morning and set it up for you, if you want," he offered.

"No hurry," she assured him. "Anytime you get a free minute will be fine."

"What about our gift?" Denny inquired. He and Danielle had bought Nikki three decorative geese for her yard. "Have you decided where you're going to put them?"

"Sure," she replied with a wink. "They'll go great in my bathtub, don't you think? Of course, they'd go even better with a hot tub. Maybe I ought to put one of those on my Christmas list this year. Hint. Hint."

Danielle laughed. "Your chances of getting a hot tub from these three tightwads is about as good as winning the lottery."

"That reminds me," Nikki said with a snap of her fingers. "I wonder what happened to those tickets I put in with the letter. I have no idea why Thorn would need them, but it's driving me crazy thinking I might have had a winning combination."

"Not likely," Sam put in. "But if you do find them and if they are worth something, can I get a loan? I have my eye on a new combine, but it's a little out of my pocketbook."

"Stand in line, baby brother," Jack told him. "I could use an updated computer first."

"What about me?" Denny challenged. "What lawyer worth his salt doesn't deserve a new Lexus?"

"You don't!" came the chorused, laughing answer.

A little while later, Nikki's mother, Paula, sat down beside her. "How are you doing, pumpkin?" the older woman asked.

"I'll make it," Nikki said. "The baby helps. Whenever I get to feeling too blue, I think of that tiny life growing inside me."

Paula nodded and smiled. "I know. There's nothing quite like it, nothing quite so magical and marvelous as knowing you're going to be a mother." She chuckled and added, "Even David Copperfield can't top that! Let him make the Empire State Building disappear, or the Grand Canyon. He still can't give birth, can he?"

"I bought some paint and wallpaper trim Friday evening," Nikki said. "I'm going to start working on the baby's bedroom in my spare time. Sheree has volunteered to help."

"She's a wonderful friend," Paula commented. "I'll help, too, whenever I can. And if there's any major work to be done, we'll draft your Daddy and Sam." She hugged her daughter close, then pulled back to give her a loving, maternal look. "You're not alone in this, honey. Just remember that when you get to feeling down. We're all here for you, and we'll help you any way we can."

"I can't believe you would even suggest such a thing!" Nikki exclaimed in disbelief. She held the phone out from her ear and eyed it as if it contained something evil. In a way, it did—the reprobate on the other end of the line, one ex-husband by the name of Scott Derringer. "That's vile, Scott, even for you."

"Oh, grow up, Nichole," he chided. "Open your eyes and live in the real world for a change."

"The real world?" she echoed. "You must mean the one you inhabit, where everybody changes bedpartners like a game of musical chairs. And why did you think I'd be willing to do likewise, Scott? I didn't like it when we were married, so why would I go in for that sort of thing now?"

"Well, I just figured that after that little jaunt you took to Mexico with your lover, you might have loosened up a bit since I last saw you," he told her. "It was worth a shot."

"I'd like to give you a shot," she retorted disgustedly. "A twelve-gauge in the vicinity of that zipper you can't keep fastened. What's the matter, dearie? You horny? Running short on fresh meat? Thought you'd tap the old tried-and-true stuff again? Well, forget it. You make me sick. I wouldn't have you in my bed again if you were the last man on earth. I'd order a dildo first, and teach it to mow the lawn, which is more work than you ever did around the house. What's more, how did you get my phone number? I just had it changed."

"I have a friend who works for the phone company. Nice little buxom redhead with a tattoo of a tarantula on one breast that looks like it's moving when she breathes hard. And I can get her breathing really hard, too."

"You always did go nuts over boobs. I'm not just talking breasts here, either. Your friend sounds like a real class act, Scott. She's also about to be unemployed. First thing in the morning, I'm calling the phone company and having her fired. I'm sure you're not the only one who's seen that spider jump. Then I'm getting my number changed again; and if you dare try to get it, to call me, or to show your face anywhere near me, I'll slap you with a restraining order so fast it'll make your head spin."

With that, Nikki slammed the phone in his ear. "God! What a scuzz-bucket!" she ranted. "Someone ought to staple his zipper shut, with him in it!"

September dragged by. Even as busy as she was with school, grading homework afterward, and decorating the new nursery, Nikki had too much time on her hands—too much time to think and to worry.

Her house was an older two-story frame set in an earlier-established division with large lots and plenty of big shade trees. Nikki preferred the area and the house to those in the newer subdivisions. For one thing, there was both more privacy and more neighborliness, which should have been a contradiction but wasn't. It was somewhat like living in a Norman Rockwell, old-town painting.

Here, she had neighbors who watched out for each other and really seemed to care. She wasn't as isolated as she would have been in a more rural setting—the mall was only a short drive away—but neither was she living in a busy section of town. The homes were older, but well kept, as were the lawns. Children could run and play and ride their bikes without fear of being run down by speeding motorists. Folks, old and young, visited across flowered borders and backyard fences. Families got together for block cookouts. Front porch swings were the norm rather than the exception. It was a very friendly place to live.

Her home suited her. It was large enough to accommodate the family she'd hoped to have someday, yet small enough to be cozy. It wasn't fancy and ultra-modern, but it was comfortable and it hadn't cost her the earth to buy. Best of all, Scott had never set foot in it; she'd bought it a year after their divorce.

Not counting the screened-in patio/mud room off the rear of the house, the downstairs consisted of four rooms— a living room and dining room linked by a wide archway, a moderate-sized kitchen with a window seat eating area, a smaller room in the back that she'd turned into a study, and a tiny bathroom. Upstairs, there was a larger bathroom and three good-sized bedrooms, above which was the attic. The basement was nothing to rave about, just a cement-block hole in the ground housing the furnace, water heater, and her washer and dryer; but Nikki had hopes of one day remodeling it and making a den or playroom down there.

Outside was the requisite front porch, complete with swing, a two-car detached garage, a stone driveway, and a huge fenced-in back yard. The fence never kept Her Nibs corralled, but it did give the cat a safe haven from neighborhood dogs, lots of trees to climb, and an alternative to her litter box. Nikki had encircled the house with flowers of every type and hue and had spent a small fortune making sure she would have blossoms from early spring until frost.

With Silver Thorn in mind, Nikki viewed her home with a fresh, critical eye, wondering what he would think of it. Would he find it too cramped, too cluttered, too enclosing?

Would he appreciate the appliances and carpeting and old oak woodwork, not to mention the convenience of a furnace, electricity, and indoor plumbing? Would he think the lampshades were too fancy, the furniture too soft, the curtains too frivolous?

She wasn't too concerned with the bathrooms, the kitchen, or her little office. There wasn't much she could do to alter or improve them anyway. The nursery was coming along nicely, and the remaining spare bedroom was currently just a catchall. Mainly, it was the living room and her own bedroom that troubled her. Somehow, she just couldn't envision Silver Thorn relaxing in either of them. The decor in each seemed too feminine, too frilly, now that she surveyed them with a more discerning eye.

Wanting to change them, but needing to do so on a limited budget, Nikki was stymied. Her mother and Sheree came to her rescue, only too glad to contribute their opinions, as well as their time and talents. However, Paula thought perhaps Nikki was rushing things, that she should wait until Silver Thorn appeared to lend his own ideas to the decorating scheme.

"You could misjudge what he would like, and all your efforts could be for nothing," Paula said. "You don't really have to do much of anything to it immediately. The nursery, yes, but the rest could wait awhile."

"I have to do this, Mom," Nikki tried to explain. "It's not merely to keep busy, but more something to bolster my hopes right now. To assure myself that he really will come."

"Besides," Sheree put in, "I really can't see any man being comfortable in a living room like this. A woman, yes. A man, a real man, no way. It's altogether too froufrou, if you get my drift. Too many ruffles and frills, too much rose and mauve and berry, and the furniture is entirely too delicate. For one thing, that loveseat has to go, and that chair with the curved legs and tapestry cushion.

A deep, long couch and an overstuffed recliner would be loads better. And a coffee table and end stand that are solid and stable."

"Fine, but my bank account isn't going to allow for all that, I'm sure," Nikki reminded her. "And I certainly don't want to go into debt by putting everything on credit."

Sheree smiled. "You don't have to. Haven't you ever heard of garage sales? First, you have one of your own and unload everything you don't really want or need. Then, you watch the newspaper for the items you'd like. You can find some great bargains, and not all of that stuff is junk, either. Especially when someone is moving and has to get rid of a lot of their furniture."

"Also, if you can't find the curtains you want on sale, we can always buy some material and sew them ourselves," Paula contributed. "The same with the lampshades. It's not all that difficult to recover them if you can't find what you're looking for."

It took some doing, and three weeks of solid browsing by all three women, but they finally pulled it together. By the time they were done, the living room and master bedroom had been overhauled, and on a shoestring budget.

The formerly mauve walls in the living room were now a neutral sand color, which blended wonderfully with Nikki's brown-and-cream-shaded carpet and the splashes of brighter colors throughout the room. Nikki had found a teal-green couch and a recliner and rocker to compliment it, all with thick puffy cushions. Sturdy oak-block endstands and cocktail table, another moving-sale find, flanked them.

The new drapes she and Paula had sewn were ivory with flecks of pale sage. Sheree had scarfed up a set of ceramic table lamps with a western-Indian motif in soft, swirling hues of aqua and copper that echoed the colors in the diamond-designed wallpaper border banding the top of the walls. The shades were of wheat-colored linen, with nary a ruffle in sight. Nikki had even found a trio of inexpensive framed prints to highlight the walls, one picturing a collection of colorful Indian pottery, another a misty forest waterfall scene that reminded her of the small cascade at the caves, and one depicting an Indian maiden and her brave standing by a river.

The bedroom had been less of a challenge. There, they had only to change the color scheme, the curtains, and the bedding. They'd gone with indigo-blue walls, with coordinating shades of blue in the geometric designs of the bedspread and curtains. Chunky jar lamps had replaced the flower-bedecked globes on the nightstands on either side of Nikki's queen-size waterbed.

They were all sublimely pleased with the final result of their labors.

"Comfy, cozy, restful, easy on the eye," Nikki commented approvingly.

"Basically childproof, or as near as you're going to get," Paula added.

"And an overall Native American theme. Thorn should feel right at home," Sheree offered. "Just don't let him put up a totem pole or drag in those awful stuffed animals hunters are always carting in from the taxidermist."

Nikki heaved a long-suffering sigh. "He can bring live animals inside if he wants or build a firepit in the middle of the living room floor. If he'll only come to me, as long as he arrives safe and sound, I won't care. I just want him here with me as soon as possible. Tomorrow is the first of October. If he hasn't convinced Tecumseh in the next few days, history will play itself out as written."

"And then he'll come," Sheree assured her with a fierce hug. "You'll see."

A chattering at the window drew Sheree's attention. With a frown, she pointed to the squirrel perched outside Nikki's windowsill. "Speaking of animals, I hope Thorn has some way to chase off that pesky little varmint that's been hanging around the house. If that thing ever gets inside, even in the attic, it will make a mess. I've heard of squirrels and chipmunks chewing through wiring and setting homes on fire. And this little pest definitely looks like he wants indoors."

Nikki's smile was misty. "That's *Aneekwah*, my spirit guide. He showed up about a month ago. He's here to protect me, I think."

"That wee beastie?" Paula scoffed. "He couldn't frighten off a flea—which I'm sure he's infested with, by the way."

Nikki shrugged, her grin growing. "Maybe not, but he's sure scared some of the sass out of Her Nibs. I found the prissy feline quivering under the chair the other day, looking for all the world like a gigantic Angora dustball! I was truly tempted to spray her with Endust and use her for a feather duster! I might yet, just to put her to some good use."

Twenty-eight

The anniversary of Tecumseh's demise had come and gone, and still there was no word from Silver Thorn. Nikki was as jittery as a bug on a hot rock. Her concentration was next to nil. She hoped her students would not suffer because of it, but it was so hard to keep her mind focused on her classes these days. It had been two months since she'd last seen Thorn, and she was totally miserable. She couldn't sleep, and she had to force herself to eat, for the baby's sake.

She was showing now, her pregnancy obvious to anyone who cared to notice. In a few days, a week at most, Nikki figured she'd be halfway through her term, four-and-a-half months along. The previous weekend she'd broken down and gone shopping for maternity clothes. Not that she'd gained much weight as yet, but what she had gained was going straight to her tummy, creating this round little bulge that everyone seemed to take great pleasure in poking fun at.

"You resemble a twig with a volleyball glued to it," Sheree told her. "All stick arms and legs, and this lump in the middle."

"Hey, sis, you'd better lay off the sauce," Sam had teased. "You're getting a nice little beer belly there."

Her dad joked that she could play Santa this coming Christmas. Her mom just frowned and fretted. But her obstetrician seemed satisfied that all was well. Nikki was just glad the bouts of morning sickness were a thing of the past.

It was Tuesday, the eighth of October. Third-period classes had just begun, and Nikki was looking forward to her only free period of the day. She was headed for the teachers' lounge when the oddest feeling swept over her. If she'd had to describe it, she'd have said it was like a wave of—not really dizziness or disorientation, but something akin to awareness or precognition, maybe. A funny, fuzzy sort of sensation that enveloped her and sent her emotions in a tailspin. Suddenly she had to get out of there. Out of the hall. Out of school. Immediately, if not sooner.

Nikki didn't stop to notify the office that she was leaving. She grabbed the first kid she saw and sent him to the principal with a message that Mrs. Silver was ill and had gone home for the day. She didn't care what they thought or if they grumbled at having to find someone to substitute for her on such short notice. She simply raced for the parking lot, and her car.

Her fingers were shaking, and she had to aim for the ignition three times before the key went into the slot. Then she almost flooded the engine trying to get it started. Finally, she was out on the road and heading west, toward her mom and dad's farm. It wasn't a totally conscious decision. Rather it was as if she were being drawn there, called there by some heretofore untapped intuition. The only thing she knew for sure was that it was imperative that she go to the tree. Now.

By the time Nikki pulled the car to the side of the road near the tractor lane next to the river, she couldn't have said if she'd run six stop signs, passed a dozen burning properties, or hit a herd of cows. She recalled very little of the drive into the countryside other than her need to get there quickly.

She abandoned the car, scarcely remembering to kill the engine. In her haste, she left the keys in the ignition, her purse on the passenger seat, and the door wide open. It had rained the night before, and the heels of her pumps sank into mud. She hardly noticed. Nor did it slow her headlong dash for the fallen tree. Once there, she flung herself into the hole where the roots of the oak had once been buried, and began clawing at the wet dirt, disregarding any damage to her clothing or her nails. Anyone who chanced to see her would have thought her mad, but Nikki knew, beyond a doubt, what had impelled her there.

Within minutes, her fingers found what she sought. Half sobbing, she pulled the rawhide packet from the earth. "Yes! Yes! Oh, God, let it be! Please let it be!"

Quickly, she unwrapped it, and for a moment was stunned to find nothing inside. Then she saw the writing on the soft inner side of the skin and nearly wilted with gratitude. "Of course," she told herself. "What was I thinking? He wouldn't have ready access to paper."

Swiftly, her heart thudding a mile a minute, she scanned the brief note. Then, when she'd determined the contents, she reread it more slowly, lingering over every precious word. It was brief, and to the point, and it looked as if Silver Thorn had printed it with his paints in lieu of pencil or ink. It read:

Neeake. Mission failed. Brother walks with the Spirits. Must go to mother now. I come soon. One or two moons. Wait. I will come. Your Silver Thorn.

Nikki sank back on her heels and clasped the letter to her breast. Tears of joy streamed down her face, unheeded. "Silver Thorn!" she whispered. "Oh, my darling! Thank you. Thank you. You can't know how much I needed this sign from you. Or perhaps you did. Hurry, my love. I'll be waiting. Your son will be waiting."

As if stirred by her words, the baby moved slightly, a mere fluttering deep inside. Her hand flew to her stomach, her eyes round with surprise. This was the first she'd felt the baby move since that time with Thorn at the cave, when the blue arrow had appeared on her belly. The mark was still there, something Nikki hadn't bother to explain to her curious obstetrician.

As if her words could carry across the years and the miles from her heart to his, Nikki said softly, "Your son lives, Thorn. I felt him move just now, for the first time in all these months. Perhaps he felt your presence somehow and was responding to it or to the joy that has leapt into my heart just by reading your letter. I prefer to believe that he knows you, that he senses you reaching out to us. Join us soon, dear heart. Join us soon."

Ohio—1813

The tie between them was strong, perhaps made stronger by their separation and the fact that it was their only link now. Silver Thorn knew the exact moment when Neeake retrieved the message he'd buried at the oak tree. He felt her urgency, her elation—and he felt their baby stir within her. How this was so, he did not know. Nor did he question it. He simply knew that the quivering flutter in his heart was his son moving within Neeake's womb.

His own joy at sharing this miracle of life pierced the veil of sorrow which had enveloped him since Tecumseh's death. His brother had fallen in the Battle of the Thames, just as Neeake had said he would. He'd died instantly. But before the battle, Tecumseh had spoken to his followers, and to Silver Thorn, with prophetic words of parting.

"Do not grieve when I leave you to walk with the Spirits, for I shall return another day. There will come another time when my people need me to lead them. Then I will come again to show them the way."

Knowing he would die that day, and proud to do so as a Shawnee warrior, Tecumseh had rejected his British general's red uniform-coat in favor of the traditional buckskin garb of his brethren. Because he'd gone into combat dressed no differently than any of the other warriors, perhaps even less elaborately than some, the American soldiers had not been able to identify Tecumseh's body on the battlefield. Had they done so, they would surely have mutilated it, taken his clothes and his flesh for souvenirs. But except for the wound which had killed him, Tecumseh's body was unmarred when Silver Thorn and several others stole back to retrieve it. Honoring his pledge, Silver Thorn had borne his brother's remains to a secret location far from the site of the battle, to a place Tecumseh had always treasured deep in his heart, and there had lain him to rest.

Now, Silver Thorn had another mission, one he prayed would be more successful. He was leaving immediately to join his mother and other relatives at the Cherokee village far to the south in hopes of convincing them to remove themselves safely to Mexico, where they would escape the trials to come, most particularly the dreaded Trail of Tears of which Neeake had spoken with such sadness. He would take his family there, if they would agree, and then, finally, he would be free to join his love . . . the woman who held the other half of his heart in her small white palm.

Ohio—1996

"Denny! Denny, I need your help!" Nikki rushed into her brother's private office in a rare panic.

"What is it? What's happened?" Denny was out of his

chair and rounding his desk in a flash. He'd seldom seen his sister so flustered. Her wide violet eyes held a frightened look, and her face was as pale as death except for two bright spots over her cheekbones. He ushered her toward a chair. "Sit down. Calm down. Do you want some water? Tea?"

"No. I can't sit. I'm too upset. And I don't want anything to drink. What I want is for you to find a way to make Brian Sanders leave me alone and stop prying into my private affairs."

"Brian Sanders?" Denny echoed. "The reporter you once dated?"

Nikki gave a jerky nod. "The same. Three dates, and the dumb son-of-a-sewer-rat thinks he has some sort of claim on me. Can you believe it? I've all but told him to take a running leap off a short pier, but he keeps coming around, bugging me, asking me out, sending me flowers.

"What is it with some men?" she exclaimed in exasperation, slicing her fingers through her hair and mussing it. "Scott called me awhile back, too, wanting to *get together for old time's sake*. Don't they understand the meaning of fidelity at all? You'd think it was a completely foreign concept that someone would wish to honor her marriage vows."

Denny frowned. "How far has Sanders actually gone, Nik? Is he stalking you?"

She stopped pacing. "No, not precisely, but I wouldn't be surprised if it came to that. He's pissed, Denny. Truly pissed that I would prefer another man over him. I think, with Silver Thorn nowhere around, Brian half convinced himself that there was no other man, that I'd simply made him up for some reason. But now, with my pregnancy so apparent, he's more irate than ever. Since this wasn't a second Immaculate Conception, it's driving him nuts that another man got into my bed, succeeding where he'd tried and failed."

"Okay, so he's jealous," Denny conceded. "As long as you don't go home to find a dead bunny boiling on the stove, I don't think we're dealing with any real crisis, sis. I'll talk to him, if you want. Tell him to back off. Maybe he'll take the hint if it comes from a man. In fact, I'll even imply that he could meet with bodily harm if he persists. Does that meet with your approval?"

"This might not seem like a crisis to you, but it certainly is to me," she informed him tersely. "And there's more, Denny. Brian now seems obsessed with trying to prove, at least to himself if not the entire world, that I had a vacation fling, got pregnant, and invented a fake husband just to cover my rear with the school board. He admitted to me that he's been nosing around and that he can't find any physical evidence that a man by the name of Thorn Silver even exists. He's already checked public records and computer listings for a social security number, driver's license, and God knows what else and come up empty. Denny, we've got to do something! We've got to create some sort of background, some records to prove Thorn is real or Brian will just keep digging. He's like a damned dog with a bone!"

"Uh-oh."

"Understatement, brother dearest."

Denny waved his hands in front of him. "Okay. Okay. Just calm down and let me think a minute."

He was silent for so long that Nikki was ready to shake the words out of him. At last he said, "Your idea of making Thorn an archaeologist, particularly one who works exclusively in foreign countries, is going to come in very handy. If he's never worked or claimed a permanent address in the U.S., that would explain why there is no record of his ever filing an income tax return or having a social security number or a driver's license. He could even be a citizen of a foreign country, for that matter."

"No. That would necessitate even more legal paperwork and red tape, wouldn't it?"

"You're right. It would be much better if he were a native-born U.S. citizen—which he is, of course. Unfortunately he's from the wrong century. Okay, let's see. When and where was he born?"

She did some fast mental calculations and announced, "March 9, 1768, in Xenia, Ohio."

The words were scarcely out of her mouth when Denny burst out laughing. "If you'd tried for aeons, you couldn't have come up with a better place for him to have been born! He's what, forty or forty-five years old?"

"Forty-five, but we could shave a few years off his age if we have to. Hell, I've already changed the poor man's name, why stop at that?"

"It's perfect!" Denny declared delightedly. "Do you remember that tornado that swept through Xenia back in 1974?"

Nikki shook her head. "I'd only have been about eight years old then," she reminded him.

"Well, it's one of the worst ever recorded, and it destroyed at least half the town, including the downtown business district. I think it tore the roof off the courthouse, if I remember correctly, but I can't be sure. They claimed that none of their records got lost or ruined, but who's to say there weren't a few that got sucked up and carried off or lost in the shuffle of renovation? Like Thorn's birth records, for instance? And remember that computers back then weren't nearly as sophisticated as they are now. Cut the power lines, and zap! Scads of valuable information could have disappeared into the netherworld, never to be found again."

Nikki's eyes widened appreciatively. "Thorn's records, his parents', all literally wiped out. That would account for a missing birth certificate and other local data, but what about a passport?" Nikki asked. "Surely he'd have one of those if he worked in all those different places. Also, there's the small matter of our nonexistent marriage certificate. Anyone who really wants to dig deep enough— Brian Sanders for instance—would expect to run across something of that sort sooner or later. If he doesn't, it's only going to make him all the more suspicious, don't you think?"

"No problem," Denny assured her. "We can get Thorn a whole set of fake I.D. Passport and all. Illegal aliens do it all the time."

"What?" Nikki shrieked. "Are you out of your ever-lovin' mind? Denny, you're a lawyer, for heaven's sake, and here you are contemplating something totally unlawful!"

"Shhh! Keep your voice down, will you?" he cautioned. "If it comes to that, we don't want the entire world to know it, do we? Now, as to my being a lawyer, you can thank your lucky stars that I am, sweet pea. How do you think I know about all these neat little tricks? I've defended some of the smartest damned criminals you'd ever care to meet, and I have to admit they've taught me a lot. I just never thought I'd ever put any of it to use for personal reasons."

"And about half of those defendants are behind bars now, serving ten to twenty in the big house!" she hissed. "We could go to jail, Denny. We're not talking small potatoes here."

"Just let me take care of everything, Nikki. It will work out fine. Trust me."

"This from the brother who swore to catch me at the bottom of the slide and left me to skin my knees when Shirley Abbot flashed a mouthful of braces at him?" she scoffed.

"That was Jack," he reminded her with a mock glower. "I was the one who bloodied Billy Brown's nose after he pushed you into the mud puddle and ruined your new Easter dress."

Nikki shrugged. "Sorry. Guess I got that mixed up. Still, I don't want any of us to get into trouble with the law. Especially you, Denny. You could lose your license, and you have a family to support."

"Just the birth and marriage certificates for now, then," he said. "And a passport. We'd need proof of that first, I imagine, for him to allegedly have flown into the country to join his bride. You do have some decent snapshots of him as I recall."

"In what, a breechcloth?" Nikki threw up her hands. "Oh, God! This is suddenly getting so blasted complicated!"

"Not really," he claimed. "Jack can do wonders with that computer of his, which is going to make things a whole lot simpler. He's a master hacker."

"Now you're talking about involving Jack, having him break into computer records, I suppose? Where will all this end?"

"With you and Thorn living happily ever after, I hope," Denny told her. "Now, get out of my office so I can get some work done, will you? I'll speak to Jack and get the ball rolling. I might even have a nice little chat with your snoopy reporter friend, too. Just to let him know whom he's dealing with when he tries to screw with our baby sister."

"In his dreams," she muttered. "Only in his dreams."

Twenty-nine

Ohio—The Caves—Late November 1813

The Moon of the Beaver, the month the white man called November, was drawing to a close. The winds were cold and brisk from the north, shaking the last of the leaves from the trees. Soon the snows would come, more than a few fluffy flakes now and then, wrapping the earth in a blanket of white. The rivers would freeze. The falls would cease their singing until spring brought warmth to the land again, awakening it from its winter slumber.

Silver Thorn could not wait that long. He must reach Neeake before this happened. If he failed now, as he had in his previous attempts to join her, he would be forced to stay here without her until spring thaw, or perhaps forever. He knew that much of his magic had to do with the time of the year, the position of the moon, the sun, the stars. Perhaps they would never again align in a pattern favorable for traveling to another time. He wasn't sure, but he feared it might be so.

Already he'd made four attempts to go to her. Each time he remained in his own world. He must succeed soon. Perhaps now, tonight. The moon was full, as it had been when he'd first cast the spell that had brought Neeake to him. Perhaps it would aid in transporting him to her. He prayed that it would be so, for time was short and he was nearly out of spells to try, incantations to sing, and various combinations of the two.

Bracing himself against the chill of the night air and the cold water, which would soon turn his limbs and flesh numb, Silver Thorn divested himself of his shirt and leggings. Clad only in his breechcloth and moccasins, he stepped carefully along the rocky path until he stood at the foot of the rushing falls. Clasping the amulet in his hand, he raised his eyes and arms to the moon, now near its zenith, and began to chant. Though shivers racked his frame, he dared not hasten the ritual.

The moon had passed its highest point when Silver Thorn finally ended his plea to the Spirits. He stood alone, half frozen and desolate on the rocks, knowing he had failed once more. His heart felt as if it were shattering in his chest. Pain filled him.

"No!" His cry bounced back at him, echoing off the barren land. With trembling hands, he opened his spirit bag and brought forth the picture of Neeake, his precious lovely bride. It was slightly tattered now, worn from the many times he had handled it, stared at it. Now, by the bright light of the moon, he peered at her image and wondered if this would be his final remembrance of her—a still face upon a shiny piece of paper.

He rubbed his thumb over it and jerked in surprise when the sharp corner of the photo pricked his skin. A bead of blood fell, staining the picture, and Silver Thorn quickly wiped at it, fearful that it would ruin the photo altogether. He succeeded only in smearing it worse, so badly that he could scarcely discern Neeake's likeness.

"No!" he shouted again, his grief all the worse. He rubbed at the blotch, his anger and frustration growing, the anguish tearing at him like gnashing teeth. Tears sprang to his eyes, blurring her image all the more. One salty droplet fell, mingling with the blood and Neeake's fading face, and Silver Thorn fell to his knees, overcome with agonizing sorrow.

That's when the earth began to spin, setting the moon dancing overhead until it became a whirling white wheel amid a dizzying blur of stars. Stunned, Silver Thorn clung to the rock in an effort to maintain his balance. But his hands slipped. He felt himself falling, reeling, caught up in an ever-tightening spiral that threatened to suck the last breath from his body. Just as the dizziness defeated him, he felt the amulet snag on something. He could not react fast enough to keep it from being ripped from his grasp, along with the treasured photo of Neeake.

His final conscious thought was, "If this is not the path to Neeake, let it then be death, for I do not wish to live without her."

Ohio—November 1996

It seemed as if Nikki had just gotten to sleep when she awoke with a jolt. Her waterbed, the one guaranteed not to slosh, was weaving back and forth like a ship in a hurricane. In those first moments of disorientation, Nikki wondered if she were experiencing an earthquake, perhaps one of those infrequent-but-not-unheard-of tremors along the New Madrid Fault. If so, this was the first one she'd felt, and all this bobbing about was making her nauseous.

Gradually, the bed rocked to a halt, and Nikki exhaled cautiously. Then, as she lay perfectly still, waiting for her stomach to calm completely, she heard it. Breathing! Heavy breathing! Coming from the other side of the mattress! Right next to her!

Her heart thumped to a halt, then resumed at warp speed. Her mind raced, sifting through all possible explanations. Only a couple popped into her brain, and they were ridiculous. The cat? Had Her Nibs developed an asthmatic problem? Possible, but not probable. A narcoleptic burglar? Highly unlikely.

Her night visitor moaned, and Nikki, scared out of her wits, let out a shrill shriek even as she clambered clumsily out of bed. Or tried to. Which wasn't easy for a woman who was nearly six-months pregnant and entrapped in a body-snatching waterbed!

"Oh, God! Oh, God! Oh, God!" she screeched hysterically, grabbing for the side rail and hauling herself over it. As she tumbled to the floor, the man—she was sure it had to be a man's voice—groaned again. She was fumbling in the dark for the bedside phone when he mumbled something. Her hand halted in mid-movement. She froze in place. Listening. Praying. It came again, that rumble that sounded like her name.

Her breath caught in her throat. Afraid of what she might find, but more afraid of not knowing, Nikki groped for the bed lamp, her eyes trained on the bed all the while. The moment she snapped it on, what she saw had her shrieking anew—this time in soul-consuming jubilation.

"Thorn! Thorn! Oh, dear Lord! Is it really you? Are you truly here? Oh, God! Oh, gosh!" He was still half unconscious, and she was shaking him now, trying to bring him around to full awareness. "Are you all right? Speak to me, Thorn! Wake up, sweetheart! Look at me!"

His eyelids fluttered. "Neeake?"

"Yes! Yes! It's me, Thorn! Wake up!"

Slowly, afraid he might be dreaming, Silver Thorn opened his eyes—to the most beautiful sight in the world. Neeake. His Neeake. Smiling down at him. Dripping happy tears on his bare chest. Gripping his arm so tightly that he could not doubt that she was real, for her finger nails were piercing his skin.

In the next instant, he had her in his arms, embracing her so hard that both of them could scarcely breathe. Laughing with her. Crying with her. Smothering her with kisses. Wanting to feast on the sight of her, but at the same time reluctant to release her even that briefly.

"Neeake, my love. My sweet, sweet love. How I have missed you!"

"Oh, Thorn, I feared I'd never see you again, never get to hold you close to me. Love me. Oh, darling, love me. It seems like years."

His soft chuckle was nearly a sob. "It has been, dearest heart." He kissed her deeply, his hands stroking across her thinly clad body. They came to rest on her rounded belly, and he felt their child move within her. "What of the baby?" he asked.

"He won't mind, I'm sure." The baby kicked once more. Nikki smiled. "I think he's trying to say hello to his papa. Why don't we give him a closer visit?"

For all the time they'd waited, their lovemaking was slow and tender, a lingering exploration as they savored this glad reunion, this renewal, to the fullest. There was no place on her body he did not touch, no part of him she did not learn again. She filled her senses with him, and he with her, reacquainting themselves with the feel, the taste, the scent of each other.

When he entered her, ever so gently, he filled more than her body. He filled her soul. Her blissful cry echoed his. "Welcome home, my darling," she sighed.

Her silken warmth surrounded him, bathing him in the dew of her love. "Yes," he murmured huskily. "I am home. You are and ever will be my home."

Some time later, when their immediate passion had been satisfied, Silver Thorn kissed the tears from her face. "I pray that these are joyous tears, for I would forfeit a limb before I would hurt you."

She nodded. "I'm fine. More than fine. My heart is bursting with happiness."

"As is mine. I also feared that I would never reach you. I tried many times these past days and met only with fail-

ure. I knew I had to find a way soon, before the falls
froze, for I did not think anything would succeed then."

"Whatever you did this last time, it worked. Thank
God." Her hands stroked over him, relishing the texture of
his bare flesh. She threaded her fingers through his ebony
hair only to stop abruptly as she suddenly realized what
she was feeling. "Good grief, Thorn! You're soaking wet!"

"I was standing at the foot of the falls. I recall kneeling
on the rocks when the dizziness came upon me."

"For heaven's sake, it's November, Thorn! It must have
been like standing in ice water! And you nearly naked!
We've got to get you dry, and warm, before you catch
your death."

"I am plenty warm," he said. "But I have made your
blankets wet."

She hadn't noticed until now, but they were damp and
clammy. Especially where he'd first landed in the bed—
sopping moccasins, breechcloth, and all. These had long
since been discarded and now lay in a sodden heap on the
carpet alongside her nightgown.

"No problem. We can change the sheets. But you really
do need to towel-dry your hair. Better yet, you can use
my hair blower."

Nikki squirmed to the edge of the bed and tried to lever
herself out of it. Her efforts set the mattress to wobbling
again.

Silver Thorn braced himself against the swaying motion.
"What manner of bed is this, that moves so? I swear,
Neeake, it was like mating in a rocking canoe. Not that
we did not manage quite well, but it would have been
easier if the bed had remained still."

She grinned at him. "It's a waterbed. The mattress, below the covers, is filled with water. I'm still trying to get
used to it myself, which is all the more difficult the bigger
I get. I don't think these things were invented with a pregnant woman in mind. If you don't like it, they make regu-

lar, firm mattresses to fit the frame. We can always buy one of those if you prefer."

Silver Thorn pressed against the mattress with his hand, testing its give. "We shall see. Why does it not feel cold?"

"There is a heater to keep the water warm," she explained. "I'll show it to you later. Right now, I think it's time I introduced you to another marvel of modern technology: The hair dryer."

She pulled him along with her into the bathroom and switched on the light. He gaped in awe. His fingers reached toward the toggle hers had just left, and he flipped the light off. Then on . . . and off . . . and on again. A slow grin curved his mouth. "This is truly wondrous, to have such light when it is dark outside. How is this possible?"

"I can't explain the technicalities of it, but it has to do with electrical current running through wires in the walls. This electricity is a source of power to run all kinds of modern appliances, including the lights. See these plugs?" she gestured to a wall outlet. "We're going to plug the hair dryer into one of these, and it's going to produce hot air to dry your hair."

Silver Thorn was less interested in Nikki's explanation than he was in the vanity lights framing the bathroom mirror. He walked up and touched one, pulling his hand back immediately. "Hot," he commented. Leaning closer, he examined the bulb. "Is the fire inside this ball?"

"No fire, Thorn. Just wires, filaments, and electricity."

He glanced down at the shell-shaped sink and its fixtures. "And this?"

"A sink and faucet. Water comes out the spigot when you turn these knobs. The right one for cold water, the left for hot." She demonstrated how it worked.

"Where does the water come from? How does it get here? How does one side produce hot water?"

This conversation suddenly reminded Nikki of her

nephew at age three, when his favorite thing had been to ask questions nonstop. "The water is piped from a reservoir miles from here. The plumbing also runs up the wall. There is a water heater in the basement."

"Why are there two sinks?"

Nikki frowned. "I don't understand. There's only one sink, Thorn."

He pointed to the tub. "Is that not a sink also? It has a faucet, does it not?"

"That is a bath tub, for bathing. You plug the drain, fill the tub with water, then get into it and bathe. When you're done, you release the stopper and the dirty water drains out. That gizmo near the top is a shower head. You can make the water come out there, in a spray, instead of the spigot. Most men prefer a shower to a bath, so I've heard."

His attention was already veering toward the only large fixture left. "This is a seat of some sort?"

"That's the toilet. Remember, I mentioned it to you before, when we had that conversation about indoor outhouses."

His brows rose as recollection dawned. "Yes, but I wish to see how it works."

She lifted the lid, showed him how the seat raised on its hinges, and pressed the handle. "The water flows from this tank into the bowl, forcing the waste out through the bottom hole and the plumbing. After you flush, it takes a few minutes for the tank to refill, so you can't flush twice in the same few seconds. Also, I want to warn you not to leave the seat up when you are done urinating. Always . . . always . . . put the seat down again, even if you leave the lid open."

Thorn looked the apparatus over and couldn't figure out why she was insisting on this, for it seemed to have nothing to do with the operation of the toilet. After a moment, he asked, "Why must the seat always be put down again?"

She gave him a wry smile. "Because women never have

to raise the seat to go potty, darling. Therefore, we don't automatically check each time to make sure the seat is down, especially if we toddle off to the toilet in the middle of the night and half asleep—which I'm doing more often as my pregnancy advances. If, by some chance, I should plunk my bare butt down on cold porcelain and fall through to that cold water, I would not be a happy camper. And then I would want your head served up to me on a platter. Does that answer your question sufficiently?"

He grinned down at her. "I have missed that sassy mouth of yours, wife."

She flipped the toilet lid down and shoved him onto it. "Sit, you big lunk. Let's get your hair dry so we can change the sheets and go to bed."

She took the hair blower from its rack beside the sink, plugged it in, and turned it on. The sudden noise made Thorn give an involuntary start. "It's okay," she told him over the mechanical roar. "See?" She aimed the dryer at her own head and then at his hand, letting him feel the rush of warm air. Then she directed it toward his head, ruffling his hair with her free hand to aid the drying process.

A short while later, they were snuggled together beneath dry bedding, as cozy as two peas in a pod. Nikki yawned and reached to turn off the lamp switch. Her gaze fell on the big red numbers of her digital alarm clock. "No wonder I'm so tired. It's three o'clock in the morning, and I'm supposed to be up at six-thirty to get ready for school."

"You have lessons tomorrow?" he asked, his disappointment evident.

"Yes, tomorrow and Wednesday. Then we get four days off for Thanksgiving weekend. However, I'm going to call in sick in the morning so that I can stay home with you."

He smiled. "This is good, as long as it does not cause trouble for you at your school."

"They can easily get another teacher to take my classes for two days," she told him. "For the next week, I want to concentrate on nothing and no one but you."

Thirty

For the second time in just a few hours, Nikki jerked awake, her ears assaulted by a loud wailing. Beside her, Silver Thorn sprang upright into a sitting position.

Nikki pawed for the alarm. "It's okay. It's just my alarm clock," she muttered. She punched the button, but the screeching continued. "Damn hard rock!" she grumbled, slapping at the buttons again. "I only set it to this station because I'm afraid I'll sleep through anything less raucous."

The din continued, and she peered at the clock through bleary eyes, wondering why the blasted thing wouldn't shut off. The dial read 5:45. She frowned. "Huh?"

"It is not your clock, Neeake," Silver Thorn told her after the fact. "If my ears do not fail me, that is Macate we are hearing, in another part of your wigewa."

"Macate?" she repeated dumbly. "Don't tell me that dratted lynx came forward with you!"

"I did not bring him, wife. He must have come on his own."

"Nuts!" Nikki clawed her way out of bed and stumbled toward the hallway. "If he's hurt Her Nibs, I'm going to turn him into a throw rug!"

"Her Nibs?" he echoed.

"My cat."

Nikki trudged downstairs, Silver Thorn right behind her. The racket was coming from the living room. When she

cleared the arch, Nikki stopped so suddenly that Silver
Thorn bumped into her. She stood gaping, hardly able to
believe her eyes. "Oh . . . my . . . lands. They're . . .
they're . . ."

"Mating," Silver Thorn supplied.

"But they can't!" Nikki exclaimed in a fluster. "They
mustn't! Her Nibs is a full-blooded Angora! A very special
and expensive breed."

"Evidently the cats do not know this or they do not
care," he commented. "Moreover, did you not tell me that
in your time a lynx is very rare? Would that not make
Macate as prized as your pet?"

The cats had finally separated, and were now eyeing the
two humans with like expressions of disdain, as if chiding
them for their untimely voyeurism. Her Nibs looked like
a bedraggled, badly mauled stuffed toy. Her fur was damp
and matted into globs, as if she'd just been through the
spin cycle of the washer. Her round green eyes still held
a glazed look, one with which Nikki could readily empa-
thize.

"I know just how you feel, baby," Nikki commiserated.

"I do not wish to hurt your feelings, love, but that creature you call a cat more resembles a hairy rat. She is very
homely and small. Is she yet a kitten, perhaps?"

"She's a full-grown house cat, Thorn," Nikki huffed. "A
domestic pet. She's supposed to be small. Unlike that unruly, wild beast of yours, she lives indoors. And she's
trained to use a litter box and not claw up the drapes and
furniture, which I'm sure is more than you can say about
Macate."

"If I tell him to behave properly in the house, he will,"
Silver Thorn informed her.

Nikki's brows arched in open skepticism. "Oh, really?
Then tell him to keep his big paws, and other assorted
and sundry parts, off of my pedigreed pet!"

Silver Thorn chuckled. "Neeake, I think perhaps it is

too late for that; and even were it not, Her Nibs seems to enjoy Macate's attentions. Much as you enjoy mine, little goose."

Without giving her the opportunity to argue the point, he swept her into his arms and carried her back up to her bed. There, he made passionate love to her until she was too sated to think about much of anything, let alone two horny cats.

Nikki could swear she heard water running. These days just the thought of water, let alone the feel of it, and her bladder sent emergency signals to her brain. She fought it as long as she could, but the discomfort grew, rousing her from sleep. Her eyelids drifted open, and she automatically reached toward the other side of the bed, seeking Silver Thorn. He wasn't there. But for her, the bed was empty, and for one dreadful moment Nikki thought she'd dreamed the whole thing—his unexpected arrival in the middle of the night, their lovemaking, all of it. Then she heard the toilet flush and more water running, and her heart resumed its normal rhythm. He was here, in the bathroom. He really, truly was here with her after all.

Smiling, she rose and walked to the open bathroom door. Her grin grew as she saw what he was doing. Absorbed as he was, he didn't notice her right off.

"Ahem." Nikki cleared her throat loudly and waited.

Silver Thorn's head snapped up, and he gave her a sheepish grin. "I was seeing for myself how they work."

"So I assumed," she said. The lower vanity doors were open, exposing the plumbing below the sink, and the taps were open full bore. The lid was off the toilet tank, and Silver Thorn's arms were wet to his elbows. "I hope you satisfy your curiosity before my water bill rivals the national debt."

She went over and shut off the faucet. "I think I ought

to mention that we're charged a fee for every gallon of water we use. I don't try to conserve all that much, but it's not a good idea to deliberately waste water, either. It's like throwing money down the drain."

Silver Thorn could scarcely conceive it. "You must pay for water in your day?" He shook his head in disbelief. "Do they also make you pay for the sunlight and the air you breathe?"

Nikki gave a dry chuckle. "Not yet, but it might come to that someday. As soon as they can figure out how to measure the amount each person uses and tax it."

She gestured toward the tub. "Would you like to take a shower this morning?"

He gave her a questioning look. "Are you sure I would not be using too much water?"

Nikki was immediately contrite. Going up to him, she pulled his dark head down to hers and planted a soft kiss on his lips. "I'm sorry, sweetheart. I don't mean to be such a bitch. There's just so much that you have to learn about life in the twentieth, soon-to-be-twenty-first century. I want to help you, but if I get too bossy, just tell me to tone it down, okay? Now, about that shower . . . ."

She showed him how to operate the levers, handed him a towel and washcloth from the cupboard, and indicated the soap and shampoo. "Take as long as you like and enjoy it," she told him. "Just be sure to keep the shower doors closed so the floor doesn't get wet."

He eyed the big tub, then turned his luminous gaze on her. "Do you not wish to shower also, Neeake? Surely this bathing tub is large enough for the two of us."

She smiled. "I suppose I could join you," she said, her own eyes alight with deviltry. "We might even conserve water if both of us bathe at once." She waggled her eyebrows at him playfully. "Then again, maybe not."

* * *

He looked fabulous in his new blue jeans and pullover shirt. The denims hugged his thighs and buttocks as if he'd been poured into them. The knit jersey molded itself across his massive chest and shoulders. Nikki nearly drooled.

"I had to guess at your size," she said. "Maybe I should have gotten a size larger. Oh, well, we can go shopping later. I just wanted to have something on hand and ready for you because I didn't know when you would appear. I'm sorry, but I couldn't begin to estimate your proper shoe size or I'd have at least bought you some Nikes, like mine. I suppose your moccasins will suffice for a couple of days."

"I think these things you call briefs are too small, also," he informed her, tugging at his crotch.

She shook her head. "No, they just take some getting used to, darling. If you prefer, we can buy you a different kind of men's underwear called boxer shorts. They are less restrictive."

"Do they also have the hole and flap in the front?" he inquired. "It feels strange, as if I could pop through it at any moment."

Nikki laughed. "I know it must feel odd after wearing a breechcloth, but you must admit the slot is convenient. I've always wished women had a similar setup so we didn't have to half-undress just to go to the bathroom."

"I like this zipper better," he said, peering down at the fly of his jeans.

Nikki'd had to laugh at him when she'd first shown him how it worked. He'd been like a kid with a new toy, working the zipper up and down repeatedly, fascinated by it.

She grabbed his hand and pulled him along after her. "Let me give you a tour of the house, and then we'll have breakfast. You can admire all the newfangled kitchen gadgets while I'm fixing our food. It will be a treat to prove to you that I actually can cook a meal without burning everything to a crisp."

Nikki showed him the rest of the upstairs first, starting with the newly decorated nursery. "This is the baby's room. Do you approve? My friend Sheree helped me choose the border. I was delighted to find those little Indian guardian angels. I like them much better than any of the cartoon figures or a lot of cutsie ducks and teddy bears."

Silver Thorn stood in the center of the floor and turned in a slow circle. "It is very nice, but it seems strange that our son will have a room of his own when he is but a babe. How will you hear him when he is hungry?"

"It's not as if he'll be living on the next block, Thorn," she chided with a chuckle. "I'm sure any son of yours will have a healthy set of lungs, and our room is only a few feet away. Also, if we don't get one as a shower gift, I intend to buy a baby monitor. It lets you hear everything going on in the nursery from anywhere in the house. How do you like the cradle? I got it at a yard sale. Babies grow out of those so fast I couldn't see paying full price for a brand new one. Dad sanded it down and repainted it for me."

"The bigger bed, the one that looks like a cage, is for later, when he no longer fits the cradle?" Silver Thorn deduced, walking over to inspect the crib.

"Yes. It also turns into a toddler bed. When he's big enough to crawl out of the crib by himself, the side rails remove and the mattress lowers so he can manage more easily without the risk of falling so far and possibly hurting himself."

"I must make him a dream catcher," Thorn decided, "to hang over his bed. It will catch the bad dreams in the web and allow only the good dreams through to him."

Nikki nodded. "A dream catcher would certainly be more unique than a run-of-the-mill mobile."

* * *

Silver Thorn had glimpsed the living room earlier. "I'll show you how the stereo and television work later," she promised. "And the VCR." Her study was too cluttered to bother with at present, other than to let him take a quick peek. Nikki actually dreaded having him discover her computer, for she couldn't imagine trying to explain it to him when she didn't really understand it that well herself.

The dining room wasn't that dissimilar from the one at the Galloways' house and didn't hold much interest for him. It was the kitchen that enthralled Silver Thorn, from the moment he stepped into it. He gazed in wonder at the many cabinets, the counters, and all the shiny, intriguing appliances in every corner of the room. Nikki showed him the stove, the refrigerator, the dishwasher, the microwave and smaller appliances—briefly explaining the use and convenience of each. She tried to limit her admonitions to the most important issues.

"Never put anything metal into the microwave," she warned him.

He grinned. "Is this another thing which would make you require my head on a platter?"

"Absolutely. More than that, it would totally ruin the oven. Metal causes electrical arcing, or some such thing. All I really know is that microwaves are not built to work with metal. It might even cause the blasted thing to blow up or start a fire and burn the house down. Also, if your bread gets stuck in the toaster, you must remember to unplug it before trying to pry the bread out. If you don't and you stick a knife or fork in there and connect with the coils, you're going to get one hell of an electrical shock, which could very well kill you. It would be similar to being struck by lightning, I'd guess."

"Anything else?"

"Too much to mention at one sitting," she replied. "I'm just glad you're so intelligent, because trying to learn all of this in such a short time would certainly be beyond my mental capacity. Now, why don't I teach you how to make coffee?"

He took to the favored American brew like a duck to a June bug. As he sipped, he watched Nikki as she prepared the batter and poured it into the waffle iron. Minutes later, she presented him with two perfect blueberry waffles, along with heated syrup and a tub of butter. "Dig in," she told him, setting the plate on the table before him. "There's plenty more where that came from."

Silver Thorn wolfed down half-a-dozen waffles before settling back in his chair with a gluttonous groan. "I greatly regret poking fun at your cooking, Neeake. In truth, you are a wonderful cook."

"As long as I'm on familiar territory," she admitted with no false modesty.

While she cleared the table and loaded the dishwasher, Silver Thorn played with the kitchen gadgets. He was particularly intrigued with the can opener and had opened three cans of peaches before she could get him to stop. The refrigerator was another fascination. He could not get over how cold it was inside that big box when it was so warm in the kitchen. He repeatedly opened and shut the door and that of the upper freezer compartment, exclaiming over the gush of frosty air that rushed out.

Finally, Nikki called a halt to his antics. "Enough of that. The food won't stay chilled for long if you keep letting all the cold air out."

She started the dishwasher. Silver Thorn, who had seen her depress the handle and push the buttons, reached out, tugged on the lever, and quickly opened the door. He peered inside, frowned, and told her. "Start it again."

She did. Again he stopped the machine in mid-cycle, jerked the door open, and looked. His frown deepened. "Why does it stop?" he asked. "I want to see the wheel go round and clean the dishes."

"Thank goodness it does stop when you open the door

or we'd be knee-deep in water right now," she said. "It's designed to spray the dishes, not the floor, Thorn."

"Why do you need so many dishes?" he questioned, throwing open one of the cabinets and gazing at the array of plates and bowls. He opened another, filled with cups and glasses. And a third, stuffed with cans and bottles and boxes of food. "And all this food," he marveled. "Do you have so many guests?"

"Not really. I suppose I could get by with fewer dishes, as could most families, but this is what we're used to. And food which can be stored for long periods without perishing is not only convenient, but a very practical necessity, especially in the dead of winter." She gave a helpless shrug. "What can I say? Modern Americans are spoiled. We prefer variety, abundance, luxury, and convenience whenever possible."

It took most of the afternoon and early evening to catch up on what had happened to each of them in their time apart. Silver Thorn related how he'd escorted his mother and sister and several other members of his family and tribe safely to Mexico. His sister's husband and other capable warriors had gone along and would be there to take care of the elders and children as they set up their new village.

For her part, Nikki told Silver Thorn how Sheree, her parents, and her brothers had rallied round her. She also filled him in on his new persona and the problems she'd encountered with Brian Sanders. Silver Thorn was not pleased to learn about the nosy reporter.

"You say you dated this man prior to meeting me. Explain this word *dated*. Does this mean he was courting you?"

"Definitely not, at least not as far as I was concerned. It never went that far, Thorn, I simply went out with the man three times, to dinner and a couple of movies. He kissed me good night at my door, sent me some flowers and a box of candy, and that was all. And before you get your briefs in a bunch, let me say that in today's society, sharing a meal with a man does not constitute marriage or any other binding relationship."

"Yet he seems to think he has some claim on you, does he not?" Silver Thorn persisted.

"Hey! That's his problem, not mine—or it wouldn't be if the idiot would leave me alone."

"He will leave you alone now, Neeake," Silver Thorn promised darkly. "If he does not, he will find himself buried up to his neck in an anthill."

"Now, that I'd like to see!" she crowed with delight, flashing him a pert smile. "And while you're at it, could you save a space next to him for my ex-husband?"

"Gladly."

"At any rate, Brian wouldn't bother me at all if I were certain he was going to accept this story about you. But he's already tried to pry into your past, and he finds it odd that he can't dig up any background information on you. I'm afraid he's going to persist along these lines and really make waves. That's why Denny and Jack are trying to invent a new and credible past for you. It's also why it is so imperative that you learn to cope in today's world as quickly as possible. If you display what people consider normal behavior, they won't think to question it. On the other hand, if your behavior seems strange or foreign to them, it provokes their natural curiosity—and that is precisely what we want to avoid."

"Then I shall become what everyone thinks I am," Thorn assured her, drawing himself up proudly. "I shall be Thorn Silver, this archaeologist who digs up old Indian weapons and pots and other artifacts. I will study your history. I will learn your modern ways. I will make them believe all the tales we must put forth to them. But they will also learn one steadfast truth among the lies—that you are my wife and carry my child. I will abide no other man attempting to trespass upon my territory or to steal that which is mine."

Thirty-one

When the telephone rang later that evening, Nikki nearly had to peel Silver Thorn off the living room ceiling. "It's just the phone, Thorn. Remember? The instrument that lets people talk to each other over long distances. We can just let the answering machine catch the call. That way we don't have to answer if it's someone we don't want to talk to."

The answering machine picked up on the third ring, and Sheree's voice said, "Nik? It's me. Sorry I couldn't call sooner, but I had to hurry for my date with Dave. I just wanted to make sure you were okay and not awfully sick. Hey! Are you there? If you're listening, answer me. I'm really worried about you, kiddo."

Nikki picked up the receiver. "Okay, so you caught me playing hookey. Satisfied?"

"Are your really all right? Nancy said you called in with the flu. Have you seen the doctor? Can I bring you some chicken soup or something? Do you think you'll be better by Thanksgiving? As much as I love your family, I'd really feel odd about going to dinner at your Mom's without you."

"Sheree, shut up and I'll explain everything in three words. Thorn is here."

"Oh, God! You're kidding! You're not kidding!" Silver Thorn could hear Sheree's shriek from where he sat, several feet from the phone. "Can I come over? I'm dying to meet him."

"Get real, girl!" Nikki told her. "It's almost eleven o'clock. Time for all good teachers to climb into their beds, and that's just where Thorn and I were about to head when the phone rang. And you're not invited to join us. You can meet him tomorrow. Believe me, Sheree. He'll still be here, and he's anxious to meet you, too."

"But I have school tomorrow," Sheree wailed. "Maybe I can call in with the flu, too."

"Nothing doing. They'll think they have an epidemic on their hands. Listen, I'm going to take Thorn out to meet Mom and Dad tomorrow. Why don't you drive out after school?"

For all her previous enthusiasm, Sheree suddenly wavered. "Are you sure, Nikki? After all, it has been awhile since you've seen the big guy. I'll understand if you want to keep him under wraps for a while."

"Tomorrow afternoon will be fine. Just don't tell anyone else, please? Once word gets out, everyone will want to meet him and we won't have a minute's peace."

"Uh . . . that reminds me. Dave and I ran into Brian this evening at the restaurant. He must really be desperate to approach me in public, when the two of us can't stand to be within spitting distance of each other. Anyway, he made a point of asking about you and whether or not you'd heard from your long-lost hubby. I told him to flake off."

"Thanks. I owe you one, Sheree. I'll talk to you later."

"Yeah. Sweet dreams, and other stuff, you two."

After breakfast the next morning, Nikki called her parents and all three brothers to inform them of the news of Thorn's arrival. Her Mom and Dad wanted her to bring Thorn out to the farm immediately, but Nikki politely declined.

"We've got a lot of other matters to take care of first. We'll see you this afternoon. I'll stop by the bakery and pick up one of those cherry cheesecakes you like so much."

One of those other matters was teaching Thorn how to operate the T.V. and VCR. "I've got a whole library of video tapes on American history," she told him. "I find they're a great learning tool—much faster than reading a book when you're in a rush. Next week, when I'm back at school, you can review the tapes, and when I get home I'll answer any questions you have. Also, television itself is very educational, depending on what you watch, of course. I don't think you're going to get a true image of the average American home by watching daytime dramas or game or talk shows. Still, there is the educational channel and the national news—and the sports channel for pure entertainment. And, lest I forget, football. I just know you're bound to love that. Then there's the Discovery channel and documentaries, and I'm sure we can rent a few tapes on archaeology."

"Are you certain I will live long enough to learn all you have planned for me?" he teased.

"Black Hoof lived to the ripe old age of one hundred and nine," she informed him smartly. "I'm going to take very good care of you, and I plan to have you around for many years to come sweetheart. I can't guarantee that you won't end up with bifocals and a pacemaker, but I'll try to keep your cholesterol down to a dull roar and I can promise you lots of exercise—even if most of it is conducted in bed."

With his introduction to television that morning, Thorn was completely captivated. "It is like your photographs," he marveled. "But in these the people speak and move."

On the average of every two seconds, he asked her to explain something he'd seen. Nikki obliged.

"That's a car. You remember me telling you about them, don't you?"

"No, that's a truck. Similar to a car, but built to haul cargo."

"That's a scene of the New York City skyline. Yes, amazingly enough, there really are that many people living there. Look at the tall buildings—like huge wigewas."

"That's a train."

"A boat—think of it as a big canoe."

"That's Washington D.C., where all the major crooks hang out. Sorry, just kidding. That's where our government seat is located. The Congress, the President, the Supreme Court."

"That's enough of this for a while. Hand over your remote control, buster. We're taking a break."

"Fasten your seatbelt." Nikki reached across Thorn's lap and helped him buckle up. "I know it's somewhat uncomfortable to be strapped in like this, but it's for your own safety. Besides, it's the law and we don't want to be stopped by the police and given a ticket."

After buckling her own belt, Nikki glanced across at him with a wink. "Ready?"

Silver Thorn gave a stiff, silent nod. He was nervous about riding in this strange metal horse Neeake called a car. On the other hand, he was brimming with excited anticipation, looking forward to experiencing this new mode of speedy transportation.

Nikki started the engine and backed slowly out of the garage. "Don't worry, Thorn. I've been doing this for years, and I'm a very careful and conscientious driver. Just relax and enjoy the scenery."

Fortunately, the speed limit in this quiet neighborhood was set at twenty-five miles per hour, which gave Thorn a few minutes to accustom himself to the movement of

the car at a slower pace. With one big hand tightly clamped
to the console and the other grasping the passenger door-
grip, he forced himself to concentrate on the view beyond
the windows. Though his grip remained firm, within seconds he was amazed at what he saw.

"So many cars, all these big wigewas," he marveled.

"Houses," she corrected automatically. "Of course, this
is an older division, so these houses aren't nearly as modern and fancy as some of the newer ones you'll see."

"What are these poles with all the cords on them?" he
wanted to know.

"Utility poles for the electrical and telephone lines. See
how the wires run to each house?"

"Why do we stop here?"

"See the red sign? It's a stop sign instructing drivers
that they must stop at this street intersection before going
on. Such road signs are designed to keep motorists from
all trying to go through the crossing at the same time and
hitting each other's cars. Not that it always works; but
without them, driving would be much more confusing and
quite hazardous."

Some time back, Nikki had mapped out an itinerary of
local historical sites which would be of most interest to
Thorn. With nearly three hours until they were due at her
parents' house, they had plenty of time for a small tour.
Their first stop was to be the small mall on Ft. Amanda
Road.

Along the way, they followed the Ottawa River, the old
Hog Creek, driving past the oil refinery with its huge
steam stacks and dancing orange flame. Even enclosed as
they were in the car, Thorn could smell the rank odor of
crude oil.

"What a stink!" he said, wrinkling his nose. "It smells
worse than Windbreaker."

"Windbreaker?" Nikki inquired. "Who, or what, is
that?"

Thorn grinned at the memory. "He was a boy we grew up with in the village. His real name was Little Horse, but he was forever passing farts, so we all called him Windbreaker."

Nikki laughed. "I'll bet that made courting something of a trial for him. Did he ever overcome his digestive difficulties?"

"Only when his mother died. Most likely it was her cooking that provoked the problem."

Nikki pulled into the entrance to the mall and headed the car into the drive-through lane at McDonald's. "I won't promise that this meal won't give you gas, but it's high time you got your first taste of America's favorite foods. A cheeseburger, french fries, and a milkshake."

She pulled up to the speaker, and Thorn watched in amusement as she placed their order. They inched forward behind several other cars, eventually reaching the window, where Nikki exchanged money for a sack of food and two frosty drinks in big paper cups. Cradling them carefully in her lap, Nikki swung into the mall parking lot, stopped, and cut the engine.

After demonstrating how to use the plastic straw, she placed their drinks in the handy cup holders jutting out from the console and handed him his sandwich and box of fries.

"Do you know where we are, Thorn?" she questioned, gesturing out the window at the mall, the roads, the traffic.

He shook his head, the most he could manage with a mouthful of burger and bun.

"We're parked in the center of what used to be Peahchaete's village. See? There's the river. You know, I always did wonder how it came to be called Hog Creek, especially as far back as your time. Your people weren't into raising pigs, as I recall."

Silver Thorn gazed around dazedly, scarcely able to comprehend that this busy, bustling place, with all its buildings and pavement, was the site of the old village. He answered Nikki's inquiry almost absently. "Many years ago, perhaps two hundred years from this date, there was a British agent who lost his hogs while fleeing from Logan and his warriors. From that day on, the river was known as *Kushko Theepe*, Hog Creek. The warriors had a fine feast that night."

"Pigs and all, I know the river was a lot cleaner than it is now with all this industrial pollution," Nikki lamented. "It's a rotten shame that modern man, as intelligent as he professes to be, has to ruin his own environment, and most of everyone else's. At the rate we're going, in a few decades the air, the rivers, the oceans, the land and forests will all be just one huge garbage dump."

From there Nikki headed the car south. She made a short detour to show him the school where she taught, but didn't stop. "I'm supposed to be home sick with the flu," she reminded him. "I'll take you inside another day and show you around."

Their next destination was some miles away. As they rode along, Thorn drank in the sites in ever-growing amazement. Even the rural areas, with their cattle, barns and fences and silos, fascinated him.

At length, Nikki flipped on the radio, which was tuned into a soft rock station. Thorn listened attentively and finally settled back as if deciding that the music, though definitely different from any he was used to, wasn't bad at all. Nikki wondered if the drums' providing the background rhythm weren't the deciding factor. She would eventually introduce him to all the varying types of music—classical, hard rock, country western—so he could determine which he liked best. She just hoped it wouldn't be rap!

Just outside a small town, they turned into a little corner cemetery. "I thought you might like to see Black Hoof's monument," she told him. "It's rumored that he was buried around here, perhaps in this very cemetery, but no one knows for sure. They did erect his monument here, however. A lasting tribute to his life."

After paying their respects—which was decidedly odd for Silver Thorn, since in his own era Black Hoof was still very much alive—they headed west. "We don't have time today or we'd drive on to Indian Lake and look around a bit. We'll do that another day, though, and perhaps go on to Bellefontaine, which is Blue Jacket's old stomping grounds. Then there're St. Mary's, known as Girty's Town in your day, and Piqua, of course—when we're not so pressed for time."

Shortly, they arrived at Wapakoneta. Nikki parked behind the row of businesses that backed up to the Auglaize River. "Remember me telling you about this place? I know it can't appear very familiar to you now, but those stores sit approximately where Black Hoof's village used to stand. Somewhere along here, you lounged beneath a tree while I picked berries and got into a nice patch of poison ivy."

"May we get out of the car here?" Thorn asked.

"If you want."

Huddled into his new sweatshirt for lack of a heavier coat, Thorn strolled along the riverbank, deep in thought. Nikki walked silently at his side, not wanting to disturb him as he sorted through his memories. Some minutes later, he knelt down and scooped up a handful of cold dirt.

"It is strange, but I can feel the heartbeat of my people here, in this earth beneath our feet. This was their home, their river. In some way, though they no longer live here, this land is still theirs, imprinted with their lives. It shall always be so, no matter how many buildings the white men erect over it or how many of their hard roads they lay down. The footprints of my people will never be erased from this place."

Nikki knew without being told that whenever Silver

Thorn became restless or homesick and needed to touch home again, he would come here—to this spot where the essence, the spirit, of his Shawnee brethren lingered still.

Thirty-two

There was a bakery in a little strip mall in Wapak where Nikki planned to pick up the cheesecake she'd promised her mother. Again, Silver Thorn was highly interested in the traffic, the stores, and all the people coming and going.

"It's not normally this busy on a weekday," Nikki informed him. "But tomorrow is a holiday, when a lot of the businesses will be closed, and people are trying to get last-minute projects done before the long weekend. Not only that, many ladies may still be picking up their Thanksgiving turkeys and pies for tomorrow's big dinner. I know Mom will be baking like crazy, trying to get everything done on time."

"She is making the meal for so many by herself?" he asked.

"No, but she always insists on doing the lion's share, even though each of the other women in the family will bring a dish or two to add to the fare."

Nikki spotted a driver pulling out of a parking space and whipped in after him, beating another motorist out of the spot. Silver Thorn appeared quite stunned at the sudden move. His fingers were digging grooves in the upholstery, and there were white lines of tension around his tight mouth, as if he were barely constraining a scream.

"Sorry. I didn't mean to scare the peanut butter out of you," she apologized. "But sometimes you have to be really quick." She reached for her purse. "Do you want to stay out here and people-watch or would you like to come inside with me?"

The opportunity to finally glimpse the inside of a building other than Nikki's house was too good to miss. "I will accompany you."

As Nikki had known it would be, the bakery was packed with patrons, all eager to make their purchases and escape with their goodies. She and Silver Thorn had to wait several minutes before someone could serve them. Meanwhile, Thorn got the chance to observe the customers and the bakery personnel at close range, to note the way they were dressed, their mannerisms, and eavesdrop on a variety of conversations.

When they finally walked out, cheesecake in hand, Nikki declared, "I swear I must have gained five pounds just inhaling the air in there! Didn't it smell absolutely scrumptious?"

Silver Thorn agreed and added, "It made my stomach rumble and my mouth water. I cannot believe how many different sweets they have there, all in one place."

"Yeah, it's a dieter's nightmare and idea of heaven all rolled into one. I noticed you watching several people quite closely. Any comments?"

"The lady with the hair like a ripe plum. Is that a normal color for a white woman's hair?"

Nikki laughed. "No. That particular shade comes straight from a bottle, darling. And from the looks of it, she did it herself, without the aid of a decent hairdresser."

"And that boy with her. He had writing cut out of his hair in patches. It said *bulldogs*."

"He's probably on the football team at a nearby high school. Their mascot, something akin to your totem, is a bulldog. A lot of the young football players get their hair cut that way, but I believe it's a dying fad, thank God. You're not the only person who thinks it looks stupid."

* * *

Thorn paid particular attention as they pulled into the long driveway at the Swan farm. The house, similar to Nikki's but somewhat larger, was set well back from the road. A big white barn sat across the drive from it, and a large machine with two huge wheels and two smaller ones was half-in and half-out the open double doors. "That's Dad's tractor," Nikki said. "The farming's pretty much done for the year, as far as harvesting and plowing the fields go, but Dad can still show you around the place, if you want.

"And that's Shep," she added, pointing to the black-and-white dog loping toward the car. "He's part collie and part mutt. He's a good guard dog and great with kids. More bark than bite. As soon as he knows that you belong to us, he'll accept you as a life-long friend."

Nikki's dad met them at the door and ushered them inside. "Get in here out of the cold before you turn blue. Good grief, boy, where's your coat?"

"We haven't gotten him one yet, Dad," Nikki hurried to explain. "I thought maybe we'd hit K-mart on the way home. He needs some shoes or boots, too."

She continued with the introductions. "Dad, I'd like you to meet Silver Thorn. Thorn, this is my dad, Henry Swan."

The men shook hands. "I am pleased to make your acquaintance, Mr. Swan," Thorn stated formally.

"Likewise," the older man said. "But friends and family call me *Hank*. That or *Dad* will do nicely. Let's go on into the kitchen. Paula's in there cookin' up a storm, and there's no way I'm gonna pry her out of there anytime soon. Don't want to, either," he added, patting his stomach.

As they entered the kitchen, Paula wiped her hands on a dish towel and held one hand out to Thorn. "Forgive the flour. I just can't cook without making a mess of myself. Welcome to the family, Thorn."

"Thank you, Mrs. Swan." Thorn took her hand rather awkwardly, not entirely sure what to do. He wasn't used to greeting a woman in this manner.

Sensing his discomfort, Paula helped him off the hook by saying, "Call me *Mom*, or *Paula* if you prefer. These first meetings are so blasted difficult, aren't they? Just give me a hug, Thorn, and sit yourself down." She tugged him into her arms for a quick, hard embrace. "I hope you're planning to stay for supper. We're just having a pot of spaghetti since we've got such a big meal tomorrow. Sam is coming by in a little while."

"So is Sheree," Nikki said. "I hope you don't mind. She's pitching a fit at having to wait this long to meet Thorn."

"She's welcome anytime."

"Do you want some help, Mom?" Nikki offered.

Paula nodded. "You can toss the salad, if you would, and get these two helpless men a cup of coffee. Otherwise, they're just bound to get in the way."

The two men drank their coffee while the women cooked and Nikki related the day's activities. Comments and questions flew back and forth, and soon everyone was much more at ease. Half an hour later, at precisely 3:30, a car barreled into the barn lot and stopped with a squeal of brakes.

"That's got to be Sheree," Nikki commented with a grin. "Little Miss Speed Demon. Believe it or not, Thorn, her driving is much worse than mine."

Thorn looked doubtful, but replied prudently, "Then I do not think I will ever wish to ride with her."

Everyone laughed and agreed with him, and Nikki headed for the door to greet her friend.

With scarcely a how-do-you-do to Nikki, Sheree hurried into the kitchen, took one long look at Thorn, clasped both hands over her heart, and sighed dramatically, "You're everything Nikki said you were. Under other circumstances, I'd ask if you had a twin; but I've seen pictures of the Prophet, and frankly the idea of coming face to face with him gives me the willies. You and Tecumseh must have inherited all the good looks in the family, not to mention the brains. Welcome to 1996, Thorn."

"Thank you. Also, for being such a loyal and trustworthy friend to my wife."

Sheree shrugged off his compliment. "It's nothing, really. Nikki would have done the same for me."

Nikki poked Sheree in the arm and teased, "Hey! You must be slowing down these days. I expected you at least ten minutes ago."

Sheree screwed up her face. "I would have been here sooner, but I remembered at the last minute that my gas tank was edging on empty and I had two video tapes to return before they were overdue. But I did make good use of the delay." She reached into the large satchel hanging from her shoulder, withdrew three tapes, and handed them to Nikki. "I rented these for you. They're the only ones I could find on archaeology. You can make copies of them and Thorn can review them at his leisure. Just make sure these are back at the store in two days. I've been late returning tapes so often they're ready to revoke my card if it happens again."

Sheree plopped into a chair. "So, Thorn, tell me how you like the modern world so far."

This provoked another lively round of conversation which carried into the dinner hour. Sam, who was notoriously late for everything but a free meal, arrived just as the ladies were placing the food on the table.

He didn't wait to be formally introduced, but walked right up to Thorn, stuck his hand out, and said, "Hi. I'm Sam, Nikki's youngest brother. I live right down the road." Before Thorn could reply, other than to shake his hand, Sam claimed a chair and bellied up to the table. "Let's eat. I'm starved."

"Samuel Swan!" Paula scolded. "Where are your manners? You know I taught you better than that, and I don't appreciate your making me look bad in front of Thorn. Goodness! What he must think! Now, go wash your hands."

The others chuckled as Sam raised his hands and waggled them in front of him. "I already did, Mom. See? Clean as a whistle. I didn't even stop to pet Shep on the way in. Do I get an extra serving of dessert for being such a good little boy?"

"You keep tormenting your Mom, and you'll get a knot on your head," Hank predicted good-naturedly.

Thorn had never eaten anything resembling spaghetti and was not altogether sure how to get the long strands from his plate into his mouth without feeding his lap. The others, seeing his problem, graciously offered instruction. Though not terribly proficient with a fork, he soon learned to twine the spaghetti onto the utensil with the aid of his spoon. Within minutes, he was actually getting more in his mouth than was falling back onto his plate. To his surprise and delight, the strange looking meal was delicious. He especially liked the thick, chewy Italian bread, which had been brushed with butter and garlic and toasted.

When Thorn professed a desire to learn to drive, Sam immediately volunteered to teach him. "Nikki will be busy at school; and now that the crops are all off, I'll have plenty of free time."

"That's fine, son, but don't forget we've got that old combine to repair. It barely made it through the season," the elder Swan put in.

"That reminds me, what ever happened to those lottery tickets of yours, Nikki?" Sam inquired. "The ones you were going to redeem to help me put a down payment on a new combine. Remember?"

"Oh, I'd forgotten about those."

"They are here," Thorn said, pulling his spirit bag from

beneath his shirt. He opened the little pouch and extracted the tickets. "I believe these helped to bring me forward to the correct year, which is why I retrieved them from Neeake's letter to you."

"Well, if they did the trick once, maybe they'll be lucky a second time," Sheree suggested. "You know you can still check the winning numbers at almost any lottery sales location, and the tickets are good for six months."

"It would probably just be a waste of time and energy," Nikki stated. "What are the odds of having a winning ticket? I don't know why I bothered to buy them."

"No matter what anyone else claims, I say your odds are always fifty-fifty," Sam challenged. "You either win or you don't. If you don't want to check on them, I will—for a cut of the winnings, say forty percent."

"Ten," Nikki said.

"Thirty."

"Twenty, and that's final," Nikki stated.

"Sold." Sam held out his hand, and Thorn handed him the tickets. "Now, won't you be surprised if one of these does turn out to be a winner?"

After dinner, Hank loaned Thorn a jacket, and he and Sam showed Thorn around the barn lot while the women cleared the table and did the dishes. Then Nikki suggested that they leave.

"We still have to go shopping, and I have to fix a couple of dishes for tomorrow's dinner. Besides, I need time to rest up. It's going to be a madhouse with Jack and Denny and their families here, and I want to come early and help Mom finish the meal."

Department store shopping was another amazing revelation to Silver Thorn. Though he hadn't realized it at the time, that tiny bakery had only been the tip of the iceberg. It was mind-boggling to view all this merchandise under one roof! The colors, the fabrics, the varying array of items—everything from ready-made clothing to plants, from toys to tools, the uses for many of which Thorn hadn't the foggiest notion.

With Thorn stopping every few feet to examine one object or another and asking dozens of questions, it took them the better part of two hours to outfit him with a sheepskin jacket, three pairs of shoes, jeans, dress and sport shirts, slacks and belts, and a pair of winter gloves. Nikki winced at the total, but resolutely whipped out her handy charge card.

They exited the store pushing a fully loaded cart. "I'm bushed!" she declared wearily. "Still, it was better to get this done tonight. Traditionally, the day after Thanksgiving, which officially kicks off the Christmas shopping season, is the busiest retail day of the year. From then until Christmas, the stores will be thronged with holiday shoppers, not to mention the passel of kids lined up to talk to Santa Claus."

"Who is this Santa Claus that all the children wish to speak with him?"

"Well, he's rather a combination between a real man who lived many years ago named Saint Nicholas and a mythical character who is supposed to live at the North Pole and makes toys for children. He drives a sleigh pulled by flying reindeer, and on Christmas Eve he delivers toys to all the good little boys and girls the world over. He's fat and jolly, with a white beard and . . ." Nikki stopped in mid-sentence, drawing in a harsh breath. She stood as if turned to stone, staring across the parking lot, her mouth working soundlessly.

"Neeake, what bothers you?" Thorn inquired worriedly. "Neeake? Answer me!"

She pointed a shaking finger. "Th . . . there! I saw . . . I saw . . ."

"What? What did you see?" Thorn prompted anxiously.

"The Prophet!" The word emerged as a muted, strangled shriek. "I saw him, standing right over there, by that green van."

Thorn's head snapped around in the direction she was pointing, but he saw nothing but cars and a few ordinary twentieth-century citizens. Abandoning the cart for the moment, Thorn took her by the shoulders and turned her to face him. "That is not possible, Neeake. Surely your eyes and your mind are playing tricks on you. These past days have been most busy and trying."

Nikki got mad. "Damn it, Thorn! He may not be there now, but he was. I know what I saw. And my brain is fully intact, thank you! It was him! I know it. There couldn't be two men that ugly, that fearsome. It was Tenskwatawa. He's here!"

"But how can that be?" Thorn wondered. "It was nearly impossible for me to come to your time, and my powers are much greater than his. How could he have managed it?"

Nikki's violent shiver had nothing to do with the falling temperature. "I don't know, Thorn, but he did. Somehow, he did. And it can only mean trouble for us."

Thirty-three

When they arrived home, they found Macate pacing the house and growling. His tufted ears were on the alert for the smallest sound.

"See?" Nikki said. "Even Macate knows something is up. Now do you believe me?"

"It is not that I doubt your word, Neeake, but perhaps that I don't want to believe that Tenskwatawa has followed me here. The entire reason for sending you home last summer was to keep you safe from him. And now, somehow, I have led him to you again."

To further agitate matters, Nikki found a message from Brian on her answering machine.

"Hey, babe! Brian here. I just want you to know that I'm here for you if you need me. Don't get mad, but I've done some more checking on your long-lost hubby and I'm still coming up empty. Chances are, he fed you a line of bull twelve-miles long—false name and all; and despite what he led you to believe, I'm willing to bet your marriage to him isn't even legal. Face up to it, babe. The phony's been stringing you along. He's probably done the same with other women; and if he hasn't shown up by now, he probably never will. Good riddance, I say. Now, how about giving me a break, doll? I'm busting my butt trying to help you, and all I'm getting is the cold shoulder. Call me."

"When Hell freezes solid," Nikki muttered angrily.

"Lord, but I wish he'd poke his reporter's nose into someone else's affairs! We don't need him making any more
waves. We have problems enough."

"I would like to give him a break," Thorn commented
curtly. "I would take great pleasure in breaking his face."

After an extremely restless night listening to Macate's
endless pacing, it was a relief to escape to the farm again.
There, Nikki and Thorn were immediately enveloped in
the warmth and security of her loving family. Denny and
Jack, with all their clandestine collaboration, were eager
to present them with the fruits of their efforts. The others
were equally eager to be included in the conspiracy, and
their Thanksgiving holiday soon resembled more of a high-
tech defense council than the average family get-together.

"Here's what we've got," Jack told them, spreading several documents out on the coffee table. He selected one
and presented it to Thorn. "This is your birth certificate,
complete with the official state seal. It's bogus, of course,
but no one will ever know that. The stamp is an exact
replica."

"Now," Denny chimed in, "you'll need a certified copy
of that in order to apply for a social security card. This
may create a slight fuss because they aren't going to be
able to locate your original birth records in the Xenia
courthouse. But, thanks to Jack-the-Hacker, when they
check the state computer records—voila! They'll hit pay-
dirt! With your birth certificate and social security number,
you can apply for your driver's license. By then, Sammy
should have you ready to take your driver's test."

"I'm going to start him out on farm lanes and old back
roads," Sam contributed. "It might seem odd that a grown
man in this day and age doesn't know siccum about driving, and that way there'll be less chance of attracting attention."

Next, Jack gave Thorn a small book. "Your fake passport, listing all the different countries you've worked in," he explained. "It's totally worthless, so don't try to use it for any foreign traveling. I just thought it might come in handy, in case someone decides to get really snoopy, like that reporter, for instance. It looks authentic enough to pass a cursory inspection, but I wouldn't chance presenting it at any actual international port of entry."

He selected another document, handing it to Nikki with a flourish. "This is yours, sis."

It was a marriage certificate, stating that one Nichole Anita Swan and one Thorn Silver had been wed at 4:45 P. M. on the tenth day of June 1996, in some unpronounceable town in Mexico with at least twenty letters in its title. Likewise, the registrar, or priest, or whoever had supposedly performed the ceremony, had a full eight names and terribly illegible handwriting.

Nikki had to laugh at her brothers' ingenuity. "I'll treasure it always," she told them.

Next, Jack sorted out several pages and presented them to Thorn. "I took the liberty of creating a resume for you. It lists all the places you supposedly worked, and for whom. As an added precaution, I included several written references from your former employers, and I must say you're an exemplary employee," he tacked on with a chuckle. "Needless to say, these chaps, working as they do in the outback of nowhere, are ridiculously hard to find when it comes to verifying references and such. Hence, the written recommendations. You'll need them, and the resume, when you try to get a job here in the States."

Thorn nodded. "I intend to find work of some type as soon as possible that I may support my family. It would not please me to do nothing while Neeake teaches at her school."

This led to an intense discussion on what sort of position Thorn might hope to find.

"What did you include on his resume, Jack, concerning his education?" Nikki inquired.

Jack chuckled. "Leave it to the schoolteacher to ask that. Don't worry, sis. I've got it covered. Thorn's mother taught him via mail-order courses similar to the home-study programs available now. He concluded high school in that manner with the equivalent of a GED from somewhere in Australia. Very hard to verify that, naturally. As far as his professional expertise is concerned, he learned his trade from his archaeologist parents as he grew up around the digs and in the wilds. You can't beat hands-on experience in a career like this. He's more or less a parental-taught, self-taught expert, very well respected by his fellow archaeologists, as proven by those glowing references."

"But surely he had some formal schooling in the profession," she argued.

"From where?" Denny questioned. "The minute we list a university he's supposed to have attended, anyone can check the school records. Not to mention yearbooks, old professors and classmates, et cetera. It's too risky. Much better the way Jack and I devised it."

He turned to Thorn. "So, what sort of work would suit you? Preferably, something that will put your natural skills to good use."

"Which ones?" Sheree interposed. "His Native American skills or his supernatural ones? He'd make one heck of a magician, you know. Big money there, too."

"That's a bit of a stretch from archaeology, though, don't you think?" Mari put in. "Wouldn't people wonder why he gave up his life's work, something he's so good at, to do something so drastically different?"

"I believe I would like to try something similar to this archaeology," Thorn said thoughtfully. "But I do not want to travel and be away from Neeake."

"What about something to do with museums?" Danielle suggested. "Their Native American exhibits, in particular.

Don't they usually employ someone to verify the artifacts, or at least consult an expert in that field?"

"That's a marvelous idea, Danni," Paula commented.

Everyone echoed the sentiment, including Thorn.

Denny grinned and gave his wife a hug. "Have I ever told you how much I admire your brain? I love your body, too, but it's your brain that really turns me on."

"It strikes me that nearly every town, no matter how small, has some sort of museum or fort or historical site. This part of the country abounds with them," Hank pointed out. "Maybe Thorn could get a position as a regional consultant on Indian relics." He frowned and asked, "Is there such a profession, I wonder?"

"If not, we can always create one," Jack proposed. "Lord knows, we've fabricated Thorn's entire background. Inventing a new position for him should be a piece of cake. And who better to verify Indian effects from this area than a Shawnee who actually used them? He's a natural!"

Nikki nodded. "What do you think, Thorn? It might mean minimal travel, but nothing more than a few hours' drive from here."

"Yes, I would like this work very much," Thorn said, approving the notion. "The only thing better would be to minister to my own people. Already, I miss being a shaman."

"Why can't you combine the two, Uncle Thorn?" This from Denny's teenage son, Steven. "There must be lots of folks in these parts with Shawnee ancestry who wish they knew more about their heritage. Stuff like the old ceremonies and dances. And I'll bet there isn't a single person in the whole state who knows how to speak the language. Except you."

"Out of the mouths of babes!" Paula declared.

Hank's eyes lit up with excitement and yearning. "Yes.

You could teach us our native tongue, Thorn, and all the old ways that have been lost and forgotten all these years."

"It would be a great service to your people," Sam added.

"And nontaxable, to boot, if you supplied an educational and religious need and simply took donations," Jack couldn't help noting.

"Wow! I think we're really onto something here!" Sheree exclaimed.

"I think so, too," Nikki said. "As long as it makes Thorn happy."

"Nothing could give me more pleasure than aiding my people," he assured her, his eyes aglow with enthusiasm. "Nothing but loving you."

Thorn enjoyed not only the wonderful Thanksgiving feast, but the warm, open companionship of his new family. Even in his own time, among the Shawnee, Thorn had felt set apart from the majority of his fellows—mainly due to his unusual skills. Many of them had been wary of him. Others had set him above themselves, almost as they would an idol or a spirit figure. Here, none of that seemed to matter. These people accepted him as one of their own, completely dismissing his peculiar talents. They even deigned to tease him without fear of some awful retribution. This pleased him immensely. It put him at ease and warmed his heart. For this affectionate kinship, he was truly thankful.

The table had been cleared, and dessert and coffee were being served when the doorbell rang. Paula frowned. "Who can that be? No one was expecting anyone else, were they?"

Everyone replied to the negative.

"I'll get it," Hank said, rising from his chair.

In a few seconds he was back, and now he was frowning. "Nikki, there's a man at the door wanting to speak with you. It's Brian Sanders."

Nikki froze in place. All around the table, silence fell.

Steven broke it first. "Uh, oh. Now the stuff's gonna hit the fan."

Nikki rose slowly, her glance sliding toward Thorn. "I suppose the only way to get rid of him is to talk to him."

"And to let him see for himself the husband he claims is a . . . what did he say? A phony?" Thorn, too, had risen and was striding from the room.

"If you need any assistance, call out," Denny offered. "I've already had one not-so-pleasant discussion with him, but I'm game for it again."

"I thank you for the offer, but we will need no aid, brother," Thorn stated tersely. "However, this reporter-man might, if he truly angers me."

Brian was standing just inside the door in the entrance hall. The smile he was about to offer Nikki died half-born on his lips. "Uh, who's the aging hippie with the long hair, Nikki? Don't tell me this is the errant husband?"

"How perceptive of you, Brian," Nikki grated through clenched teeth. She turned to Thorn. "Thorn, this is Brian Sanders, the reporter I've told you about. Brian, my husband, Thorn Silver, who I'm sure is contemplating how well his hands will fit around your throat. Be forewarned. Everything you say can and will be held against you. Now, if you would kindly state your business and leave, I would appreciate it. You've interrupted our meal."

Brian was evidently taken aback and at a loss for words, which in itself must have been a novel experience for him. It took him a moment to collect his thoughts. "I . . . uh . . . you've been avoiding me, Nikki. I thought today would be the best time to catch you and have a little talk."

"About Thorn," she surmised.

"Y . . . Yes, actually," he stammered. Heat climbed into

his face, staining it red. "I suppose you got the message I left on your answering machine last evening."

"We did, indeed," Thorn told him, spearing Brian with a glacial glare. "I do not appreciate having my wife's ears assaulted with your lies."

Though obviously intimidated, which was precisely what Thorn had intended, Brian defended himself. "Most of what I said was the truth, at least as I see it. I've done my best, but can't glean even the smallest bit of information about you, Silver. That's rare enough to raise my suspicions, which might prove to hold more than a grain of truth. Everyone has a past, some sort of record on file in a computer somewhere. So where is yours? Who are you? What are you? An underworld spy? A mobster with ten aliases? Or maybe you're simply an illegal alien trying to gain U. S. citizenship by charming an innocent woman into a hasty marriage."

Thorn took a step toward Brian, his hands aiming for the man's neck. Nikki quickly stepped between them and clasped Thorn's arm. Not that she could hold him back if he didn't want to comply with her wishes. "Why would Thorn need to do that when he's already a United States citizen by birth?" Nikki questioned.

"That's what your brother said, but I don't believe it. I've checked, and I can't find a birth certificate on file."

"Then I suggest you check again," Thorn growled. "I was born in Xenia, forty-five years ago. If I have a copy of my birth records, surely the state does also."

"Okay, so why haven't you ever filed an income-tax report?" Brian persisted. "Why doesn't the social security office have any record of a number for you? Or the DMV, for that matter?"

"Surely Denny told you that Thorn and his parents lived and worked outside the U.S. Why would they possess social security numbers or driver's licenses for a country where they neither live nor work?" Nikki shook her head at him.

"Your reasoning just doesn't make sense, Brian. Maybe you should consider taking a long, restful vacation. Get away from the pressures of the job before you burn out entirely."

"Oh, no you don't," Brian argued. "You're not going to get rid of me that easily. This situation stinks to high heaven, and I'm not going anywhere until I get to the bottom of it."

"We are going to get rid of you," Thorn assured him grimly. "One way or another. Now, you will leave my wife alone in the future or I will be forced to harm you. While I would take great pleasure in it, Neeake would most likely plead for your life. Therefore, I will issue this one warning. If you do not heed it, the fault will be yours. Do I make myself clearly understood?"

"Yeah," Brian grumbled. "I can recognize a threat when I hear one." He backed toward the door. "I'm leaving. For now. But the minute I can get the goods on you, Silver, I'll sic the cops on your tail. Bet on it, buster. Then Nikki will see that I'm right."

"If you're planning on my gratitude, think again," Nikki told him. "And Thorn doesn't make threats, Brian. He makes promises—and keeps them."

She slammed the door in his face. Hard.

Thirty-four

Nikki and Thorn were halfway home when Thorn suddenly inquired, "Where is this place out west where you say most of the Shawnee now live?"

"I wasn't sure myself, so I did some research once I got back here. I found that the major concentration is in several communities around Oklahoma City. One town is actually named Shawnee, Oklahoma, and one is called Tecumseh."

"How long would it take to get there in your car?"

Nikki tried to calculate it. "Around a day and a half, I suppose, driving a twelve-hour-day and stopping at night. Why?"

"Will you take me there? Now."

Nikki steered the car to the side of the road, shifted into park, and faced him before answering. "Okay, Thorn. What's up? Why this sudden urge to go to Oklahoma immediately if not sooner?"

"I do not know why I need to go there, only that I must. It is as if something or someone is calling me to go. I feel that it is most urgent that I get there as soon as possible."

Nikki shook her head in wonder. "I knew better than to ask and to expect an ordinary answer."

"Will you drive me there?" he queried again.

"I'll do better than that," she told him. "If we can get seats at this late hour and if my credit card will stand the strain, I'll get us both airplane tickets. Flying is much faster, and we can rent a car on the other end."

"Fly?" he repeated incredulously. "How does a person fly? And what is this airplane you speak of?"

"It's a machine with an engine and wings that is aerodynamically designed to be capable of flight. A trained pilot *drives* it, so to speak, and there are many seats on the inside, making it possible for numerous people to ride in it at once."

"Is this airplane thing safe?" he asked doubtfully. "What happens if it decides to fall from the sky?"

"If a plane malfunctions that badly, it crashes, burns, and all aboard are usually killed," she admitted bluntly. "However, statistics generally show that more people die in car accidents than in airplane crashes every year. Millions of people fly every day and arrive at their destinations safely."

"And you feel assured that we could do so?" he prodded.

Nikki nodded. "I wouldn't have suggested it, otherwise."

Thorn mimicked her nod. "Then we will do this. How much faster will it be to go by flying than by driving?"

"That depends on when the next flight is scheduled and whether or not we can get tickets for it. Many times, the seats are all taken weeks in advance. If we can get seats and a flight tonight or tomorrow out of a nearby airport, we could arrive in Oklahoma City within a couple of hours of takeoff, I imagine."

"How does one check on this information?"

Nikki put the car back into gear and guided it onto the road again. "By telephone. I'll call as soon as we get home. Then, depending on what we find out, we'll pack some clothes and drive to the airport. By the way, do you have any idea how long this mysterious mission of yours might take? I'm supposed to be back at school first thing Monday morning."

"No, but I do not think it will take long. Perhaps a day or two, but I cannot be certain."

Nikki sighed. "Okay. I guess we'll just play this one by ear."

After half-a-dozen phone calls, Nikki found an open flight from Dayton International to Oklahoma City. It departed at 9:00, which gave them just enough time to pack an overnight bag and dash off to the airport. It was a rush; and she knew that if they got held up in traffic or encountered an accident, they'd never make it on time—which could mean forfeiting nonrefundable tickets that had cost a bundle! She also took a few minutes to call ahead and reserve a rental car and secure a motel room for the night—and to notify her parents of their last-minute plans.

They made their flight—barely. Knowing that time was of the essence, Silver Thorn did not dally, though he would have liked to have gotten a better impression of the bustling airport. As it was, they were the last passengers to board the aircraft. After quickly stuffing their coats and bag into the overhead compartment, they took their seats. Nikki, knowing how exciting it was to fly for the first time, offered Silver Thorn the window seat. While he would have gotten a much better view on a daytime flight, she figured he would still be enthralled by the sight of the city lights dotting the landscape below them.

Silver Thorn was understandably nervous. Though he did his best not to show it, Nikki could tell. The tense lines around his mouth were back, and he sat stiff and still in his seat, his hands clutching the armrests.

As they taxied toward the runway, engines rumbling, Nikki patted his white knuckles comfortingly. "It will be fine, Thorn. We'll be in the air in just a few minutes."

Perversely, she couldn't help teasing him just a little. "Be brave, darling. The flight attendants frown on sniveling passengers."

He spared her a scowl, but said nothing in reply. His jaw was too tightly clamped to allow for speech.

They lifted off with a boost of power, and the ground fell swiftly beneath them. It was a dizzying, exhilarating moment.

Nikki leaned over him. "Look, Thorn, see all the lights down there? Isn't it beautiful?"

He swallowed the lump in his throat and dared to look. It was a stunning sight. As were the stars above. "So this is what the eagle sees as he soars upon the winds," Thorn murmured in awe-filled wonder.

When the stewardess came by to offer them refreshment, Thorn absently declined. He was much too enthralled with watching out the window to bother with anything so trivial. They flew though a cloud, and he exclaimed softly, as thrilled as a child at Christmas. Nikki shared his delight, enjoying it all the more through his eyes and reactions.

It was over all too soon. They landed in Oklahoma City with a couple of bumps and a squeal of tires on pavement. It wasn't the smoothest of landings, but Nikki was glad the weather was cooperating. There was no snow or ice with which to contend. Just the chill of the crisp night air.

They'd packed lightly and thus were able to avoid the crush and the lengthy wait at the baggage carousel. Their first stop was at the airport car rental. Within half an hour, they were zipping through interestate traffic, headed toward their nearby motel.

Interstate travel was another novel event for Silver Thorn and one for which he wasn't sure he cared much. Now, he stated decisively, "I believe I like flying in that huge metal arrow better than riding so fast in a car."

Then came the motel, and he was intrigued anew, especially with the elevator that took them to the fourth floor, where their room was located. When he grabbed at his stomach, Nikki laughed. "Yeah. It makes your tummy tickle, doesn't it?"

The room had a huge king-size bed, a T.V.-radio combination, a microwave ensconced in an armoire, and a mini-bar. Almost all the comforts of home. In the bathroom was a basket of complimentary toiletries, another wall radio, and a hair dryer.

Like the majority of travelers, Silver Thorn tested the bed first. "I like this firm bed," he informed her. "I cannot seem to adjust to sleeping atop water."

"I'm not too keen on it myself," she admitted. "As soon as we can afford it, we'll replace the mattress."

"I would prefer a big one like this. My feet stick out of the end of your bed."

"Our bed," she reminded him as she hung the last of their clothes on the rack. "And if you want a king-size mattress, we'll have to replace the entire bed. That will cost more, so we may have to wait a bit. With the baby coming, we'll have more pressing expenses that must be considered first."

Nikki's stomach rumbled. "I'm hungry, aren't you?" At his nod, she suggested, "The restaurant is closed, but the snack bar will still be serving. Why don't we mosey on down and grab a bite to eat? That or we can run out for a pizza or order something from room service."

"Room service?"

Nikki showed him the menu card near the phone. "It usually costs more, but you can call down and have the food brought to your room."

Silver Thorn shook his head. "I would rather see more of this place if you are not too tired."

She grinned at him and grabbed her purse. "You can't kid me. You just want to ride in the elevator again. Just give me a minute to freshen up."

The snack bar didn't affect him much, but he was curious about the nightclub they passed along the way. They stopped for a second to poke their heads inside and give him a peek. He came away nearly dazed. "The music is so loud it assaults the ears," he said. "And so much smoke, I thought the room was on fire."

"There was a day when I would have enjoyed that," Nikki confessed. "It's only been a couple of years since I quit smoking cigarettes. You do get somewhat accustomed to the noise after a while, though it does make conversation difficult. However, as much as I enjoy dancing, I really don't care to be around a bunch of drunks."

"That is what the nightclub is about?" he questioned. "Dancing and smoking and drinking firewater?"

"Basically. That and picking up women—or men, for that matter."

"Why would a person want to lift another person?" he asked in some confusion. "Is there some reason for this?"

Nikki chuckled. "Sorry. To *pick up* a person in a bar means that you introduce yourself to a stranger and invite him or her to come to your room—to your bed. It's a practice that can be very hazardous to your health, in more ways than one."

After a light meal, they took an alternate route back to the elevator and passed the heated indoor pool. Nikki gazed at it with longing. "I wish I'd thought to pack my swimsuit. It sure would be nice to soak away some of the travel kinks. See? They even have a whirlpool. Being pregnant, I don't think I could indulge in that. The water's probably too hot, but you'd adore it—if you had a pair of swim trunks."

A maid overheard Nikki's lament. "You two want to go in, I can get you a couple of suits," she offered. "That fancy boutique up front would charge you a fortune, but we got some stashed away in a back room—stuff previous guests have forgotten to take with them when they checked out. They've all been properly washed, if you don't mind wearing other folks' leavings."

Nikki indicated her bulging stomach. "I doubt you'd have any to fit me, but I'm sure Thorn would appreciate a loaner."

The maid laughed and gestured toward her own rotund build. "Honey, we have some suits back there that would go around both of us twice. Must have been made at the tent-and-awning company! You wait here, and I'll get you fixed up in a jiffy."

As Nikki had predicted, Thorn revelled in the whirlpool, letting the jets beat at his tense muscles. The hour was late, nearly midnight, and they had the place to themselves. They swam for a while and, when Nikki began yawning, finally returned to their room, leaving the borrowed suits and a nice tip behind.

After their hectic flight and the late night, morning came too early to suit Nikki. But with all the racket in the hall— guests moving about, laughing and talking; the cleaning staff clattering cleaning equipment and running vacuum cleaners—there was no going back to sleep, even if Silver Thorn had been of a mind to let her. He was up and eager to be about his business.

"Have you figured out why we're here?" she grumbled, grimacing at her reflection in the mirror. Then, "God! I look like road-kill! Promise you'll protect me from vultures."

Thorn laughed. "I pledge it. As to my mission, I have this wish to seek out a shaman, though I do not yet know who or why. Perhaps he will be able to enlighten us when we find him."

A few hours and several miles and inquiries later, their shaman turned out to be a *sha-woman*, or more correctly, perhaps, a, Shawnee medicine woman. She lived in a small cottage on the shore of Lake Thunderbird, between the towns of Tecumseh and Norman. She was also a full-fledged professor at a nearby institute, specializing in the study of paranormal psychology.

Gaze Starpath had her door open before they were half-way up the walk to her porch. "Welcome, my brother and sister. I have been expecting you."

Nikki didn't know precisely what she'd expected to find inside the cottage—maybe a crystal ball or two, tarot cards spread out on a table, strings of beads and a couple of black cats. She discovered none of this. The little house was neatly furnished, with nary a cat or anything particularly unusual in sight. At first glance, the oddest thing was the vast number of bookcases filled to overflowing with reading material about extra sensory perception, mental telepathy, and other subjects relating to parapsychology. There were also several books on Native American history, assorted medical tomes, and—surprisingly—a whole section crammed with romance novels!

"Sit, please," Miss Starpath invited, leading them further into her small living room. "I will serve tea." Indeed, the tea was already steeping in a pot on the coffee table. Next to it on the tray were three cups. Nikki's eyes widened.

As the other woman poured the tea, Nikki studied her openly. And enviously. She judged Gaze Starpath to be in her early to mid-thirties, and, she was beautiful. Her jet-black hair swung in a sleek pageboy, playing hide and seek with her high cheekbones and tawny complexion. Huge hazel eyes dominated her face. And she was as slim as any fashion model could hope to be.

Gaze looked up and caught Nikki's avid perusal. "Do not worry, Neeake," she said in her soft, sweet voice. "I have not summoned your husband here to claim him for myself. At least not the way you may think."

Nikki's brows inched upward in shock. Had she been that obvious, or had this woman actually read her mind?

And how did she know her name? The name only Silver Thorn applied to her.

"Then I was summoned," Thorn concluded, "by you."

Gaze nodded. "I have been waiting to do so for years, Silver Thorn."

"How? Why?" Nikki asked.

Gaze's smile was serene. "Perhaps you have heard of the studies which have determined that there is a strong empathy between twins or other products of multiple births, be they identical or fraternal. We have found that there is also a telepathic link between them. That, among other factors, is how I contacted Silver Thorn."

For the first time, she focused her clear, luminous hazel eyes directly at Thorn. "Don't you know who I am? Don't you recognize me at all? Let me help jog your memory. I asked you to remove my body from the battleground, to bury it in a secret place."

Nikki's jaw dropped. Silver Thorn stared at the woman seated opposite him. "Tecumseh?" he questioned. "How can this be?"

Gaze chuckled. "How does one explain many of the strange and wondrous things in the world? You, of all people, should not be so surprised, especially after the spectacular feats both of us have performed. Moreover, didn't I tell you that I would return in a day when my people needed my guidance?"

"But . . . you are now a woman," Thorn stated superfluously.

Gaze offered a careless shrug. "I do believe you would be less shocked had I returned as a bat. Be it frog or fox, pine or peanut, male or female—reincarnation is no respecter of gender, race, religion, or politics. If I come again in the future, I may be African or Asian, Moslem or Hindu. Who is to say? For now, I am a Shawnee medicine woman who simply wished to meet her brother once more. Through past-life regression, I recalled our relationship. I also recalled that you were going to try to go forward from 1813 into 1996 to join your bride. And just within the last day or so, I have sensed that you were in trouble. I want to help, if I can. Tell me what is wrong."

"Nikki believes she has seen Tenskwatawa near our home. If this is so, then he somehow managed to follow me forward into this era."

"I don't merely think I saw him, Thorn," Nikki corrected. "I'd bet my last dollar on it."

Gaze nodded. "Ah, so that is the dark cloud I felt whenever I thought of you. He is forever an ill wind, instigating disaster. We should have slain him when we had the chance."

"I would be satisfied just to send him permanently back to his own time, where he belongs," Thorn declared.

Nikki agreed. "Yes, that would be best. We certainly don't want his body discovered or to have the law breathing down our necks. That would be terrifically difficult to explain."

"Especially since policemen tend to deal in cold hard facts, not paranormal theory," Gaze added wryly. "If they can't touch it, see it, or smell it, to most of them it doesn't exist."

"A few months ago, I would have understood that attitude perfectly," Nikki declared. "Now . . ." She paused, her glance wavering between the other two. "Well, now it might take a few minutes to assimilate, but nothing would truly surprise me."

"If Tenskwatawa is currently in Ohio, then that's where we must go," Gaze said. "I'll come with you and we will search him out and deal with him once and for all. I feel it's imperative that we do so before he can cause too much mischief—which is, after all, his favorite game." She rose and headed toward a connecting room. "Let me pack a bag and call my secretary."

"You might want to call the airlines first," Nikki suggested. "With the holiday, they might be booked up. Thorn and I were extremely lucky to get tickets at the last minute."

Again, Gaze graced them with a serene, mystical smile. "Luck had nothing to do with it," she told them frankly. "I will have no problem securing a ticket."

"Then you still retain your powers, as before?" Thorn queried curiously.

"Most of them," Gaze acknowledged. "But I rarely get the chance to exercise them as I did in the old days. A pity, really, because you know the adage—use it or lose it. I would truly hate to forfeit those abilities entirely."

She cocked her head at him. "What about you, Silver Thorn? Did your powers come forward with you?"

Her direct question shook him. "I do not know," he replied truthfully. "I have not attempted to apply them since I arrived."

"I suggest you try them out," Gaze proposed seriously. "Before we encounter our dear, demented brother."

Thirty-five

They arrived home about an hour and a half before dark only to find Sheree huddled in her car in Nikki's driveway waiting for them. As soon as she spotted them, Sheree leapt from the car, her blue eyes appearing as huge as dinner plates in her pale, drawn face. She ran up and clutched Nikki's arm with trembling hands. "Thank God you're home!" she exclaimed shakily. "I've been frantic sitting here waiting for you, hoping you'd come soon, wondering if you were okay!"

"What's wrong, Sheree? What's happened to upset you so?" In her heart, Nikki knew the answer before Sheree gave it.

"I saw the Prophet!" Sheree blurted out breathlessly. "Even without his nose ring and dressed in jeans and a denim jacket, I recognized him from all those horrible pictures of him. At first I thought I was hallucinating, but I couldn't have been because he was with Brian Sanders, of all people—and even in my wildest dreams, I'd never allow Brian into them. It scared the liver out of me to see those two talking to each other. They're up to something, Nikki. Something rotten!"

Nikki muttered an obscenity.

"My sentiments exactly," Gaze commented gravely.

Thorn agreed. "Those two together can only mean trouble." He ushered the women toward the house. "Come. We must plan what to do next."

Even through the front door, they could hear Macate caterwauling. Thorn frowned. "Let me go in first and check to make sure Tenskwatawa is not inside waiting," he cautioned. "We would not want to walk into a trap. Tec . . . Gaze, you stay with Neeake and her friend."

Gaze nodded. "I will guard them."

Thorn disappeared into the house, and Sheree leaned toward Nikki and whispered, "Who is she?"

"Her name is Gaze Starpath, and she's a Shawnee medicine woman and a professor of parapsychology in Oklahoma," Nikki explained quietly. "Would you believe that she is also Tecumseh reincarnated?"

Sheree gave a numb shake of her head. "At this point, I'd believe anything."

Nikki automatically introduced the two women, her attention focused on the door.

Within minutes, Thorn returned and motioned them inside. "No one is here now, but I cannot say they were not before."

"Is anything missing or out of place?" Gaze asked.

"I'll look around; but even if there were, I'm not sure I'd notice right off," Nikki responded.

"I'll help you," Sheree volunteered. "How long has it been since you dusted?"

Nikki frowned at her. "What a thing to ask your best friend!"

"Hey! It doesn't bother me. I just asked because if it's been awhile, we might be able to find a clean spot to indicate that something's been moved or jarred from its original setting."

Nikki's grin came spontaneously. "Is that the kind of thing you and Dave discuss on your dates? Pitiful, Sheree. Really pitiful!"

Nothing appeared to have been touched, but Macate was still prancing and growling for all he was worth. And the hair on Her Nibs' back and tail was ruffled, a mark of her own agitation.

"I propose that we go in search of Tenskwatawa and this reporter," Gaze said. "It would be better than sitting here like ducks in a barrel, waiting for them to come to us. At times like this, the best defense is an immediate offense."

Thorn turned to Sheree. "Where did you see them together, Sheree?"

"At the American Mall." Nikki gave a nervous giggle. "They were just outside Baskin-Robbins, eating ice cream cones, of all things!"

"We will start there, then. And the parking lot at the place where Neeake and I shopped the other evening."

"If we don't find them there, we might try Brian's house or his office," Nikki suggested. "Lord help us if he's filing some wild news story even as we speak! Can you imagine the uproar if the truth came out in print?"

"Who in his right mind would ever believe it anyway?" Sheree countered. "He'll look like the prince of fools!"

Nikki shrugged. "Maybe, but maybe not. Especially if he has Tenskwatawa here to back him up. I'm not on top of this sort of thing; but I know there are tests to scientifically prove the age of artifacts, and Tenski himself would certainly fall into that category. As would his clothing and anything he brought forward with him. If nothing else, it would certainly provoke some interesting questions which would be better left alone."

Sheree shot Thorn an irritated glower. "Boy, you really stirred up the muck when you decided to pry into the future."

"I will settle it as well," he vowed grimly.

He faced Nikki. "Tell me where Sanders lives and works, and Gaze and I will begin the search."

"What about us?" Nikki inquired, indicating herself and Sheree.

"I would feel more assured of your safety if the two of you would go out to the farm and stay there until you hear from us," Thorn said. "There, you will have your family, your father and brothers, to protect you. If you were to accompany me, you might place yourself in more danger or distract me from my duties, if even unintentionally."

"He is right," Gaze concurred. "Do not fear, Neeake. Thorn and I make a formidable team, but we must be able to fully concentrate on the task at hand."

Sheree was more than willing to comply, and she urged Nikki to do so. "I don't know about you, but my nerves have had just about all the excitement they can stand for a while. And you have the baby to consider."

It was agreed, then, that Gaze and Thorn would take Nikki's car, with Gaze at the wheel, and Sheree and Nikki would use Sheree's. "What about Macate?" Nikki inquired as they headed for the cars. "Shouldn't he accompany you? Maybe you could put him to use as a search dog—or cat. He surely won't do you much good locked up in the house like this."

"If I need him, he will come to me," Thorn assured her. "You forget, he is of the spirit world. Walls and locks cannot confine him."

Nikki rolled her eyes. "For a spirit, he sure was humping Her Nibs like any mortal male! I didn't think they allowed such base urges in the afterworld. I guess there's always room for hope, huh? Chocolate and sex in heaven; what a nifty thought!"

The four of them climbed into their separate vehicles. Since Nikki had parked behind Sheree, Thorn and Gaze backed out first. They waited to make sure Sheree's car started, and she pulled out after them, leaving with a toot of the horn and a final wave.

At that moment, Aneekwah dropped from the tree at the end of the drive onto the hood of Sheree's car. "Speaking of weird animals," Sheree commented. "What the devil has gotten into your nutty squirrel? Shoo him off my car before he scratches the paint, Nik."

Nikki was reaching for the door handle when she felt the sharp jab at her side just below the short hem of her jacket. "Stay as you are," growled a gruff voice from the back seat.

Nikki recognized that voice and froze. Beside her, Sheree let out a strangled squeal. Her eyes were wild with fear as she gazed at a spot behind Nikki's seat.

"You, with the yellow hair," Tenskwatawa rumbled. "Drive where I tell you or I will cut your friend's child from her belly here and now."

"O . . . o . . . okay!" Sheree stammered. "Ju . . . just tell me where we're going."

"Not far," came the brusque reply. "Turn around. We go in the other direction."

"You won't get away with this, Tenskwatawa, whatever you have planned," Nikki said, drawing a careful breath. "Silver Thorn knows you followed him. He'll find you."

He gave an evil laugh. "I intend for him to do so. You are the bait that will draw him into my snare."

Nikki's heart fell. "Give it up, Tenski. You should know by now that you can't win against him."

He poked the knife more firmly against her lower ribs, emphasizing the immediate threat. "But with you as my hostage, I have the upper hand, do I not?"

Nikki said nothing in reply, and he took her silence as mute agreement.

Indeed, they did not have far to go, which was fortunate considering how badly Sheree was shaking. Within the span of three minutes, they were pulling up a long lane so near to Nikki's house that they could have handily walked the distance. It was a spot familiar to everyone in the neighborhood, an old abandoned sanitarium that had once been used to treat tuberculosis patients. It was long empty now, in a sad state of disrepair, its original purpose made obsolete by drugs that had all but banished the dread disease. Many of the windows were broken out, others boarded up. Weeds grew profusely on the spacious, once-immaculate lawn. The pond where swans used to swim was reduced to an expanse of slimy, stagnant water.

No one ever came here now, not even a rare prospective buyer. No one, it seemed, but Tenskwatawa. And now Nikki and Sheree. No one would think to look for them here—or hear them if they cried out for help.

On the off chance that someone might drive past and become curious, Tenskwatawa directed Sheree to pull her car into the enclosed garage area formerly used to house ambulances. Nikki's spirits sank further. For someone so new to the twentieth century, her evil brother-in-law was coping incredibly well in the modern world. Apparently, he had a knack for sniffing out those things which would be to his best benefit.

Their captor led them, at knifepoint, into the dark interior of the building and up three flights of stairs to an inner hallway devoid of windows. There he lit two small candles with a lighter he pulled from his jacket pocket. His blade never straying from Nikki's side, he retrieved a length of rope he had stashed away and quickly tied the two women to a long counter which was bolted to the floor, a former nurses' station. Then he gagged them.

"I wouldn't want you to cry out and lead Silver Thorn to you too soon," he gloated. "But neither do I wish that you not be able to breathe, which is why I am careful not to cover your noses."

He stood over them, his one dark eye gleaming with malice, his demonic grin revealing his rotting teeth. "I will also leave you with light." He gestured toward the votive candles on the countertop. "You will note that I have placed them on the ledge. Unfortunately, the wood is very dry and likely to catch fire very quickly if the candles burn down enough for the flame to reach it." He let loose a fiendish cackle. "Those are very small candles, are they not? They should burn most rapidly."

He checked their bindings once more, assuring himself that they were tight, taking an extra moment to savor the fear mirrored in their eyes. Then he rose and started down the hall toward the staircase. "I can smell your fear from here," he called back to them. "I would stay to enjoy it further or perhaps to avail myself of your white flesh, but I have bigger fish to fry." He laughed at his own joke.

"Did I say that I am preparing other fires as well, all through this place?" He paused for a dramatic sigh. "Ah, so many rooms, so many corners Silver Thorn must search for you—if he lives to do so. Surely, the smoke will suffocate you long before anyone discovers your charred bones."

Left alone, the two women stared at each other through terror-glazed eyes. Nikki tested her bonds, tugging at them frantically, but they wouldn't budge. Nor would Sheree's when she tried. They were sitting a few feet from each other, huddled beneath the desk of the nurses' station in the narrow knee space where the desk chairs no doubt sat at one time. Their hands were bound behind them, tied to metal support posts, with their ankles lashed together in front of them.

After several minutes of futile struggling, the women collapsed against the posts, knowing it was useless. Though they could not see the candles from this position, they could see the reflection of the tiny, flickering flames on the opposite wall. They stared at the wall, the fluttering light, and each other with bleak, despairing expressions. Their helpless tears said all that they could not voice.

Gaze and Silver Thorn had searched high and low and could find no sign of their brother. They finally managed to track down Brian Sanders at his apartment complex

The reporter, who had been so eager to communicate his views before, was now most unwilling to speak with them.

"Look, Silver, I'm staying away from Nikki, just as you want me to. You've got no beef with me on that score."

"Perhaps not, but there is another matter that I would discuss with you. This man, this Indian, with whom you have been seen."

Brian smirked. "Oh, you mean old Tenska-whoever. Yeah. He sure gave me an earful."

"I'd take whatever he told you with a grain of salt," Gaze put in. "The man is a drunkard. His word is worthless."

"That's not the way I see it," Brian debated smugly. "I'm of half a mind to believe his wild tale. And if I can gather enough proof to convince enough other people, this could be Pulitzer material."

"Try using the other half of your brain," Thorn suggested somberly. "The part which hopefully still functions normally. This man is dangerous. We must find him immediately, and we need you to help us. He has attempted to harm Neeake more than once. Would you put the life of the woman you claim to love at risk for an uncertain chance at fame?"

"In a heartbeat," Brian stated flatly.

Gaze fixed him with a hard glare. "Then you don't love her, Mr. Sanders. Let me put it to you another way, one that might sink through those Pulitzer plums dancing in your head. If this demented Indian harms Neeake and you could have led us to him in time to prevent it, you could be brought up on criminal charges. Aiding and abetting. Withholding information. Harboring. Any number of other charges that carry a hefty prison term. Now, I ask you, do you have any idea where we might find him?"

Brian hesitated. "Is he really that dangerous?"

"He would kill her," Thorn announced curtly. "If you know where he is, if you care at all for Neeake, you must tell us all you know. All that he told you and that you told him."

Brian looked sick. "I . . . I . . . Oh, God! I showed him where you live. I drove him right past your house last night!"

"Did you also take him to the farm?" Thorn pressed.

"No, just Nikki's house."

Thorn could breathe again. "Do you know where he's staying?"

Brian shook his head. "Not exactly, but he did laugh when I showed him the house. He said something about spotting the perfect place nearby. He didn't say what kind of place or what he was doing there."

"Thank you, Sanders. I shall put this information to good use." Thorn turned away, eager to be on his way.

Gaze grabbed his arm, halting him. "Wait. There is one more thing left to do here."

She returned her attention to Brian. Her voice, when she spoke next, was soft and compelling. "Look at me, Brian Sanders. Look deeply into my eyes, and tell me what you see there."

Brian complied. "I see your eyes, of course. And my own reflection in them."

"Look closer," she urged quietly in a soothing, sing-song tone. "See yourself as I do. Describe what you see."

"My face," he replied slowly. "I need a shave. My front teeth are crooked. I never got braces." Each word emerged more slowly than the last, as if it were an extreme effort to coordinate his brain and speech.

"Your eyes are very tired," Gaze informed him in a murmur. "You can barely hold them open. You want to close them. You need to close them. Now."

Brian's lids fluttered, then closed. He swayed dizzily, then leaned back against the door frame.

"Brian, lift your right arm and hold it out before you," Gaze instructed. His arm rose slowly from his side.

"Good. Now, listen very carefully. You did not meet the Prophet yesterday. Nor did you drive him past Neeake's house. You've never met Tenskwatawa, Brian. Therefore, you will forget anything he told you. As far as you will recall, you went home alone last night. Straight home and to bed. Anything you wrote for your news column concerning the Prophet will seem nothing more to you than an idea you had for a future book. When next you read your notes, you will consider them pure drivel. You will destroy them and anything having to do with them that you may have entered on your computer or elsewhere. You did not speak to me or to Thorn today. Our conversation will be erased from your mind. Do you understand all that I have told you?"

"Yes," he intoned.

"Repeat to me what you know to be true," Gaze said.

As he did so, Thorn whispered into Gaze's ear. She nodded and grinned. "One more thing, Brian," she advised when he had repeated her former instructions. "You no longer have any interest in Neeake, except as a casual acquaintance. Nor do you wish to investigate Thorn's past. It is of no concern to you whatever."

"Not my concern," he agreed drowsily.

"Now, in a few minutes you will awaken. You will not recall this conversation, but you will abide by all that I have told you. You will enter your apartment, attend to any business I have indicated, and go directly to bed and sleep soundly until morning. You may put your arm down now."

Gaze motioned to Thorn that they should leave. They were out of the parking area and several blocks away before Brian awoke.

By mutual agreement, they drove back to Nikki's house. As they pulled up, nothing appeared out of the ordinary. Sheree's car was gone. She and Nikki had most probably arrived at the farm hours ago. Still, Thorn felt uneasy; and Gaze's intuition was sounding an alarm in her head. Something was dreadfully wrong, and they both felt it.

"Can you work the telephone for me?" Thorn asked. "I wish to call Neeake's parents and make sure she and Sheree arrived safely."

"Yes, and while you're confirming that, I'll take a closer look around the property. Something doesn't feel right."

Gaze dialed the number and left Thorn to speak with Nikki while she toured the house. Again, Macate was nearly wild. Gaze found nothing inside and decided to go outside to inspect the garage. As soon as she opened the back patio door, Macate was out like a shot.

Gaze entered the garage and knew instantly that Tenskwatawa had been there. She would have known it even if she hadn't found the lance with his feathers bound to it—and the note dangling from it. The Prophet had inscribed signs on a piece of paper, a message as clear as any written language.

Gaze raced for the house, note in hand. She met Thorn coming toward her.

"Neeake and Sheree are not there," Thorn exclaimed. "They never reached the farm."

"I know." Gaze handed him the message. "Tenskwatawa has them both. He is holding them in an empty building nearby. He doesn't say where this building is, but he must know we are bound to find it soon. He'll be lying in wait for us, Silver Thorn. Make no mistake. He means to kill you, and most likely me, too, if he has any idea who I am."

Thorn contemplated this. "Perhaps he knows nothing about you. Perhaps that will be our best advantage."

Gaze's eyes lit up. "Yes," she agreed. "He may not expect the two of us, but only you. We must find this place and scout it out. Maybe you can gain his attention while

I enter from another direction and take our brother by surprise."

"First we must find where he is holding them," Thorn said. As if on cue, Macate let out a loud yowl. Thorn's smile was tinged with satisfaction. "Macate knows. He will lead us to this place."

Thirty-six

The candle on the counter was sputtering. Nikki prayed that it had one of those little metal discs on the bottom and that it would be enough to keep the open flame from direct contact with the parched wood. Otherwise, it would go up like tinder and she and Sheree would burn with it—as surely as if Tenskwatawa had bound them to the stake.

One candle gutted out. The other was fluttering feebly, giving off almost no light now. Nikki smelled something. She hoped it was only the extinguished candle and not the counter starting to smolder. She couldn't tell. And she sure couldn't ask Sheree. She could scarcely see her friend. In the encroaching gloom, Sheree was just a dark blur several feet away.

Something furry brushed Nikki's lower arm, and she jerked in surprise. Her scream echoed only in her head, thoroughly muted by the cloth Tenskwatawa had shoved into her mouth. She felt the furry thing again and would have screamed anew, but then she heard it. She squinted and thought she saw something move on the floor next to her. It chattered, and Nikki could have bawled with relief. It was Aneekwah, her squirrel spirit guide.

Then the little animal did something truly amazing. It leapt into her lap, balanced itself on her tummy, carefully took hold of the end of the rag protruding from Nikki's mouth, and tugged it free. Nikki sucked in a welcome breath.

"Sheree?" she whispered, not wanting to alert the Prophet if he were lurking nearby. "Sheree, Aneekwah is here. She just pulled my gag off. I'm going to see if I can get her to loosen the ropes with her teeth, if that's possible. If I can get loose, I'll untie you and maybe we can escape."

Nikki thought she saw Sheree nod. At any rate, the squirrel must have understood what was expected of her, for she scampered around to Nikki's backside and promptly began gnawing at the rope. A short while later, Nikki's bonds were loose enough that she could pull her hands free. She took a minute to massage the blood back into her numb fingers and quickly went to work untying her feet.

Aneekwah helped, then raced over to Sheree before Nikki had restored enough circulation to move. Nikki crawled to her friend and eased the cloth from between Sheree's dry lips. "Are you okay?"

"I'll be better when we're out of here," Sheree croaked. Nikki worked at the ropes binding Sheree's ankles while Aneekwah tended to those at her wrists. Within minutes they were both free.

Sheree rubbed her wrists. "Check the candles."

Nikki eased upward, peering over the top of the counter, afraid she'd find Tenskwatawa leering at her from the other side. He was nowhere in sight. But that didn't mean he wasn't just around the corner in any of more than a dozen rooms. Nikki checked the candles and felt the wood at their bases. It was slightly warm, but not alarmingly so. Hopefully, if their captor had lit others, they had done as little damage.

As she was looking at it, the second candle sputtered out, leaving them in total darkness. "Crap!" she hissed softly.

"Ditto," Sheree muttered. "How are we supposed to find our way out now? And what, God forbid, if the Prophet comes to check on the candles . . . and us?"

"I'll crawl out of here on my hands and knees if I have to," Nikki declared softly. The squirrel brushed her ankle, and she barely restrained a shriek. "I think Aneekwah is trying to say that she can lead us out."

"Super. You grab her tail, and I'll grab yours—your shirt tail, that is—and let's vamoose!"

It was slow going, but they persisted, inching along on hands and knees along the wall facing the nurses' station. Every few feet, they encountered a doorway, and beyond that more wall. On and on it went, until Nikki swore the hallway went on forever. At least they were headed in the opposite direction from the way Tenskwatawa had led them in, or Nikki assumed they were. Her sense of direction wasn't the best in this inky darkness.

"So where are all those candles Tenskwatawa promised to light?" she grumbled softly. "We could sure use one right about now."

Behind her, Sheree grunted her assent.

Finally, Aneekwah bore to the left. Nikki and Sheree followed suit. Another few feet, and Nikki rasped a hushed shout. "I see a window ahead, Sheree. Stand up."

They fumbled forward and found themselves at the end of the shorter hallway, facing a window with its pane missing. Nikki thought she'd never seen such a welcome sight. Until she leaned down for a look out the window. She withdrew with a frustrated moan.

"What?" Sheree demanded.

"Have a look," Nikki said, gesturing her forward. "We're three flights up, with nothing between us and the ground but a rickety, rusty fire escape. I'm sure Aneekwah meant well, but she weighs a lot less than we do and I'm not sure that old thing will bear our weight. It doesn't look too secure; and even if it would hold us, it's bound to make a racket. I'd hate to get all the way to the bottom, if this metal contraption even goes clear to the bottom, only to find Tenskwatawa waiting to escort us back inside."

"I'm willing to take that chance," Sheree insisted. "Even if I fall and kill myself, it's a darn sight better than burning to death. If you want, I'll go first. Test the waters, so to speak."

"Okay. Just be careful."

"Care to tell me how to manage that?" Sheree scoffed.

Several seconds later, Sheree was standing outside the window on the top step of the fire escape. "Wish me luck," she whispered nervously. "I'll yell up at you when I reach bottom. If I do a swan dive off this thing, I'll just yell."

Nikki reached out and clutched at her sleeve. "Sheree? Have I ever told you how much I love you? How much I treasure your friendship?"

Sheree sniffed. "Don't go getting maudlin on me now, dearie. But I should tell you, you're in my will. You get my leather jacket and my goldfish."

With that, she was gone, creeping precariously down the creaking, swaying stairs. Though the night was cloudy, the sky was still considerably brighter than the inside of the building. Even so, Nikki lost sight of Sheree somewhere near the first-floor level. She literally held her breath, listening as hard as she could.

There was a muffled thud, followed by an even more muffled groan. Then . . . "Come on! I made it! Except for that last step. It's a doozy. About six feet off the ground."

Nikki climbed out cautiously, clinging to the windowsill all the while. "Here I come, ready or not," she hissed. She crept down the fire escape, one slow step at a time, praying for all she was worth.

It seemed an eon before Sheree called out softly, "Hold

it. That's the last step. Unless you want to jump for it, which I wouldn't recommend, I'd say you should try to maneuver yourself around so you can hang from the bottom step by your hands. That way, your feet should reach the ground."

Sheree's advice was more easily given than applied. With nothing supporting her feet, Nikki felt as if her arms were about to be torn from their sockets. But, as Sheree had pointed out, anything was better than burning alive. At last, feeling like an aging acrobat, with Sheree trying to steady her from below, Nikki felt her feet touch solid ground.

She heaved a hearty sigh and hugged her friend. As fast as their tingling, quivering limbs would carry them, they loped around the corner of the building and barreled straight into someone else coming from the opposite direction.

As she fell, Nikki felt her ankle twist. She knew she stood little chance of escaping again. "Run, Sheree!" she gasped.

"Neeake? Sheree?"

"Gaze?"

"Thank God!" Nikki whimpered. "I thought for sure you were Tenskwatawa! Where's Thorn? How did you find us?"

"Macate led us here. Thorn is entering another way. I am to take the rear entrance and try to sneak up on Tenskwatawa from behind. How did you get out?"

"Down the fire escape on the other side."

"You stay here," Gaze ordered. "Better yet, hide in that clump of trees. We'll come for you when it's safe. If we don't come within half an hour or if you hear shots or something equally dire, head for your home." She pointed them in the right direction. "Lock yourselves in and phone the police."

Gaze disappeared around the corner, and Nikki limped

toward the trees. Halfway there, she stopped and turned to Sheree. "I can't do this. I'll die of fright, not knowing what's going on. You go ahead and hide."

"Not on a bet," Sheree grumbled. "We're in this together, pal. Besides, I'd sort of like to be on hand to see the old Prophet get what's coming to him."

They stole back the way they had come. When they reached the fire escape, it was still wobbling, but Gaze was already inside. They continued slowly onward toward the other side, Nikki favoring her ankle with every step.

As they neared the corner, Nikki spotted the parking garage. This is the way we came in," she hissed.

Sheree nodded. "I'm scared spitless!"

"Me, too!"

They hunched down below window level and crab-walked toward the door. It stood open, and from somewhere within, they heard loud voices. The loudest was Thorn's. Cautiously, they followed the sound.

"I would kill you this instant if I could," Thorn shouted. "I only spare your worthless life so that you may tell me what you have done with my wife and her friend. However, for every minute that goes by that you do not grant what I wish to hear, I shall break another of your bones until you are begging me to put you out of your misery."

Nikki peered anxiously around the door frame into a huge kitchen. Sheree's head popped up beside hers, and they both gaped at the sight before them. Thorn was standing in the center of the room. Tenskwatawa was slumped against a wall several feet from him. The Prophet's nose was gushing blood. His left arm hung at an odd angle. His good eye was fast swelling shut. All in all, he looked as if he'd just met up with a cement truck and lost.

Even as they watched, Thorn raised his arm and pointed at his brother. Without advancing near enough for physical contact, he broke Tenskwatawa's right leg. Nikki and Sheree heard the sickening crack of the bone from clear

across the room. That wasn't what caused Nikki's stomach
to roil, however. It was the sight of the knife protruding
from Thorn's back, approximately in the middle of his left
shoulder blade. Even through the thick sheepskin jacket,
blood dripped in a steady stream from the wound, staining
the light leather crimson.

She tried to stifle her gasp of horror, but Thorn heard
her. So did Tenskwatawa. The moment Thorn turned his
head toward her, the Prophet wrenched another knife from
inside his jacket.

Nikki screamed a warning. Sheree's shriek echoed it.
Before their screams had died away—before Thorn could
return his attention to his brother—before Tenskwatawa
could launch his weapon—his wrist went suddenly and totally limp. The knife clattered to the hard tile floor, and
Gaze stepped forward through a side doorway to kick the
knife away.

"You!" she bellowed at the Prophet. "You have brought
us nothing but misery from the moment you first drew
breath! Now you shall reap that which you have sown all
these many years. To slay you now would be a kindness.
Rather, you will return to your own time to live out your
remaining years in agony. You will be bent and broken,
your bones aflame with aching, for they will never mend
properly. You shall draw not one breath that is not tor-
mented. Even your beloved whiskey will not tame the pain.
You will be scorned and reviled by your own people, and
none will take you in. That will be the price of your wickedness and treachery against your own brothers."

With a wave of her hand, she rendered him unconscious.
Only then did she turn to the others. "Bring the car
around. We must remove this piece of offal to a place
where Thorn's spell will work."

Sheree stepped hastily forward. "I'll help you if you
think the two of us can manage him. I don't think you've
had a chance to notice, but Thorn has a knife sticking out

of his shoulder blade and Nikki is certainly in no shape to lend a hand."

"Just bring the car," Gaze repeated. "I will manage this one." With astounding ease, she hefted Tenskwatawa across her shoulder in a fireman's carry. She chuckled at the stunned look on Sheree's face. "Powers such as Thorn's and mine do come in handy at times like this."

Sheree recovered with equal wit. "If you were really good, you could just zap all of us home and not need the car at all."

Minutes later, they were gathered in Nikki's upstairs bathroom, which wasn't built to hold four adults at once. Tenskwatawa, still unconscious, lay sprawled in the tub. Gaze stood over him, as if daring him to waken. Thorn sat astride the toilet seat minus his coat and the knife, which Gaze had deftly removed. A few chanted words from her, along with some mysterious movements of her hands, and Thorn's wound had been reduced to little more than a deep scratch—to which Nikki was now applying anti-bacterial ointment. Sheree hovered in the doorway.

"Thorn told me how he came to be here, how the waterfall may have enhanced the magic. I think you were correct, Neeake, when you said it had something to do with the ionization of the molecules in the air. If that is so, your shower should suffice just as well to send Tenskwatawa back."

Nikki nodded, then frowned. "But if he came forward once—and I still don't understand how he did it—what is to prevent him from doing so again?"

"He will not have the charm," Gaze told her. "Nor does he know the spell. It is my guess that he rode in on Silver Thorn's coattail. For a few brief moments, the door to the future was left open, the window of opportunity if you will. Tenskwatawa grabbed up the amulet before it closed and was thus transported into the present right behind Silver Thorn. This will not happen again."

"I hope not," Sheree muttered.

Gaze looked at Thorn. "Are you ready?"

Thorn nodded and took his place at the side of the tub. The others watched as he brought Tenskwatawa to a state of semi-consciousness. Softly, he submitted the hypnotic suggestion the Prophet would soon obey. "You will reach the other side and immediately release the amulet, Tenskwatawa. If you do not, it will burn a hole through your hand. While you may recall your visit here, you will remember nothing of the spell necessary to perform traveling through time. Nod once if you understand my directive."

The Prophet responded with a small nod of his head.

"You will not fully awaken, under any circumstances, until you have reached your own time and dropped the amulet," Thorn added for good measure.

He then reached out his hand to Nikki, who placed into his palm the snapshot of Tenskwatawa that she'd taken on the sly. "While I would not want you to make a habit of trying to deceive me, Neeake, it is fortunate that you disobeyed me on this one matter," Thorn said. "Without this, it might be impossible to send him away. This picture shows him in his own time and was taken in his own time. I believe it is necessary to the spell to employ something affiliated with the proper era in order to produce the required results."

Thorn reached over, tucked the snapshot into Tenskwatawa's pocket and placed the amulet in his hand, then turned the shower on full force. Then he commenced to chant. The three women joined hands and minds, focusing on a single thought—sending Tenskwatawa permanently back to 1813.

Many minutes elapsed. The minutes became half an hour and more. Then, just as they were about to admit defeat, Tenskwatawa disappeared in a puff of steam.

No one moved. No one spoke. They simply watched and

waited. They all jumped when the amulet came clattering back into the porcelain tub. Thorn grabbed it up with a shout of triumph as if he were afraid that Tenskwatawa would somehow retrieve it before him.

"It is done!" he exclaimed, holding the amulet high, as one would a trophy. "He is gone for all time."

"Maybe not for all time, but certainly for a long while," Gaze said wryly. "Who knows if someday he, too, may be reincarnated."

"He's much too evil for that, isn't he?" Nikki questioned. "Didn't I read somewhere that in order to be reincarnated you need to have done something good in your life?"

"There is that theory," Gaze allowed. "Another is that a good person comes back as a higher life form while a bad person may emerge as a lesser one."

"Then the Prophet is definitely headed for the lowest rung of the food chain," Sheree predicted drolly. "And I intend to step on every worm and bug I see from now on!"

They were still celebrating their success, when the phone rang. "My gosh!" Nikki said. "I completely forgot to call Mom and Dad back to let them know we're okay."

"I did that while you were tending to Thorn," Sheree told her.

"Then who can be calling?" Nikki wondered. She picked up the receiver just ahead of the answering machine.

"Hi, sis!" It was Sam. "Did I call at a bad time?"

"Couldn't be better," she informed him happily.

"Is Thorn there?"

"Sure is. Do you want me to get him?"

"No, but if he's within earshot, why don't you put me on the speaker-phone?"

"Okay, but watch your language. Sheree and Gaze are here, too."

Nikki hit the button, and Sam's voice came through the speaker. "I've got some bad news and some good news. Which do you want first?"

Nikki sighed. "Don't play games. Sam. You always say that, and then you give me the bad news first anyway. So out with it."

"Okay. I checked your lottery tickets, and you were right. You didn't win the big one—which was a cool twenty million, by the way."

"What else is new?" Nikki intoned.

"Weeell," Sam drew the word out, then paused for dramatic effect. "Your numbers matched one of those in the June's Millionaire of the Month drawing. You have until December first to collect your winnings, so if you want your three hundred thousand, you'd better hurry on down to claim it. You've only got a few days left."

"Omigod!" she yelled. Then, not certain her rascally brother wasn't putting her on, she said breathlessly, "Samuel Swan, you'd better not be kidding about this or I'll tell Mom. She'll never feed you again."

"Hey! I'm the guy you're gonna split this money with, remember? I wouldn't joke about that kind of cash. In fact, first thing Monday morning, I'm placing an order for that new combine!"

"With my blessings!" she told him excitedly.

"So, what are you going to do with all your loot?" he inquired.

Nikki laughed. Her eyes were sparkling like the brightest amethysts as they met those of shining silver. "I think I'll really splurge. I'm going to buy the largest flea collar I can find for Macate. And a wee tiny one for Aneekwah. From here on, our pets deserve nothing but the best!"

"And a big, firm bed for us," Thorn added decisively.

Epilogue

Nikki set her romance novel aside and reached over to turn up the volume on the baby monitor. Thorn's deep voice, crooning a Shawnee lullaby, came over the speaker. It was followed by a soft, snuffling sound which brought a ready smile to her lips. Their son Sage was snoring!

He'd arrived right on schedule, three months ago, and was as healthy as a child could be. Which had been a tremendous relief after all her worrying that his time-travel experience might have harmed him in some way. Sage had coal-black hair, Nikki's violet eyes, and a good dose of Thorn's masculine charm. Only time would tell if he'd inherited his father's mystical powers as well.

Nikki relaxed back into the comfort of her patio lounger and pushed her sunglasses up on her nose. For a moment, she debated whether or not to apply more sunscreen, then decided she'd wait and let Thorn do it for her when he came downstairs. Besides, she reasoned, today was their first anniversary, and she intended to enjoy it to the fullest. Evidently, Thorn had similar notions, for he'd awakened her that morning after having transformed their bedroom into an enchanted glade. They'd made slow, delicious love in a paradise filled with rose petals and fluttering butterflies.

For the coming evening, Nikki and Thorn had booked dinner reservations and a motel room complete with its own private hot tub. Sheree and Dave, who were engaged to be married later this month, were coming over to babysit and to claim the latest of Her Nibs' kittens. The first had made its lone appearance late last January. It had been the oddest-looking animal Nikki had ever set eyes on, with fluffy gray-and-white-striped fur, tufted ears like its papa, and huge green eyes. Thorn had insisted on keeping it. This time around, there had been a litter of two, equally homely. One was to go to Sheree and the other to Gaze.

Gaze now lived just down the street, at least until she and Sam decided to tie the nuptial knot. Sam had taken one look at Gaze and tumbled head over heels in lust. Love followed shortly behind, but Gaze was making him wait for the "I do's" before moving in with him. Besides, just now she was very busy setting up her parapsychology clinic in the old tuberculosis sanitarium.

Luckily, the place hadn't burned down; and with all the renovation it needed, Nikki and Thorn had been able to purchase it for a song. Thorn was using part of the building to conduct his classes on Shawnee culture and language. Only those closest to Gaze and Thorn were not stunned at how quickly they had restored the building to better than its original condition. Moreover, most of the repairs hadn't cost a cent—just a twitch here, a nod there, and some magical Shawnee incantations!

Thorn's classes and his consulting job for regional museums and historical sites kept him happily occupied. For herself, Nikki would resume teaching at school after a lengthy maternity leave which had conveniently run into summer vacation. In her time off from classes, she and Thorn were collaborating on a book—a factual history of the Shawnee tribe.

Thorn joined her on the patio, interrupting her musing with a long, stirring kiss. He perched on the side of her lounger. "What time are Sheree and Dave coming?" he inquired as he lazily stroked his hand up and down her leg.

Nikki cocked an eyebrow at him. "Why? Getting anxious to start celebrating? Again?"

He slipped his fingers inside the hem of her short shorts, teasing her. "You know I am always eager for you, Neeake. I stay that way, which is most uncomfortable much of the time."

She grinned at him and lowered her sunglasses, the better to appreciate the heated gleam in his mercury-hued eyes. "You really should buy some of those boxer shorts, darling. We don't want Sage to be an only child simply because your briefs are too tight to allow a proper flow of fluids to your intimate regions."

His teasing smile matched hers. "There is no worry of that, little goose. Have you forgotten your vision? There are three more eggs to hatch in our nest. There is every possibility that we will begin our next child this very night."

"Oh, no. Not quite yet," she told him. "I need some time to devote myself to Sage first. Besides, I like fitting into size-ten clothes again. Let me savor it awhile longer."

He leaned down to claim another kiss. "Then we will simply practice making babies. It is a most pleasant activity."

"Yes, I can tell you enjoy it *immensely,*" she joked, wriggling against his big, hard erection. "And practice does make perfect."

"We are already perfect. Together."

Nikki gave a contented sigh and pulled him more fully into her embrace. "Yes, my love," she agreed. "So we are."

If you liked *CHARMED*, don't miss
HORIZONS,
coming in 1997 from Zebra books.
Turn the page for a glimpse of . . .

HORIZONS

One

Kelly Kennedy stashed her carry-on in the overhead compartment and settled into her seat with a sigh. It was going to be a long flight from New Zealand back to the U.S., and hopefully a quiet one. With any luck she'd sleep most of the way.

She was exhausted—physically, emotionally, and mentally drained. The past few months had been a hell she never wanted to relive, fraught with one traumatic event after another. In the midst off trying to launch her newest beauty-and-fitness boutique in Australia, the third in a fledgling chain she called Courtesans, Inc., she'd been forced to deal with a messy divorce. Three weeks ago, with the ink not yet dry on the divorce decree, she'd flown from Phoenix to Sidney, leaving the smoldering ashes of her marriage behind her, hoping to find some sort of relief from all the heartache and anger.

It hadn't worked out that way. Simply fleeing the scene of the disaster hadn't been enough. Even with all that distance behind her, and the rigors of getting the new store ready to open, of ironing out last-minute problems, she'd kept bumping up against the residue of her failed marriage. The wounds were too fresh yet, and would take time to heal. Mentally, rationally, she knew that. Emotionally, she kept hoping for a miracle cure, some type of super-injection that would jerk her off of this endless, energy-robbing treadmill of misery and rage, recriminations and tears.

But for now, it was back to Phoenix, via Auckland, Hawaii and San Francisco—back to sorting out the strange mix of his-and-her friends, relatives, and acquaintances that had arisen in the wake of the divorce. Back to listening to well-intentioned advice she didn't want to hear. Back to attempting to adjust to the role of the single female after five years of playing doubles. God! It was simply too wearisome to contemplate!

She was staring out the small, dingy window, trying to muster the energy to buckle her seatbelt, when a strident voice at her elbow claimed her attention—and everyone else's.

"Seat four A! That is what my ticket says! This woman is in my seat! I demand that you make her move!"

Kelly looked up, recognized the indignant pain-in-the-ass Mexican starlet, and gave an inward groan. Geez! Once Life decided to dump on you, it just wouldn't quit!

"Miss Gomez, please understand," the harried airline attendant said, "when a person doesn't arrive prior to half an hour before boarding, his or her seat is allotted to someone else. Especially in the case of an unconfirmed reservation, such as yours. If you read the instructions with your ticket, you should have been aware of this. There are seats at the rear of the plane . . ."

"No!" Alita Gomez stamped her spike heel in demonstration of her ire. "I paid for first class, and that is what I will have. How dare you think you can treat me this way! Me! I could cause you to lose your measly little job with a mere snap of my fingers! Do you know this?"

Kelly was in a lousy mood at the moment herself, and Miss Hot-to-Trot was the last straw. "I didn't think it was possible to snap your fingers with nails that long and weighted with that many layers of enamel," she piped up, drawing Alita's regard back to her. "You might not want to chance it. Those claws of yours might break off all the way back to your wrist."

"Oh, it's you!" Alita sneered. "The manager of that hole-in-the-wall beauty salon at the hotel. I cannot imagine why such a highly-rated hotel would allow you to set up your shabby little shop there."

Kelly smirked back. "Probably because it's such a treat to annoy snobbish clientele such as you."

"Well, you won't last long," Alita predicted airily. "Whoever heard of combining a fitness center, a beauty salon, and a boutique in one business? Bah!" Her nose rose in disdain.

"If you gave us a chance, Attila, even you could benefit from our services. For one thing, we could teach you how to apply your make-up without a trowel."

Just across the aisle, Zach Goldstein didn't even try to hide his grin. What had promised to be just another boring trip was starting off to the contrary. Here he sat, with a ring-side seat at a cat-fight between two irate beauties. One hot Mexican tamale and one cool, tart-mouthed blonde. He'd never considered himself a womanizer, but the thought crossed his mind that if they started yanking hair and tearing at each other's clothes, it would be almost as good as a female mud-wrestling match!

Personally, he was rooting for the strawberry blonde with the long French braid and big green eyes. She really was quite attractive, with a clean, naturally-pretty look about her. Of course, the Gomez woman was no slouch either, but Zach had always been drawn to a less flamboyant type of beauty. More wholesome, less artificial.

Like Rachel. Rachel had been his concept of the ideal woman, the perfect mate. Somewhat shy in public, a little bold in private; more prone to listening than speaking, though she didn't hesitate to take a firm stand on issues important to her. Zach used to tease her about being a closet zealot. He'd give his right arm to be able to do so again.

God, he missed her! Three years since her death, and

that soul-deep ache still lingered. There seemed to be no escaping it, especially when, with each passing year, their daughter was maturing into Rachel's mirror image. Same huge brown eyes, same nose, same stubborn chin. Becky was twelve now, teetering on the threshold of womanhood, but still young enough to be Daddy's little girl at least half the time. Mostly when she wanted her own way.

His job as an architectural engineer kept him away from her more than he'd have liked, but his mother and dad and two sisters helped fill the gap so that Becky could remain at home with family and friends. He tried to schedule time off from his work to coincide with breaks in her school term, and in summer she'd often join him on site for several weeks. It was rough going, but somehow they were making it work. As soon as he got settled in Las Vegas and got this latest project off the ground, so to speak, he would send for her again. In the meantime, his telephone bill would soar to new heights, and he'd continue to worry that his baby would soon be wearing lipstick and developing a figure, and, God-forbid, dating!

His attention veered back to the matter at hand as the airline hostess tried to reason with the two women passengers. "Ladies, please. The plane is nearly ready to debark, and everyone must find his or her seat and get buckled in."

She turned a pleading gaze toward Kelly, who seemed the more amenable of the two. "Ma'am, if you would agree to give up your seat, I promise you a first-class meal and complimentary drinks from here to San Francisco."

"Throw in a free ticket for a future flight, and you've got a bargain," Kelly told her.

"I'll do my best," the stewardess promised. "Thank you."

"What about my manager?" Alita Gomez persisted. She gestured toward the short, rotund man waiting silently behind her. "Eduardo was to have a seat with me. We have much business to discuss."

"I'm sorry, Miss Gome, but . . ."

"No problem. Make me the same deal that you did for the lovely lady, and Miss Gomez's manager can have my seat," Zach offered.

Alita graced him with a brilliant smile, her eyes quickly assessing and approving his dark good-looks. "At last!" she purred. "A man who knows how to be a gentleman! I will have Eduardo reward your generosity by providing you with a free ticket to the concert I will be giving in Hawaii this weekend."

"That's very gracious of you, Miss Gomez. Unfortunately, my lay-over there will only be for as long as it takes to refuel." His regret was genuine. Though Alita had yet to prove her worth as an actress, she was indisputably one of the best recording artists to come along in the past decade. Her rich alto voice, low and sultry, turned a simple song into a seduction. Zach already owned two of her latest discs, and was looking forward to the release of the next.

"I wouldn't mind an autograph for my daughter, however," he suggested as an alternative. "Her name is Becky."

"And what is yours?" Alita asked with a come-hither look.

"Zach."

"Do you really have a daughter, or is the autograph for you?"

"Oh, for heaven's sake!" Kelly groused. "If you want this seat so badly, Lolita, I suggest you postpone the flirtation and let me out of it. You're blocking the aisle."

Alita's smile instantly transformed into a glare, which she turned toward Kelly. "My name is Alita. Alita," she stressed.

"And mine is Kelly. Kelly," Kelly mimicked. "And

you're still in my way. Unless you've changed your mind and want to sit elsewhere."

Though the starlet's glower remained, she stepped back just far enough to allow Kelly to vacate the seat. As Kelly reached for the overhead compartment, the stewardess offered, "I'll be happy to bring your things back to you later, Miss."

"No thanks," Kelly told her. "Unlike some people, I'm used to *carrying* my own weight, as opposed to throwing it around."

Collecting his briefcase, Zach relinquished his own seat and followed Kelly down the aisle to the rear of the aircraft. As he settled once more into an empty seat directly opposite hers, the young black serviceman next to him leaned nearer and whispered, "Is the fox with you?"

Zach gave a low chuckle. "No such luck."

Familiar with the phenomenon that frequently compelled travelers to converse with complete strangers—often to the point of revealing intimate details their captive audience had no wish to hear—Zach quickly precluded such an event. Removing a sheaf of papers from his briefcase, and his reading glasses from the pocket of his sport jacket, he began to study the notes on the hotel complex he was to build in Las Vegas.

Across the aisle, Kelly was biding her time until take-off. White-knuckle flyer that she was, she knew she would not be able to relax until they were airborne. Reminding herself that, statistically, more people were killed on highways than in air disasters, didn't help ease the jitters much. To alleviate her own nervousness, she concentrated on her fellow passengers, wondering with envy how so many of them could seem so calm.

Kelly had always been an inveterate people-watcher. Not that she was particularly nosy; other people and other cul-

tures simply intrigued her. She found the varying customs,
modes of dress, languages, foods, and mannerisms fascinating. While someone else might be bored to tears upon
observing a Japanese tea ceremony, Kelly would have been
totally enthralled. She'd once sat practically mesmerized
through a day-long presentation of Native American
dances—complete with drums, chanting, and authentic
costumes. Afterward, she'd incorporated some of the
unique Indian artistry, the colors and patterns, into a special line of clothing for her boutique. At the Olympics in
Georgia, a virtual global melting-pot, she'd been nearly ec-
static, and had garnered many additional ideas for her business.

Now, she sat observing those around her, her sharp green
gaze taking in all the subtle nuances that hinted at the character of the people around her. Coming down the aisle was
a Japanese gentleman in a suit undoubtedly custom-tailored,
so fine was the material and so perfect the fit, which led
Kelly to think he was probably a very precise person. Behind
him was a fellow, either a native Australian or a wanna-be
Aussie, in a tan bush outfit and hat. Further on, blocking
the passageway, was a heavy-set woman dressed in stretch
pants and a horizontal-striped blouse which only accentu-
ated her weight problem. Kelly couldn't help but wince at
the picture she presented, her fingers literally itching to take
the woman in hand. A good diet and exercise program,
proper clothing, and a more complimentary hairstyle, all of
which were right up Kelly's alley, would make a world of
difference.

A few rows up, a young couple was trying to settle their
toddler between them. The little girl, complete with toothy
grin and dimples and a frilly pink jumpsuit, was absolutely
precious! She was also having too much fun waving and
babbling at the two elderly people in the seat behind her
to want to sit down.

Kelly's heart gave a painful twinge. She'd miscarried two

years ago, and hadn't gotten pregnant since, which was probably a blessing now, considering the divorce. Still, she looked at that darling child and felt tears stinging at the back of her eyelids. How she'd wanted a baby! A family all her own, upon which to shower all her love.

Seeing the older couple, their snow-white heads so close together, turn to each other and share an adoring smile, only made Kelly feel worse. From all indications, they had the relationship she wanted, the one she'd thought she'd had. A love so secure that it could only grow stronger through the years. Mutual devotion between life-long mates.

Kelly swiped at an errant tear, angry at herself for letting her ragged feelings get the better of her. Sniffling, she delved into her handbag for a tissue. Failing to find even one among the multitude of items overflowing the purse, she heaved a sigh of disgust.

Suddenly a white cloth appeared before her, suspended by deeply-tanned fingers. She glanced to her right, into the topaz eyes of the man who'd given up his first-class seat to Alita Gomez's manager. Zach, something-or-other. He was offering her his handkerchief.

She gave a self-conscious smile. "Your mother must be very proud of you. Gentlemen are a rare breed today."

Zach grinned back at her. "Maybe I'm not polite at all. How do you know this isn't a flag of truce, or an offer of outright surrender?"

Kelly laughed. "For one thing, I wasn't aware we were at war." She accepted the handkerchief from him. "Thank you."

"You're very welcome," he replied. With that, he turned went back to his work, affording her the privacy to properly compose herself.

Finally, everyone had boarded and the plane began to taxi away from the terminal. The steward in charge of the last several rows of passengers, a good-looking young man with red hair and soulful brown eyes, commanded their attention. He welcomed them aboard and commenced the usual speech, citing the rules about smoking, keeping their trays locked into position in front of them, and staying in their seats until the seatbelt sign went off after take-off. He continued with instructions concerning air-sick bags, flotation cushions, oxygen masks, and emergency exits, ending with, "We are here to assist you in any way we can, to make your journey comfortable and pleasant."

In the rearmost seat, which butted up to the galley, a burly passenger grumbled, "Comfortable? Hah! That's a laugh!" He jingled the handcuffs that bound his wrist to that of the detective seated next to him. "I can't even blow my nose without seeing your paw in front of my face."

"So pretend we're Siamese twins and shut up," the lawman advised brusquely. "I don't like it anymore than you do, and I'm not the one who splattered my wife's brains all over a bedroom wall, then skipped out of the country. It's gonna be a long trip back to Tennessee, Roberts, and only slightly better if you're not bitching the entire time."

"So dig out the key and unhook us," Earl Roberts suggested. "It ain't like I can go anywhere. What do you think I'm gonna do? Open a door and throw myself out into the ocean? I didn't see them handin' out parachutes when we got on this over-sized death-trap."

"Relax, Roberts. The 747 has an excellent safety record. And out of about two hundred passengers, as near as I can tell you're the only one whining like a baby."

"Maybe that's 'cause I'm the only one tied to you. And you did some big-time gripin' of your own when they made you turn your gun over to the pilot when we boarded." Earl added that jab with gleeful spite. He eyed the smaller man with a sneer. "You scared any, sittin' here without your weapon, knowin' I could strangle you with my bare hands anytime I took the notion?"

The detective met the threat with a challenging glare, not in the least intimidated. "Try it, and you're gonna wish you did have a parachute. Nothin' says I have to bring you back alive."

They'd crossed the International Date Line, thus gaining a day on the calendar, and were somewhere over the Polynesian islands, when they hit a series of thunderstorms, one after another. Though the pilot came on the intercom several times to assure everyone that there was no cause for alarm, passengers were encouraged to remain in their seats, with their seatbelts fastened. The turbulence became so great that the flight attendants had to secure the carts in the galleys. Contrarily, the rougher the weather became, the more drinks were ordered. The poor attendants were being run ragged serving alcoholic beverages to those passengers who evidently preferred being thoroughly anesthetized to being soberly aware of the frightening situation in which they now found themselves.

Many people, seasoned travelers and first-timers alike, resorted to the air-sick bags, as the aircraft lurched and bounced, and pitched through the dark, ominous clouds. The busy, friendly chit-chat that had previously permeated the atmosphere soon dissipated into whispered exchanges, quiet fervent prayers, and an ever-growing silence.

Each time the plane took one of those heart-stopping thirty-foot drops, as if the air beneath it had suddenly been whisked away, Kelly swallowed a screech of pure terror. She was clutching the armrest so hard that her fingers ached from the prolonged pressure.

Witness to her fear, Zach offered, "If it would make you feel better, we could hold hands."

Kelly shook her head and declined the gallant gesture. "I'm afraid to let go that long." A pry-bar couldn't have loosened her hands from the armrest—or wrested her from

er seat. Which made Alita's appearance all the more star-
ling as the singer made her way slowly down the tilting
aisle toward the rear of the aircraft.

Though her own face was strained, Alita cast a glance
at Kelly's white-boned knuckles and laughed. "It appears
that you, not I, will be the one with no fingernails left."

Kelly unclenched her jaw and muttered, "Slumming,
Miss Gomez?"

"I came to give Zach his autographed photos," the ac-
ress said, turning a three hundred-watt-smile on Zach. She
handed the pictures to him, and explained in a husky murmur, "The one of me fully dressed is for your daughter.
The other one is meant especially for you."

Zach had just thanked her when the beleaguered steward
appeared and curtly suggested that Alita return immediately to her seat.

True to form, Alita tossed her raven-hair and declared
loudly. "I do not care what your stupid sign says. I have
had to come all the way to the back of the plane in search
of a restroom that is not occupied. I am going to file a
complaint. For so many people, on a plane this size, there
should be more restrooms available." With that, she
flounced past him, nearly shoving the man into Kelly's
arms, pushed another passenger headed for the facilities
out of her path, and promptly claimed the small cubicle
for herself.

The door had no sooner clicked shut behind Alita than
the entire interior of the aircraft was filled with a blinding
white glare, accompanied instantaneously by a loud, deaf-
ning crack. Immediately, the plane pitched into a steep
dive.

Panic ensued. Screams rent the air, above which the attendants were frantically trying to issue orders. Though he
was standing next to her, Kelly could barely hear the steward yelling, "Secure your tray tables. Remove your eye-
glasses and any sharp objects from your pockets. If you

have a pillow or blanket or jacket, place it in your lap, between your legs. Put your arms over your head, bend over, and put your head between your knees."

There was no time to think, barely time to react. And yet in that same surreal period, everything seemed to be happening in slow-motion. Half-ripping it, Kelly struggled out of her jacket and hunched forward. The woman to the left of her grabbed a partially-knit afghan from her bag and did likewise. Across the aisle, Zach tore off his sport coat. Next to him, the soldier tucked his face into a tiny airline pillow. In the rearmost seats, the detective and his prisoner swore at each other as they tried to stretch the lawman's suit coat between them.

In those horrible, stupefying moments, sobs and curses and prayers mingled. The baby was shrieking at the top of her lungs. Above the din, the plane's engines were whining and coughing as the craft lurched dizzily downward.

Half suffocated by her tears and her jacket, Kelly raised her head slightly. Her terrified gaze met Zach's for a split instant before he reached out one large hand and roughly shoved her head down again.

His voice, shouting at her to stay down, was the last thing she heard—just before the tremendous jolt that rendered her blessedly unconscious.